# PROTECTION IN PARADISE

## By the Author

Dancing Toward Stardust

Dancing With Dahlia

The Mogul Meets Her Match

Protection in Paradise

# PROTECTION IN PARADISE

*by*

Julia Underwood

2025

**PROTECTION IN PARADISE**

ISBN 13: 978-1-63679-847-9

THIS TRADE PAPERBACK ORIGINAL IS PUBLISHED BY
BOLD STROKES BOOKS, INC.
P.O. BOX 249
VALLEY FALLS, NY 12185

FIRST EDITION: MARCH 2025

---

**CREDITS**
EDITOR: CINDY CRESAP
PRODUCTION DESIGN: STACIA SEAMAN
COVER DESIGN BY TAMMY SEIDICK

# Acknowledgments

This book would never have made it to print without the team at Bold Strokes Books. First, I owe a huge thank you to Rad and the rest of the BSB family for their continued support. They are amazing— knowledgeable, supportive, efficient, and inclusive. Sandy Lowe is always available to offer advice and support when needed. Cindy Cresap was my editor for this book, and not only did she clean up my mistakes and cheerfully share a few new writing craft improvements, she reinforced the lessons that Ruth Sternglantz, who edited my prior books, has diligently tried to teach me. Hopefully, their lessons are sinking in and those bad present participles won't show up in future draft manuscripts "like weeds." They have both been dedicated to making my current and future manuscripts the best possible. And then there are so many additional people behind the scenes who have helped bring this book to completion with clear and timely publication guidance, cover choices, deadlines, production design, and eBook design. This team of dedicated people made this publication possible.

I also need to thank my family and friends who have been understanding, helpful, and supportive as I've focused not only on writing, but also on an effort to wade into the social media aspects of becoming an author. The younger family members offer me laughs and inspiration for the juvenile minor characters in my books, and there is nothing like a canine companion with side-eye looks, the delete button attention-getter, and the ultimate laptop lid closure to make sure I stay tethered in the real world.

Without you, the reader, there would be no reason to write. I can't thank you enough for your investment of time and resources. I'm grateful to those of you who write thoughtful reviews because your insight helps make me a better writer. And for everyone taking the journey of two hearts...happy endings, always.

As a reader and writer, I'd like to dedicate this book to the alphabet, twenty-six letters that allow us to communicate across time and space, grow as individuals, and touch each other's lives. To the power of twenty-six simple shapes that can create stories that entertain us, brighten our days, and embed in our hearts.

# CHAPTER ONE

Personal time had to be carved out of Eve Maguire's calendar with a chainsaw, and she couldn't believe how quickly tonight's personal time had gone from kindling to ash. It was all because of a good deed—a good deed that had derailed another good deed and incinerated her entire carefully planned evening.

She lived by that calendar, her life organized into bureaucratic boxes of time commitments mostly dedicated to her professional life. That was how Eve had orchestrated it. She'd let the personal side go this past year because focusing on her job was so much easier, and she was so much better at that.

Eve glanced once more at her Jeep's clock before she clicked her seat belt into place and then looked back across a parking lot illuminated by lampposts bleeding eerie halos of amber. Unlike when she'd arrived, Breezeland Emergency Veterinary Hospital was now shrouded in a light fog. Eve released a slow sigh of resignation. There seemed to be no way to salvage her evening plans, so she put those plans aside for the moment while she revisited the veterinarian's last words.

"He's unchipped. I've no doubt that he'll need a new home. There's been no sign he's a biter, but he's not shy about sharing his opinion…can't really blame him for that. If you get him a ramp, he'll probably be a couch potato."

There was no canine on Eve's couch for a reason. She didn't want to wade even dog deep into a personal life right now. She was too worried about keeping her professional life on track to start trying to figure out her personal one. Eve suspected that she would have to address it at some point in the future, but now wasn't the time.

The old mutt did bring back fond memories of Minnie. That fifteen pounds of doxie had been a lifesaver. Uncle Glen and Aunt Sadie had acquired her when Eve and her brothers had first come to live with them after their parents' car accident thirty-seven years ago when Eve was ten. She could use another lifesaver, but an abandoned old dog in need of thirty-some stitches that she'd scooped up off the side of the highway in the mist-muted early evening light…no way. She'd volunteered to pay whatever was needed to take care of the injured animal and given the veterinary hospital her Visa number, but Eve had no desire to be committed beyond her credit card. She'd done her good deed and upended her entire itinerary to make sure he received adequate medical care.

"I'll come by late tomorrow morning if it works out, just to make sure we're settled up and to collect the receipt." That had been her response before ending up out here in her car. Eve hadn't needed to be sidetracked like this. On top of a few low-level open cases, she was dealing with an arsonist on the loose, her mayoral boss being up for reelection and down her neck, and an opponent—Eve's ex-girlfriend—with an agenda to appoint someone else to Eve's position if she was elected, whether Pauline openly admitted it or not. Eve knew that her job was at risk.

Yeah, a geriatric, pablum-eating canine with attitude who'd probably been dumped in the woods near where Eve had found him would fit right in. *Not.* Well, she'd pay the bill and put the entire unexpected event behind her.

Eve looked at the time once more before starting her car. She sat for a moment and contemplated her options. As for the original good deed, it had been too long since Eve had made a visit to the Bay Area senior care facility to see Sadie. With this unplanned derailing dog event, the three-hour drive to Golden Days Elder Estate had expanded into nearly five. The seniors would be turning in or already fast asleep by the time she arrived. This would be a wasted trip unless Eve found a room, stayed the night, and then made a short visit in the morning that would have to suffice. She'd already cleared her schedule tomorrow so that she could do some catching up at work, but now she'd be spending the morning at the old folks' home instead.

After she pulled into a drive-through for a quick bite to eat, Eve drove the last hour toward that string of urban cities all packed into the sea of humanity just across the bay from San Francisco. She could go for an elite hotel, but the generic place she'd seen on her phone before she'd left the vet clinic parking lot with a 4.2 rating would work. The big bonus was there was a bar nearby. That left her options open.

Eve decided she needed to let off a little steam, and that was difficult to do in her small town where she avoided publicly drinking more than a rare beer with a burger or slice of pizza. She considered for a moment. The Bay Area was huge, and there was little chance of being recognized if she headed down the street to that bar. Even if she was, so what? She was on personal time and three hours away from Paradise Pines—where she was Eve Maguire, chief of police.

❖

Eve sat on a barstool in this place named Lady Luck and ordered an old-fashioned. She hadn't had one in years, and the mix of bourbon, bitters, sugar, and a twist of citrus sounded good tonight. The lighting was low and the digital jukebox music added a background auditory component that overlayed and leveled out the bursts of congenial patron commotion. The air was drugged with the mixed aromas of french fry grease, booze, and the end-of-the-day crowd that populated the establishment tonight. This was a working person's place.

As Eve sat there sipping her drink and surveying the tables off to her left, someone took the barstool on her right. She'd been happy sitting here alone, and she hoped the person had no intention of engaging her.

"I'll have whatever she's having," the brunette told the bartender in a sultry voice with the same hint of teasing that the smile she offered to Eve conveyed.

That teasing traveled right to where Eve made contact with the barstool. Eve shifted a bit and then pinged the side of her glass with her pointer finger. "What if I'm having balsamic vinegar in Kool-Aid?"

The blue-eyed stranger raised her eyebrows. Eve was fairly certain the room full of guys who were looking at her bar companion wouldn't argue with her assessment of striking, but she had the feeling that the woman wasn't interested in them.

If Eve had to describe her, she would have gone for the facts with a bit of elaboration. Long and full-bodied, her brown hair carried caramel highlights that only enhanced her appearance. Her lush lips were the centerpiece of enticing feminine features, or maybe it was those alluring, laughing eyes. She was probably less than a decade younger than Eve's forty-seven years, but it was the aura of vitality that stoked an uncharacteristic gallop in her heart rate. How did you begin to easily define that?

She hadn't personally connected with a woman in the year since the breakup with Pauline, and had no plans to do so tonight. She could certainly pay attention, though, as part of her professional training.

"Vinegar and Kool-Aid? Then I guess I misjudged you, and I'm not in for the experience I was hoping for." Those azure eyes danced as they gazed at Eve.

Eve took another sip, buying a moment to collect herself. This woman was flirting with her, and she was completely out of practice. Eve reminded herself that was a good thing because she hadn't come here to flirt with anyone, not even with a stunning stranger who spoke to that part of her that had been in hibernation and was now stirring. There was no place in Eve's life for this—a life that was back in Paradise Pines. But maybe being three hours away from home gave her the latitude to let her guard down for a few minutes.

"The experience you were hoping for...are we talking about the drink or something else?" Eve asked. "I'm a bit rusty."

"You take me for someone who picks up women in bars?" the woman replied with that same flirtatious tease infiltrating her tone.

There was no good answer to that question that wasn't loaded with the potential for trouble. A *yes* response might offend her and seemed presumptuous. A *no* might offend someone trolling for company of a certain sort.

Eve decided to dodge the question by approaching the subject in a different way. She was having a good time. She might even try dusting off her own flirting skills in this anonymous watering hole, but she had no intention of letting things get out of control.

"It's an old-fashioned. Not a glass of Love Potion for Two. Not a Tie Me to the Bedpost." As soon as the words were out of her mouth, Eve blinked and shook her head. Obviously, she'd been alone too long, and this alluring woman ignited an uncharacteristic cheeky boldness. It was a good thing she'd never see her again.

"Good to know. For future reference." The woman's mirth tugged at the corners of her mouth. The bartender placed a drink identical to Eve's in front of the stranger. She took a long swallow and nodded.

"Future reference, huh?" Eve said. "I'm probably over my limit with the one drink."

"Only one drink, and you chose the old-fashioned. I'm a researcher at heart...so many choices. Cupid's Kiss, Sex on My Birthday, Part-time Lover." Eve's new drinking partner played up every name, the way Eve had done.

Eve choked as she tried to contain her laughter—and these feelings she wasn't prepared to experience. "Whoa. You're way ahead of me. I just came in to unwind after a tough day. As for a Sex on My Birthday, it's *not* my birthday."

"I was just listing off drink alternatives I've read about. I'm not a big drinker myself. You brought up Tie Me to the Bedpost. Not that I'm complaining, but I'm happy just sitting here chatting with you."

"Sorry," Eve said. "Let me repeat, I'm rusty at this." And she wasn't ready for this. She'd spent a year building a life that had no room for another woman, not even an anonymous stranger. But tell that to her renegade hormones because that was all this was.

They sat in comfortable silence sipping their drinks. Eve noticed the woman had a tiny scar just above her left eyebrow that offered her captivating face a touch of character that suggested she had a past. And those small creases next to her mouth and eyes mapped out traces of what would undoubtedly prove to be more pronounced laugh lines. Her face…a life story mixed with perfection.

She was so compelling, Eve thought before she chastised herself. Eve wouldn't let her mind go there, not to an anonymous physical encounter with a stranger. That not only wasn't her style, but just contemplating it reminded her that she'd have to deal with the inevitable emotions that would be churned up. She'd worked too hard to avoid those this past year.

Her drinking partner finally broke the comfortable silence. "So tell me about your tough day. The one that's *not* your birthday."

"It wasn't that terrible. Just headed to visit someone I wanted to see, but I was waylaid and had to stay over so that I can do that tomorrow. And you? Just unwinding?"

The woman shook her head and finished off her drink. "I'm in the process of moving. Packed all day and decided to get out for a bit. But I'm about ready to call it a night."

"Me too." Eve took her last swallow. It was time to head out and put a halt to this interaction and her unwelcome thoughts.

They headed toward the door with the woman right behind Eve. As they entered the parking lot, Eve turned and gave her a long last look, one that Eve knew communicated her hunger because she couldn't suppress it. Eve tried to focus on maintaining control, protecting her heart. Not that this stranger had anything to do with her heart.

The woman leaned in and waited for the objection that Eve could not bring herself to make, then brushed her lips across Eve's. Eve let the contact linger. She didn't want to end that soft and warm caress of connection, that ember of suppressed physical longing that could so easily flare to a wanton flame. The bare touch of tongues—it felt good. Natural. The rightness surprised Eve because she didn't kiss strangers. She didn't want to be kissing anyone right now.

Then that rightness ruptured Eve's resolve as she opened to the kiss and leaned into the brunette. She pressed her breasts and her pelvis into the curves of this beautiful woman, and their bodies melded in a perfect pairing. It didn't feel like a taking. Or a giving. Eve's mouth met hers in a sharing. A slow, deep exploration. Tangling tongues, breathing the same air, exploring a mutual attraction. Molten heat pooled between Eve's thighs and her heart pounded out a rapid drumbeat to the desire that drove their physical communion. Her body craved this stranger.

The door opened as two couples left the Lady Luck establishment, and the fellowship from the interior drifted out. Every alarm sounded in Eve's head as she lectured herself that she didn't have casual sex in parking lots with strangers. She needed to care for somebody if they were going to be intimate. But look at how that had worked out for her. Caring left her vulnerable and she hadn't been ready to go there in this past year. She hadn't met anyone who'd made her want to figure out what would work for her now—sex in a parking lot with a gorgeous stranger she'd never see again might be the answer, but it had never been what worked for her before.

Eve moaned and then pulled back before she couldn't—or before she invited the woman to her 4.2 rated hotel room for 10.0 sex. "Good night. It was nice meeting you."

"Nice to meet you too. *Old-fashioned.*" There was no mistaking the amusement that infiltrated the stranger's husky voice. "Not Love Potion for Two. Not Tie Me to the Bedpost." Then she added, "For future reference." Those blue eyes were still dancing, still agitating something deep inside Eve. They poked at memories of things she didn't want to desire, at memories of things she didn't want to miss.

"I rather doubt it, but just in case…remember the drink called Date Night. It's more my speed." Then Eve turned to leave while she still could, but not before letting herself throw back over her shoulder, "But I do carry handcuffs."

# CHAPTER TWO

Eve pulled into the parking lot of Golden Days Elder Estate at a quarter to nine the next morning. She couldn't stifle a yawn after a night when sleep had eluded her. She'd tossed and turned for hours. Last evening had provoked thoughts of her absent personal life and made her question if it was finally time to consider what her body needed, what her heart could handle. Maybe she should have slept with the woman—someone she'd never see again. That damn kiss meant nothing, perfect as it was. She certainly couldn't be vulnerable to a stranger, and maybe it would have satisfied this friggin' libido.

However, discretion was professionally ingrained in her. Back in her small town, Eve knew better than to think she had free rein over her life with no repercussions—there was no bedding someone local just to assuage her physical desires. And bedding a total stranger wasn't wise either. Besides, she'd always known that she needed more, and last night's bar encounter had only roared her repressions, her vulnerabilities, her turmoil back to life.

Spontaneous flirting and off-the-charts chemistry—those were about lust and not love. Eve had done a fair amount of dating and known that initial flicker of love before she'd moved to Paradise Pines, but that hadn't worked out when job demands and her girlfriend's family issues had interceded. Eve's career had been her sole focus for a number of years after that—there were professional ambitions to pursue. Then she'd tried again with Pauline, but her ex had been a master of flirtation and creating chemistry, and look how that had worked out—worked out for so many women besides Eve. Eve had been taken in and played for a fool. Now she knew what to exclude.

Finally, around three a.m., after she'd spent a year accepting that she just didn't want a personal life, Eve had conceded that long-term relationships needed a rational approach. Not that she wanted a relationship, but it was better to be prepared so she didn't get sucked in with this obviously resurgent libido and repeat the damfool mistake she'd made with Pauline. Exhausted, she'd promised herself that she'd come up with a plan. A well-thought-out, practical strategy that would steer her personal life clear of spontaneous combustion.

Before opening the door to the senior care facility, Eve adjusted the lumpy package wrapped in colorful ballerina sheep paper that she carried under her arm. The paper had been the end of the roll, and Eve reminded herself she needed to order some more. Witnessing the unwrapping was one of her greatest pleasures on these visits.

"Hey, Chief Maguire. It's good to see you. I haven't seen you in quite a while and I didn't expect to see you this early in the day." The young man in the reception area rushed over to hold the door for her.

It always surprised Eve that he remembered exactly who she was because she hadn't been here in over a month. The first thought that ran through her mind was that either he must have had a very good experience or a very bad experience with law enforcement that created such an imprint. He seemed like a nice, polite young man and she smiled at him.

"Thanks." Eve remembered his name too—an occupational hazard type of name association. A criminal…Jack the Ripper. "How's it going, Jack? Life's been a bit hectic, and I've only had time for phone check-ups, so I appreciate the quality care you provide. I'll head on back."

Taking a deep breath, she walked into the room where Sadie was sitting up against the back of the adjustable bed, her eyes closed. The soft light of the indirect morning sun filtered through the window shade and mellowed her aunt's appearance. It softened the features forged over eighty-two years.

"Hi, Sadie. It's Eve, and I brought you something."

Her aunt opened her eyes and frowned. "Eve? You're way too old to be Eve. She's a teenager."

Eve kissed her aunt's cheek. It would be a waste of time arguing with Sadie, and she probably wouldn't remember this visit by tomorrow. "Well, I'm here to see you and deliver a gift." She handed Sadie the wrapped package, one of the few things that awakened the old delight her aunt used to have for so many things.

Sadie ripped the paper free from the offering with a huge grin, then pulled the tan teddy bear to her chest. "You'll tell Eve that I'm so glad she found Rupert, won't you?"

Eve looked over at a chair in the corner of the room where a group of almost a dozen stuffed brown bears that Eve had brought on prior visits over the past year now sat. Bears that Sadie seemed to recognize the moment Eve delivered them. Uncle Glen had told Eve that her aunt had loved her collection of brown teddy bears as a child, and Eve had found a connection with her aunt through them. "I will. Anything I can get you?"

"You can tell Glen that he needs to hurry up or he'll be late for work."

"We wouldn't want that." Glen had suffered a heart attack nine months after Eve had helped him place Sadie here where she could get the care she needed. After her parents' accident, her aunt and uncle had made sure Eve and her brothers were still part of a family and helped them heal. Eve and her younger brother, Earl, at age ten and eight, had agreed to be adopted and take on Glen and Sadie's last name of Maguire, also their mother's maiden name, while her older brother, Mike, had been eighteen and on the cusp of independence. Glen's passing and Sadie's decline had hit Eve hard and added to the stress of this past year.

"Glen's the love of my life. Listen to your heart. That's my best advice. Listen to your heart." Sadie smiled before she leaned back and closed her eyes, the new bear clasped closely against her chest.

Eve sat in the visitor's chair next to the bed and watched her aunt doze. She owed her so much more than what she was able to offer. After about fifteen minutes of listening to her aunt's quiet respiration, she decided there wasn't much more she could do for Sadie today. Eve kissed her on the forehead, and as she was backing out of the room, she ran directly into the certified nursing assistant, Rosemary. Eve checked in with the CNA by phone for twice-weekly updates.

"How are you doing? How's life in Paradise?" Rosemary squeezed Eve's arm. The name Paradise Pines was frequently shortened to Paradise by people familiar with the small town.

Eve offered her a smile. She'd gone to school with Rosemary, who had supported Eve in high school when Eve had come out. Their bond had only grown with Eve's Golden Days Elder Estate phone calls and visits.

Eve appreciated their history and Rosemary's steadfast support.

Rosemary was aware of Eve's relationship to Sadie and her commitment to policing, handed down through the generations. She was one of the people who knew that Eve had made the decision she wanted to go into law enforcement at a young age. Twelve.

The year before she'd entered high school she'd lost her older brother, who had followed in their father's footsteps and became a police officer, in an off-duty motorcycle accident. It had been another blow to Eve. Her aunt and uncle had refused to discuss the incident or talk about Mike in any detail, she assumed because they'd thought she and Earl had been through enough loss. It had decided her course— she'd completed an advanced college degree in criminal justice and then gone on to pick up the law enforcement mantle that continued the family tradition.

The assurance that she had Rosemary, someone she trusted, keeping an eye on Sadie was a huge relief for Eve. It was also nice to have someone she could talk to outside of Paradise Pines.

"I'm doing okay," Eve said. "Mayoral election politics are dominating a lot of decision-making. Probably the worst in the decade I've been there. Three candidates instead of just the incumbent mayor— he didn't have challengers his previous two elections. Plenty of fallout. I certainly prefer the policing to the politics."

"Pretty bad, huh?" Rosemary gave her a sympathetic look.

"I've got good officers, so the policing aspect is fine. I even enjoy hitting the pavement and picking up the slack when needed."

"So, it's the politics?" Rosemary chuckled and rolled her eyes.

"It's not a big secret." Eve leaned back against the doorframe. She welcomed the chance to chat with Rosemary face-to-face. "At least among those paying attention. The station is small. I have an office and there's a small bullpen area that serves the officers under me. The only other office is unassigned because its function is essential. It's used for sharing confidential information, low-key interrogations, and by any of the officers needing a short-term private space. The creation and maintenance of that space, it's been a priority."

"Sure. That makes sense. So, what's the problem?"

Eve looked back into the room at Sadie, who was still sound asleep, then went on to explain the situation to Rosemary.

"With the town library burned to the ground, a small trailer's housing the salvaged books, but there's no room for a librarian's office. Mrs. Comber retired after the arson, and her replacement is due to arrive this upcoming week. Mayor Greg Sneed recently decided to house the new librarian in that unassigned police office rather than a city backroom location—a decision calculated to offer the appearance of a functional, interim library setup to minimize the fact there's an arsonist on the loose. I'll need to find a way to make it work so my officers can do their jobs."

Losing that space to politics really pissed Eve off—another *Pauline Bromwell repercussion* in her life.

"I'm sorry. So, is it a tight race?"

Eve knew she could count on Rosemary to be discreet, and while Rosemary knew she'd broken up with Pauline about the time of Sadie's placement in the facility, they'd never had the chance to talk about her.

"My ex is now suddenly running against the incumbent mayor. The third candidate—he's young with no political experience, so I don't see him standing a chance. I was hired before the current mayor was first elected, and he's had no issues with me. He's run unopposed for both of his two four-year terms, but now Pauline's on the ballot, and she's angry that I ended our relationship after I found out she didn't have the same commitment to us as I did. She'll undoubtedly replace me—if not outright fire me. She'll do everything in her power to force me out."

Rosemary nodded as Eve sighed. She'd dedicated her adult life to her job, knew it was a good fit—that she was good at it. "Pauline's label for cheating was *lapse*. The several I know of probably aren't the sum total of her lapses. I suspect part of her anger is pride…that I walked before she could."

"Well, I hope she loses. What's she got going for her?"

"Probably the things that got me involved with her in the first place. Pauline's well put together and smart. No problem being charming when it serves her. With me, she knew how to flirt and feed the feeling of connection—she zeroed in on me at one time." Eve swallowed hard and shook her head at her own susceptibility. "Our focus was our jobs, me in law enforcement and her in accounting. I thought her acceptance of our busy schedules was based on each of us attaining our professional potential and not an opportunity that gave her time to play the field."

Eve knew that success required the choices and time commitments she'd made. She'd thought Pauline's busy schedule had been focused on her own accounting career as the senior accountant at a large medical corporation's headquarters located about half an hour away in the county seat. Maybe she'd been too trusting, but now Eve could only castigate herself for being a cop who had missed all the clues.

"How long were you together?"

"Four years." Those four years had been her commitment to the relationship, Pauline's obviously less in hindsight. "I made assumptions. Not that Pauline would have welcomed a deep discussion about what we expected or needed from each other. It was a lesson—if you can't talk and clarify things, that's a clue about where a relationship is headed."

"She took a piece of your life," Rosemary said. "And a piece of your heart. I've got no doubt that the right person is out there for you."

Eve shrugged. "I'm doing fine on my own." She'd lost a piece of her heart, but she didn't know that the right person was out there. At forty-seven, she'd learned a few things, and one of them was protecting that heart in the future.

"You've had a lot of loss over the years, Eve." Rosemary offered her an understanding smile, and Eve decided to shift the subject back to the election.

"Sneed was unopposed, then my ex signed up at the last minute, as well as the third candidate. Now Pauline's zeroing in on the voters, telling them what they want to hear. How simple the solutions are to complex issues. Who's to blame and who can save them—her. You know the sound bites."

"The same story from big-time politics all the way down to local ones." Rosemary shook her head.

"It's the same people voting. Looking for what's going to improve their lives, who supports their mindset, and who's in the way of that. You can't really blame them, but they need to do their homework."

"I'll stick to these seniors, and most of them in here aren't voting. Current politics do make Wes and me worry for our two kids."

"I hear you," Eve said. "Thanks so much for taking such good care of Sadie and keeping me in the loop. I'd better head out now, but call if you need to."

"Have a safe trip home. I'll talk to you at the end of the week." Rosemary turned and proceeded down the hallway, and Eve headed out to her car. She had a vet bill to finalize.

❖

Eve wavered over stopping at the vet clinic on her way home. She'd had an hour of driving to consider that they had her credit card number and approval to charge her, and she didn't need the receipt for the care of the old dog. They could probably email it to her if she had questions. But then the car ahead of her on the highway slowed way down before turning into the clinic parking lot, and because her foot was already off the gas and on the brake, she followed.

"Are you here for McGruff?" the young woman at the reception counter asked as Eve entered the clinic.

"McGruff?"

"The old dog you brought in last night off the highway needing stitches—I was here in the back when you showed up. Staff tagged him with the name...his cranky disposition. No owner found so far, and it would be a huge surprise if there is one. We'll go through all the legal steps of looking for an owner. We already did some checking and notified animal services. If found, an owner has first claim."

Eve stood there, still kicking herself for stopping on the way home. What had possessed her?

"He'd been out there a while too, or really neglected. Dr. Kent gave you the twenty percent compassionate citizen discount. She's got the instructions ready, and McGruff's been cleaned up as best we could, considering the sutures."

"I just came in to make sure the bill was settled and get the receipt. I'm sure McGruff will find someone else to take him." She needed to stand firm.

"Are you kidding me? He'll have fought for his life out there in the woods just to come to God knows what. Foster care's scarce around here, so it's likely some chaotic shelter. He needs you." The young woman was earnest. "We put him back together on the outside. But he needs someone to put him back together on the inside."

The receptionist looked down the hallway as a young man led the scrappy old dog out from the back on a leash as he growled at everyone he passed. Another female employee trailed behind with a large bag. Eve shook her head at the terrier mix with one ear that stood at half-mast and the other missing a substantial piece, but at full alert. His ash-gray hair stood out in every direction as if he'd been plugged into an electrical outlet.

Eve sighed. She didn't need a dog who didn't even like her. "I'm no saving angel."

The growling little canine disagreed with that statement and broke free, running directly to her before sitting and looking up at Eve with eyes so sad they stung her soul. For Pete's sake. Then he thumped his tail a few times, and she hated it. Not McGruff, but her own blasted waffling. What the receptionist had just said—it hit her. She could relate. *We put him back together on the outside. But he needs someone to put him back together on the inside.*

"Whoa," the three vet clinic employees within sight said in unison.

"McGruff has a thing for you. It's meant to be," the receptionist added.

Dr. Kent came out from the back, and she smiled at Eve. "His blood work checked out okay. So, are you going to take him on the contingency nobody claims him, which I seriously doubt? He hasn't warmed up to anyone until just now with you. He hasn't snapped or bitten, but just grumped." The vet took the bag from the woman who'd carried it out. "A few cans of soft dog food. Antibiotics since some of the wounds were becoming infected. A complimentary towel for transport. And we had a spare bed we've washed up that was left by a prior client, so he's set there."

Eve was overwhelmed by how fast this was progressing. She'd never expected the blasted mutt to pick her out as the only human he found acceptable.

Dr. Kent looked down at the paperwork she'd picked up from the counter and read it. "Eve Maguire." Then she looked at Eve. "McGruff Maguire—it has a certain element of dignity to it, don't you think?"

Dignity? Eve didn't know whether to snort or just smack herself. This good deed was taking on a life of its own—with an effort at attachment to her life.

Dr. Kent cleared her throat. "Look. If you can't take him, I get it. He's going to need a good home. You check out in the compassion department and in being financially capable of supporting his needs. You're the only person I've seen him show an ounce of affection for. But it's up to you. If you take him, we'll continue to look for an owner and contact you if we find one, but he's been on his own for a while or was severely neglected. And you can bring him back if it doesn't work out."

Ten minutes later, Eve was driving down the highway with the canine in his new bed in the back seat of her Jeep—she was caught between calling herself a sucker and saying "Oh shit." McGruff Maguire didn't seem to mind one bit.

❖

McGruff had followed Eve around the house until she'd settled in her family room last evening. When she was finally ready to turn in, Eve had moved his bed to a spot on the floor next to her bed and he'd fallen asleep for the night, snoring loudly. Now, with her cup of morning coffee in front of her, Eve decided he needed a nickname that wouldn't prejudice others against him when he was introduced at work.

*Mac.* At least at work. Better than McGruff, although she was becoming attached to that name—it suited him. There was no way that one look at the mutt wasn't going to guarantee a shake of everyone's head at work. She was going to take her licks, but she needed to try to mitigate the damage. Curses on her waffling—the mutt wasn't going to help the image she tried to portray as a decent but disciplined boss. Not a pushover.

After she'd perused the morning news on her laptop, Eve ordered another three dog beds. A totally practical purchase, so that she'd have one for the family room, one for her bedroom, one for her car, and another for work. She ordered a ramp so he could be a couch potato—she didn't want to have to be at his beck and call when he wanted up or down. She'd also call from work to set up someone to install a dog door out to her backyard. Eve assured herself that she wasn't getting way too invested in McGruff—all these things were for her convenience. Then she loaded the canine, a water bowl, and his bed into her car and headed to her office because she had a professional life to tend to.

Unloading the pooch and his accommodations when she arrived at work, Eve prepared herself for the inevitable razzing.

"So, is that the new K-9 unit, Chief?" Officer Grady Lopez asked as Eve and McGruff entered the building. McGruff growled at him as the kidding continued from the others who had stopped to look.

"I think it's a large rat…Cadaver dog—he's the cadaver…Looks like a drug detection dog who oversampled the goods…"

"Highly trained to take down most everybody, so give him a wide berth," Eve said. "You can call him…Mac."

Looking at McGruff, Eve shook her head as Grady took the bed and water bowl from her and carried them to her office while she kept the dog on a tight leash.

"My cousin's a canine behaviorist. If he really is vicious, she could probably help you," Mona, the dispatcher, volunteered.

"You can get me her contact info, although they told me he hasn't bitten anyone. He's just vocal about his displeasure. *Do not* ask me how this happened." Eve scowled as she tried to figure out how she could justify how she'd ended up with the cranky critter, not only to those looking on but to herself.

Everyone who had gathered in the growing audience of onlookers was keeping a safe distance. McGruff looked from one person to the next and offered each a deep-throated growl. Eve tracked his progress as his head swiveled from person to person until he suddenly jerked free and headed over to someone standing by the entrance. Like he'd done with her at the veterinary clinic, he sat and thumped his tail. Eve looked up to see who had his approval and was shocked. *Oh, fuck.*

She'd seen those blue eyes recently. She'd kissed those full pink lips. She knew the curves of that body. Eve was looking at the striking brunette from the bar, into her sapphire eyes, and they were still dancing.

Eve offered a minimal nod before taking a deep breath and collecting the mutt as she tried to collect herself, heading on to her office where the dog bed was now located behind her desk next to her chair. He settled right in. She did not. What the hell was the woman who had infiltrated her dreams the last two nights doing here, infiltrating her police station, infiltrating her space, and charming McGruff?

# CHAPTER THREE

Shaye Hayden headed down the hall to the office where the engaging hazel-eyed blonde from the bar had headed with the scrappy dog, noting the sign posted outside her open door that read *Eve Maguire, Chief of Police.* Oh, hell no.

She hadn't had a clue, never suspected the law enforcement status, never even thought *cop.* Shaye had done some internet reading on the current state of the town she'd left behind when she'd turned eighteen, but she was now back for good. She'd never thought to specifically check out the current chief of police in Paradise Pines, or just Paradise, as so many locals called it. She hadn't reflected on the shortened name in a long time, but this new revelation wasn't working to the positive.

*"Old-fashioned."* Shaye muttered the name she'd been calling Eve in her head whenever she'd thought about the stranger from the bar encounter—and it hadn't been infrequently. Eve had connected with her—mature, layered, witty…and by her own admission, rusty. Shaye had felt the chemistry and had seriously thought about Eve since then. She'd made an impression—she was a contradiction of captivating shows of assertiveness interwoven with a propensity to retreat from those enticing displays. She was intriguing…and alluring in a subtle, fascinating way that Shaye swore she would not try to explore further now that she knew Eve's profession. They had no future.

As Shaye stood in the chief's office doorway, she couldn't help but notice Eve's black pants stretched tightly across her shapely backside as she bent down to the dog bed. With her white button-down shirt tucked in, the view was unimpeded.

As Eve straightened, Shaye looked her up and down. Her golden blond hair was now pulled back into a loose bun and she wore more work-appropriate clothing. Shaye felt the physical draw she'd felt the other night, but she also felt a desire to get to know the person who had made her laugh in the bar, and who obviously had a soft spot for such a disaster of a dog, even though Shaye had the impression she was trying to hide it. Eve had sparked something in Shaye, but no woman could cause her to throw caution to the wind and ignore all the experience-based warnings she had in place about cops. Absolutely not.

She glanced around the space. A college diploma from somewhere, but a coat rack with the black blazer she'd seen her wearing out front and a bagged dress uniform on a hanger blocked Shaye's view of the school's name and exact degree. There were various certificates too—probably an academy certification, maybe some additional training certifications or commendations.

An open cupboard door caught Shaye's attention. She saw half a dozen stuffed animals, all brown teddy bears lined up on a shelf, still with their price tags attached to their ears. The police chief was a contradiction to what Shaye expected from someone in her position. But still a goddamn cop.

Aside from her profession, Eve wasn't even her usual type these days. Shaye's current type had been someone eager and younger, girly-femme, and happy to settle for a one-and-done good time, but she couldn't ignore that she was feeling a need for more than what she'd been recently pursuing.

After her divorce, Shaye decided she didn't want any more pain in her life. She'd pursued meaningless encounters, but now notions of a solid successful relationship were resurfacing. She was feeling the void that she'd once thought she'd partially filled with her marriage…after she'd let Cynthia into her life and then proved herself wrong three years ago. She'd taken a huge risk and convinced herself that with Cynthia she'd at least found lasting love, if not peace from her past. That had turned out to be an illusion.

Now, hitting forty, Shaye had finally started considering her future, admitting she needed to make changes after discussions with her library mentor and friend, Annie. She wanted that elusive happiness that others seemed to have, or at least not the rut she'd started to call her life. She wanted what Annie had with her husband, Thomas.

Shaye had fled this town half a lifetime ago, but the guilt and pain had come with her. Annie had convinced her that she needed to finally face the baggage of her past or she'd never heal—she certainly hadn't fully found peace anywhere else. That was the reason for this move back to Paradise Pines, along with the fact that her mom was aging and would need more help. So now here she was, standing in the office of the chief of police.

Eve was watching her. When she noticed that the cupboard door was open and the teddy bears were visible, she walked across the room and shut the door, giving Shaye the impression that she didn't want to reveal that she had a collection of stuffed animals in her office. Interesting, and too late now. Eve was an enigma and still off-limits.

"I didn't know *for future reference* would happen this soon. You stalking me?" Shaye fought to keep her tone accusatory, but couldn't prevent a hint of the same teasing that had been there the other night. She just seemed to bring it out in Shaye.

"Yeah. Me and my tracking dog." The edges of Eve's lips quirked upward, causing Shaye to stare at that mouth.

"Eve, is it?" Tracking dog her ass…Eve definitely had a sense of humor that Shaye appreciated.

"Eve works. You have me at a disadvantage. There's no wall sign for me to read."

The name *Eve* worked for Shaye too. *Eve.* A name symbolic of womankind. And it was a straightforward name—Eve might have her walls, but she hadn't come across as superficial or duplicitous or anything less than genuine.

"I'm Shaye. Shaye Hayden. When you said you had handcuffs, I was thinking of something else—besides being arrested." She raised her eyebrows and offered a suggestive look before she caught herself and sobered.

A suppressed chuckle escaped from Eve. "Who says I only use them professionally?" A pink hue infused her cheeks and she cleared her throat. "Or do I need to arrest you?"

"You know, you're not nearly as rusty at this as you tried to convince me in the bar." Shaye was going to have to be careful. She was drawn to Eve and she didn't want to be. Couldn't be. And that blush indicated Eve wasn't full of herself either. She was way too appealing.

Eve straightened as she rubbed the back of her neck, but there was the same hunger in her eyes that Shaye had seen before their kiss. A kiss Shaye had relived way too many times. There was also uncertainty in those eyes—almost a humbleness. Eve was the chief of police, owned the ugliest dog Shaye had ever seen, and had a collection of teddy bears in her office. She was sexy as all hell in an engaging way. Not in a girly hours-at-the-mirror way, but in an attractive, dignified way that included her not even seeming to know it—which made her even more appealing. And dangerous. Shaye hadn't taken this new job to end up involved with a cop.

"So, Shaye Hayden. Who are you and what are you doing here in my office?"

"I'm the town's new librarian. The mayor gave me an empty office just down from yours…with what's left of the library in a trailer and no office space."

Eve's brow furrowed as she shook her head and frowned.

Shaye knew what she had against cops, but what in the world could Eve have against librarians? "You have a problem with librarians or just me?" Shaye was working hard to stay on topic and not divert to her own feelings. This wasn't her ideal situation either.

Eve let out a sigh. "I don't have a problem with librarians."

Shaye blinked. "And what did I do…besides sharing a moment of mutual passion in a parking lot? It was mutual, wasn't it?" She remained silent while she waited for Eve's answer.

"It was." Eve's color flushed deeper, but her eyes darkened too, and Shaye took that as a positive reflection on the memory. Eve continued, "You're a political pawn. You shouldn't—"

Shaye clenched her jaw. She'd thought that she liked Eve. She already knew she'd walked away from the bar desiring at least a night with her…*past tense* she told herself now. But she was afraid that like the other cops who had let her down in her life, Eve Maguire was no different. Political pawn? She hadn't even been in town for twenty-four hours.

"I shouldn't…what?" Shaye asked, struggling to maintain a neutral tone and hear her out.

"It's not you specifically." Eve's tone carried no reciprocal irritation targeted at Shaye, and she relaxed a bit.

Eve touched her hair, maybe buying herself a minute to consider what to say, and Shaye remembered how it had hung thick and unrestrained the other night. Long silky layers that fell well below Eve's shoulders and covered all but the front of her neck—so easily whisked aside to lay lips to the back curve of that jaw. Shaye cleared her throat, trying to also clear the thought. "Not me specifically, but still me. Again, I shouldn't…what?"

"The mayor runs the town. He can do what he thinks best," Eve replied.

"And that upsets you because…?" Shaye could see that Eve was in cautious mode. Professional mode. You probably didn't get to her position unless you had that streak of political animal in you that avoided confrontation with your superiors. But for Shaye, this wasn't about the mayor right now. She was dealing with Eve and the obvious frustration that she'd directed at Shaye...*political pawn.*

"Let me spell it out for you. It's an election year, and for the first time since he became mayor, Sneed has opposition—three people are running," Eve said. "The library's in a trailer with no room for the librarian because of an arsonist we haven't caught. So, to try to normalize the library system and divert focus away from an arsonist on the loose, the mayor gave you the office that my officers need as a private space."

Okay. So maybe Eve wasn't such an ass after all—at least not in her explanation of why she was upset. But she was still a cop. Shaye cleared her throat. "I had no idea."

"It's done. Not your fault. I'll deal with it—part of the job."

Shaye nodded. Eve clearly wasn't happy with the arrangement, but there wasn't much Shaye could do about it, so she changed the subject. "What's with the dog? It looked like the other cops hadn't met him before, so he's new?"

Shaye advanced into the office and around the desk. She moved closer to the pooch who stepped out of his bed and headed toward her, tail wagging. Eve leaned back on the edge of her desk and watched.

"No offense," Shaye continued as she dropped to a knee, "but he's probably the ugliest dog around. He looks like he's been tied up and not so kindly interrogated. Or a Mary Shelley creation—Frankenstein's monster. What's with all the stitches? Maybe you should call him Frank."

"I found him on my way to the Bay Area the night I met you. On my way back home the next morning I stopped at the vet's where I'd left him to finalize the bill that I'd told them I'd pay—ended up with him too." Eve didn't sound unsettled about spending money on the dog, but if Shaye was reading her correctly, she was adjusting to ending up with him. "I'm hoping they'll find his owner, but it seems he was dumped."

"So along with the old-fashioned label, I can add *pushover.*" For crying out loud, Eve was growing on her, and Shaye couldn't let that happen.

"The vet staff named him McGruff—sweet name for a *sweet* little dog," Eve dryly noted. "I introduced him to everyone here as Mac, his undercover name. I hadn't thought of calling him Frank. Appearance and growling disposition are part of his undercover identity, and I'm sure he'd appreciate you calling him Mac here at work and not blowing his cover. Seems only you and I know the delightful, real McGruff." Eve returned her face to passive, but the twinkle in her gaze told Shaye that she was enjoying this exchange. Shaye was too.

"Got it. His nasty growling undercover persona is Mac and we need to stick with that when addressing him while he's working. But the charming side he presents to you and me is the authentic McGruff Maguire. And I use the term *charming* liberally." Shaye couldn't prevent a grin at the absurdity of this dog having an undercover identity, and then she could have kicked herself for enjoying Eve so much. Shaye didn't want to be the least bit attracted to her.

Eve studied her. "Because for some reason, he's chosen the two of us to demonstrate that *charm*."

McGruff nudged Shaye's hand and leaned into her, clearly requesting that she pet him. Eve watched as she decided to sit all the way down on the carpet and let him climb into her lap. She actually liked the tough old fellow, and she needed to do something to distract herself from Eve. He looked up and licked her chin, and Shaye cocked an eyebrow at Eve as she accepted McGruff's approval.

"First you steal my spare office." Eve still sounded a bit stern, but then a ghost of a smile touched the corners of her mouth. Shaye reluctantly registered her dimples and reconfirmed how attractive she was. But it wasn't just the physical—it was the connection and ease of their interaction. "Now it's my canine cop you're stealing."

The reference to *canine cop* slammed into Shaye and made her pause to consider the situation. She was getting way too cozy with both Eve and McGruff. The dog was so outrageous that he was hilarious, and those soft, moist lips of Eve's that kept offering Shaye that suggestion of amusement were so hard to ignore—especially because Shaye knew how well they could kiss. It was time to shut all this down. She gave McGruff a final pat and stood.

"I'd better get to work—in your stolen office." Shaye couldn't stop herself from poking at Eve. Much as she disliked cops, she was having way too much trouble disliking her. Eve was making inroads, and that set off loud alarms.

"Office stealing…don't make me come to your temporary library and arrest you." There was amusement in Eve's tone.

"Why not arrest me here at the police station?"

"I kind of like the idea of handcuffs in the stacks. More to check out in the library than books." As soon as the words were out, Eve looked unsettled, as if she didn't know what had possessed her. "Damn...sorry."

Shaye shook her head, biting her cheeks to prevent another grin. They definitely had chemistry, even if she wanted nothing to do with cops and Eve was upset at her for losing the office to Shaye. It fed the deep quiver at her core. "I'm holding my breath, Chief." As Shaye turned to leave, she said, "See you around, Mac." Then she whispered, "McGruff."

She had no business flirting with Eve, but she couldn't seem to help herself. Well, she'd just have to do better. There was no way this could go anywhere. Shaye was back in Paradise Pines for a reason, and not only would Eve Maguire, chief of *fucking* police not be a balm to her wounds, she would undoubtedly exacerbate them. Shaye decided she had no business using the shortened town name—this wasn't her version of Paradise.

❖

Eve's phone rang and she saw it was Doug Hooper, the county fire inspector. He was located at the county seat about twenty miles away and handled the investigations of cases like the library fire in Paradise Pines, which only had a small local volunteer fire department. Hooper had been working with Eve, and she'd been waiting for a more official update.

"Eve here. How are you?"

"I'm fine, Chief. Just calling to touch base and go over what we've got on your library fire."

"Good. As you know, there were no fingerprints on the note mailed to me, common papers, computer-generated so no handwriting to analyze. And nothing else," Eve said.

"I know you're dealing with an election year and the pressure is on to catch the person."

"The mayor is beside himself. He's never been opposed before, and two new candidates signed up after the fire. He's moved as fast as he could with a temporary trailer and a new librarian when the previous one retired." Eve felt an internal fluttering of pleasure as she thought of Shaye and she tamped it away. "It would be good to catch whoever did this before the election, but I already know you're doing everything you can. I've been poring through old cases and info as time allows, watching possible suspects, and my officers are paying attention."

"You know the usual arson motives—vandalism, excitement, revenge, crime concealment, profit, extremism, the indiscernible," Hooper said. "And I've already mentioned the infamous fire captain John Orr who started nearly two thousand fires—he set them because he allegedly wanted to be a hero when he showed up to put them out. He's now locked up for arson and murder. His simple incendiary timing device—burning cigarette and three matches wrapped with a rubber band—we've verified from what we collected that it's the same method used in your library. This info is all online for anyone to find."

"Good to know, but not sure how available-to-anyone info will help us catch the arsonist," Eve said.

"Lab analysis IDed the accelerant as gasoline. The cover of darkness and malfunctioning cameras haven't helped. None of the forensic evidence gains us a suspect either."

"I sent you copies of everything I have. The note I received… mailed to me, arriving a day after the fire." She pulled a photocopy from a file on her desk and read it out loud. "*If you won't ban the books, bitch, well then, burn, baby, burn.*"

"It seems they want us to believe it's tied to extremism and book banning, thus the library site. But that *bitch* piece…might be personal, Eve. You be careful."

"I've pored back through old cases," Eve said. "I know I've got my enemies out there…years of testimony against people, arrests and lockups. The only recent arson was a couple of kids and a trash can. There are a few parolees I'm trying to keep an eye on, but no one in violation that I know of. The city was leasing the burnt library building and I'm researching that. A ninety-nine-year lease signed almost fifty years ago and tied to a ninety-something-year-old, out-of-state resident, so I'm not seeing her as a likely suspect, but I'll keep digging."

"All you can do is keep your eyes and ears open."

"I know." Eve sighed. "Another possibility is election related. Losing the town library by arson isn't good for the incumbent mayor, but it seems pretty extreme. It happened before the other two candidates had signed up and entered the race."

"You have anything special at stake regarding the election—small town and all?"

Eve hesitated. She'd been acquainted with Hooper from a distance for years and they'd become friendly, but she didn't want to let their conversation drift too far into the personal—this whole mess was political. Well, personal too with Pauline in the race.

"You know small-town politics," she replied. "I'm appointed by the mayor, the mayor is elected by the citizens, the citizens care about what impacts them—for example, someone on the loose who burned down their library."

"Are you worried about your job?"

Eve took a moment to reply. "The mayor's most serious opponent, Pauline Bromwell, might have her own chief of police in mind. I don't think the third candidate has a chance, and I have no clue what he'd do with my position." That was all Eve was going to say about the risk to her job—nothing specific about her ex-girlfriend to Doug Hooper, as much as she liked him.

"Well, let's catch the SOB before the election, then."

"I'll vote for that." Eve leaned back in her chair and frowned as she concluded the call.

## Chapter Four

It was late Friday afternoon, and Shaye struggled to bend down and then heave another box onto the table so she could examine its contents, the same motions she'd been going through since the surprising police station encounter with Eve Maguire a few days ago. There were two reasons that she was spending as much time as possible in this little tin box triaging books—some the salvageable warped casualties of a firehose spray-down, some with singed corners, and many marinated in smoke.

Shaye loved books and had pep-talked herself into the mindset that she was a bibliophile on a rescue mission. This town's torched library had helped save her sanity when she was a kid. That was the first reason.

The second, less noble reason was that with her libido fighting with common sense, it was best to avoid her new office and the temptation of Eve. *The temptation of Eve.* Memories of a painting with that title surfaced from an art history course she'd taken years ago. Female nude. Shaye shook her head. If she thought of Eve that way, she was screwed.

As Shaye lifted another pile of books from the box, her phone rang. She looked at the caller ID, smiled when she saw it was her best friend, and took the call.

"So, you actually survived the move from the Bay Area," Annie said. "I gave you a few days to settle in, Shanelle Desiraye Hooligan."

"*Hooligan*?" Shaye faux-huffed. Annie often had a new name for her, related to her real name or not.

"It has a certain appeal, don't you think? And Shanelle Desiraye is the truth. Blame your parents."

Shaye wanted to avoid any discussion about her fathers, so she commented on her mother. "I've neglected my mom—you know that I need to catch up with her."

Shaye could hear Annie's response—a distinct "Mm-hmm" without further comment.

Annie already knew why she was back in town. She'd been a major advisor to Shaye's decision to return, so no reason to retread that territory right now. Shaye redirected her comments back to her name, and hopefully, a lighter conversation. "How about just Shaye Hayden? Might even get me not to hang up on you."

"Okay, I'll concede that it's Hayden. But you're no fun," Annie said.

"Oh, I'm fun." Shaye let her voice drop a suggestive octave.

"So, are you having fun there in Paradise Pines yet? As your library professional mentor and friend for too many years to count, I want the details…what besides scorched books is hot in the boonies?"

Shaye hesitated too long.

"Holy cow. Who is she?" Annie asked, not keeping the amusement out of her voice.

"No one I'm interested in."

"So, tell me who *aren't* you interested in?"

Shaye bit her lip, remaining silent while she decided what to say about Eve. She might as well talk to Annie. It wasn't like she was going to get advice or therapy from anyone in this town, except maybe her mom, and she knew she was going to need support if she was going to stay strong.

"This is not the time to be quiet." Annie used her authoritative librarian voice. The one they both had perfected to tell unruly teens who were breaking the rules of library etiquette to do just the opposite.

"The mayor gave me an office in the police station. One that's needed for police work."

"Is he mad…the police chief? Are you already in hot water?" Annie asked.

Shaye cleared her throat. "*She*."

"Aha. My mistake. Good for her…police chief. Is she hot?"

"Not my normal type."

Annie chuckled. "Not your normal type—so you're saying she's mature, sophisticated, has leadership skills…"

"Yes," Shaye replied. "All those things. But she's a cop. You know how I feel about cops. Not in a million years am I getting involved with one, and this one is the freaking chief of police."

"So don't get involved. Your loss."

Shaye remained silent again.

"Oh my God. What did you do?"

"I might have sort have kissed her, never having met her before, not even knowing her name, who she was. At a bar the night before I moved. I was three hours away from bumfuck nowhere."

Annie hooted. "You're my hero, Hayden. You've launched. You know we bibliophiles love a good hero's journey—in your case, heroine."

"I'm thrilled to be so entertaining."

"Shaye…the hero's journey. It's epic. The departure, the initiation, the return. Moving to the sticks on a savior mission—saving a library, but more importantly, yourself. You made a departure, although in your case that means a return. You know, the call to an adventure—your refusal of that call when you didn't want to go. The influence of the mentor—me—convincing you to take the job, and more importantly, to face your past. The wise counselor…Obi-Wan Kenobi, Gandalf—that's me."

Shaye was laughing now.

"I'm serious. But that kiss—now there's a call to adventure in its own right, and I'm hearing you refuse that call—your refusal to follow up on that kiss. I'm mentoring you to go for it. Give this cop a chance," Annie said.

"And I always thought you looked more like Yoda."

"My advice, give the romantic journey a shot…moving to the remote wilds isn't the journey, it's just the setting."

"Not going to happen," Shaye said. "I'm here for a reason. And finding out I kissed a cop. Even unknowingly…a cop has no place in my life."

"Think on it. Anyway, I'm just calling to confirm that on my trip north to see my folks, you're going to drive to semi-civilization and meet me for coffee tomorrow morning at that coffee house that I sent you the address to, about half an hour from you. I'll call you when I'm forty minutes out. That'll give you time to drive over there."

"Yup. I've got it on my calendar…Saturday morning…coffee with Annie," Shaye replied. "Can't wait."

"I've gotta go, but I'm following this amorous odyssey—you and the bumfuck nowhere chief of police. You're my hero, *Homer.*" Annie hung up, still laughing.

❖

Eve went over recent events as she drove through the open space out of town. Last evening, she'd been watching the crowd disperse after the football game, making sure everyone was staying safe. She'd seen Pauline's daughter, Cassie, in a group of kids and parents as they'd exited the high school stadium. The sighting had poked Eve in that sore spot she worked so hard to bury. It was over a year into Eve's post-Pauline period, and even though she'd been the one to call it quits, occurrences like seeing Cassie reminded her of what she'd thought she'd had. At what she'd failed at.

She missed Cassie, who was now eleven. From what Eve had heard around town, Pauline had used the mayoral run as an excuse to park her daughter at Pauline's stepmother's house for the long term. Eve actually thought that might be best for the kid. Ginny Bromwell was a good person. Although of retirement age, she job-shared a kindergarten teaching position at the elementary school in town and was great with kids.

She and McGruff had been up early this morning so she could stop at the police station before she'd headed to her current destination to meet her brother, Earl, for coffee at their halfway spot. She'd wanted to make sure everything was running smoothly at work. And even though it was a Saturday, Eve had checked to see if Shaye might be sitting in the office she didn't belong in, half hoping she'd be there, telling herself it was probably better that she wasn't. She hadn't seen Shaye since that day after returning from Sadie's with McGruff—she was either totally tied up in that little trailer or she was avoiding the police station on purpose.

Trying to tamp down her thoughts about Shaye, Eve turned left off the highway onto a smaller road. She needed to sort out her life, not get involved with someone new who she could attest to being a masterful flirt. And who she knew to be a superb kisser after a little barstool chatter and just one drink. If she hadn't learned anything from Pauline, she had no common sense. No sense of self-preservation either. She needed to figure this out and not just fall for somebody. Not that she was falling for Shaye. She needed to keep her eye on her job.

Shaye was a hazard too—not her fault, but the spare office was still gone. Plus, Shaye seemed to have something against her for being the police chief. Eve had worked her ass off and devoted her life to become the best chief of police she could be, so Shaye's attitude perplexed her.

McGruff growled from the back seat and brought Eve back to

the moment. It was a where-the-hell-are-you-taking-me growl, and Eve had a hard time not offering him a response—maybe a peal or two of uncontrolled hilarity because of how ridiculous this was. Who would have thought she'd be translating the growls of a canine curmudgeon as the only significant component of her personal life?

"Hang in there, McGruff. We're here."

Eve pulled into an empty spot out in the middle of the Daily Grind parking lot, then climbed from the car and lifted McGruff out of the back seat. She walked him to an adjacent wooded area where he snorted his way through the weeds to find the perfect spot to lift his leg while Eve stood there and waited.

She wanted Earl to meet McGruff in case she was desperate for an emergency dog sitter sometime in the future. Earl had been too busy Roto-Rootering clogged plumbing and fixing unexpected leaks in his thriving business to drive over to Paradise Pines, so they'd agreed on midmorning coffee today at a spot about half an hour away from Eve's place since he had a job near the coffee shop where they'd met on other occasions.

Joye, Eve's friend and hairdresser, had agreed to be the first responder for dog care after McGruff's half-hearted grumble of minimal tolerance—probably the piece of cookie she'd given him. Joye had a big heart, and after telling Eve she'd never seen a critter more in need of a makeover—personality-wise and appearance-wise—she was on board for dog-duty backup. When Joye had left Los Angeles and a bad divorce behind almost seven years ago, Paradise Pines had acquired a top-notch hair stylist who hadn't only delivered the best haircare for miles, but she'd befriended Eve as well. Besides her salon, she'd decided Paradise Pines needed a local weekly newspaper, which she'd named the *Paradise Pulse,* frequently shortened to just the *Pulse*—she'd started it and was now the journalist and publisher of local news.

"Okay, McGruff. Time to wrap it up. I really need you to be on your best behavior. I know Earl wears that baseball cap and has a completely different take on politics than I do, but he likes dogs and loves a macho man—and that's you. Besides, you're part of the family now. It doesn't matter how that family got pieced together—even including an unplanned canine roadside acquisition."

As she finished resettling McGruff into his back seat bed, Eve heard the deep rumble of an approaching pickup truck that pulled in next to her. Earl let the deep rumble of his huge, six-wheeled work vehicle continue to resonate across the parking area for another long moment before he turned off the engine and climbed down from the black elevated cab.

"Showtime, McGruff. Be cool." Eve patted his head.

Earl came over to where Eve was standing at her vehicle, back door wide open and McGruff offering a deep-throated groan of concern.

"Hiya, sis. I didn't peg you for ending up with a mutt." Earl remained standing back from the open door and bent low, smiling in as the groaning continued from the car's interior.

"Long story, but it seems he's mine now. His name is McGruff. But I'm trying to call him Mac at work—don't ask."

"McGruff." Earl chortled. "Cool name. I sure hope he's got bigger balls than that Minnie princess that Sadie and Glen had."

Eve gave Earl a disapproving look, knowing he was working hard to offer her a show of brotherly poking. "Minnie *never* had any balls—may she rest in peace. Maybe that's why I'm the one with the detective credentials. And McGruff here doesn't need the ones he's missing. Once you meet him, you'll realize he's no princess. Not exactly a gentleman either, so be prepared."

Earl adjusted his cap, continuing to lean down and peer into the car. "Hiya, buddy."

McGruff took one look at him, stood up on the back seat, and then howled like a wolf. A head-thrown-back, full-throated serenade unlike anything Eve had heard come out of his mouth to date.

"Holy smokes. He's my kind of ball-less dog. If they're going to make you a eunuch, don't let them shut you up," Earl said to him. "And that don't-mess-with-me exterior...God, he could be a WrestleMania mascot."

Eve couldn't help but be amused. Of course Earl would appreciate McGruff's obnoxious disposition and I've-been-through-hell look.

"Does he bite?" Earl asked as McGruff continued his brother-in-arms call to the wild. At least he had Earl's approval.

"Nope. Not that he's confessed to anyway." She couldn't keep the tease out of her voice with her little brother. All six foot five, two hundred and thirty-some pounds of him.

"Well, that's a shame. Showing your teeth on occasion beats the blinkin' heck out of prissy-ass, commie kumbaya crap."

"If he could vote, I'm sure he'd be checking the same boxes you do," Eve drolly suggested.

"Okay. I'm in if he ever needs a spot to land for a few days."

"Thanks, Earl. You know I love you. Except for canceling out my vote…you're my favorite sibling."

"You're my favorite sibling too." Then he grinned. "Nothing to do with the fact you're my only sibling."

"Nothing at all."

"Shall we leave McGruff here to sing his song of despair at the state of the world and go get some coffee?" Earl asked.

"Not sure that's what he's singing about, but let's go fill a mug."

They entered the café and Earl headed toward an empty table. There were display cases scattered throughout the space filled with bags of coffee and other merchandise for sale. The place was packed, and Eve was happy they found seats.

"I'll go get us drinks if you hold the table," Eve said. "You want your normal with two sugars?"

At his agreement, Eve headed to get in line. As she stood there with two people in front of her, the person behind her whispered in her ear.

"They don't serve old-fashioneds here. I guess it's a little early for one anyway. Same question as Monday. You stalking me?"

Eve paused in surprise as she realized who was standing there. She tried to ignore the rush of pleasure and spoke back over her shoulder, "Same answer as Monday. Sure am…me and my tracking dog. Gave up our Saturday morning, traveled over hill and dale, all to spy on you at the Daily Grind."

"So, where's that *charming* little undercover McGruff, then?"

"Snoring in my vehicle. After he interviewed my brother as a prospective ally and emergency backup option, howling his opinion like the leader of the pack at a full moon to the entire parking lot, Earl and I came in for a little coffee. That was, of course, just extracurricular to stalking you here."

"Nice undercover outfit too." Shaye's breath warmed Eve's neck, then she stepped back and made a point of appraising Eve in her tight jeans from behind. "Are you armed and dangerous?" Shaye paused her assessment, then continued. "Yup…extremely dangerous."

She didn't want to be, but Eve was enjoying herself. Shaye knew how to take her places she hadn't been in way too long. But it wasn't just the physical surge. She couldn't deny that she liked Shaye, and that created internal anxiety.

Eve stepped to the counter for her turn as Shaye diverted her attention to the muffin case. Eve placed her order and paid. She quickly handed the kid behind the counter an extra twenty-five dollars and told her that she was paying for the brunette's order behind her and she could keep the change. Receiving an appreciative grin from the barista, she headed to collect her two drinks and Earl's packets of sugar before nodding at Shaye on her way back to her table. Dang if she didn't feel compelled to add a little extra sway to her hips.

"Who was the gorgeous chick in line with you?" Earl asked when she plunked the drinks down. He was still staring at Shaye. "You going to introduce me?" He turned back to Eve and suggestively licked his lips before smoothing the front of his T-shirt across his broad chest. Eve knew he was teasing her with the show.

"Don't be a jerk."

Earl grinned. "Okay. But she does look like my type."

"She's the new Paradise Pines librarian. She's only interested in people with library cards." She enjoyed teasing her brother too, who clearly relished portraying his version of a macho male.

"I just might be motivated to get one. For that stunner, I'd be willing to learn to read." Earl winked at Eve. "Maybe hit up the story hour…oh, the places *we* could go."

Eve chuckled as she shook her head. "She didn't call you a jackass, but I'd swear she was thinking it. Hate to tell you this, pal, but she plays for my side."

"Sits with the political crowd on the left, huh? I could work with that under the circumstances." He danced his eyebrows.

"Sorry, but she—"

Earl interrupted with a mumbled, "She likes girls." He was looking across the room. "Obviously she does."

Eve followed his gaze. There was Shaye with her arms around a redhead who must have just walked in. They hugged and laughed, and Shaye's eyes sparkled with delight. The exuberant redhead spoke into Shaye's ear. Eve felt a surge of jealousy she had no business feeling, and the smack of being played. This was probably why Shaye had taken the job.

# CHAPTER FIVE

Well, this was the address, if Shaye was to believe her online search. She stood on the porch and looked once again at the new Mercedes-Benz GT in the driveway. She surveyed what was professed to be the nicest neighborhood in town. Then Shaye turned and stared at the front door as she took a moment to pull in a few deep breaths through her nostrils and slowly blow the air back out through her pursed lips. She chastised herself for hesitating because this was a step she knew she needed to take.

Annie had advised her, or to be honest, given her encouragement again yesterday at the Daily Grind regarding Shaye's need to face her past. "You've already taken the library job—deciding that returning to and living in Paradise Pines was part of coming to terms with your childhood. No heroine's journey without the road of trials," Annie had reminded her while Shaye rolled her eyes at her. "And I think the circle is symbolic, even if you don't exactly match the story template. Circling back to Paradise Pines will hopefully help you finally sort things out and mend. You need to mend. Maybe I'll even hear you calling it just Paradise one of these days."

Annie was aware of Shaye's past. The series of three men married to her mother. The guilt Shaye carried. The fact that the cops had shot her first stepfather by accident when she was five. Shaye's birth father, Jay Hayden, had passed away before she was born, and she had no memory of him. Her first stepfather, David, had married Shaye's mother when Shaye was three—he'd loved Shaye and her mom the two years they'd been a family, and she had memories of his love. He was the man she'd called Dad and was still the man she considered to have been her father. They'd been on a weekend getaway trip to San Francisco, he and Shaye inside a convenience store paying for gas when there was a holdup. A responding rookie cop had fired wildly and shot him because of her. It was her fault—she'd yelled "Gun!" when she'd seen the cop pull his weapon, and the rookie had panicked and fired, hitting her dad. A friggin' rookie who acted before he assessed the situation—who had lost his cool and taken away the dad she'd loved.

That also made it all her fault that they'd barely scraped by until her mother had finally remarried a man with two kids. Not a man like David, but it put a roof over their heads and food on the table. Joe Bromwell had passed away seven years ago, and she hadn't seen her stepsiblings in ages.

She'd only called her mom on rare occasions and visited twice after she'd attained her library science degree in San Jose, settling in Berkeley, where she'd eventually met someone. She'd actually married a cop, albeit a persistent one who had pursued her. On her part, maybe the marriage had been a failed attempt to make peace with her cop anger and move on. She now suspected that Cynthia had been taken with her looks. The marriage had lasted a few years and ended three years ago. Shaye had believed she'd given the marriage her best effort, so the divorce had added to her pain, reenforced her disdain for cops.

She'd hunkered down after her marriage was over and had only called her mom occasionally and visited twice since she'd left after high school. Seeing her mother was on Shaye's list too, but she needed to work up to that because her heart had so much more at stake with her mom. Being available to help her mom as she aged was another reason Shaye was back. Andy, her stepbrother, had never made the list.

After letting out one last drawn-out exhalation, Shaye knocked. She heard footsteps and then the door opened just a crack.

"Leaving no trail is critical." Her stepsister had a phone to her ear and looked startled as she swung the door open wider and saw Shaye. She held up a finger. "Gotta go." She shut the phone down and straightened her shoulders. "I was expecting someone else." The disconcerted look transformed into the old familiar mask of charm and benevolence that Shaye had seen come and go so many times in her past, depending on what would best serve her stepsister.

"Is that you, Shanelle? I'd heard you were back in town. Librarian, is it?

"Hi, Pauline. I just stopped by to say hello. Yes, I'm the town's new librarian." Shaye would have recognized her stepsister anywhere, even after all these years. She was the same platinum-coiffed, face-painted, and meticulously packaged person she'd always been style-wise, just with years more living under that presentation. Her flashy jewelry, the luxury car, the neighborhood. It was all window dressing, but undoubtedly important to Pauline. Pauline had always disdained their mundane middle-class upbringing and certainly seemed to have managed to leave it behind. Her mom had told her that Pauline had a high-level accounting job.

"So, I'll be your boss if things go according to plan. I'm running for mayor, so you'd better stay on my good side."

Shaye made a show of studying Pauline from right to left before asking, "And which side is that?" Pauline was still the same person on the inside—full of herself.

"I can see you haven't lost your sense of humor, even if your ex did more than enforce the law. Can't trust those cops, based on the gossip that filters back this way from the big city," Pauline said.

"That's one of my rules. Never trust a cop."

"I don't blame you. I've got my cop issues too. Top cop issues," Pauline replied.

Shaye had no idea what that "top cop" comment meant, especially coming from Pauline, but talking about cops wasn't on her agenda that afternoon anyway. Her current agenda was fulfilling the promise she'd made to herself to make contact with Pauline rather than end up in an awkward unplanned encounter, and to also ask about her mother.

"I've got a campaign event in twenty minutes, or I'd ask you in." Pauline remained blocking the open doorway, Shaye on the porch.

"That's okay. I just wanted to touch base since I'm back in town. Have you seen Mom lately?"

"Sure. I check in with her," Pauline said. Her eyes darted around, avoiding direct contact with Shaye's, a sign Shaye had learned years ago meant there was probably something she was withholding.

"And?" Shaye asked in her prodding tone.

"She's doing okay. Older, but okay. She'll probably be thrilled to see you. At least I think she will. You know how Ginny is…maternal. Ginny *Mommykins* Bromwell. Always willing to help those in need." Pauline's tone wasn't complimentary.

Shaye hated the way her stepsister derided her mother's maternal instincts. Made that sound like a bad thing. She might as well have used the word *chump*. Her mom had always been nothing but kind to Pauline and her brother after she'd married their father and become their stepmother.

"Not a bad trait to have, and it certainly can't hurt your campaign to have a Bromwell in town who wants to help those in need," Shaye replied.

Pauline smiled sweetly. It was her perfected sweet smile, the one that Shaye knew was way more calculated than sweet. "Well, Shanelle, considering the disaster of your youth, then your marriage falling apart, I can see why you've stayed away."

Pauline had always known how to slip in the knife. Then twist it. When she wasn't putting on her charismatic charade.

Pauline's facade made Shaye think about Eve's dog. Shaye appreciated McGruff. No pretending—he liked who he liked, and he let everyone else know how he felt about them. Shaye wanted to growl at Pauline, but she bit her cheeks because it would serve no purpose. Annie would be proud of her. Pauline had a vindictive streak right through to her core.

"Well, I'll let you get to your event, then. I'm sure that with the election I'll see you around town." Shaye started to turn away. She certainly wasn't going to wish Pauline good luck in the mayoral race.

"You didn't ask about Andy," Pauline said.

He was Pauline's younger brother, Shaye's stepbrother, and fell halfway between the six years that separated Shaye from Pauline's forty-six years. Six additional years that Pauline once lorded over her when they were younger. Now six years that were showing on her stepsister.

"So how is Andy?" Shaye asked.

"Still always broke, always willing to be a mercenary. But there are advantages to that when you're running for office."

"Advantages?" Shaye wasn't surprised at the broke or even the mercenary description. Her stepbrother had struggled with his issues. She remembered Joe Bromwell being a father who put in long hours at work, and Pauline had been a derisive sister. Shaye also remembered her mother's efforts to help him, but he'd been rebellious. Now she wondered what "advantages" meant.

Pauline shook her head and cleared her throat. "You know, putting up and relocating campaign signs, stuff like that. I try to help him out when I can."

Shaye had decided to ask about Cassie too, but a woman in a scant bathrobe suddenly came up behind Pauline. She gave Shaye a scowl and then said, "Hey, babe. My girlfriend is off work in a little while and expecting me home, so I need to get dressed and head out. Have fun at the campaign event, and I'll see you tomorrow afternoon." The woman disappeared back deeper into the house, out of Shaye's view.

"I've gotta go." Pauline waved good-bye and swung the door closed.

Shaye walked back to her car and sat there a minute. Forget the growl, she wanted to howl like Eve had said McGruff had done in the car outside of the Daily Grind. Awooooo. But she didn't have the energy for it right now. The next challenge—her mother, but not today.

❖

It was barely past four thirty on Tuesday morning, and Eve had finally crawled out of bed because she couldn't sleep. She hadn't slept well since Saturday. She told herself it wasn't because of what she and Earl had witnessed in the coffee shop—that Shaye had what certainly appeared to be a girlfriend. No, Eve was upset with herself.

Not that she was falling for Shaye, but that she'd allowed chemistry and attraction and the best flirting encounters of her lifetime and that flawless, irrevocable kiss to push her into this state of letdown when she hadn't carefully analyzed what her next relationship should even look like. She only had herself to blame.

Eve had resisted doing it because she despised stalkers, but she finally opened her laptop while she drank some coffee and did some quick every-joe-citizen type of cybersleuthing on the internet—she refused to use her professional resources. The information she found was linked to *Shanelle* Hayden's professional life as a librarian. After a bit of exploring, Eve was also able to deduce that she was likely the same person divorced from a Cynthia Dunbar, and maybe the same Cynthia Dunbar who was an Oakland police officer. An ex-wife as a cop certainly might explain the hostility to law enforcement if it had been a contentious divorce—if she had burned Shaye the way Pauline had burned Eve.

Eve showered, dressed, and collected McGruff before heading to work, even though it was barely six a.m. She'd just entered her office when she received a call from a county dispatcher who handled nighttime calls for Paradise Pines during the hours when Mona, the Paradise Pines dispatcher, was off.

"I wanted you to know that we just had a call from someone who said they're outside your mayor's campaign office. A fire alarm is going off, and they can see smoke and flames through the mail slot in the front door. Firefighters have been alerted, but I wanted you to know too, Chief."

"Thanks for the call. I'll head over now."

Eve contacted Grady Lopez, who was the officer on shift and a block away. She knew that the other officer she'd normally call for backup was probably at home preparing to give testimony in a burglary case at the county courthouse later that morning. She and Grady agreed to meet at the campaign office as soon as possible. "No one goes in except the fire crew. Detain the 911 caller if you can so we can see if they witnessed anything. I'll get there as soon as I can."

Then she called the county fire inspector's office to leave a message for Doug Hooper. She was surprised when he picked up so early. She explained what was going on, and he told her he'd head down to Paradise Pines immediately.

She stood and grabbed McGruff's leash. "Come on, boy. You can go for a ride and wait in the car where it's warm."

The police department was a few blocks west of the heart of downtown. As she turned onto Main Street, it was still too early for most of the shops to be open. Downtown Main Street was lined on both sides by rows of commercial enterprises—retail shops intermixed with other small businesses like the local real estate and insurance offices, all with darkened windows.

Eve passed her friend Joye's hair salon, the Cutting Edge, and noted that the lights were out. Joye had a large room in the back that served as the publication headquarters for the *Paradise Pulse*. Eve continued to cruise to the far end of Main Street where Sneed had headquartered his campaign. As she pulled into a spot directly in front of the office, her phone rang. Seeing that it was the county fire inspector, Doug Hooper, she took the call and listened a moment before leaving McGruff in his bed in the back seat and moving to join Grady, who was containing the small crowd that was gathering as the fire crew finished putting out the blaze.

"Hey, Chief." Steve, the head of the volunteer fire crew greeted her. "Not much of a fire. A burnt pile of debris—looks like paper. Maybe wadded, but small enough to shove through the mail slot in the door. My first impression is that someone pushed it through the slot and then dropped in whatever they used to light it. Didn't look like it was all turned to ash either—a bit of unburnt material at the periphery that the flames didn't consume. Looks like it was all done from the outside—through the door slot. It was pretty easy to snuff the small blaze. It's out."

"Thanks, Steve. I'm glad it wasn't big enough to need the full county fire crew. You know Doug Hooper, their fire inspector. He should be here in about ten minutes or so."

"Well, he's the expert, so since the danger is over, I'll leave it in you guys' hands." As Steve headed out, Eve walked over to Grady, who had taken charge as the officer on the scene.

"Chief, I can handle the lookie-loos here if you want to talk to the jogger over there, our witness and 911 caller." Grady pointed to the back of a person in a blue knitted beanie sitting on a bench several feet away.

Mayor Sneed came walking up, surveying the scene before addressing Eve. "What the hell is going on? I want you to look at Pauline Bromwell for this."

"Hopefully, we'll get to the bottom of it." Eve would need to remain impartial and hand any police aspect of the investigation off to the county sheriff if there was any real evidence that Pauline was involved. She didn't need a conflict of interest. "Inspector Hooper should be here soon, and he'll undoubtedly step in considering the library fire. You'll want to work out of another place for at least the day, and Hooper and I will take care of this. You're going to need a cleanup crew after we finish."

Sneed nodded as his campaign manager joined him. "Bret and I are going to go get a cup of coffee and regroup. Here's the office keys. Call me when you know something. I'll have my phone handy." They turned and headed down the street toward the Paradise diner.

"As if his phone isn't superglued to his ear," Grady said, then pointed toward the back of the jogger still waiting on the bench several feet away. "The witness."

"I'll take that interview. You watch the place until Hooper gets here, then go see if anyone was around in the neighboring shops and saw anything."

With her car in a spot right in front of the campaign office, Eve checked on McGruff through the slightly lowered car window. He was snoring in his bed in the back seat, so she let him be. Then she walked over to the bench to talk to the 911 caller. As she approached, she realized from her shape that the jogger appeared to be a female. She walked around to face the seated witness.

Eve and Shaye both raised their eyebrows in unison.

"I didn't expect the chief to show up." Shaye pulled off her beanie.

As Eve watched Shaye shake out that head of gorgeous hair, the early morning light enhancing the caramel highlights, she gulped and did her best not to let the wave of attraction that pulled at her chest and traveled lower override her professional demeanor.

"A fire in the mayor's campaign office will do that," Eve replied. "I didn't expect the town librarian to be jogging down Main Street at the crack of dawn on a cold morning."

Shaye was wearing running shorts and a T-shirt over her lean body, her long muscular legs providing evidence that she was a regular runner—and also evidence that Eve's initial assessment of *striking* was more than Shaye's face. Eve reminded herself that Shaye, who had so enticingly flirted with her...awakened long dormant feelings...expertly kissed her...also appeared to be involved with someone else. She was exactly the kind of person Eve would be excluding if she finally decided that she was willing to take the risk of considering a future long-term relationship with someone. Eve made sure her face was schooled to impassive.

"You look cold. It's not exactly weather for sitting around outside in running attire. Are you okay with sitting in my car right there?" Eve pointed. "To tell me what you saw."

As she worked to keep her focus on her job, Eve reflected on what Hooper had told her about John Orr, a firefighter who set fires for the excitement. She knew in her gut that Shaye was simply a witness, but she still had to keep an open mind that a 911 caller could be involved and seeking attention. Shaye wasn't living in town when the library was burned, one look at her body supported the fact she was a regular jogger, and McGruff liked her, whatever that meant. But everyone was a suspect until they weren't.

"Sure. Always willing to help those dedicated to protecting and serving." Shaye's words carried an undertone of sarcasm.

For Pete's sake. What did she have against *all* police? Eve considered her laptop search and Shaye's divorce. She had her own issues with Pauline, but she didn't blame all accountants. Eve led Shaye over to her car and opened the front passenger door for her. McGruff was now curled up on that front seat and looked at her through one squinted eye before he let out a soft grumble and closed that eye again.

Shaye looked over Eve's shoulder into the car and chuckled. "Looks like your canine sidekick is riding shotgun."

"He was in his bed in the back seat a moment ago. He's never been interested in riding shotgun before. I can move him."

"Let the old man be," Shaye replied. "I'm not going to freeze to death."

"You've got goose bumps. Shall we sit in the back seat?"

Shaye looked Eve up and down, her blue eyes darkening like they had in that bar. Her disdain for cops didn't show in her hungry gaze. Eve watched Shaye come to a decision, put on an air of bravado, and wiggle her eyebrows. "I'm game if you are."

Eve rolled her eyes. The darn flirt. She wasn't going to be distracted. She shut the front passenger door, leaving McGruff in peace, and opened the back seat door. Hooper had arrived and was talking to Grady. "I'll be with you, Hooper, when I finish here," she called to him.

"I've got it, Chief. A county forensics tech is due any minute too, so we'll handle it."

Eve waved and turned back toward the open back door, leaning way in and pushing the empty dog bed to the far side of the seat. She suspected Shaye was watching as she bent into the car—fair enough, she'd have a hard time not checking out Shaye if the roles were reversed. She accepted that they were physically attracted to each other—but she absolutely wasn't going to act on it. She backed up and nodded at Shaye to go ahead and have a seat.

"I'll grab you a blanket from the back. Warm you up a bit."

Shaye started to offer Eve a comeback, probably at the "warm up" reference, but then pressed her mouth closed. Eve chastised herself as she retrieved the blanket. She needed to watch even her innocent remarks—there was already too much chemistry between them. Shaye had scooted to the middle next to the dog bed when Eve returned and handed her the blanket before she climbed into the space that was left. Shaye was struggling with the blanket, so Eve, whose entire left side was pressed against Shaye's right side, twisted sideways and helped her wrap the covering over her scant running outfit. Eve needed that scant outfit covered.

"Just protecting and serving," Eve muttered.

A suppressed snort escaped from Shaye before she actually laughed. "I'd think you'd planned this, but your shade of pink suggests otherwise."

"I'm going to kill that dog," Eve muttered some more.

"Oh, I get it. Not only is he a tracker and an undercover canine, but he orchestrated this close encounter too." Then Shaye smacked her forehead in an exaggerated manner. "Maybe it's worse. Maybe he orchestrated that highway encounter of yours so we'd end up sharing old-fashioned drinks in a bar." Shaye leaned forward and spoke to the front passenger seat. "Sorry, McGruff, but wasted effort. I don't like cops."

A long, low objecting moan came from the front seat.

Eve wasn't going to discuss Shaye's divorce or her dislike of Eve because of her career, but she couldn't suppress a lip twitch at the damn dog. Then she took a fortifying breath and grew serious again as she fought to ignore her thrumming pulse, a static beacon in her turmoil of feelings as she concentrated on questioning the witness. "So, tell me what caused you to call 911."

Shaye and Eve spent fifteen minutes exchanging information.

"When I came around the corner onto Main Street off Lupine, several blocks down," Shaye pointed down the street, "I saw a figure in dark clothing close to here, but I was too far away to know if it was right here at Sneed's campaign office. It could have been the place a door or two down on either side of his place, and I couldn't tell you much of anything about the person. They took off and left in the direction I was jogging, so I never got closer to them."

Eve didn't learn anything else except that Shaye hadn't seen anyone else but had heard a smoke alarm as she had passed the office and thought that she'd smelled smoke. She'd pushed on the mail slot and seen the smoldering paper down on the floor, so made the call.

Eve told her to stay there in the car, then went to the open office door and attracted the attention of Hooper in his personal protective equipment, his forensic tech in similar PPE attire.

"I'm going to drive our 911 caller home," Eve told him. "You want me back here or shall I get on with the day?"

"We've got it. There's nothing more you can do here. Your officer said he was going to check for more witnesses, so I'll touch base with you later. Let you know what we've got and when we're done. I suspect that mayor of yours will be breathing down your neck."

Eve nodded and headed back to the car. She climbed into the front seat, surprised to see that McGruff had returned to the back seat bed next to Shaye.

"I'm taking you home. You want to move up here, or are you okay being chauffeured?"

"McGruff and I are good back here. It's 421 Chestnut."

"Not a short run for you this morning—that's across town," Eve said.

"A neighborhood I knew before I rented the place." Shaye looked away when Eve gave her a questioning glance in the rearview mirror. It only made Eve more curious. Curiosity was part of her job, she assured herself.

Ten minutes later, they pulled into a driveway with a small house on the lot. Shaye scooted out of the back seat, leaving the blanket behind.

"Thanks for the ride."

"My pleasure," Eve responded, conflicted because it totally was.

## CHAPTER SIX

Later in the morning, the fire inspector called Eve at her office. "Hey, Chief. So let me bring you up to speed on what I know."

Eve was listening to Hooper when she saw Shaye walk past the open door on her way to her office.

Hooper continued to talk and Eve had to concentrate to keep her attention on what he was saying. The incendiary device appeared to be the same type as the prior one used at the library, and that information had never been released to the public.

Eve watched McGruff take off and turn down the hallway toward Shaye. She walked to the doorway with her phone to her ear as she monitored his progress while Hooper continued talking. "Hopefully, we'll be able to confirm or deny a match to the library fire arson."

Eve tracked McGruff as he trotted right into Shaye's space, and she struggled to bring her attention back to the phone conversation. Traitorous mutt.

"Damage to your mayor's campaign office was minimal—not much fuel and the area below the slot was barren. I doubt an accelerant, but we'll do lab analysis. Your guess as to the motive is as good as mine—poorly planned, political, or something else?" Hooper asked.

"I don't know. While this probably isn't playing out well for our mayoral incumbent, Sneed would love to be able to blame his election opponent. He's unhappy," Eve said. She was unhappy too. And frustrated. She was pretty sure her job was contingent on who won this election. This was additional motivation to solve the arsons.

"That's all I have for the moment." Hooper concluded his rundown of the situation.

"So far, there's been no note like I received after the library fire. The *Paradise Pulse* publisher called me for information. I'd like to keep politics out of it. I'm not going there without proof."

"Sounds good. Let's keep each other updated."

"Thanks, Hooper." Eve finished the call and headed down the hallway to Shaye's office to catch up with her disloyal dog. Her phone rang again, and because it was the mayor, she took the call standing in Shaye's doorway as she watched Shaye sitting in her chair with McGruff in her lap.

He lifted his face and licked Shaye on the chin, making Eve think about that kiss she and Shaye had shared. Eve nodded at her. Shaye looked good in gray slacks and a pale pink blouse, but Eve couldn't lose the image of her in in those running shorts and T-shirt—testimony to the great shape she was in. Well, all the future kissing was going to be up to the pooch.

"Hello, Mayor. I just got off the phone with Doug Hooper. Let me bring you up to speed." Eve proceeded to tell Sneed what Hooper had told her, Shaye listening in. Eve waited patiently while he rattled on, claiming the fire must have a linkage to Pauline. She was ready to finish the call, but before she could end it, the mayor changed the subject.

"You know the city is having a citizens' commendation presentation on the fifteenth. A Thursday, late afternoon. Just happens to be my fiftieth birthday too. It's important I have a good turnout for appearances' sake, so I'm expecting you to attend. I've got a lot of people to call, to make sure they show, so I'll leave it to you to pass the message on to the new librarian in that office next to yours. Gotta go." He hung up.

Eve shook her head, and her heart rate elevated as she took in Shaye. There was no getting around the fact that their paths were going to cross. Eve just had to keep her eye on her personal mission—to find time to establish some personal guidelines for herself so if she did eventually consider dating, she wouldn't repeat her mistakes.

"The mayor said to tell you he expects you at the city's commendation presentation on Thursday, the fifteenth. For outstanding citizens," Eve said. "Mandatory for his big crowd expectations. It also happens to be his fiftieth birthday, so I'm sure that won't slip by unnoted—probably actually the basis for the timing. I'd bet money on cake."

"You don't sound happy."

Eve shrugged, knowing it was part of doing the job she didn't want to lose. "Not part of the official job description, but part of small-town unofficial duties. Recognizing influential citizens during an election year. I bet you didn't know that eating birthday cake was as important as running the library."

Shaye cocked a brow at Eve. "I'm not a total innocent. Are they serving alcohol? Maybe old-fashioneds? To make it worthwhile."

"I never mistook you for an innocent. I know better. And I hate to disappoint you, but my guess is coffee or tea." Eve chuckled as she added, "When it comes to 'Happy Birthday to You,' sing your little heart out."

"Got it. Will I get fired for singing off-key?"

"Not if you're flashing those pearly whites and grinning like a Cheshire Cat for the photo op."

"Like this?" Shaye did just that, and Eve felt her heart in her throat, triggered by more than those gorgeous pearly whites. Triggered by the aura of exuberance projected across Shaye's stunning face, dancing in her animated azure eyes. It was a mix of feelings harder to explain than simple physical attraction. So much more complicated. Eve struggled to suppress the magnetism of Shaye Hayden, especially when Shaye momentarily freed herself from whatever weighed on her.

"That'll probably do," Eve said, fighting for a carefully controlled tone with no hint of her side of this invisible connection that she felt in their exchanges. "Come on, McGruff. I need to drag you along on some errands."

"If we bring his bed down here, he can stay with me. If you think he'll be happier."

"I think there's a law against stealing my dog. Severe consequences for you."

"For me, huh?" Shaye's tone was infused with fake innocence.

Eve did her best to ignore where this conversation could go and addressed what she'd meant. "You'd have to put up with growling. Maybe even howling."

Shaye laughed, and then raised and lowered her eyebrows suggestively. "Exactly what I was thinking, but glad you clarified it for me, Chief."

Blast it, but Shaye was a menace and an enticing flirt, but Eve couldn't help but join in the laughter through her embarrassment. "You knock it off." She pointed at Shaye before redirecting her attention to McGruff and pointed at him too. "And you can count yourself lucky I don't haul your traitorous canine carcass to the pound." Eve turned on her heel before calling back over her shoulder, "I'll be back in an hour or so. Leave him in my office if you have to go before I get back."

"I've got library hours at the trailer this afternoon and need to continue the cleanup, so I'll do that if necessary."

Heading back down the hallway, Eve chastised herself. Shaye hated cops, maybe for a good reason if the online information about Shaye having a cop as her ex-wife was correct. She was already involved with someone else. She was an expert at creating off-the-chart chemistry. Eve needed to keep reminding herself of those facts. Leave Shaye and the kissing to McGruff. She still had a job to keep her plenty busy.

❖

Eve dropped by the Cutting Edge. Joye had called her for a fire update for the newspaper, and Eve wanted to get out ahead of the news because it would only add to election tension. In addition, Joye was one of the best clearinghouses in town for what was happening— even before it happened. Her contribution to Paradise journalism was informally shortened to the *Pulse* for good reason. Maybe they could exchange information.

With no customers at the moment, Joye greeted Eve with a cup of coffee. "Where's that deputy dog disaster of yours?"

"He preferred to stay at the station with the new librarian. The one who stole the spare office space next door to mine."

"And you're blaming her for that office assignment instead of the mayor? Maybe you should blame Pauline for running for mayor— that's what Sneed's reacting to." Joye pursed her lips as she considered. "Yeah, don't vilify the librarian. Blame Pauline. Eve's bad apple."

Eve rolled her eyes at Joye's characterization of Pauline. It wasn't far off-base. Then she shrugged, and Joye studied her before she raised the corner of her mouth in a sign of affectionate amusement and gave Eve a nod. She knew Eve too well, and that expression signaled she knew there was more to the situation than the office assignment.

"She has a girlfriend from what I know. End of discussion," Eve said.

"We never began the discussion…and that tells me a whole lot."

"You know as well as anyone that I need to face where I went wrong with Pauline. And Shaye would be exactly the same mistake, although I saw her with a woman, and they were pretty darn close. Looked like a girlfriend relationship to me…when I drove over and met

Earl for coffee at the Daily Grind, so I'm already the wiser." Eve gave Joye a warning look, hoping that would get her off the topic of Shaye.

Joye threw up her hands. "Okay. Are you here to book a hair trim or to spill the latest on what you and Doug Hooper found at the fire this morning?"

"News travels fast."

"Smoke signals," Joye replied. "Spelled out a direct hit on Sneed's campaign office."

"Yup. There's not a lot I can tell you, but he should be back in the office before the day is over."

"Good to know. I didn't want to have to report it out as a major item to feed campaign gossip. I have to treat it impartially, though."

"Do what you have to do." Eve shrugged and then smiled. "Keep giving me decent hair trims, put up with my dog, and I won't hold it against you."

"Thanks." Joye took a sip of her coffee. "I should tell you that I'm going out with Earl. He came in for a haircut and asked me to go to dinner with him on Friday night."

Eve choked on her drink. "You and Earl? He's a good guy and I love him, but I think your world view might be a bit more to the left than his."

"True. But I don't think either of us has politics on the agenda."

"I don't want to hear about it—at least not any bedroom details. Not now. Not later. Not ever. Not you and my baby brother," Eve said. "I just came by to quash rumors about the fire. It was small. No break-in. Happened through the mail slot of Sneed's campaign office with very little fuel on a bare floor, so there was little chance of spreading. No more clues as to who or why. That's all I've got for you."

"Okay. Thanks. The location at Sneed's headquarters has people suggesting that it kinda makes Pauline look suspicious. Maybe I won't quote the info as coming from the chief of police to save you the wrath of Pauline—in case she gets elected. Sneed's office fire makes her look bad."

"There's no evidence of Pauline's involvement. I'm likely toast if she wins, so a quote on the facts isn't going to matter." Eve felt a pang of exasperation at this consideration of the role that Pauline was having on Joye doing her reporting job, and the fact that quoting Eve from her official role as chief of police seemed so politically charged.

"I've got Faye Brown due to arrive in about five minutes for a color and cut, but I'm glad you came by. I did want to pass something else on to you. Unofficially and not in your cop role. Just rumor."

"I'm listening," Eve replied.

"I know it's a sensitive issue for you, but I also know you care and you keep tabs on her, so I just want you to know that I heard that Pauline's daughter, Cassie, has been climbing Coyote Hill. Up to the big rock at the top late at night and sitting up there alone. Nothing terrible, just not very safe. I also heard that she's living with Pauline's stepmother, Ginny."

"Thanks. I'd heard she was with Ginny too. I hadn't heard about her being out alone late at night, though." Eve sighed. She'd had a relationship for four years with the girl while she was with Pauline, from the time Cassie was six, until a year ago. Eve cared for Cassie. She'd become attached to her, but putting her in the middle when Eve had left Pauline a year ago hadn't seemed right, so she'd backed off. The entire situation had put Eve in a tough position, so simply keeping tabs on Cassie from a distance had been her solution. Now she'd have to think about what to do. If Cassie was staying with Ginny, that might make things easier.

Faye Brown came in, which was Eve's cue to leave. She refused to think about the Joye and Earl tryst—they were adults—but Cassie was just a kid. Eve would need to address the issue.

❖

As Eve stepped out of the Cutting Edge, she realized her day wasn't improving. Sometimes she wished she lived in a big city because the chances of running into your ex would be significantly reduced compared to a small town like Paradise Pines. Since their breakup, Eve had managed to give Pauline a wide berth and had avoided directly encountering her for longer than she probably had a right to expect. Well, there Pauline was now, not fifteen feet away and headed in Eve's direction. There was no evading her. Eve immediately decided that her goal was to keep the encounter brief and not draw attention to the two of them if she could prevent it.

Pauline wore a well-tailored white pantsuit, black heels, and a neck scarf. Her hair and makeup had received her usual meticulous attention. Eve noticed the increased ostentation of the bling she wore—she hadn't seen her recently. Large diamonds hung from her ears and more diamonds flashed from the multiple rings that adorned her manicured fingers, and she had what appeared to be an expensive gold watch on her left wrist.

Eve wondered if the finery was even real, or just another element of Pauline's facade. She'd heard that Pauline had recently moved to the upscale Regal Heights area of town, so she obviously was making progress toward the lifestyle she'd craved. Eve considered that maybe she had a new girlfriend with money that Eve hadn't heard about yet, or maybe she was doing very well in her senior accounting job and maybe even making some good investments too. However, when it came to Pauline, the only factor that really mattered to Eve these days was who won the mayoral seat.

"Well, if it isn't the *current* Paradise Pines police chief." The purr in Pauline's voice was practiced and perfected. Eve wondered how she hadn't seen through Pauline before she'd wasted four years of her life. This first volley was a reminder that Eve's job was on the line, and the almost imperceptible flare of irritation in Pauline's eyes backed that up. Pauline likely wouldn't blatantly threaten her. She was much more subtle than that.

"Hello, Pauline. It's been a while. You look like you're doing well." Eve ignored the churning in her stomach.

Pauline pursed her lips, coated in her signature deep red hue, *Diva Indulgence*. The things you learned when you lived with someone, Eve thought...and fitting. Then Shaye's full moist lips, minimally glazed if at all, came to mind—so much more appealing.

"I am. I was just running some downtown errands before heading to my campaign office to drop a few things off. I heard about Sneed's office fire." Pauline gave nothing away in her tone, but when Eve considered how well Pauline had fooled her in the past, she didn't have much faith that she'd be able to detect any suggestion of guilt on Pauline's part, even if she was involved in the arsons.

Eve wasn't sure if Pauline was fishing for information or not, but she wasn't prepared to disclose anything that wasn't common knowledge. "We're working with the county fire inspector on the arsons." That information had been in the *Pulse* after the library fire.

"Well, I bet Sneed is getting impatient for you to solve this." Pauline paused before she added, "You are *his* chief of police."

"Actually, I was the chief before he was elected. I serve the community at the pleasure of whoever the mayor is. The mayor answers to that community through election."

"Exactly. At the pleasure of the mayor," Pauline echoed.

Eve was reaching her limit. "I get it, Pauline. If you're elected, my job is in jeopardy."

Pauline dipped her head, discreetly making it clear where she stood, not that it was novel information to Eve. Eve had known this from the time Joye had called to let her know Pauline had entered the race.

It was time to change the subject. "Cassie. I heard she's staying with Ginny." Eve toyed with mentioning what Joye had disclosed about Cassie's nighttime escapades but wanted to hear Pauline's reply before she said more.

"She is. I just don't have time, and Ginny's a born mother. I've been busy...the campaign and all. In fact, I've got to go." Pauline moved past Eve, then threw back over her shoulder, "Cassie's out of my hair and doing fine with her."

Eve wasn't surprised by Pauline's response, but it still angered her. She decided that she'd need to follow through on her own.

❖

Late the next afternoon, Eve stood for a moment, reflecting on how there didn't seem to be a way to leave her past behind. She'd been there on rare occasion before—this was where Pauline's stepmother lived, and she'd had reason to come here on occasion with Pauline. Taking a deep breath to calm herself, Eve knocked on Ginny Bromwell's front door. She hoped Ginny and Cassie would be here before their dinner hour.

She'd thought about Cassie last night and decided she needed to check up on her because while she'd avoided direct contact before, she now had information that pushed clarifying the child's safety into the scope of her job. She realized that there was a good chance if she really wanted to help Cassie, this was just an initial step. A more sustained presence might be needed, contrary to how she'd handled Cassie recently because of Pauline. Just knocking on the door triggered all sorts of heart palpitations, but Eve wouldn't forgive herself if something happened to Cassie and she hadn't followed up on what Joye had told her.

"Why, if it isn't Eve." Ginny greeted her with a huge smile as she opened the front door wide. "I wasn't expecting you, but you're a sight for sore eyes. Come on in for coffee, and you can tell me what I can do for you."

"I've got my newly acquired canine unit in my car, so I shouldn't stay long."

"Fiddlesticks. You go get him, or her, and I'll share a biscuit or two I bought for my neighbor's dog. I won't take no. I want to meet…?"

"McGruff. Male. A little worse for wear, but we're working things out." Eve strode back out to her car, leashed McGruff, and walked him to where Ginny stood at the entrance to the house. Maybe he'd be an icebreaker with Cassie.

"Come on in and join us. This is the afternoon for visitors," Ginny said as she led them across the living room to the dining area.

Eve could see Cassie at the table with a soda in front of her, talking to a ponytailed female whose back was to Eve. She focused on Cassie, who pushed her too-long blond bangs out of her eyes, scowled, and then gave Eve a hard glare. Eve sighed. She probably deserved it, at least from an eleven-year-old's point of view.

"Eve, McGruff, of course you know Cassie, Pauline's daughter. She's living with me and I'm delighted." Ginny gave Cassie a smile. "And I think my daughter left town before you arrived, Eve, but I'd like you to meet Shanelle Hayden—also the new town librarian."

Eve locked eyes with Shaye, who had swiveled around to face her. Eve's chest squeezed tight, then she felt her heart stutter before picking up speed, pounding as she fought to show no reaction, to not close her eyes and take a deep breath. Ginny's daughter? She'd known Ginny was Pauline's stepmother, although as an adult, Pauline rarely spent time with extended family. Pauline had once mentioned she'd grown up with a stepsister who had been married to a police officer. Eve had never met that stepsister, but she had to be Shaye.

Eve swallowed and refused to blink. She allowed herself a moment to absorb this revelation. She and Shaye had nothing in common except her law enforcement profession and Shaye's aversion to it…and a magnificent, impulsive kiss that was turning out to be a huge mistake… and an undeniable chemistry that would blow up in her face…and now this newly disclosed Pauline linkage. Goddamn stepsisters. Eve couldn't believe she'd ever even considered for a nanosecond letting Shaye shift the focus in her own life from strictly professional—that's what she was good at. This couldn't get much worse.

"Shaye." Eve nodded, concentrating on appearing unaffected by what she'd just discovered. Eve never would have suspected this, and she had to assume Shaye hadn't had any knowledge of her personal history either.

"If you're calling her Shaye, then you two have met. Of course you have, both employed here by the town." Ginny beamed.

"Yes, I've met the chief of police," Shaye said, obviously working to keep her tone neutral as well, but Eve could discern a guarded undertone.

Okay, Eve thought. No disclosing to Ginny any more than a passing professional encounter. Fair enough, that worked for her too, especially with this new stepsister revelation. As Eve's emotions warred between attraction and revulsion, she chastised herself. She needed to take this disclosure as the gut punch gift it was. She and Shaye didn't have a snowball's chance in Hades of a future, and the sooner she accepted that, the safer her traitorous emotions would be.

"Coffee will be done in a minute. Are you staying, or should I fix it to go? Cream or sugar?" Ginny asked from over by the coffeepot before she handed Eve two dog biscuits.

"Black is fine. To go, please." Eve walked over to the table and set the biscuits in front of Cassie. "You willing to do the honors?" she asked. Eve watched the tug-of-war play out, Cassie glaring at her and then offering McGruff a softer look. Eve turned her back on them, giving Cassie space while she directed her attention to helping Ginny in the kitchen. Ginny winked at her, so maybe she was doing something right.

Taking quick glances, Eve observed McGruff sidle up next to Cassie and offer his sorrowful, starving dog look. Cassie rolled her eyes before handing him a biscuit. After consuming the second one, he gave Cassie an appreciative grunt and then headed around the table to Shaye.

"At least the dog is happy to be around me," Cassie said, looking at Eve. "Is there a reason you're here? Can't be for coffee and dog biscuits." Then she tilted her head toward Shaye. "You here to arrest Aunt Shanelle? Or do you call her Shaye?"

Eve decided to play it light. "Think I should? And yup, I call her Shaye, but I'd have to book her as Shanelle."

Shaye was concentrating on the drink Ginny had placed in front of her.

Cassie broke a smile. "Naw. She's okay. Now as for my mom..." She shook her head, tossing those long bangs to the side. "Just in case you don't know, Eve's my mom's ex-girlfriend," Cassie told Shaye.

Eve watched Shaye's eyes widen in disbelief before she shook her head like she'd heard wrong. A frown flashed across her face before she controlled it back to an indifferent presentation. Eve wasn't going to address that now. Cassie didn't deserve to be part of Eve's explanation or commentary about her mother. After a prolonged moment, Shaye sat back in her chair, indicating she was resolved to just watch the show. Pressing her lips together, Eve focused on Cassie.

"I owe you an apology, Cassie. I've missed you, but I didn't want to make life harder for you."

"Or for yourself," Cassie shot back.

"Cassie," Ginny said in a warning tone.

Eve held up a hand. "You're right, Cassie. I took the chicken-shit route."

Cassie hooted at "chicken-shit," just as Eve had suspected she would. Ginny bit her cheeks, clearly understanding exactly what Eve had done to try to connect with her.

"If you quote me, I'll deny it." Eve made sure she infused her tone with a touch of levity.

"It'll cost you," Shaye said. "I'm a witness. I think you owe Cassie an outing. Place of her choice."

Eve glanced at Shaye. She'd appeared to be sideswiped by the "my mom's ex-girlfriend" announcement, but Eve had to give her credit, she was taking the high road. Or more likely, Eve's past really didn't matter to her because Eve didn't really matter to her. Eve buried that thought as her stomach roiled, then she placed the focus back on Cassie and today's mission to come up with a way to reconnect.

Eve studied her and raised an eyebrow. "You game? If it's okay with Ginny. If she has the authority to give permission."

"I do. I have a legal power of attorney agreement since Pauline isn't always available," Ginny said.

Eve nodded, not wanting to know all the reasons Pauline was unavailable. She had no doubt Cassie was better off with Ginny.

Cassie gave Eve a dissecting gaze and twisted her mouth toward a frown. "I want to go to BurgerTown for a double burger and fries. Then I want a new hairstyle at the salon. Then I want to see where you and McGruff live, maybe pizza there for dinner." Cassie slumped, like she'd just asked for the impossible.

Eve nodded. "Is that it?"

Cassie's eyes lit up, giving Eve a calculated grin. "Well, we could go to the beach in bikinis. And then hit karaoke night with you singing some Taylor Swift."

"I think your first few are a good start if Eve's game," Ginny said as Eve coughed into her forearm.

"I kinda liked the second round," Shaye muttered.

"I've got to go." Eve made a point of ignoring Shaye and picked up the thermos of coffee Ginny had made for her.

Shaye stood up with the leash in her hand, indicating she was going to walk Eve and McGruff out.

"Hair, and maybe we can get hamburgers before and have pizza after," Eve said. "You think about a movie we might watch with the pizza. I'm sure Joye will be booked this Saturday. What about the next one?"

Cassie stared at her, then asked, "So you're not bullshitting me?"

Ginny gave her a reproaching look. "There's probably a nicer way to ask that question, Cassie."

Cassie rolled her eyes. "So, there's no bovine manure involved? Just chicken droppings." She gave Ginny a challenging grin, but Ginny wisely slipped out to refill her coffee cup, avoiding further off-the-topic conflict.

"You've got Stacy's sleepover that next weekend, Cassie," Ginny called from the kitchen. "You're open the one after."

Eve decided she needed to nail down the date so she could book the hair appointment with Joye. But more importantly, Eve needed to prove to Cassie—and to herself—that her desire to spend time with Cassie wasn't "bovine manure."

"Okay then, I'll make the appointment for the Saturday after your sleepover. I'll call you to confirm. If you have your own phone, shall we exchange numbers? I don't give my cell number to just anyone, but I'd like you to have it in case you need it." Eve figured if she was going to do this, she might as well go all the way and start changing the kid's mind that she was just another unreliable adult.

Cassie's eyes widened, then she closed them as she clearly forced her face into what appeared to be a practiced pose of indifference. She pulled out her phone and entered the number that Eve recited before taking a minute to type Eve a text so she'd have Cassie's number too. Glancing down at her cell screen, Eve read, *No big deal if u change ur mind.*

Eve pocketed her phone and looked at McGruff, bonded against Shaye's solid leg. She knew that Cassie wasn't much different from McGruff. Vulnerable and wearing armor, even if she wasn't outright growling. Effing Pauline—what had she ever seen in her? Or maybe she just hadn't looked.

"In the meantime, you be careful. It's a pretty safe town, but no going out alone at night," Eve said as she refocused. "I'm looking forward to our girls' day out."

Eve didn't mention the nighttime escapades because she didn't want to make Cassie feel defensive. Bringing up something that specific might destroy what rapport she hoped she was building with Cassie. She'd get to Coyote Hill and the reasons Cassie went there alone in the dark sometime in the future.

"I'm glad you came by, Eve. You're welcome any time," Ginny said.

Eve held up the thermos. "I'll get this back to you. Thanks."

Shaye followed Eve to the car and boosted McGruff into his back seat bed before she shut his door with a sharp bump of her hip. Eve headed around to the driver's door, trying to convince herself she just wanted some distance from the reunion with Cassie, a child with whom she'd had a loving bond. And while Pauline had seemed to avoid extended family, Eve realized she'd missed her occasional encounters with Ginny too. But they weren't the real issue.

Eve's distress was a result of the stepsister news. Looking over the car roof, she started to get in, then decided to at least nod. She could handle another ten seconds of being polite. She shut her eyes as her throat tightened. She'd seen those great-at-flirting, master-at-conjuring-chemistry, who-cares-if-I-have-a-girlfriend signs before—Eve hadn't wanted Shaye to turn out to be another Pauline, but that had been figurative, not literal. Now she knew the two of them had a direct connection, a history. Maybe Shaye was smoother, but then Pauline had been really smooth too, once upon a time.

"I dropped by to catch up with Mom, and I'm thrilled to see Cassie here," Shaye said, looking over the car top. "I've been negligent." She hesitated and then added, "This isn't the time for a discussion and you don't owe me one—"

"That's right. I don't owe you anything. You're Pauline's little stepsister. You don't like cops, and I'm one. It looked to me like you're already involved with someone. End of discussion." Eve wanted to take off. To not feel anything for Shaye. She'd tickled Eve's dormant interest in pursuing a long-term relationship, and it all added up to disaster.

"Involved with someone?"

"A girlfriend." Eve wondered if Shaye was being honest or just playing ignorant. Pauline had been skilled at playing ignorant.

"A girlfriend? That's you—you turn out to be Pauline's ex-girlfriend. Holy crap...*Pauline*?" Was that disgust in Shaye's tone? Or maybe it was just incredulity. "That's a statement in itself. How long?"

"None of your business...four years...for me. Not sure how long for her." Eve had difficulty swallowing, the bad taste of history constricting her throat.

A quizzical look flitted across Shaye's face.

"Meaning in a monogamous committed relationship. Me. Not her." Eve needed to just drive away.

Shaye snorted. "You've either got fortitude or you're a fool."

"I'm a fool, Hayden. And a cop, so that ought to cover some of my worst negative traits." Eve climbed into the car, slammed her door, and pulled away from the curb. She looked up at herself in her rearview mirror. "No more being a fool," she told her image. Shaye had just suggested that she was one and Eve had to agree, but it didn't make it any easier. Then she shifted her focus to the street scene behind her car—to Shaye's receding image. That was exactly where Shaye Hayden needed to stay—in her rearview mirror. Eve pounded her steering wheel as McGruff howled. Just fucking perfect.

# CHAPTER SEVEN

Shaye was home alone trying to read a current mystery. It was a series she loved and just her luck that it contained a fictional cop named Eve, but no way was Shaye going to let the Paradise Pines police chief ruin her Friday night book date. She'd already spent too much time invading Shaye's thoughts.

She'd spent the entire past week after their encounter at Ginny's house avoiding Eve by working in the library trailer. A week of trying to separate and reconcile the feelings Eve stirred in her. Admittedly, there were those based in pure primal desire, even if she was experiencing other confusing emotions as well. She needed to make this about her hormonally fueled response to Pauline's ex-girlfriend and then forget her—there was a world full of eligible women out there who weren't Eve Maguire.

However, Shaye had had an impossible time ignoring those more complex, emotional feelings rooted in facts she could identify—some based in wanting to get to know Eve better because there were so many things to like about her. When those feelings surfaced, she'd reconfirmed her previous conclusion that her reasons for crossing Eve off any option for romance were spot-on. Shaye had already known that cops had no place in her future, and this new information...anyone who had been Pauline's ex had to be bad news. Her stepsister was toxic. Forget Eve Maguire. Shaye was done with her. She picked up her book and started to read chapter two for the third time.

Shaye didn't know what time it was when a high-pitched screeching sound startled her awake. She must have fallen asleep reading because her book was splayed across her lap on the couch. Looking around in the low glow of the side table lamp, she realized she was hearing the shrill outcry of the smoke alarm and that she smelled smoke.

She stood, headed to the back door, and flung it open, only to face an inferno. Waves of scorching heat emanated from the bright red-orange searing flames that consumed the wooden structure. Dark thick smoke billowed into the house and Shaye choked on the particle-laden air. She turned and ran through her small rental to the front door and tried to pull it open, but it wouldn't yield.

The vapors from the burnt fuel of the back porch filled the house to a degree that it was becoming hard to see, hard to breathe. Shaye coughed as the irritation to her throat and lungs escalated. She pulled open a side window in the dining room, then she pushed out the screen and threw herself through the opening before she made a jarring landing on the hard dirt below. The choking air left her lungs with a whoosh, and she blacked out for a moment. When Shaye came to, someone was kicking her in the ribs. She rolled onto her side and did her best to cover her head with her arms.

"You want to remain healthy, you don't have a clue who you saw at Sneed's office. One wrong move and you're finished. Got it, bitch?" The voice was a whispered mid-pitch snarl filled with anger and maybe fear, and delivered from behind a black ski mask and bandit-style kerchief. Shaye was too dazed to even tell if her attacker was a man or a woman.

Focusing on protecting herself, Shaye didn't answer. Whoever they were, they terrified her. They sounded so angry. She struggled to grab an ankle or a foot. A distant siren drew closer, and she figured it was the local volunteer fire department. Shaye finally managed to seize the denim of her attacker's jeans. She fought to hold on and not let go.

A blow landed on her ribs, then another on her shoulder. Fighting for air and groaning as the loud fire vehicle pulled up in front of her house before killing the siren, Shaye couldn't hang on when her attacker fought to pull free and then took off toward the backyard where they could escape over a low fence. She stretched out on her back and attempted to take deep pulls of the cool night air into her lungs as she looked up at the night sky and labored to regulate her breathing. Tears streamed down the sides of her face.

"I'm Steve, volunteer with the local fire department. We've got you." A man with a kind face and wearing a helmet leaned over Shaye. "The county fire department is coming too and is just a few minutes out since the 911 call went through their dispatcher. Our guys are bringing the fire under control. Anyone else or any animals still in there? And do you need an ambulance or are you good with an EMT looking at you first?"

"Just me, and I'm okay. I just need to catch my breath." Shaye started to sit up as another figure approached.

"I've got her, Steve. Go do what you need to do."

Shaye recognized that voice. Steve nodded and headed around to the back of the house.

"You just can't seem to stay out of trouble, can you?" Eve kneeled down and gently brushed Shaye's wet cheek with her fingertips.

"What are you doing here?" Shaye's first reaction was that Eve was a welcome presence, familiar and calm, but then the conflict inside Shaye surfaced and raged. Eve was there in her police chief role, as a friggin' cop. Not because she cared.

"Can I help you move away from the burning building, or do we need a stretcher? It's not safe here." Eve carefully pushed Shaye's hair back from her face.

Shaye tried to ignore the sudden surge of attraction to Eve. She could blame it on her current state of duress, but she had to admit that for the entire past week she hadn't been able to ignore her confounding feelings. It had been a long week—a difficult week.

"I can move." Shaye tried not to grunt with the effort it took to stand.

"I'm going to help you. We're going to take it slow. To answer your question, Denise, the county dispatcher who took the 911 call, contacted me because I'd specifically requested to be notified if there were any more fires in town."

Eve was just settling Shaye into the front seat of her car when the county fire truck arrived. The EMT with the team examined Shaye before he advised that they get Shaye's ribs checked out, so Eve drove Shaye to the regional emergency clinic where she was found to have multiple bruises but no fractures.

"You're lucky" was the doctor's comment.

Lucky was a relative term, Shaye thought as she limped out to Eve's car. Maybe this was one of those trials Annie kept telling her about, especially because she couldn't see how getting the crap beat out of her was going to make her a better person or how it fit into her journey.

"You'll be on the mend in no time," Eve said.

*Mend.* Wasn't that the label Annie had given the reason for this whole upheaval in her life? Just wait until the next time she talked to Annie.

❖

They were finally in the car heading back to Paradise Pines from the hospital, Shaye leaning back with her eyes closed as Eve drove.

"I've been in contact with the crew back at your house," Eve said. "The blaze was set at the back porch door. The front door was tied from the outside to the porch pillar so it couldn't be pulled open from the inside. That's why you had to go out the window. Do you feel up to giving me a quick rundown of what happened?"

Shaye gave Eve a summary of her evening as they drove. She concluded with her thoughts on what had been said. "If I'd seen anything at Sneed's office that could identify the person, you would have known when you first interviewed me, so I don't see the point of tonight."

"Maybe they fled town and are back. Maybe they got to thinking of the consequences if you did identify them—you could be familiar with the person, or they are with you, or they think something might trigger your recognition later if you run into them. Or maybe giving you a warning, if a bit late, was something they felt compelled to do. Guilty people do strange things—especially if they have a lot at stake," Eve said.

"They were barely a shape in the distance and I couldn't see their face, so they're pretty safe."

"They don't know what you saw. They gave you a warning, maybe more emotional than rational, and it could have killed you. We have no clue who this is, but they're dangerous." Eve paused for a moment as she considered the situation.

"I should tell you that that first day I stopped to see Pauline, she was on the phone. She was telling someone that it was critical not to leave a trail as she opened the door."

"I'll file it, but it's not real evidence. She's on my suspect list, but I don't see this person being her, even if she's behind things," Eve replied.

"I agree," Shaye said. "I just thought you should know what I heard."

"You're coming home with me. You need protection until we

figure this out, and that's the easiest solution." The words were out before Eve had time to consider them.

Eve ignored the increase in her heart rate and tamped down the sudden visceral rush of pleasure that flooded her body, followed by disquiet. This was a purely logical professional decision about keeping Shaye safe.

Since arriving home from Ginny Bromwell's house a week ago after running into Shaye there, Eve hadn't encountered Shaye and concluded that she was avoiding her. At first, Eve had felt disappointment mixed with her anger, but as time passed, she'd focused on the facts because they were so much less confusing.

Eve had even gone out of her way to be objective. Though the situation irritated her, Eve knew that the assignment of the much-needed police station office to Shaye wasn't Shaye's fault. So she'd focused on the evidence.

The good news was that Eve was confident that she could cross Shaye off the suspect list—she couldn't see Shaye as the arsonist after the attack. Shaye was a master at flirting and creating chemistry, the same things that had attracted Eve to Pauline, who'd used her skills to attract so many other women—it should have been a blaring warning sign, but Eve hadn't paid attention like she was now. Shaye had certainly attracted her. However, she also needed someone stable and honest and loyal. And how could someone with a probable girlfriend she hadn't disclosed offer those? Crap, maybe Shaye even had girlfriends...plural.

However, it was the finding that Shaye was Pauline's stepsister that had shocked Eve the most, and she had spent the last week since their encounter hammering out what she wasn't going to do. She *was not* going to let Shaye into her personal life. There was no place for her there, where she could easily find herself repeating her past mistakes.

This attack on Shaye's property and person fundamentally changed the situation too, at least for the short term. Shaye was now a person who Eve was in charge of keeping safe while searching for the perpetrator. There was no room for a romantic relationship in that affiliation. It violated her professional code of ethics if she was going to give Shaye no choice but to come home with her in order to protect her.

For the time being, having Shaye off-limits on a personal level would buy Eve some time to put this unwelcome attraction in long-term perspective. It would help her move on to what her life really needed to be—without Shaye in it. Once she had Shaye settled safely for the night, Eve promised herself that she'd make some bigger decisions about what she *was* going to do about her lack of a personal life. And professionally—she'd consider her options for a plan that would keep Shaye unharmed until they caught the SOB.

"I don't want to put you out," Shaye said.

"This is a professional decision—to protect you. I have a guest room, and McGruff likes you."

"McGruff, huh?" Shaye gave Eve a tired smile.

"You need a watchdog and a support dog tonight. He has discerning tastes in humans…seems you're someone he's decided to tolerate. *The ugliest dog around,* if I remember your description of him."

"He's growing on me. As for me, what's not to like? Homeless, black-and-blue, reeking of smoke. How about taking me to my mom's house?"

Eve had already considered and rejected this option. "It's really late and we don't want to wake your mom. Besides, Ginny has her hands and her house full with Cassie living with her—it's a small place. But more important, someone set your house on fire after rigging your front door so it wasn't easy to escape that way. We don't want to put Ginny and Cassie in danger too." Eve glanced over at Shaye as she drove. "We can both sleep at my place, or I can sit in my car outside of wherever you land, doing my job of seeing you're okay and hardly sleeping at all." Eve repeated, "You can use the guest room."

"Thank you, Eve." Shaye didn't open her eyes or look at her, but her tone was sincere.

Eve smiled at the fact Shaye was willing to comply and even seemed appreciative. She decided to try to lighten the mood if she could. "Thank me after you've spent a night."

"Really? Is the guest mattress bad?" Shaye sighed and didn't put up any objection, her eyes still shut. "With these pain meds, I could probably sleep on the floor tonight."

Eve chuckled. "It's a new bed. But McGruff's an old dog and he snores loud enough to rattle the entire house."

"And I let you talk me into this." The amusement in Shaye's voice warmed Eve's heart. It warmed her heart in her professional capacity, she told herself.

❖

After they'd made it inside the house and McGruff had greeted them, Eve quickly collected a spare T-shirt, sleeping shorts, and a toothbrush for Shaye before pointing her toward the shower.

"Toothpaste, shampoo, and a clean towel are in there already. Anything else I can get you?"

Shaye shook her head. She looked so exhausted. Eve carefully turned her around and guided her to the bathroom door before leaving her.

Eve made sure McGruff went outside one last time, then settled him back in his bed on the floor in her room. When she heard Shaye open the bathroom door after cleaning up, she escorted her to the guest room before collecting her dirty clothes to throw in the washer.

"Steve called me and the fire's out. The county fire inspector and his forensics tech will check things out tomorrow. I'll see you in the morning. Let me know if you need anything."

Shaye wasn't exhibiting her usual energy, but she offered Eve a weak smile.

After running the wash and throwing the load into the dryer, Eve headed to her own room and prepared for bed. As late as it was, she didn't fall asleep right away. She'd grown accustomed to all the objectionable sounds McGruff made while he was sleeping, so he wasn't keeping her awake. It was thinking about Shaye that wouldn't let her mind shut down. All this loss of sleep was exactly why over the past week Eve had sworn that she'd leave Shaye Hayden in the rearview mirror. She didn't want all the tumultuous feelings Shaye aroused in her.

As Shaye slept just down the hallway from her room, Eve pondered how she'd let this situation come to pass. While she'd recognized 421 Chestnut as Shaye's address when the dispatcher had given it to her, Eve had needed to respond because of the arson aspect—although she knew that she'd driven even faster knowing it was Shaye's place. And putting Ginny or Cassie in danger tonight had been off the table. All her actions were judicious.

Eve acknowledged that she'd been in a bind because she had both professionally and personally wanted Shaye protected and this seemed the best answer until she came up with a longer-term solution. The professional aspect was defined by her job, and Eve decided the personal aspect could be defined as the fact that Shaye wasn't a complete stranger. Labeling it *official* would hopefully keep Shaye at a distance because Eve couldn't let Shaye use proximity, even if it was only a night or two, to grow on her the way Pauline had done with orchestrated charisma and seduction. Eve was wiser now. She had to remember that she'd already made the prudent decision about what she *was not* going to do—there was no place in her personal life for Shaye.

As all these thoughts churned in Eve's head, she decided that the time had come to consider what she *was* going to do about personal relationships in the future. That wasn't so hard. She was going to be reasonable. *Reasonable* was the key word. As she lay there, Eve decided that she would rationally analyze the women she dated. There needed to be some level of attraction, but attraction was overrated. At forty-seven, that had to be further down the list than the things she was now considering as reasonable requirements: stability, honesty, loyalty. In fact, those could not be overrated.

Eve also decided that she'd accept the next date invitation she received from a *reasonable* woman just to prove to herself that she had common sense and was ready to move on. It was time. Dating somebody who was reasonable would prove she was making major personal progress. With that settled, Eve closed her eyes and drifted off.

After several hours of sound sleep, Eve woke up confident that if she relied on logic and reason instead of the chemistry that was driving this physical desire that Shaye seemed to provoke, she might find what she needed in a long-term partner, or at least protect her heart. It was a well-thought-out conclusion. Eve was grateful that she was a mature, intelligent person.

She stretched and then headed to the bathroom for a shower. As the warm spray hit her, Eve thought about the day. First on her list, she needed a long-term plan to protect Shaye. She would need round-the-clock protection with the obvious threat made against her last night, and Eve needed to solve that—part of her job, sworn to protect and serve.

She considered that she didn't begin to have the manpower to assign an officer to Shaye, and there was no way during an election season that Sneed would increase her budget to add any personnel. In addition, her gut told her that going through channels to try to get Shaye parked in a safe house would be rejected by Shaye…besides the fact that she probably wouldn't qualify as someone with information that another law enforcement agency would deem worth the effort and expense of protecting.

Because she'd finally made her decisions about what she was and was not going to do in her personal life for the long term, she was feeling much better this morning. With the new criteria defined for dating, Eve decided that she could do the generous thing and keep

Shaye there while she got back on her feet and they figured out who was setting the fires. She'd view this as implementing purely official protection.

Feeling pleased and confident, Eve turned off the shower and dressed. McGruff hadn't been in his bed like he usually was in the mornings, so she headed to the kitchen, following the enticing aroma of fresh baking mixed with caffeine.

Shaye sat at the table still wearing Eve's T-shirt and shorts, a cup of coffee in front of her and McGruff at her feet waiting for the gift of crumbs from the slice of coffee cake she was so ineptly trying to eat. She kept her eyes on him as she merrily missed her mouth and let small chunks descend to the floor, where they did not remain.

"I hope it's okay that I made a coffee cake," Shaye said as Eve stood there taking in a scene that fit the domestic image of what she knew she wanted.

Eve frowned. Shaye was gorgeous in what little attire she was wearing, and her antics with McGruff were heartwarming. She didn't trust her voice, so Eve nodded as she reminded herself of the conclusions she'd reached and the promises she'd made to herself, then she went through the kitchen to the laundry room and emptied the dryer of Shaye's clean clothes as she bought a little time to collect herself.

"Here are your clothes," Eve said as she set them on the kitchen counter.

"I was hoping you might enjoy sitting down to a warm slice of breakfast right out of the oven and a little coffee, Saturday morning and all. If not, I made it for the dog."

Eve fought to be grumpy—at least not touched by Shaye's cooking efforts. But looking at her with a light bruise on her cheek and more deep purple spots on her arms didn't allow indifference. The contusions made Eve livid at whoever had done this damage to Shaye. And she felt not only reasonable empathy but an unsettling level of worry and caring. Her reaction was to take on a reserved, distancing demeanor—it was self-protection, considering her need to safeguard Shaye wasn't only professional but visceral. Eve settled on being polite.

"You like to bake?" Eve asked. That was polite, wasn't it?

"On occasion. Too much baking and there wouldn't be enough miles to jog off the consequences. But this morning, there's an appreciative pooch."

"So, there's no end to the lengths you'll go to bribe my undercover canine into your good graces?"

"The dog spoiling is just a side benefit," Shaye replied. "But I'll be careful. No doughnuts for your canine cop. Just crumbs. Now, his boss might be a different proposition." Eve could read the twinkle in Shaye's eyes as she drawled that last word.

"No propositioning his human handler." Eve shook her head. How had the conversation so easily become flirtatious? And how come she was enjoying it so much? Eve decided that she needed to change the subject. "I hope you slept okay. You've obviously been up a lot longer than I have."

"Your new mattress was fine. Just a few aches and pains from last night's encounter woke me up. A couple of days and I'll be good as new."

"It might take more than a few days," Eve said. "But I'm glad it wasn't worse. Now I just need to catch the bastard who's setting the fires so we can all get on with our lives."

"Speaking of getting on with our lives, while I appreciate your hospitality, I need a plan now that my house is uninhabitable," Shaye replied.

"Let's talk about today's plan. You need to take the day off, recover a bit. I need to catch up with the fire inspector. Doug Hooper will be on-site this morning, if he isn't already there." Eve paused for a moment as she considered the rest of the day's plans. "I should be able to go inside the burnt house and retrieve some of your belongings with Hooper's approval—hopefully later this morning. I can send them back over here to you. You might need to wash any clothing, get the smoke and ash out—you can use my washer and dryer today."

"I have Saturday library hours this afternoon." Shaye said. "Two to five o'clock. I need to be at the trailer for those. I don't want to let anybody down."

Eve admired Shaye's determination to carry on with her job, but Eve wanted her to heal. She gave her an admonishing look. "Don't make me lock you up to keep you from overdoing it. Last night, the ER doctor said you need to take it easy for a while."

Shaye held up her hand, palm out, in a halt gesture. "Mayor Sneed won't think letting an arsonist prevent the librarian from doing her job is good for his reelection campaign. I thought the plan was on keeping things as normal as possible for the voters."

Eve considered this, pressing her lips together as she weighed Shaye's condition against politics. Shaye seemed to be doing okay today, and she had a point. But more heartening, she didn't seem to want Pauline to win.

Shaye added, "I'll need a bit of bruise-covering makeup for the afternoon library hours today. Or for the mug shot—a girl's gotta look her best, no matter the reason for the photo op."

Eve looked at McGruff to keep from chuckling. "Demanding as all get-out, isn't she?"

"You haven't seen anything," Shaye retorted, giving Eve an exaggerated suggestive look.

The easy flirting and the chemistry jolted Eve back to her convictions again. "So, returning to today's plan...I'll probably need to stay with the fire inspector or at least be knee-deep in the investigation and repercussions from the fire. And dealing with the mayor. I'll have my officer, Grady Lopez, bring you what I can after I do what I need to do with Hooper, including bringing you a laptop—yours or the library's. I'll make sure you get to the library this afternoon. And tonight, you need protection, so you're coming back here."

"We need to talk about that," Shaye said.

"We can talk more tonight. For now, I think we have a plan for today."

"Damn, you're bossy. You think you can just lay down the law?" Shaye's tone had shifted to one laced with irritation.

"I am the chief of police," Eve noted in exasperation. She needed to know that Shaye would be safe before she left to join Hooper. "Just in case you forgot." Eve held Shaye's piqued stare, then acknowledged to herself that she found the huffy Shaye sitting in that skimpy outfit so much more alluring than she wanted to find her.

"I'd like to forget, but obviously that's not happening," Shaye replied.

Eve wondered how they'd gone from flirting to confrontation so fast. *Flirting*...she couldn't do that while protecting Shaye. Clashing wasn't her style, but maybe it was a good thing. If she could keep her focus on how infuriating Shaye was, and on her well-reasoned conclusions and guidelines for personal relationships, maybe she could save herself from her own infernal libido.

"I know you don't like cops, but I'm doing my best to protect and serve." Eve let out a sigh. She didn't want to fight with Shaye. She was trying to help her.

"All in the line of duty," Shaye muttered.

"Exactly." Eve filed that away. "In the line of duty" was a good phrase to remember if she needed to remind herself what her mission was.

Shaye let out a long, slow breath of obvious frustration and shut her eyes for a moment, then made a point of addressing McGruff and not Eve. "You're the only police presence I want to be around right now."

"That's good, because I'm out of here. Shall I leave Deputy Dog or bring him with me?" Eve was hoping maybe McGruff would help with Shaye's distress. As she spoke, Eve noticed the glow of tears in Shaye's eyes. They hit her hard. "I'm sorry. For what's happened to you, Shaye. Can we talk tonight? Discuss what's best for you?"

Shaye nodded through her sniffling. "I'll watch him."

"Then I'll leave. You need to lock up and don't answer the door except for Grady or me. I'll show you how to set the alarm." Eve had an excellent alarm system including outdoor motion detection, and trouble would reach the dispatcher on-call, so Eve was comfortable leaving Shaye there for the day. She'd have her house patrolled as well, just to add to the protection, although this arsonist seemed to work in the very early hours or at night.

"Thanks." Shaye wiped her face with the hem of the T-shirt, exposing smooth, pale abdominal skin. More skin than Eve wanted to see with her pledge of personal indifference.

"You have your phone, so use it if you need to." Eve made sure Shaye had her direct cell number. The desire to kiss her was growing. Not a romantic kiss, of course—just a comforting one. But that wasn't in the line of duty.

❖

After Eve left, Shaye sat and allowed herself the luxury of feeling miserable—she let herself cry some more. She reminded herself that she had other issues that had been making her miserable for years, and she'd come back to Paradise Pines to resolve those. That was her purpose for being in her hometown. She'd have to expose old wounds if she hoped to heal. That meant a heart-to-heart with her mother. Shaye hated that she'd cried in front of Eve, let her emotions seesaw so much after suddenly finding herself in this situation. She'd wanted to walk away from Pauline's ex, not move in with her.

"Okay, McGruff. How about I let you out for a bit while I clean up the kitchen?"

McGruff agreed, or at least didn't verbally cross her, but he ignored the newly installed dog door in the kitchen and headed to the large sliding glass door in the dining room and waited there. Shaye let him out and settled at the dining room table, taking in the backyard and her current situation.

She was in someone else's house. Hers was gone. It had been rendered unlivable, ash combined with the charred debris of her former dwelling—torched on purpose. Shaye knew that if she really was going to eventually move on with her life, she needed to find the positive, so she struggled to be grateful. There was the view out to Eve's backyard. The spring rays of sunshine falling on that wooden trough of blooming wildflowers, green foliage sprinkled with pinks and purples and yellows. She watched a blue jay drop to the deck, harassing McGruff, who was being his usual killjoy canine self, growling and moaning his territorial displeasure, more bark than bite as the bird boldly laughed in his face. She wiped the residual distress from her eyes and laughed for a moment too, taking in the two unencumbered critters. Then she considered McGruff—he might be in good hands now, but he'd probably shed his share of dog tears too.

God, she'd love to be unburdened by the feelings that weighed on her right now—the fear, the attraction, the anger. To just be sitting on a beach, watching the rhythm of the water playing out on the sand. She could visualize the scene—items resting on a blanket. There was a bottle of wine, a container of her favorite sesame seeded crackers, but then her incorrigible mind's eye didn't stop at that. There were two wine glasses waiting to be filled. One for her, and one for Eve—the cop who was protecting her. The cop who had been on her mind since that night at the bar. Shaye shook her head, trying to force her thoughts to somewhere further away. To Hawaii, or maybe Alaska. Places nowhere near Eve Maguire, chief of *fucking* police.

# CHAPTER EIGHT

Eve lay in bed on Sunday morning and studied the ceiling. McGruff's bed was empty and she could smell coffee, so she knew Shaye was up. She hadn't planned to sleep so late, but she hadn't planned to be working until after midnight either.

She'd learned that Shaye's car had been torched as well, and knowing that the news would upset Shaye, she'd decided the professional thing to do was to tell her in person. Now Eve would have to do that this morning, and her belly felt a twinge of anxiety.

Yesterday, Eve had made sure Shaye had received the belongings she'd promised to retrieve from the damaged house as well as rides to and from the trailer for library hours. She'd only texted Shaye off and on as her day filled up because Shaye might need something at the house, and the hot dinner she'd had Grady pick up and deliver was only because she'd been called out on a search for a lost child and she wanted to make sure Shaye ate. Her continued texting during the search was simply to assure herself Shaye had set the alarm and was safe, as was her readiness to head home at the slightest sign of trouble. Yesterday, she'd justified her actions as all part of the job. Yesterday, she'd told herself that of course she'd do the same for anyone under the same circumstances.

Shaye had already been asleep in the guest room when Eve had finally hauled her exhausted derriere home last night, so she'd dropped into bed after a granola bar she'd shared with McGruff and a glass of milk. Studying the rays of morning light on the ceiling this morning, Eve considered that this was the life she'd chosen and she rarely resented it. However, yesterday she'd been torn between duty and Shaye as the day had worn on, and if she was being honest with herself this morning, that had been drifting too close to personal.

Yawning, Eve climbed out of bed and pulled on sweatpants

over the shorts she'd worn to bed. She wanted to find Shaye. No, she corrected herself...she needed to find McGruff.

She was surprised to find the kitchen empty, no Shaye and no dog—only a full pot of coffee, a bag of scones, and two clean, empty mugs. After walking out and searching the backyard, Eve decided to check the guest room. As she headed down the hallway, she found the bathroom door slightly ajar with the sounds of Shaye cooing, McGruff moaning and growling, and running water coming from within. What was going on?

There was a lot of loud clattering and splashing, followed by some low swearing—both human and canine, if Eve was translating accurately. She touched the door and it swung open a bit. She could see Shaye leaning over the tub, only her shorts-clad ass and the back of her bare legs showing as she struggled with McGruff. Eve couldn't help but stare at the heart-stopping, sexy-as-hell view she'd just stumbled upon...reality far exceeding any of the unprofessional dreams she'd been trying to ignore.

Suddenly, Shaye stood and stepped into the tub, then sat down with her bare legs, shorts, and lower torso submerged. She pulled the squirming dog into her lap, her white T-shirt immediately soaked by the wild antics of a swimming, splashing McGruff. The subsequent wet T-shirt presentation eclipsed any wet T-shirt images Eve had ever seen—transparent cloth clinging tightly to full round, breasts. Firm mounds peaked by darker round circles ringing nipples on full display, alert and so alluring.

Shaye looked up and locked eyes with her. Eve knew that arousal was behind her own likely pupil dilation, but also suspected that surprise at Eve's presence was at least partially behind Shaye's indigo stare. There was no place for arousal on her own part, and she wanted to stick with surprise as the official explanation for Shaye's reaction too.

"Well, are you going to make yourself useful and hand me the dog shampoo that Grady's wife brought?" Shaye took control of the situation first, maybe because Eve couldn't think of anything to say— libido overload.

Eve stood frozen. She seriously considered climbing into the tub with Shaye until McGruff barked at her and common sense told her now wasn't the time for the things she'd been thinking. *Never* was more like it. Thank God for McGruff because she'd almost thrown her carefully reasoned conclusion—that there was no place for Shaye in her personal life and this arrangement was purely professional—out the door and climbed into the bathwater with Shaye and that squeeze bottle of soap. For God's sake, this was Pauline's stepsister…a Pauline knockoff.

Eve pulled herself together. "Trying to drown my dog?"

"Don't tempt me. The little charmer is a holy terror in the tub. Grady's wife is a vet tech, and he brought her by this morning with a delivery of scones and the expertise to remove McGruff's sutures. And she left some dog shampoo. I didn't want to wake you—after *protecting and serving* half the night—so because he was good to go, I decided it was time for me to help him have a bath."

Eve suspected Shaye's shift in tone on the protecting and serving phrase was to remind both of them of Eve's role, but she ignored that for the moment. After yesterday's grueling day, she didn't want to be the chief of police this morning.

"And here I was, thinking *he* was helping *you* have a bath." Eve couldn't help but chuckle.

"Well, he succeeded."

Eve grabbed the bottle of shampoo and handed it to Shaye, then collected two large towels from under the cabinet before leaning back on the counter to watch.

"You know that you're going to ruin his reputation," Eve said.

Shaye gave her a quizzical look.

"Ugliest dog in town."

"I think addressing that might take more than a bath." Shaye squeezed out a palm full of shampoo and started lathering it into McGruff's coat. Eve watched Shaye's hands work their way up and down the mutt—watched those massaging fingers.

After a thorough scrubbing, Shaye opened the tub drain and then rose. She pulled the shower curtain mostly closed before turning on the overhead flow and rinsing off McGruff and herself. Eve did her best not to look through the few inches of open space the curtain didn't cover.

She never thought she'd be grateful to be handed a sopping wet dog, but Eve needed the diversion. As she wrapped him in the waiting towel when Shaye handed him out, Eve glanced at her, still clothed under the spray. She could see the darkening bruised areas over Shaye's lower ribs through the wet fabric.

Intense anger overtook her again at realizing the extent of Shaye's injuries, but Eve decided it was an emotion she was more prepared to justify and deal with than the attraction she'd been fighting. She was going to catch the bastard who had hurt the town librarian, not because it was Shaye but because she was a member of the community Eve had sworn to serve. And she'd protect her from further harm. That was Eve's job, and it was the only reason Shaye was standing in her house, standing in her shower, standing in a wet T-shirt that revealed way too much.

❖

"Let's agree that you need this protective arrangement until we catch whoever hurt you, set your house on fire and—"

"I'm not agreeing." Shaye took in Eve's professional demeanor, a major shift from the sensual connection that she'd felt twenty minutes ago during the dog bath. While Eve's shift irritated her ego, she embraced it for the slap back to reality it offered.

Eve pursed her lips and waited instead of continuing with what she had been saying before the interruption.

"I'm not agreeing to any of it. I came to town for a reason, and it wasn't this." Shaye fought the indulgence of crossing her arms over her chest. Stomping her foot under the table crossed her mind too. She was so tempted to resort to overt, immature acts of conveying her displeasure, only because she didn't know how much more she could deal with. She refrained and let her tone disclose her mood.

They were at the kitchen table with coffee mugs in front of them because Eve had said that she wanted to talk, and now Eve was playing the role of good cop, even if there was no bad cop present taking the adversarial stance—Shaye didn't want to fall for the concerned caring officer Eve was projecting, but it was better than falling for Eve, the person beneath that cop badge.

The main reason she was here in Paradise Pines, besides her aging mom, was to make peace with her past, like she and Annie had discussed. This wasn't about some friggin' rookie cop's role in her dad's shooting because that was unforgivable—this was about trying to come to terms with her own role. Nothing could get in the way of that or her move back would be a waste. She certainly hadn't considered there would be a personal threat to her well-being that she'd have to deal with too.

"And set your car on fire." Eve frowned as she quietly finished her earlier comment.

"Shit!" The hits just kept coming. "So my car is gone?"

"I'm sorry. It's totaled." Not just her tone, but Eve's eyes also conveyed sympathy as she reached out and touched Shaye's hand.

Shaye closed her eyes so she didn't have to look at Eve. When Eve pulled her touch away, the loss of physical connection deflated Shaye like that touch had been a plug holding in what bravado she still possessed. Her throat constricted as she suppressed the escalating longing that she suddenly had for Eve to hug her, hold her. Attributing her neediness to being at her stress-overload maximum, Shaye knew that she should take the sympathy touch for what it probably was—just part of that good cop role, and she didn't need that. Hell, she absolutely didn't want that.

"I know you don't like cops...don't like me," Eve said. "I'm trying to keep you safe with the resources I've got available, find a solution that protects Ginny and—"

"Cassie," Shaye finished. The magnitude of what had happened at her house, the damage and threat, filled her eyes with tears. She couldn't put her mom or Cassie in that kind of danger. She picked up a napkin and dabbed. She didn't see a better plan than Eve's, short of leaving town.

Eve waited while Shaye processed the situation. She handed over another napkin as they sat in silence, and then the very clean McGruff moved in close and sat on the floor next to Shaye, the entire side of his body connecting with her leg.

"Okay. I hear you." Shaye reached down to gently acknowledge the dog. "But now you need to hear me. This only works on my terms. This isn't official cop stuff—I don't like cops. I'm only doing this by choice. It's only because I don't need to put others in danger by refusing your offer. We'd be two regular citizens with a common goal: Shaye and Eve seeking safety and catching a scumbag." She wasn't going to be locked into some binding witness protection setup with Eve in charge when she hadn't really witnessed anything useful. Not with Eve Maguire, chief of police. She could walk whenever she wanted. "And just so we're perfectly clear, this isn't about professional roles or ethics on your part, even with our lack of a personal relationship. It's about me making choices about my life—nothing to do with your cop role. This is about me focusing on the reasons why I came back home to burning, bumfuck Paradise Pines."

Eve's eyes widened and she pressed her mouth closed. Then simmering irritation flashed across her face, the same slow-to-surface anger Shaye had witnessed out in front of Ginny's house before Eve took control and masked her agitation.

"Say it," Shaye said. "I want to hear it. If it's about choice for me, it's the same for you. No official call-of-duty crap."

"Okaaay." Eve softly drew out the word, making it obvious that she was going to be more reserved in her response than Shaye had been. "I make my own choices about my relationships too, and this isn't personal. I'll have to live with *not officially professional* if that's what it takes to protect you, but this is not about you being part of my personal life."

Shaye nodded. She should be happy with what Eve had just clarified, but Eve's confirming rejection of a personal relationship didn't seem to settle well with Shaye either. It had to be her hormones talking again because Shaye had plenty to sort out in her life without Pauline's ex muddying her mission.

"So now that we understand each other…" Eve sighed, leaving no doubt that she was taking Shaye's cooperation however she could get it. "Thank you."

Eve moved toward the sink, creating some space between them. She gave Shaye a long look that didn't hide what must be a reflection of her hormones too. Eve appeared disconcerted, like maybe the thought of hugging her, holding her, had also crossed Eve's mind.

Eve cleared her throat before she spoke again. "I'm most worried about nights or early mornings because that's when the crimes have occurred—not midday. I'll do my best to make this as easy on you as possible."

That might be Eve's intent, but even if this wasn't under the *policing* umbrella, Shaye knew spending so much time with Eve was going to be a challenge. Not because she was an ass. Because she wasn't.

❖

It was Thursday and they'd all just come from the citizens' commendation ceremony where Joye had received an award for her publication of the *Paradise Pulse*, affording the town an informative and appreciated local news source. The mayor had accomplished his photo ops and a birthday cake celebration, and now Eve was sitting at a table with Shaye, Joye, and Earl at the local pizza parlor.

Eve suspected that Shaye was avoiding her after the discussion and tears on Sunday. Giving Shaye space after all she'd been through was something Eve could do, letting her officers keep an eye on the library trailer during the daytime and simply sharing the same roof at her house with Shaye while a mutt paraded back and forth between the two of them in separate rooms in the evenings. With Shaye reading in Eve's guest room, Eve had been in the kitchen at night, trying to create a draft of the basics of her annual budget needs so she could reconfigure it into a submittable proposal. She would have normally returned to work in the evening rather than work from her kitchen table after dinner, but she didn't want to leave Shaye alone if she could help it.

Eve had convinced herself that this living arrangement worked for her because she'd been counting on her ability to fall back on professional ethics to avoid any dilemmas about the arrangement. That was until their discussion clarifying that this wasn't even remotely an official professional arrangement had flattened that ethics box where Eve had hoped to simply confine herself because she was good at staying inside boundaries, especially officially defined ones. Now she'd have to dig deeper and remember all the reasons for keeping an emotional distance when the two of them interacted.

She'd transported Shaye to work and back these last several days, a comfortable quiet settling into the space between them. Maybe the shock of the Pauline factor was diminishing—reaching a truce would be a good thing. She'd just have to figure out how to deal with the blasted chemistry she knew was still there, simmering below the surface. But for now, Eve didn't want to overanalyze it. She'd try to act professional and settle for the fact that the current situation benefitted McGruff.

There had been a surge of joy—or more appropriately from a professional perspective, an acknowledgement of satisfaction—when Eve had watched Shaye saunter into the ceremony venue a few hours ago after sending Eve a text that Grady would collect her at the library trailer and drop her at the event. Eve had saved her a seat right next to her own. *Only being polite* she'd tried to convince herself. She'd had to admit that it was more than that as her heart rate had accelerated when Shaye walked in the door. Worse, she'd had to admit that the thrumming that coursed through her veins was triggered by feelings significantly deeper than an appreciation for the looks of the stunning Shaye.

The buzz in the Paradise Pizza Parlor was low as a crowd much smaller than on a weekend gathered for dinner. Eve recognized a few people from the city event who'd had the same idea. The four in Eve's group were seated at a small square table with Shaye to her right, Earl to her left, and Joye directly across from her.

"Just so you know, I'm buying tonight in honor of the best rag in the state." Earl made the announcement before he fished his credit card out of his shirt pocket, flashed it, and then returned it.

"*Rag?*" Joye shook her head as she pulled a small framed plaque out of her oversized handbag. "This illustrious award proves otherwise."

"My apologies. In honor of the most esteemed weekly small-town periodical in the country. And its publisher." Earl grinned, obviously proud of his rephrasing.

Eve realized that Joye and Earl's Friday night date wasn't a one-and-done. She wasn't going there—she was going to enjoy this dinner. She knew that Earl was a serial monogamist, enjoying one girlfriend after another. She just didn't want either her brother or her friend to get hurt.

By the time their server had returned with their beer orders, they'd all agreed on two pizzas and a salad bowl to share.

"Aren't you the chick we saw at the Daily Grind a few Saturdays back?" Earl had turned his attention to Shaye. "With your girlfriend."

Shaye cocked her head toward Eve's brother, and from her expression, Eve suspected she was trying to visualize how they came from the same family.

"That would have been me," Shaye confirmed. "And if you mean a friend who is a girl, that would be Annie, my library mentor and good friend. And just to be clear, also happily married to Thomas."

Eve choked on her beer. Had she just heard that right? The redhead at the Daily Grind having coffee with Shaye was just her good friend and not a girlfriend. She experienced a wave of conflicting emotions. Eve was shocked that she'd been so wrong. Then she was thrilled that she'd been so wrong. Then she told herself that she had no business being thrilled—this news changed very little except to emphasize that she'd never suspected Pauline had other girlfriends and now she'd mistakenly suspected that Shaye had had a girlfriend when she hadn't. Somehow, her detective skills tanked when her heart was involved. Then she corrected herself—her heart was not involved with Shaye.

Earl pointed at Shaye. "Hallelujah. So, if that wasn't your girlfriend, then you're not on Eve's team, so to speak. I'd ask you out, but I'm an honorable man—only one woman at a time." He shifted his index finger to indicate Joye. Eve and the others rolled their eyes, and then Earl continued, addressing Shaye again. "Not to say that you aren't an excellent specimen of a woman."

"Thank you, Earl. I'm taking that as a compliment, although I've never been called 'an excellent specimen' before—at least not to my face. But just so there's no misunderstanding, this *specimen* is a lesbian." Shaye's lips twitched in an obvious effort to contain the amusement Earl's uncensored male declarations triggered. She'd probably spent her adult life dealing with drooling men. Eve had spent her life around Earl, so she was used to him. She was relieved that Shaye wasn't offended but seemed willing to accept him as he was, even showing signs of being entertained.

"That's a blooming shame. No shadow of a doubt—you're a real looker." As Earl wiggled his brows, Eve shook her head at her irredeemable brother and detected an effort at suppressed laughter from Shaye and Joye. She couldn't help but register his statement— yes, Shaye was gorgeous, but she was so much more. Leave it to Earl to blurt out his superficial male opinion, as if she was a bug tacked to a display board. And in a public place in front of Joye, who he was seemingly dating. Eve had a huge soft spot for Earl, but then she wasn't dating him. She wondered how long Joye would tolerate him.

Shaye, who hadn't shown much of the vitality that Eve had come to appreciate before the arson attack, now had a mischievous light in her eyes. If Eve was reading it right, it was the manifestation of mirth. As tempting as it was to say "uh-oh" out loud, she bit her lip and waited for Shaye to respond.

"Didn't your sister tell you? Eve and I are living together."

Now it was Earl's turn to choke on his beer, and Eve tried to simply watch as Shaye and Joye shared a conspiratorial glance while nobody clarified further.

"Slay me, sis." Earl was speechless as he looked at Eve in awe.

A flood of internal conflict hit Eve—her conviction that no place for Shaye existed in her personal life, the thrill of the image of really living with Shaye, the revelation that Shaye did not have a girlfriend. Eve was aware of the chiseling that was eroding that first one and she knew she'd have to keep reminding herself of the multiple reasons for her conviction because she could feel herself waffling. She wasn't a waffler—except for maybe McGruff. Her heart told her that hadn't turned out so bad, then she chastised herself. Shaye had nothing to do with her heart, no prospective place in her heart. Eve couldn't let that happen because she didn't want the heartbreak when it all fell apart.

Their attention shifted as they filled their plates with the aromatic offerings that had been delivered to their table. They all dove in, chewing and chatting. As they were finishing, Earl received a phone call and then apologetically informed them that one of his clients had a burst pipe and he needed to go take care of it. After being assured that nobody needed any additional food or drinks, he apologized to Joye and stood. Looking between Eve and Shaye, he offered them a knowing look. "And don't do anything I wouldn't do."

Eve suspected that left a lot of territory open that she'd never consider, but she remained silent. She wasn't discussing her love life with her brother, or more accurately the one that didn't exist.

"It's nice to officially meet you, Earl." Shaye broke the silence. "And thank you for treating us all to dinner."

Earl beamed. "My pleasure. See you all later." He gave Joye a quick parting peck on the lips before heading out to pay the bill and leave. He could be a jerk, but Eve knew she loved him the way you can only love family, flaws and all. Underneath all the displays of manliness, he was a good guy.

As they sipped their drinks, Joye looked at Shaye. Donning her journalist's persona, she asked, "So can I ask you some questions?"

Eve waited for the answer, wondering if this was the night for revelations and surprises. She leaned back to listen, wanting to believe this was just professional interest on her part, but knowing it wasn't. She wanted to know more about Shaye, who was *living with her*, even if it wasn't in the way her brother thought.

"Off the record, or on?" Shaye asked, studying Joye.

Obviously making professional calculations, Joye pursed her lips and paused for a moment. "Smart woman. Off the record, but that doesn't mean I won't unknow whatever you tell me."

Shaye dipped her chin in agreement, keeping her eyes on Joye.

"Okay, how about telling us what you find hardest about this situation. The need for constant police protection until they catch the arsonist? Or maybe it's sharing so much time with the chivalrous chief?" Joye smiled as she inclined her head toward Eve. "We all know how difficult she is."

"First of all, the protection. It's by choice and *not* official. Simply in the best interest of keeping everyone safe for now, and hopefully the

SOB will be caught. I confess to shedding a few tears when she hauled me to her house right after the attack." Shaye paused as she lightened her delivery. "But sharing space with that little ill-mannered scruff of a poor excuse for a pet balances the worst out."

"I think that's probably the nicest compliment McGruff will ever receive," Joye drily noted, and they all laughed. "Seriously though, what's the hardest?"

Shaye focused on her beer mug, as if she was mentally running through a list of challenges. At one point, a slight smile countered the frown she entertained and momentarily conveyed that maybe there was an amusing thought associated with the list. Then she seemed to switch gears and locked Joye with a measured neutral look. "Okay, I'll give you this…not going jogging at least a few mornings a week. Maybe I'm an endorphin addict, but I've been a jogger my entire life and I miss it."

"Isn't that how you ended up in this situation? Out early morning jogging and witnessing the mayor's campaign office being set on fire?" Joye asked.

"It is, but that doesn't mean I don't miss it. This little town doesn't even have a gym where I can go run on a conveyor belt, although I think part of the joy of the experience is the fresh air and scenery."

They all drained the last of their beers and Eve thought they'd probably leave, then Joye continued. "Before we go, tell us about yourself."

Shaye sat for another long moment. She seemed to be weighing what she was willing to say. That caused Eve to wonder what events in her life might have created Shaye's guarded response. *Tell us about yourself* wasn't usually fraught with caution.

"Okay. I can tell you my mom is Ginny Bromwell, which I think you know, and I was born and lived in Paradise Pines until I left for college at eighteen. My birth father, where I came by my last name, Hayden, was killed in a construction accident before I was born. My mom remarried when I was three and David was the man I've always considered to be my dad, but then he was killed about two years later…" Shaye momentarily paused, looking away from them. "He was killed in San Francisco on a family vacation weekend when I was five. My mom eventually remarried—Joe Bromwell, who I never considered to be my father, and he's now gone. That's how Pauline and Andy Bromwell became my stepsiblings. I got my library degree at San Jose State, was married—now divorced. Who wouldn't come home to a job in their field that was near their widowed, aging mother?"

Eve nodded along with Joye, and Shaye offered a tenuous smile. "And that's the overview of my life, summarized to make a boring story short."

Joye seemed to take Shaye's recounting at face value, not commenting, but Eve had a feeling that there might be more based on Shaye's initial paused response. *Sanitized,* Eve thought. She could understand that. As an adult, she still carried her own childhood losses, as would most anyone.

Her parents' car accident when she was ten had changed her life, although Sadie and Glen had been wonderful. Losing her older brother in an off-duty motorcycle accident when she was twelve had been another life-altering event. Sadie and Glen had refused to discuss the issues she'd inferred were there that had upset Mike, contributing to his recklessness and preceding the event. She knew they believed that she and Earl had been through enough loss in their lives. That loss would have been part of any thorough answer she gave to an inquiry for her to tell someone about herself. She'd picked up the family law enforcement tradition because the events of her childhood had steered her life to this police chief role that she was trying to fulfill to the best of her ability every day.

As they stood to leave the pizza parlor, Eve's instincts were telling her that Shaye had censored this telling. Fair enough, it was Shaye's story to tell, but she was still curious. Eve attributed it to professional curiosity. That was the cop in her.

# CHAPTER NINE

When Shaye heard Eve's alarm go off the next morning, her room was still so dark that she could barely make out furniture shapes. She was in that suspended enjoyable place of being warm and relaxed that existed between being sound asleep and fully awake. She could easily roust and crawl out of bed because she'd turned in soon after arriving home from pizza last night. Shaye had enjoyed the evening and had to remind herself on the ride home that she needed to maintain control of her feelings. She'd come to town to sort out some hard truths and to heal.

Most mornings she'd been out of bed and had the coffee made before Eve surfaced. Admittedly, Eve was usually up later at night than she was. Shaye's purposeful offset of their schedules helped limit their interaction. That was advantageous in diminishing the temptation of Eve, which was how Shaye was now labeling this disturbing attraction to her—*the temptation of Eve*. And that dovetailed with the tamer designation Joye had presented last night, *the chivalrous chief*. So, what the heck was Eve doing awake so early?

The click, click, click of McGruff's nails came down the hallway to Shaye's bedroom door a few minutes later, and then he nosed the door open and charged in.

"Are you out there, Eve, or just the dog?" Shaye quietly asked.

"I thought maybe I'd do a little biking this morning. See if you wanted to run along with me?" Eve knocked and then entered behind McGruff. "My joints aren't happy with jogging these days, but biking helps keep me in shape. I need to stay in shape—so I can *protect and serve*."

There was no missing the tease in Eve's tone. That tease flared those embers of desire Shaye kept contained. Just her annoying, smoldering cravings.

"I haven't noticed any problem with your shape." Shaye couldn't keep from offering Eve a full body assessment. She was wearing skin-tight biking shorts, and the fit was provocative, even if Eve was completely unaware. "And I haven't seen you up this early in the time I've been here."

McGruff yawned with a high-pitched moan thrown in at the end, and they both laughed at the mutt, then Eve yawned too. Shaye found it interesting that Eve had heard her tell Joye last evening how much she missed jogging, and here Eve was, setting her alarm and volunteering to accompany her. Shaye didn't want to appreciate the gesture as much as she was. She didn't want these simmering feelings of wanting to know Eve better to grow.

"The crack of dawn. That's dedication. Related to police work, protect and serve. Not just a job—it's a calling." Shaye teased her back.

Shaye climbed out of bed and started collecting her jogging clothes while Eve watched her, continuing their conversation. "I need a bit of stress relief too. This election's a bit challenging—Sneed's down my neck to try to pin the arson on *your stepsister*, or at least insinuate it was her."

"Yeah, it might be to your advantage to link it to *your ex*." They both knew that linking the arson to Pauline would knock her out of the mayoral race, but Shaye didn't want to think about Pauline. She peered under the bed, looking for her jogging shoes. She made sure that Eve got a full view of her sleeping-shorts-clad backside, if only because Eve's form-fitting biking attire wasn't the least bit innocuous.

"It would," Eve replied, suddenly a bit hoarse.

"But you won't. Not without evidence. Not even if it meant keeping your job. That's what I like about you." Along with the view of you in that cycling gear, Shaye thought. That Eve was honorable as well as attractive was becoming evident to Shaye, and she wasn't sure how she felt about that. She only knew it was becoming harder to ignore.

"You like me?" Eve injected a full dose of incredulity into the question, and when Shaye took a quick glance at her, she could see the amusement on Eve's face.

"It's still dark out there—I think I must be talking in my sleep," Shaye replied.

Eve laughed. "I think I'm going to set my alarm in the middle of the night more often."

"Are we going to hit the pavement or not? Because if we are, you'd better let me get dressed." Shaye shifted her delivery to a drawl. "Unless you want to stay for the show."

Eve left and McGruff stayed. Fifteen minutes later, they were out in the cool air, the sun just initiating its climb into the cloudless sky with a soft glow at the horizon, the early rays offering a minimal tick up in the morning chill. Eve had turned the route and pace over to Shaye, pedaling easily behind her.

Shaye took note that Eve wasn't riding a skinny-tire, backbreaking-handlebars, backside-bruising seat sort of bike. Eve's bike was definitely built for a female, with a step-through profile, substantial frame, handlebars that didn't require slouching over while hiding her feminine chest, and it had a seat that could meet and support Eve's shapely derriere. The frame was a lavender hue, and Shaye had to reflect that it was perfect for Eve, a forty-seven-year-old police chief...the same Eve who looked so good in her bicycle apparel...the same Eve who had set her alarm so she could offer Shaye accompaniment during a morning jog that she knew Shaye wanted. Yes, it was the perfect bike for Eve.

Shaye donned her beanie to contain her hair and tied a light sweatshirt around her waist to cover her ass, although she debated leaving the fleece jacket home to taunt Eve. She'd remembered the morning of the mail slot fire and Eve's overt assessment of her in running shorts, but then she'd reminded herself that this was a chance for a morning run. Flirting would only cause problems, as if their conversation a few minutes ago hadn't felt like flirting. Well, flirting was off the agenda, even if just being in Eve's presence didn't tend to provoke it.

Shaye pounded out four miles before she plopped down on one of the downtown benches to take a moment's reprieve. Eve pulled in behind the long seat and parked her bicycle. They were only about half a mile from Eve's house, but Shaye wasn't ready to give up the fresh air yet.

"If you'll watch my wheels, I'll get us each a coffee if you'd like. We can drink them sitting here while enjoying the early morning setting." Eve glanced across the street at the coffee shop. "We can even walk the last blocks home afterward if you don't want to continue to jog after a latte."

"A latte? How do you know I want a latte and not some six-word, froufrou coffee concoction? Or simply black?" Shaye asked.

"You can pick whatever you want. My treat. I was just channeling the amount of milk you add to your caffeine every morning."

"You noticed." Shaye knew she shouldn't be, but she was pleased that Eve had paid attention to how she liked her coffee. She'd noticed that Eve lightened her morning beverage as well but tended to drink it black at other times.

"I'm a cop. Hazard of the jo—*calling*." Eve winked at her. A bewitching wink that only reminded Shaye of their killer kiss. "Well, what'll it be?" Eve cocked a brow, tapping her foot in an exaggerated fashion as she waited for a response.

"Sooo many options." Shaye put her hand on her chin and rolled her eyes upward, as if this was a difficult decision that she was contemplating. "You talked me into it. A latte, please."

"Sounds good to me...so two lattes coming right up."

Ten minutes later, Eve was back with two paper cups. She sat next to Shaye on the bench after she handed one to her.

"So what do you have planned today. Trailer or office?" Eve asked.

"I'm still sorting and shelving books, so probably the trailer. I thought you were going to come to the library—as I remember, you said there was more to check out than books." Shaye danced her eyebrows at Eve.

"I was being a smart-ass," Eve replied.

"A blushing smart-ass, as I remember."

Eve's color bloomed now at the memory, and Shaye suspected that she was thinking about the handcuff remark too.

"So are you going to come visit me in the stacks?" Shaye asked. "I've got the lightly warped section and the heavily smoked section. Even a few books with mild singeing on the edges. Still readable, so I'm trying to figure out what to do because there's not enough money coming from insurance or the city budget to replace all the damaged ones."

"Is this the job you expected? I'm just trying to understand why you became a librarian."

"Is that the cop asking or my landlord?"

"Could it be your friend?" Eve asked before pausing and clearing her throat. She blinked a few times, then covered her actions by picking up her drink and sipping. Obviously, she hadn't planned on offering Shaye that, and Shaye had no idea what she really wanted. She needed to sort herself out first, and becoming the target of a dangerous arsonist hadn't helped. Her feelings were confusing, but she knew that her first priority wasn't to get involved with anyone, at least not romantically.

"Okay, friends." She hadn't expected to give Eve that response.

Shaye wondered how this friendship agreement was going to work out. Honesty had her admitting that *if* she was going to pursue a relationship with Eve, simply friends wasn't how she would have defined it. She held back a snort and took a sip of her own latte to cover her thoughts.

"To answer your first question, I've always loved books." Shaye pushed herself back to the librarian topic. "I must have been about nine or ten when I discovered the town library. I'd had a difficult childhood and my mom had married Joe Bromwell, so Pauline and Andy were in my life. You had siblings, so you know the significant role they can play in things—not always positive. Andy and I did okay together, but Pauline…well, she was Pauline."

Eve nodded. "I get it. I'm interpreting that to imply the reason you spent a lot of time at the library?"

"You must be a cop. Good deductive skills. Yeah, the library was my savior. Plus, I learned to love reading—being in someone else's head. I could escape to other worlds. I'd like to offer that to other kids."

Eve shoulder bumped her. "A little *public service* of your own, huh?"

Shaye nodded. "So, what are you up to today?"

"Well, at the top of my list is to catch an arsonist, but I have the feeling it probably won't happen today. I'll touch base with Hooper. And then there's always the normal, everyday protecting and serving of my own—line of duty stuff. I guess we each have our calling."

"You know, I'm finding this is a great way to have my morning coffee," Shaye said. "Thank you, Eve."

"You're welcome. It is a good way to indulge in our lattes, isn't it?" Eve grinned, then changed the subject. "I've been meaning to ask you…tomorrow's Saturday, and Cassie has that hairstyling appointment at two o'clock with Joye. Hamburgers before. Do you want to come with us or stay home and I'll have whoever's on shift patrol by? We'll be back before dark with pizza and a plan for a movie. Ginny will pick her up afterward."

Shaye slowly sipped her drink, considering the next day. "If she's free, I'd like you to leave me at my mom's while you take Cassie to lunch and the Cutting Edge. If it's okay, maybe you can pick me up and I'll go home with you for pizza and the movie."

"I can make that work," Eve said.

"I came back to town for a reason, and Mom's part of that."

"Sure, I can see that. She's getting older."

"That's not all of it." Shaye took her time, and Eve didn't push her. "You know about my dislike of cops?"

Eve nodded. "I've been assuming because of your divorce." Eve glanced down and fiddled with her shirt hem. "I confess, I looked you up online."

Shaye wasn't surprised. "The cop in you."

"I didn't use any of my police resources. Just a plain old Google peek." Eve shrugged and looked apologetic, but Shaye would have been surprised if Eve hadn't done a little digging, considering that she was living in Eve's house.

Shaye made a decision and decided she could trust Eve enough to give her more of an explanation about her life than she'd revealed at pizza last night. She paused a moment, considering…trusting a cop. Well, it was only trusting her with information, not her heart. And then it hit her that maybe there was a little bit of her heart involved. She knew this cop was growing on her, but she had things to sort out.

"How it turned out with Cynthia, my ex-wife, hurt me. But there's a lot more to what's troubled me since I was a kid. If you recall, I mentioned last night at dinner that my dad had been killed on a family vacation when I was five." Shaye studied Eve. "He was shot by a cop."

Eve set down her coffee and put an arm across Shaye's shoulders and squeezed. "I'm so sorry, Shaye."

Shaye accepted the hug. A hug laced with the closeness of Eve— the faint scent of vanilla and spice, combined with the delicious scent that was uniquely Eve. If the topic weren't so disconcerting, their proximity was. She focused on Eve's kindness. The sympathy made her choke up with the recounting of her past. She cleared her throat. "There's more. It was my fault. It was a robbery and when the cop pulled his weapon, I yelled 'Gun,' causing him to pull the trigger—my dad was hit. His name was David. While he was actually my stepdad, he was the man I knew as my dad. It changed our lives. Mine, but even more, my mom's. Annie convinced me that the guilt and pain that have plagued my life since then might be easier to address if I faced things, so I took the library job and moved back. I've seen shrinks, but that's not going to fix this. I need to talk to my mom." Shaye gulped. "Maybe tomorrow's finally the day."

"Whatever you need. You set it up with Ginny and I'll make it work. I'd love for you to join Cassie and me for pizza and the movie, but I understand that it should be whatever you're feeling like. Whatever works for you."

"Thanks." Shaye offered Eve a smile. She knew it was lopsided, but she hoped Eve knew it was sincere.

"Sure. You ready to head home and rescue the beast before we head to work."

"The beast," Shaye murmured, but it was the word *home* that stuck with her. She didn't have one, and she wasn't just thinking of the roof over her head. She knew she wanted something other than the one-and-done relationships she'd pursued these past three years, and she was making an effort to change. She was imagining something more. What Shaye couldn't believe was that it was the cop and her "beast" that were infiltrating that image.

## CHAPTER TEN

Okay, darling. Here's your coffee the way you like." Her mother set the mug in front of Shaye and took a seat across from her at the kitchen table with her own drink.

"Thanks, Mom." Shaye took a sip and offered her a nervous smile. "So, I guess you want to know why I invited myself over."

"You know you're always welcome. If you need somewhere to stay after the fire, you know that I'll always find a place here for you."

"That's not what I want to talk about. You know that I'm staying at Eve's place. I don't want to put you or Cassie in danger when it was a targeted attack on me." Shaye wasn't going to elaborate on the complexities of her feelings regarding her current situation. She needed to focus on why she was there.

She'd intimated to her mother when she'd dropped by that first time why she was back in town—to try to address what had happened to her dad. Cassie had been there, so they hadn't had a real discussion. She knew that she needed to if she was going to address her guilt. The impact of her actions on her mom was a significant part of that guilt.

"So, let's talk. What's on your mind?" Her mom looked over the top of her mug as she sipped and waited.

"I want to talk about what happened when I was five. I want to apologize for what happened to you. I know you loved Dad... David. That I changed your life." Shaye felt her throat constrict as she addressed the guilt and pain that she'd carried with her all these years. She'd been a troubled teen, and her mother knew she'd left home at eighteen because even therapy hadn't helped her resolve her view of things. She'd never addressed the subject directly with her mom as one adult to another.

"I've wanted to talk for a long time, but you were never ready." Her mom smiled. "Apology accepted, but you don't owe me one. You were a child. What happened impacted you too—I know you loved David. Regrets don't change anything. I moved on and I've had a good life. I've loved and been loved. And whether you believe it or not, crotchety grump that he liked to portray, Joe Bromwell loved me and we had a good life together. I have no regrets."

"So, you're not going to tell me that it didn't cause you significant pain?" Shaye could feel the self-recrimination that she had lived with for so many years evidenced in her question.

"Of course it caused me significant pain. I loved David. But you were five years old, and your reaction to seeing a drawn gun during a robbery was normal. David would never have wanted you to blame yourself. If there's blame to be had, it's the armed robber."

"I don't know, Mom." Shaye had lived with her memory of the event for so many years. It had become a part of who she was, almost an internal growth, a malignancy, that had become a part of her. She'd come to realize how much its toxic repercussions had overshadowed her life. She knew she'd never be able to completely excise it, but she needed to take that memory and put it in perspective. Maybe her mom could finally help her do that better than all the shrinks because her mom had lived an aspect of it too.

"Mistakes were made, darling. You can be sorry for what happened, but you can't carry the blame. What would you expect a five-year-old's reaction to be? What would you think if you had heard about it happening to another five-year-old?"

Shaye studied her mom's kind eyes, and she could see that her mom meant every word. "I just want for it to never have happened."

"I can give you a long list of things I wish hadn't happened. And a list of things I wish had. That's not life. Nobody gets to control it all. I hope you've seen me make the best of things and love the tarnation out of my life. I'm happy."

"The tarnation, huh?" Shaye chuckled. She'd seen her mother always working to enjoy her life, being positive.

"I think maybe this was the right time to talk about it—that you're in a place to benefit from a discussion. Do you feel better?"

"I do." Shaye didn't hesitate. "You're giving me a perspective that I've avoided considering. Your perspective. I thought I'd ruined your life. And while I know I was only five, I haven't really considered what that meant, maybe because I've always looked at it from whatever age I was, and that didn't start until I was older because I couldn't." She'd probably need to spend some time digesting her mom's words. She knew that she wasn't going to forget, she didn't want to forget the man who had been her loving dad, but she wanted to find some peace with the guilt and pain.

"Come visit my kindergarten class. Maybe a group of five-year-olds can help you. We can arrange for you to come for a visiting librarian story hour. I've got a book you can read to them."

Shaye nodded. She'd done her share of story hours, but some time paying attention to how five-year-olds interacted with the world couldn't hurt.

"You know we can talk anytime you want. Now if you're done for today, I'm going to have you text Eve to pick you up so you two can spend some time with Cassie."

"Is it about Cassie, or are you trying to play matchmaker, Mom?"

"I believe in the power of love."

"It can put some pretty big cracks in your heart." Shaye thought about Eve and Pauline, about herself and Cynthia, about all the heartbreak in the world.

"And I've read that cracks are where the light gets in. Maybe those cracks help a person appreciate love more. Love is everything. And for you, Shanelle, look at everything—the beginning of everything. I consider myself a strong woman, and I can do without a lot of things, but I cannot live without love. You've always given me that, even when I've lost it elsewhere in my life. Even when you were away, I knew you loved me. That mattered. And romantic love, it can complete you."

"Dope AF. You're the best, Joye. Hella yeah."

Shaye and Eve had just walked into the Cutting Edge, and the grin on Cassie's face as she looked in the mirror and gushed over her makeover made Shaye realize how much Cassie had needed a day like this. Eve's role in this good deed didn't escape Shaye either—a day Eve had arranged.

Joye had even applied some light touches of makeup to Cassie's youthful face, although she didn't need it, and Shaye was pleased for her. Meeting Eve's eyes in the mirror, something exchanged between them. Maybe only something they could trade in a reflection. The glass offered a plane of protection that a face-to-face encounter didn't. Shaye wasn't ready for what that face-to-face might convey about what she was feeling for Eve, who was standing right next to her. The mirror offered her a degree of distance, an echo of Eve's simple elegance and kindness and allure. *Dope AF.* There was no disagreeing with Cassie's phrasing.

Shaye would still do her adult duty. "Language, Cassie. You'd never catch a grown-up saying that." *Just thinking it.*

"What? *AF?*" Cassie's image in the mirror was an orchestrated display of innocence. That was before she offered a smug smile. "Atrial fibrillation. You know, an altered heartbeat. The result of having this makeover, Aunt Shanelle."

Shaye could see that Eve and Joye were fighting their amusement too. "I'm so pleased that you're such a whiz at biology. Cardiology." Shaye looked from Cassie to Joye. "And what you've done with her hair. Perfect. It does affect my heartbeat too…must be atrial fibrillation."

"I love your new look, Cassie." Eve's approval made Cassie beam. "So, are we ready for me to settle up with Joye? And then we can go pick up the pizza and watch a movie at home with McGruff."

"This one's on me. I've been wanting to try this cut, and all my customers have been more worried about covering their gray." Joye waved her hand, shooing Eve's offer of money away, and then winked at Cassie. "You did me a favor."

"Maybe you should be paying me." Cassie giggled, giving Joye the side-eye.

"Don't push it. But I'll tell you what. You're good at biology. How about English…can you write? I need an occasional kid perspective for the *Pulse*—so it's not just an old farts' rag. Haircuts in exchange for your occasional input."

Cassie threw back her head and laughed. "You've *so* got a deal. Yes, yes, yes. Thank you, Joye. And I promise, they'll never confuse my writing for some *old fart's.*"

Looking at Shaye and the chuckling Eve, Joye handed Cassie a lollipop. "I don't give these to old farts. Now, get on out of here. Go save the pooch with one of those pepperoni-topped, cheese-smothered dinner dough circles."

"You do know that McGruff and I will be chaperones tonight, don't you? These two are totally into each other." Cassie looked at Joye for her reaction while Shaye felt heat climb into her cheeks and Eve locked her attention on the door, obviously plotting an escape route.

"Totally." Joye's eyes didn't hide her mirth. "I can tell already— you two ladies are going to have a terrific evening with my new star reporter." Then she turned to Cassie. "You know the *Paradise Pulse* is just called the *Pulse* for a reason. We keep up on the current state of things here in Paradise, or Paradise Pines if you're being formal. I'm counting on you, Cassie, to keep me informed on these two."

"You got it, *boss*." Cassie gave Joye an exaggerated amateur wink that scrunched up the entire right side of her face as Shaye led the way out of there.

❖

The movie credits were running, and Eve's coffee table was strewn with the aftermath of a Saturday night pizza party. All four of them sat on the couch, Eve and Shaye bookending Cassie and McGruff.

"Do you want to text Ginny or should I?" Eve asked. She knew that Ginny was standing by to come collect Cassie.

"I will," Cassie replied. "Not yet, though. I'm taking socket dog out."

Earlier in the evening, Cassie had decided McGruff needed another nickname besides the Mac that Eve had told her was his work name. She'd run *rocket dog* past them, but they couldn't contain their laughter at the suggestion of calling an old dog who needed a couch ramp in order to be a couch potato any name related to speedy, so Cassie had informed them she was going with the electrocution theme she'd heard Shaye use to describe McGruff at Ginny's house a few weeks ago after Eve had left. "It's not an insult," she'd told him as she tried to smooth down his porcupine appearance before lifting him off the couch. "A little gel and I can now have the same look. *Lit.*" She glanced at Eve and Shaye. "That translates to *hip* in old lady speak."

"You think I'm old enough to know what *hip* means?" Eve teased her, enjoying the kick Shaye was getting out of the exchange.

"Your couch potato didn't want to miss the ending, but I know he needs to visit his favorite bush." Cassie had formed a bond with the mutt and had already escorted him to the back yard twice that evening. "I looked up that movie star on my phone, so you two scoot closer and read the article so we can talk about her when I get back inside." She handed her phone to Shaye, not succeeding in the least at acting nonchalant as she headed outside with McGruff.

Shaye looked across the couch at Eve and rolled her eyes. "Are we going to disappoint the kid or are you going to do the assignment?"

Eve remembered not only sitting next to Shaye on that downtown bench yesterday morning while Shaye shared her retelling of the trauma of loss, but also the connection of close contact. Not just the undeniable physical stirrings, but the emotional. The need to comfort Shaye, the desire to know her better, the invasion into her heart. She moved over next to Shaye and they shared the phone, heads tilted together and hands touching as Eve tried to read. She hoped Shaye was absorbing more about this movie star than she was because she stood no chance of carrying on an intelligent conversation with Cassie when her full attention was on Shaye.

As time passed, Shaye whispered, "I think the kid set us up."

"For what?" Eve knew *for what*, but she wanted to hear Shaye's take. Then the sounds of their commingled, ragged respiration made it clear enough. Drat Cassie. Or maybe she should blame McGruff for needing to pee.

Shaye turned her head the slightest amount at the same time that Eve did and they were eye to eye, lips only a few centimeters apart, the warmth from the air they shared not only reaching her lungs, but registering low in Eve's abdomen. It was probably a mistake, but not only did she close her eyes—she closed the space between them down to less than a single centimeter, and then she felt Shaye's soft moist lips barely brush her own.

"Oops," Shaye murmured, not an ounce of remorse in her tone.

God, Eve remembered the caress of those lips from the bar. And more. "We can't."

"I know."

"I want to." Eve shook her head. Did she just say that out loud? She cleared her throat. "*Friends* don't kiss."

"Nope. *Friends* don't."

They brushed lips again, a shared caress, but the sounds of the return of Cassie and McGruff had them pushing apart—with no time to re-bookend on the couch.

It hit Eve like a train—the certainty that she'd end up in bed later that night with Shaye unless she did something to derail it. Last week when she'd stopped at the bank, Eve had agreed to a dinner date with that teller, Audrey, who'd asked her out at least a half dozen times. She'd turned Audrey down every time except this last one, and only accepted because Eve had reminded herself that she'd promised to accept the next date invitation from a reasonable woman that she received, and so she had. Part of her introspection. Part of her personal progress. Part of her plan to get past her attraction to the flirty, chemistry-generating

Shaye. She was slowly proving to be someone more than Eve had surmised—so much more, but still Pauline's stepsister, and Eve hadn't decided what that meant. She was so enticing, and she was scaring the hell out of Eve. Shaye was overwhelming her as she thought about her recent convictions versus what she was feeling. She needed to sort it all out.

"I have a date. Tuesday night." Eve wondered if she could have blurted it out more awkwardly. The shock on Shaye's face suggested that she couldn't have. She was rather shocked herself.

"I miss something?" Cassie returned with McGruff and clearly wasn't oblivious to the undercurrent in the room.

It was the undercurrent of the divide Eve had just created, but so suddenly that their mutual attraction still hung in the room too. Their friggin' chemistry. "Nope. You didn't miss a thing." She hoped Cassie couldn't hear the husk in her voice, overlaid with the new strain she'd just put there.

"Mm-hmm. You two ready for me to call Ginny? Leaving only McGruff here as your chaperone?"

"Ginny's probably waiting for the call," Eve responded as Shaye collected the remains of their dinner from the coffee table and disappeared into the kitchen.

"I don't know what you did to upset Aunt Shanelle. You two are good together…the *atrial fibrillation* is obvious." Cassie studied Eve.

Before she could respond, Shaye exited the kitchen and headed toward the guest room, calling back over her shoulder, "Good night, Cassie. I love your new haircut…and spending an evening with you."

Eve turned the TV back on and they watched it in silence until Eve decided to wade in and have the talk she'd been wanting to have, making sure Cassie was staying safe. Shaye was upset with her, so she might as well go for broke and add Cassie to the list too.

"I've heard some kids have been out late, climbing Coyote Hill. I just want to make sure it's not you out at night. It's not a good idea any time, but especially not with an arsonist out there."

Cassie looked at Eve and shook her head. "Subtle, Eve. Subtle."

Eve threw up both hands. "I know I'm bad at this, but I want you safe."

"I hear you, okay?" Cassie sucked in her cheeks. "I'll do my best. You do know I'm a kid on the verge of the terrible teens, don't you?"

Eve couldn't contain a laugh. "You're not there yet. Just be careful. I care."

"So, you're not disappearing again?" Cassie asked, unable to hide the vulnerability in her question.

"I was always keeping an eye on you, Cassie, but that's not enough. I want days like today if you do too. I need days like today."

Cassie gave her that smug smile. "Well, if it's something you need, I can probably manage it."

As they finished the conversation, Ginny arrived, and Cassie gave Eve a quick hug around the waist before heading out the front door to the car. Eve waved at Ginny, and before she climbed in, Cassie turned around and pointed at Eve.

"Thanks, Eve. You need to fix this. I know…language…but you and Aunt Shanelle. Hot AF together. And it wasn't just atrial fibrillation."

## CHAPTER ELEVEN

It was Tuesday evening, and Eve cursed herself for having Shaye on her mind as she drove to her dinner date with Audrey. Shaye had done a decent job of avoiding her since Saturday night's disaster of a blurt about the date she was now heading to.

Tonight, Shaye had been back in the guest room with McGruff in the new dog bed Shaye had purchased and put on the floor for him. He'd had the nerve to give Eve a growl as she'd stuck her head in the door before heading out. The word *traitor* crossed her mind, and then she realized that maybe McGruff thought the same of her, heading out on a date. Shaye had refused to look up from her book and had simply nodded and given Eve a wave.

Even their car rides to and from work had passed with minimal interaction since Saturday, the radio substituting for conversation. Well, Eve had promised herself that tonight she'd make the best of things and see if she was any good at official dating. She could handle this. For crying out loud, she was forty-seven years old with years of experience handling difficult situations—felons, the furious, the irrational, a hostage situation or two, life-altering interviews, even Pauline. But official dating—this really scared her. And knowing Shaye was at home holding in her feelings with an outward show of indifference didn't help. Eve knew she'd hurt Shaye, even if their unofficial relationship was only related to her police chief calling, as Shaye had labeled her job. Eve knew it was becoming more.

After the thirty-minute drive from Paradise Pines, Eve pulled into the parking lot at the address Audrey had given her and emitted a bark of laughter as she read the sign: *Thai Tanic.* Audrey had texted to ask if she liked Thai food, and when she'd responded that she loved it, she received this address with *7:00?* included and she'd hit the thumbs-up. Now Eve decided that either Audrey had a sense of humor that she'd never witnessed at the bank, or the restaurant owners did and this was a sign the date might be a shipwreck. Eve figured she'd find out. She took a deep breath, unbuckling her seat belt and buckling in for whatever the gods had in store for her tonight.

Eve saw her date at a back table. Audrey was a no-nonsense sort of person—precise bob, precise makeup, precise clothing, precise speech. Undoubtedly a precise bank employee and perfect for the job.

"Good evening, Eve. Thank you for joining me."

"My pleasure." Eve looked around, interpreting the full house as an endorsement that the food was good. She drew a blank as to what else to say. She considered complimenting Audrey on her choice of restaurants, on her excellent bank-teller skills, on her meticulous appearance, but then a young waiter appeared to take their order.

Once he'd left, Eve decided to give this her best shot. She channeled Shaye and the relaxed exchanges they'd had. "So, I guess there wasn't a bank heist today since my department didn't get a call to come save you." Shaye might have made some Thelma and Louise joke, making Eve laugh.

"No, nothing out of the ordinary. I made thirty-two deposits and forty-three withdrawals for customers."

"That's impressive," Eve offered. "I suspect you're great at your job." Eve tried to apply *stable* to Audrey's declaration.

"I am. I've been there ten years."

A decade. That probably qualified as *loyal,* Eve thought. "It sounds like a busy day, lots of deposits and withdrawals."

"About average if you crunch the numbers. The weekly and monthly numbers divided by the workdays for each. Now, if we're talking holiday months, there's an uptick."

"That makes sense," Eve responded. "I'll bet December is a hectic month for you."

"Yes. Christmas season is very stressful. Probably why I start thinking *bah-humbug* as the calendar approaches Thanksgiving. Little town and a lot of old people. Old people who still use cash instead of their credit cards. We should outlaw cash and gray-haired folks."

Eve thought maybe that was a joke, but she was afraid it was just Audrey's honest opinion. Before she could respond with a quip about how that might keep Eve in her job, arresting cash users and the elderly, their waiter returned with Eve's chicken curry dish and Audrey's papaya salad bowl. Eve decided Audrey might not appreciate her commentary on why criminalizing the aged and cash users was a bad idea, so she changed the subject and asked Audrey how her food was.

"Well, the papaya could be a bit riper and the prawns are overdone. Not worth an eighteen-percent tip."

"I'm not sure it's the server's fault." Eve ventured to save the poor young man from the blame.

"If you don't send the message, they'll never improve. The tip reflects the patron's opinion of the entire experience."

Eve swallowed a bite of her delicious poultry dish. "Mine's excellent. I'm sorry yours isn't."

"Well, excellent is on the far end of a sliding scale, and while it's relative, I believe…"

Eve tuned out, nodding and offering an occasional affirmative sound as Audrey carried the conversation. She was sure that Audrey was undoubtedly a stable, loyal, and honest person, but Eve realized that she'd short-changed herself. She *so* needed flirty and chemistry too.

❖

"Well, well, well. I haven't talked to you in days. So, is this Shanelle Desiraye *Hick* calling me from the back of beyond on a Tuesday evening?" Annie answered Shaye's call with a sunny demeanor that Shaye appreciated.

"Nope. It's Shaye *Hapless*." She'd thought about *Heartbroken* for her H comeback, but she wasn't willing to go there, not with Annie, not even with herself.

"It sounds like you need to talk. What's up on this journey of yours? Is it the setting or the romance?"

Shaye gulped. She felt the pressure of the tears she was holding back. "I haven't talked to you in way too long. Let's start with the setting. I witnessed an arson—not close enough to see the perpetrator, but tell that to them. Condensed version is that my house and car were set on fire, and both are essentially gone. The house was rented, and I'm waiting for the car insurance to pay out." Shaye took a deep breath. "And I was attacked."

"Oh, Shaye. Are you hurt? Anything I can do? Where are you staying—at your mom's?"

"Just some bruises. I can't put Mom in danger. Or Pauline's daughter, who's living with her. I'm living with Eve, the chief of police…and if you laugh, I'm hanging up."

"I'm biting the bejeezus out of my tongue," Annie replied. "You're living with your nemesis."

"Well, maybe I was a bit out of sorts at coffee." Shaye knew she'd just moved to town then and had found herself assigned to Eve's spare office, frustrating both of them, although Eve had done her best to solve the issue by clearing out a supply closet at the station and even vacating her own office when her officers needed it.

"She did pay for our drinks, and when you tried to tip the barista afterward, she told you that your chief had left enough for more than a ten-dollar tip. Now, before we go on to romance, have we covered setting?" Annie chuckled.

"I talked to Mom, like you suggested. An honest talk. She convinced me that I didn't ruin her life. She even told me she's been happy, or to quote her…loved the tarnation out of her life. She offered me a new perspective. I'm still digesting it, but it was good. I should have done it years ago."

"Maybe you weren't ready. But I'm glad. And proud of you."

"She wants me to come read to her kindergartners. To pay attention to what a five-year-old's like. So maybe I can put what happened into perspective. Consider my age when it happened—five."

"That's a great idea. Do you have a date for that?" Annie asked.

"Yeah. Tomorrow."

"That's good. A wonderful idea too—seeing for yourself what your level of maturity was all those years ago." Annie's tone lightened, full of tease. "So, the other aspects of this journey of yours—"

Shaye interrupted. "Just so there's no confusion, I'm staying in the guest room."

"Oh, I wasn't confused, but if we're moving on to romance…"

"First, she's a cop. You know how I feel about cops. Working through my own childhood actions and what the repercussions were for Mom is one thing. Changing my opinion of cops after the pain they've caused me in my life is something different."

"Would you say all librarians are the same?" Annie asked.

"There's no doubt. We're all wonderful."

"Seriously." Annie didn't allow Shaye to divert the discussion.

"Okay, I get your point. But tell that to my psyche."

"All I'm saying is keep an open mind. How is *your* chief of police?"

"She's on a date tonight." Shaye could hear how pathetic she sounded. She'd been upset since Saturday night when she'd heard about the date. After such a great evening with Eve and Cassie, pizza and a movie. The kind of evening she wanted in her life. Just not with a cop.

"And you're upset. I can hear it in your voice."

"I've got no right to be. But we were growing closer, although neither of us wants that—at least I've thought we didn't—too much history in the way. I think Eve has felt the same. She's still in the aftermath of Pauline." Shaye decided she might as well be open about Eve and hear Annie's advice. "Being displaced and needing protection—she only brought me here as a solution to her *call of duty*. Although we've actually had some good times together. She made sure I had a chance to go jogging while she biked. A really good evening with Pauline's daughter, Cassie. Then we kissed. Barely kissed when she blew it all up by telling me she had this date tonight." Shaye wiped her eyes. "Shit. I don't want to care."

Annie ignored her distress, probably not wanting to embarrass her. "Let's analyze this. You've been growing close. You like her, as a person, cop and all. You kissed each other, and I know it wasn't your first kiss. I'm assuming not one-sided. And she immediately hit you over the head with this date she's going on."

"Exactly. Who does that?" As she sniffled, Shaye was happy to replace her growing attraction to Eve with ire.

"Someone who knows things are growing between you two and is afraid. What would have happened if she hadn't made the date declaration?"

"Cassie was there outside." As she said it, Shaye knew the honest answer, and that wasn't it.

"And when Cassie went home?"

"There's a good chance I wouldn't have ended up in the guest room bed. At least not alone." Shaye knew Annie was making her face the facts instead of just wallowing in her self-righteousness and the hurt related both to her past and Eve's date.

"And if she wasn't ready for that yet…well, maybe she ended up stopping things in a rather abrasive way."

"Abrasive. Exactly." Annie might be helping her achieve more clarity, but Shaye was still upset.

"Not ready *yet.* You know what that means," Annie said. "It means you two need to accomplish some things before you get horizontal together. I bet she hasn't been to bed with anybody in a while, and you've been to bed with too many anybodies."

"Okay. Okay." Shaye knew Annie wasn't trying to be hurtful—that she knew Shaye was there in Paradise Pines because she wanted change. Change in how she perceived her past. Change in her post-divorce relationship behavior.

"So don't rush her. Don't rush yourself. Give yourselves time to resolve the baggage each of you carries and get to know each other. I think you're both rusty at long-term relationships, and the last one you both had ended badly. Find out if that's what you want with her—long term. Do some dating. Some flirting."

"Oh, we know how to flirt, even if Eve actually used that word *rusty* to describe her flirting skills. The chemistry is…amazing." Shaye smiled as she considered their chemistry. It had been there from their very first encounter at the bar. "But flirting and creating chemistry are Pauline's strengths, and Eve sees me as Pauline's stepsister. And she's Pauline's ex, for God's sake."

"Her *ex*—that means she figured Pauline out."

"But four years with her." Shaye shook her head, not knowing how anyone could stand Pauline that long.

Annie chuckled. "She was busy being chief of police. Or the cheating never crossed her mind—speaks to her own character. I'll bet she has regrets over the entire experience."

Shaye nodded, thinking of the mix of feelings around her own experience with her ex-wife.

"I'm going to repeat my advice—don't go to bed with her yet. Prove you're not Pauline. Let the trust grow. You need that trust in her too. I think if you two are going to work out, you have to come to some sort of resolution with your cop issues."

"How do I know she's not in bed with her date right now?" Shaye fought to keep all the feelings that image triggered out of her voice. She'd love to get it out of her mind as well.

"You don't know. You two haven't made any commitments—she's a free woman. If she's not back before morning, you'll have your answer."

"Well, that doesn't make me feel better." She knew Annie was trying to be honest, but she didn't like it.

"Glad I could help." Annie's laughter came through the phone.

"Shut up. And be on standby." Shaye was only half joking.

"You've got it. You're doing great, Shaye. Good night."

Shaye shut down her phone and pulled McGruff up onto the bed so she could pet him. Then she picked up her book so she could read. She certainly wasn't going to listen for the alarm system letting her know when Eve arrived home.

Shaye heard a key in the door followed by a beep that signaled the code had been entered correctly. She looked at her bedside clock. Eight thirty—two hours since Eve had departed. It had either been a disaster of a dinner or a quick roll in the hay, although she couldn't see Eve doing that on a first date. She hoped like heck not. Shaye heard Eve pause at the kitchen, then head toward her bedroom and stop. The clicking of heels on hallway hardwood morphed into a softer percussion, letting Shaye know Eve had shed her heels before coming down to the guest room. Keeping her eyes on her book, Shaye's covert attention was on Eve, who was leaning against her doorframe.

"You're still awake?" Eve's blond hair was up in a loose bun, her facial features perfectly enhanced with the makeup she'd applied for another woman. Tonight, a sage-hued dress complemented her hazel eyes and didn't hide the female curves of hip bone and backside relaxed against the vertical linear border edging the opening into the guest room. Just how beautiful Eve was didn't escape Shaye's discreet glance. Not the arranged frilly-femme look she'd recently sought for superficial sexual satisfaction, but a mature manifestation of beauty that scared Shaye for its depth—for the story it told. A beauty that was just as mesmerizing when Eve was attired in those black biking shorts, or the tucked white shirt and dress slacks ensemble she wore to the office, or a T-shirt and shorts for sleeping. Shaye inhaled a lungful of air through her nostrils and locked into those gold-green eyes, hoping she didn't drown.

"It's not late enough for me to fall asleep yet. Only McGruff—he's been snoring for the past half hour. You're home early. Did you have a good dinner?" Eve wasn't the only detective around here, although Shaye didn't want to let on to the weight she knew she was going to assign to the answer.

"It was a place near the Daily Grind coffee shop."

A half-hour drive, so that meant an hour of the two hours Eve had been gone had been on the road. "Was it good?" Shaye asked again.

"Nice setting. Excellent service. My chicken curry dish was delicious." Then Eve laughed. "Thai Tanic—name of the restaurant, although I don't think it registered with Audrey...my date. Prognostic of how we did together."

"Disaster, huh? That's a real shame." Shaye laughed too. She was beginning to feel so dang good.

"You're not sounding very sincere." It was the reproach in Eve's tone that wasn't sincere. She sounded rather cheerful for a disaster of a date.

Shaye released a prolonged sigh as she went with that dang good feeling. "I was hoping you didn't kiss her." If she was going to get on with Annie's advice, she might as well start tonight and be honest.

Eve pursed her lips. "I didn't kiss her." She continued to look at Shaye, chewing on her lower lip. "She wasn't you."

# CHAPTER TWELVE

A s Eve drove Shaye to Ginny's school, she relived their encounter after the ill-fated date she'd had with Audrey last evening. The date wasn't Audrey's fault—they just hadn't clicked. But more importantly for herself and Shaye, she didn't consider her date a disaster because their brief guest room doorway encounter after she'd arrived home had clarified a few things—one being that they both seemed to know that their mutual admissions put them in a new place. A place where Eve now hoped they could talk because they'd probably done enough avoiding each other and avoiding whatever this was that was going on between them.

She'd headed back down to her bedroom after she and Shaye had shared their short exchange, afraid that lingering would lead directly to more than just talk. Those mutual admissions seemed to have put them in a new place. A place where maybe they could figure some things out because they'd probably done enough avoiding each other and avoiding whatever this was that was going on between them. After all, they were two intelligent, mature women.

Eve reflected back on how sitting there across from Audrey on their tanking date, it had become so clear that the traits she'd convinced herself were necessary in defining a future partner—stability, honesty, loyalty—weren't going to be enough. She hadn't changed her mind this morning. She'd excluded the flirting and the chemistry because of Pauline, but now she knew that she needed the entire package.

However, the even bigger revelation that had hit her on her drive home from her date last night was that she wanted all those things from Shaye. And she was fool enough, hopeful enough, to consider Shaye just might be capable of them and want them too. But they had to work past the labels they'd slapped on each other. The cop label. The Pauline label. Their years of accumulated baggage. It was a lot to get past. It would take getting to know each other, learning to trust each other.

Eve thought about what the Breezeland Veterinary Clinic receptionist had said about McGruff: *We put him back together on the outside. But he needs someone to put him back together on the inside.* Maybe she and Shaye had more in common with the rescued pooch than she'd considered. Did they each hold the final piece that would help put the other back together on the inside?

"Remember our night at the bar?" Shaye interrupted Eve's thoughts and looked sideways at her from the passenger seat as they drove toward Ginny's elementary school where Eve would drop her off so she could read to the kindergarten kids in her role as librarian.

Eve allowed her head a slight tip down in affirmation as she kept her eyes on the road, wondering where Shaye was going with this. They hadn't exchanged more than pleasantries this morning in their hurry to get out of the house, pleasantries with some new undefined undercurrent.

"I want one of those drinks you mentioned at the bar." Shaye's statement included a smile-smirk. A flirty smile-smirk.

Eve cocked an eyebrow, keeping her eyes straight ahead as she wondered where this conversation was going. "This is Eve Maguire, *old-fashioned*, who you're talking to. Don't tell me that you're suggesting Love Potion for Two, or Tie Me to the Bedpost."

The deep embers of Eve's physical attraction to Shaye sparked to life with just the visitation to those names and she considered that it wasn't just what the drink labels suggested. It was more—she didn't doubt that the recollection of that evening had been the foundation for her desire. The arousing barstool bonding, the kiss. But what fueled her now was why she hadn't pursued the 10.0 carnal escalation in her 4.2 hotel room—the knowledge that she craved so much more. She wanted to hear that Shaye wanted the same, and not just sex. That maybe there was a chance for that.

"Good memory, Chief. But the answer's nope—not those two drinks. If you remember, you told me for future reference that I should remember anther drink...*Date Night*."

"Are you asking me out?" Eve smiled, elated that she and Shaye seemed to be on the same page. A good *old-fashioned* date.

"That depends."

"Depends on what?" Eve made a turn onto the street where the school was located, not glancing at Shaye in an effort to prevent the giveaway of too much of her own need, wanting Shaye's unfiltered response.

"On whether you're going to say yes."

"*Yes* depends on a few things." Eve chuckled. "First, no sinking ships. Although it was actually a restaurant I'd return to in the future. Plus, I could give the server Audrey's half of the tip, which wasn't included when we shared the bill."

"I promise. No icebergs. What else...maybe depending on who you're with?" Looking straight ahead through the windshield, Shaye appeared to be focused on the jovial interplay of the kids traversing the crosswalk in front of them—tagging each other, good-natured pushing, the rise and fall of laughter.

"I think Audrey and I work better in a bank customer and teller relationship." Eve pulled on through the emptied crosswalk and stopped the car at the curb in front of the school.

"Bank customer and teller relationship, huh?" Shaye opened the door and turned to Eve. "Have you considered exploring a librarian and cop relationship?"

Eve heard the uncertainty in Shaye's voice. Not ambivalence, but self-doubt.

"Stumbling, bumbling, fumbling," Shaye continued. "Probably even some blundering. It's been a while."

Eve laughed. "I think you've covered the bases. At least you didn't say boring."

"We may end up being bad at this, but I don't think we'd be boring."

"Or maybe just a *you* and *me* relationship. We could consider exploring that." Eve knew that better defined what she wanted if they were going to label it. F*riends* wasn't going to work. Exploring an *us* relationship might be a better goal. If she dared hope that they could stumble, bumble, fumble, probably even blunder their way there.

Shaye nodded with a grin and touched Eve's arm before climbing out of the vehicle. "Yes. That."

Eve watched the backside of the unboring Shaye Hayden saunter off with an exaggerated sway of her hips. "Yes, that," Eve whispered. "*All* that."

❖

Meadowbrook Elementary School was in a neighborhood toward the south side of town. Heading on to her office after dropping Shaye off, Eve decided to drive farther south to the edge of town and patrol the country road loop that bordered the community rather than traveling directly through to downtown. It was a nice drive and received less attention from her officers than the populated areas of Paradise Pines. She'd been driving only a few minutes when she spotted a white pickup truck on the shoulder with its hood up. A younger man in jeans and a flannel shirt, probably close to thirty, stood in front of the vehicle. He appeared stressed. Eve pulled in behind, called her location in to Mona, and then checked that she had her weapon before she got out and approached him.

"Hi. I'm Eve Maguire—Paradise Pines PD. Need some help?" Eve studied him. He looked vaguely familiar, and while his anxiety was apparent, he offered her a slight smile.

"Thanks for stopping, Chief."

He knew who she was, but why did she recognize him? Eve was certain she hadn't seen him face-to-face. At least not recently. Maybe she'd run into him when he was much younger—late teens.

"Matthew Merchant. Call me Matt. I ran out of gas. Too much going on and I didn't fill up. That'll teach me."

As soon as she heard his name, Eve knew who he was. She'd seen a small black-and-white picture of him, and there had been a rather minimal online profile written up. He was the third candidate for mayor. The guy with terrible odds of winning against Greg Sneed and Pauline.

"You're running for mayor." Eve didn't want to dwell on the election, to think about how precarious her job probably was, so she moved on to Merchant's car problem. "Shall we make a run to the Fuel Stop? I know the owner—he'll have a spare gas can we can borrow. I'll bring you back here and you can add a gallon. With that, you can drive back into town and fill up." Eve watched him relax a bit.

"You don't know how much I'd appreciate that. I was heading to my mom's place. I promised to have breakfast with her before I sit down to start work today."

"Did you call her and tell her you'd be late? Probably a good idea. You're never too old to keep that mother figure in your life happy." Eve thought of Sadie. All their years together and the reversal from Sadie keeping her happy to her trying to make Sadie happy. The teddy bears lately.

"I didn't, but you're right. I'd better."

Eve waited while he called his mom and explained the situation. When he'd finished, they climbed into Eve's car.

"Whoa, what species is it? Some sort of fringe canine, I'd guess." Merchant chuckled when he saw McGruff in the back seat.

He ignored McGruff's growling and reached back, letting the dog sniff his extended hand before patting him on the head. McGruff leaned into the attention. His acceptance registered with Eve. Merchant, as a candidate running against Sneed, wasn't off her arson suspect list yet, but she noted McGruff's assessment. After her online checking into him, she was happy to meet him in person.

Thirty minutes later, after they'd made the run to the Fuel Stop, they pulled back up behind Merchant's stranded truck with the gallon of gas. As she'd transported him, they'd had a conversation about his childhood in Paradise Pines before Eve had moved to town. She now knew that he was thirty-one. They'd discussed his years in college as a computer science major, his subsequent years in the military, and now his recent return after a decade away, the same years that Eve had been here in the police department. He told her that he worked from his house as a website designer. She remembered from her suspect research that he lived in a small rental in a residential neighborhood, not far from Shaye's burnt residence.

"And that's the story of my life. Except for running for mayor," he told her.

"So tell me about that, since we've covered the thirty-one years of your life so far." Eve decided to initiate an election discussion. She wouldn't be surprised if someday, when he was older and probably not before she retired, Merchant might actually end up mayor. She wasn't crossing him off the suspect list because she wasn't excluding someone who was in the competition for mayor from being culpable. It was the same reason Pauline was on the list. A fire had been set in Sneed's campaign office and the library arson was detrimental to Sneed's campaign too. However, Eve seriously doubted that Merchant was involved. But damn, they needed to catch whoever was.

"My grandfather was Paradise Pines' mayor ages ago. Or maybe I should just call it Paradise, like my grandparents like to call the place." He chuckled. "Family tradition is probably part of the reason I'm running."

Eve nodded. "I've got law enforcement in my genes too." She didn't elaborate further.

"Anyway, I'm not naive. I know I won't win, but I thought I'd give it a go, learn how to run for office and all it involves, so maybe someday..." Merchant offered Eve a shrug. "It's been a great way to meet new people and reconnect with old friends—as a lonely guy back in town. Plus, I like to do my homework and I thought it would be good experience. Greg Sneed seems okay, but that Pauline Bromwell seems to have some narcissistic tendencies under that smooth exterior from what I've seen behind the scenes."

Eve nodded, but didn't say a word. The young man was astute. More astute than she'd been.

"We're a small town that elects both the mayor and the council members—people want a say in everything here. You might learn a lot from sitting on the council first."

Merchant nodded. "I was thinking the same thing. Sort of jumped in the deep end when I probably should have dipped my toe in the water first."

Eve noted that he seemed to be grounded. "I hope we run into each other again, Matt. Just maybe not on the side of the road with car trouble."

"You've got it, Chief. Thanks for the ride. And the advice. And take good care of that handsome sidekick of yours."

Eve laughed. "McGruff and I'll wait here until you get it started and follow you into town. It's been great meeting you. I'm sure we'll cross paths again."

❖

There was colorful art spread across the classroom. It was pinned to the walls, suspended clothesline-style from strings stretched across the expanse of the room, taped to the windows. There were rockets, rainbows, animals with sharp teeth that might be dinosaurs, stick people with huge smiley faces...organic and unrestrained and imaginative. Kid art.

The five-year-olds who sat in a half-circle on the floor in her mother's elementary school classroom were waiting for Shaye to start. In the meantime, they weren't wasting time—they were busy interacting. Their nonstop movement, even sitting in place, plus the sounds of chatting and giggling with the occasional snort or burst of laughter created an energetic atmosphere in the room. Shaye was happy she'd accepted her mother's invitation. She stepped forward to take front and center stage before she began and noticed one small boy tapping lightly on the lizard terrarium at the back of the room.

"If you're ready, we have a story about a girl your age who makes a jillion mistakes," her mom told the kids. They nodded and settled down. "Our town librarian, who happens to be my daughter, is going to read it to you today." Shaye's mom shifted her gaze from the kids on the floor in front of Shaye to the boy in the back. "Jason, if you pay attention and are quiet, I'd appreciate it if you would help keep Leroy Lizard company if you'd like to. Shall we begin?"

Shaye suspected that Jason was much happier in the back with Leroy, and she loved the way her mother worked with each child's individual personality and makeup.

There were several remarks and looks when the kids realized that their teacher was the librarian's mother, but the responding *yes* was loud and exuberant as the kids settled down in their semicircle so Shaye could begin, Jason paying attention from the floor back by the reptile.

Shaye took the book from her mother and showed the kids the cover, then she read each page and shared the illustrations as the heroine's mistakes tallied up.

She was about halfway through the story when one of the girls yelled "Bird" and pointed to a high window behind Shaye. Everyone's attention diverted to the window to watch a pigeon strutting on the ledge outside and looking in. A boy called out "Dove," while another loudly corrected him, asking if he didn't know what a pigeon looked like. Another boy interrupted and said it wasn't a *homing* pigeon like his uncle had, but it must be a *schooling* pigeon because this was a school.

Shaye's mother stepped up front and brought the kids' attention back to where Shaye had been reading. "Good place to pause for a moment. So far, Ms. Hayden has read about a girl who accidentally drew on the table, overflowed the bathtub, cut her bangs too short. But she found out it was okay to make mistakes. She even learned from her mistakes. Now, shall we continue?"

The kids settled back down and all eyes were on Shaye. As she continued to read, it became apparent that the book wasn't picked for the kids. Her mother had picked it for her. And she couldn't prove it, but she wouldn't be surprised if the blasted bird wasn't part of the plan too.

❖

"How's your day going?" Eve asked, knocking on Shaye's office door as the mutt scooted around her and headed for Shaye. It was late afternoon and they'd both been busy all day. "You about ready to wave the white flag of surrender?"

"Do I look like a quitter?" Shaye asked. "Hell, yes."

"We can discuss an official date night later, but how about we get a bite of dinner together this evening?" Eve didn't know how it would go, but she was hoping they could have an impromptu bite to eat and discuss their day.

"I want that date night in the future, but I'm game to grab some takeout, include the pooch, kick off our shoes, and hear about your day."

Eve nodded. "You're easy."

"Are you calling me promiscuous?" Shaye's lips twitched as she teased Eve. "I thought we agreed to take this slow. Now it seems you're talking about taking clothing off."

Eve could feel heat flush her face. And Shaye knew how to create a different kind of heat, down low and deep inside. "You're the one who mentioned kicking our shoes off. *Bare* feet. That's all you're going to see tonight."

"I'm going to see how you and I do at sharing takeout tacos with a starving fido, and I'm buying," Shaye said. "I'm going to see how we do getting to know each other by sharing the events of our day. *We*...a cop and a cop-phobic librarian...Pauline's ex and Pauline's stepsister...Shaye Hayden and Eve Maguire...we're going to see if we're compatible—more than just flirting and chemistry."

Forty minutes later, they were sitting side by side on the couch, a half dozen small tacos plated on the coffee table in front of them and McGruff on the floor watching every move they made.

"I take it Grady picked you up as planned from Meadowbrook Elementary when you were done this morning," Eve said as she swallowed a bite of her dinner. "Was your kindergarten morning good?"

Shaye took a moment before she answered. "It was good. And a setup. Mom knew what she was doing when she invited me to read. As a librarian, I've worked with kids before, but this was an entire classroom of wonderful, enthusiastic, cute—and impulsive five-year-olds."

Eve nodded. She wanted to know how Shaye had internalized those observations.

"Years of self-recrimination," Shaye continued. "Crippling. And my mom…she's helping me heal. The death of my dad, David, still happened, but now I know I didn't ruin my mom's life, and today, a bunch of five-year-olds and a pigeon offered me some insight."

"A pigeon?"

Shaye chuckled, clearly finding the incident humorous. "Pigeon lesson for the day: Five-year-olds can be rather impetuous. The bird landed outside on a ledge and was looking in the window. Besides the very loud announcement of *pigeon* that brought my reading to a screeching halt and was then followed by an impromptu juvenile commentary on the avian topic, I was astute enough to see the parallels to my childhood incident."

It sounded like the pigeon and a group of five-year-olds had precipitated the basis for a therapeutic epiphany for Shaye. A wild bird and an impulsive group of juveniles had illustrated that Shaye's actions years ago were understandable. Forgivable. Eve leaned sideways and shoulder bumped Shaye. The urge to kiss her had Eve pressing her lips tightly together. No derailing whatever this was that they were doing— it was working. They were opening up to each other, getting to know each other, learning to trust each other.

Shaye had indicated that she had moved back to Paradise Pines so she could make peace with her past and heal, so she could move on. Eve thought about how sometimes it took an event that translated into a realization to cause a person to move on. That had been the case when she'd found another woman's undergarment in Pauline's coat pocket after several prior hints of infidelity. The epiphany for Eve had been that she didn't owe Pauline the continued effort of trying to make their relationship work.

And then there was her recent revelation after her date with Audrey—that she was finally willing to take a risk with her personal life, with Shaye. That she wanted to explore a relationship with Shaye.

They had additional hurdles to overcome, but Eve was feeling optimistic. Her profession was a huge aspect of who she was, and yet Shaye carried an aversion to all cops. As for herself, Pauline had jaded her and she'd jumped to conclusions that Shaye was similar to Pauline. They needed to get beyond those prejudices. That could only occur through knowing each other better, and there they sat, starting to make that happen with a plate full of tacos.

"Okay. My turn," Eve said. "After dropping you off, Deputy Dog and I met the third candidate for mayor. We took him to get gas. He'd hit empty on his way to have breakfast with his mother."

"Well, I guess he should get votes for that—breakfast with his mother. Right up there with kissing babies. Did you like him?"

"Maybe the better barometer...he seemed to pass the McGruff test," Eve replied. "He's still on my suspect list, running against Sneed and all, but he seemed like a good person, levelheaded and sincere."

"That's good. Unlike my stepsister."

"You're really not rooting for her?" That hope Eve had been fostering surfaced and swelled in her chest.

"Eve, I wouldn't vote for her if she was the only one on the ballot. I might have grown up around her, but I'm not Pauline. She's so many things I don't want to be. That I'm not. Maybe not from a pigeon or a five-year-old, but another lesson of the day for you: If I make a commitment, I intend to keep it."

Eve's throat constricted. She hadn't realized how much she'd wanted to hear those words, and she believed them. Before she did something impulsive, she decided to change the subject.

"Thank you. I know we talked date night—an official one soon. But first I need to go visit my aunt again down in the Bay Area. Just a day trip to see Sadie unless there's an old dog to scoop up off the side of the road." McGruff thumped his tail on the floor as they both looked at him. "I'd like you to come. Maybe this weekend?"

"I have library hours on Saturday afternoon," Shaye said. Then she peered sideways at Eve, a sure sign she was considering something.

Eve was hoping that it wasn't staying overnight together in the Bay Area—well, at least her mature, rational side didn't want that. Her libido certainly voted *yes*, but Eve wanted this to work. That meant allowing time to build the trust that any chance of an *us* relationship would need.

"I received word from my auto insurance company that the claim payout for my car is approved," Shaye continued. "Maybe I can shop online this week and line up a good deal down there—more dealers, better competition for a good price."

Eve pursed her lips. She couldn't protect Shaye if she was out driving herself around. But that was the cop side of her. There had been no further sign of trouble—Shaye would probably be fine during the daytime, and this was all voluntary. She didn't want to be controlling, and she'd certainly want some independence if she was in Shaye's shoes.

"That sounds like a first step in regaining your life," Eve offered.

"I can't live with you forever," Shaye said.

Then they looked at each other as they sat side by side on the couch, sharing dinner, sharing the remains of their day. The flutter of a possible *forever* sang a few fragile notes inside Eve, and she thought that she could see it in Shaye's eyes too.

# CHAPTER THIRTEEN

Thanks for including me today. I told the car dealer we'd be there this afternoon sometime after we see your aunt, and he said there's a full Sunday sales staff on the lot, so no problem."

Shaye looked down at their two joined hands, fingers intertwined between their seats as Eve drove them south, a tactile link that felt natural. And comfortable. She'd set her hand there first, in a way Shaye had hoped would appear casual, so she wouldn't have to read it as rejection if Eve hadn't responded. But Eve had accepted her silent offering.

Still connected to Eve, Shaye shifted her gaze over her shoulder to examine the package on the back seat next to the empty dog bed. McGruff was staying with Joye, avoiding a full day of mostly back seat boredom for the old pooch. Shaye wondered what was beneath the lumpy paper that sported a juvenile zoo. It wasn't a wrapping she would have assigned to an eighty-something-year-old woman.

After three hours on the road that put them at late morning, they pulled into the parking lot of an expansive, single-story building with a sign that declared they'd arrived at the Golden Days Elder Estate.

After greetings at the reception counter, they headed back down a hallway and into a room with an older woman sitting up in an adjustable bed. Late morning rays filtered through the window and bathed her in sunlight. Eve had offered Shaye some background and the advice that it would undoubtedly be a short visit, but she still found it jolting when the first communication to Eve from her aunt was "Who are you?"

"It's Eve and I brought my friend. Her name is Shaye."

Sadie smiled at Shaye. "It's nice to meet you. How was school today?"

Eve fielded the question, not hesitating. "No school today. We went shopping, and we have something for you."

Shaye watched as Sadie reached out for the gift with frail pale hands. She tore off the paper as she chuckled the entire time. When she'd freed the stuffed animal, she laughed in delight and pulled the plush toy into a hug. "Jasper, you found Jasper."

The almost dozen teddy bears on the chair in the corner of the room and the audience of new teddy bears on the shelf back in Eve's office—they should have been a clue. Shaye had already accepted that Eve Maguire, chief of *fucking* police, didn't exist. That this complex, multifaceted Eve in no way fit the mold that Shaye had initially wedged her into. She was certainly oozing out of that mold and right into Shaye's heart.

As she observed Eve's aunt embracing the furry gift with tears of joy in her eyes, and watched Eve tenderly kiss Sadie's forehead and gently hold her hand, Shaye knew there were exceptions to the negative cop stereotype—Eve Maguire, case in point. But it had been so much simpler with her preconceived notions in place, notions that allowed her to reject the type of growing emotions she was now feeling for Eve. Feelings that put her heart at risk. Feelings with the chance of a future. A chance she wasn't ready to walk away from.

Before they left, Sadie looked at the two of them. Shaye wasn't sure who she saw or what she remembered, but Sadie told them, "Here's some advice for you two. Follow your heart. Follow your heart."

They finally said good-bye to Sadie when it became obvious that she was fading. They stopped to chat for a moment with Eve's CNA friend Rosemary, and then waved at Jack as they passed the front desk. Shaye was still absorbing all that she'd witnessed when Eve mentioned food as they pulled out of the parking lot. They agreed that a lunch stop was in order before picking up Shaye's new vehicle.

"So where shall we go?"

"Is there a place called Thai Riffic?" Shaye asked as she struggled to project a serious delivery. "Maybe we won't need life jackets."

Eve laughed as she shook her head. "Maybe we should try a place near your auto dealer. Someplace that doesn't remind me of my last date, although it wasn't all bad. Great food…an enlightening experience…"

"It got us here, didn't it? Is this an official date?"

"It's noon, so not our date night." Eve offered Shaye a quick glance as she drove. "Do you want our first date to go down in history as a visit to Sadie, who didn't even recognize me?"

"She knows you love her," Shaye replied. "And that's what matters. The love."

"I'm not going to argue with that...what matters." Eve placed her hand between them and Shaye reached over and slipped her fingers between Eve's. She could easily make this car console connection a habit.

Shaye reached her free hand toward the radio and then paused, waiting for a signal from Eve. Eve nodded, and so Shaye turned it on. She adjusted the knob that selected the station and listened to see if she could find something she liked. News, more news, heavy metal, country western, and then finally she heard a Miley Cyrus song she liked and turned the volume up. Eve squeezed her hand in time to the beat.

"Did you *see* her performance of 'Flowers' at the Sixty-sixth Grammys? YouTube it if you missed it. More than just singing..." Shaye seductively swayed in her car seat.

"I did. Not bad."

"Understated," Shaye replied with a chuckle. "I need to learn to move like that when I sing, although it just might throw my back out."

"You do know that it's a breakup song?" Eve's laughter filled the car and Shaye considered how beautiful she was. Not simply her appearance.

"I can change that." Shaye started to hum along, softly at first, but then when it hit the chorus, she threw back her head and put herself into it. She knew she had a good voice and she gave it her all. She sang it low and throaty, letting a touch of gravel add to the desire in her delivery. She altered the lyrics—sang about all the things she was going to do for Eve—all the things that Eve wouldn't have to do for herself. Eve glanced at her, hazel eyes dark and dancing along with Shaye.

"That was perfect," Eve said, her voice raspy, and she hadn't even been singing. "I can't believe how good you are."

"I think it's actually more of an empowerment song. Being able to move on past that breakup. Self-acceptance. My kind of song."

"Moving on. Can I join you?" Eve asked.

"I wouldn't have it any other way."

❖

By Thursday evening, Eve had spent much of the week in meetings or completing bureaucratic chores. Shaye was driving herself to and from work in her new Outback, and Eve knew she'd run some daytime errands and been over to see her mother and Cassie as well. Eve had picked up Cassie after school on Tuesday and taken her for ice cream. It had been shared time that Cassie needed, and Ginny had certainly been on board.

Cassie had told her about school and been so proud that she was working on her first article for Joye and the *Pulse* about current books that kids her age might like. She'd also tried to nonchalantly let Eve know how cool Aunt Shanelle was—just in case Eve didn't already know it, so why waste time dating other people? Eve had simply nodded, knowing she'd come to that conclusion too. Nothing like taking advice from an eleven-year-old.

It had been a long day and Eve was still at work toiling over her budget. She leaned back in her chair, considering her time with Shaye this week so far. They'd talked, and while she worried, Eve understood Shaye's need for more independence and the car. There was no telling how long this threat might exist, and broad daylight seemed safe enough when the arson events had occurred at night or early dawn. Shaye was still sleeping in Eve's guest room, willing to concede the need for nighttime protection for now. They both realized that Eve's profession and alarm system were assets. It was a juggling act—Shaye's need for normalcy, the recognition of a possible additional threat, their obvious and deepening mutual feelings for each other.

Eve smiled at her memory of their exchange at the car dealer as they'd stood and waited for the salesperson last Sunday.

"Crimson red pearl—not exactly an inconspicuous color. Not exactly projecting a staid librarian image." Eve had actually loved the color and was learning more about Shaye all the time.

"Hey." Shaye had offered her a fake huff. "I'm not ready for a sedate *senior citizen gray*, like someone I know who drives a job-issued Jeep." A hip bump had followed.

"Ouch." Eve had given Shaye's backside a friendly swat. "And I don't mean the hip bump. I'm not *that* old."

Shaye had bestowed a long assessing look on Eve in return, seductively running her tongue across her lower lip. "I just might be convinced, but you're going to have to prove it."

"Like showing you that my health insurance isn't Medicare? Like admitting that I've never played bingo in my life? Or did you have something else in mind?" Eve had offered Shaye an exaggerated suggestive look as she recognized just how much she was enjoying the heck out of this getting to know each other.

Shaye had returned her suggestive look. "I'm not exactly thinking *afternoon delight* means a nap in the middle of the day."

"Well, that's a relief," Eve had replied. "Because I'm probably ready for that nap by mid-morning." They'd both laughed.

Then on Wednesday, they'd shared some early morning exercise. Eve had been fairly certain that Shaye had savored their shared time soaking up the first warmth of the day on the Main Street bench, as well as the coffee, just as much as she had. They'd carved out time for an enjoyable quick dinner bite together, but with final annual budget proposals due to the city finance office, their evenings after the shared meal had them each back in their respective offices crunching numbers while McGruff ping-ponged between the two spaces.

They'd flirted, they'd teased, they'd laughed, and they'd been careful not to let the low simmering heat between them flare out of control. Not that consummating their desire wouldn't be good because Eve knew that when they became intimate, it wouldn't just be a booty call flash fire. It would be a validation that they'd expanded that initial chemistry into a much deeper connection, an appreciation of each other's qualities, an exploration of commitment, a shared and growing trust.

Eve wanted their *date night*. Not that she wouldn't love sharing hot, frenetic passion in the future with Shaye when it flared, but she wanted a significant, considered first time in bed together. She wanted slow, seductive lovemaking. She believed that Shaye did too.

They'd made a tentative date night agreement for a week from Saturday, but they still needed to step away from work for a bit and solidify a plan. The budget proposals were due at the end of next week. That should free them up to walk away from their professional commitments and offer them the opportunity to slowly and intentionally savor their connection. In the meantime, they would just continue to grow these feelings.

Eve refocused on work and was eyeball deep in numbers when her phone rang. McGruff gave her a disgusted look from his bed on the floor, rolled over, and tucked his head back down between his paws. Eve saw that it was the mayor calling, and she wondered what he wanted on a Thursday night that couldn't wait until the normal workday hours tomorrow. She decided she'd better find out. On occasion, Sneed did call after hours, often when he was home, worked up and working out in his home gym. Better to try to defuse him now than let him brew.

"Hello, Mr. Mayor. How can I help you?" Eve knew that Sneed liked being addressed as Mr. Mayor and she knew how to play the game. She also knew that it was unlikely Sneed would lead with exactly what he wanted, but would steer the conversation there.

"Chief Maguire." Sneed's voice came in measured puffs, and she could hear the steady rhythm of what she assumed were his running shoes on a treadmill. His use of her formal title with no follow-up made it clear to Eve that whatever he wanted, he wanted it from her. But first he wanted her full attention. "Just wanting to know when you're going to solve this arsonist case."

Eve pinched the bridge of her nose. If that was Sneed's lead question, he was actually wanting something more—she'd worked with him for eight years, his two terms. All she knew how to do was be honest with him and see where it led.

"Doug Hooper and I are in regular contact regarding the two recent fires—the library and your campaign office. I'm receiving everything their office can offer. My officers and I are doing all we can, including keeping an eye out for new suspects as well as keeping an eye on current suspects."

"Well, I need this solved before the election. I also hope you have Bromwell at the top of your suspect list. You know that your job's at risk." Now he was getting to the reason for his call. She wasn't positive that Sneed only meant that her job was at risk if Pauline was elected, or if it was a concealed threat that it was at risk if she didn't solve this the way he wanted it solved.

"We can only go where the evidence takes us. We have nothing except the circumstance that the fires probably will benefit her in the election, not that we are making light of that," Eve replied.

Eve wasn't going to let politics prevent her from doing her job to the best of her ability. She'd been doing this too long to not know she valued her moral compass. If there was any hint of solid evidence that indicated Pauline's involvement, Eve would step back and hand the case over to the county sheriff to eliminate any appearance of conflict of interest, either personal based on her history with Pauline or professional considering the jeopardy her job was in. Although tonight Sneed was making her question the full extent of her job security—not that she'd let him influence the investigation. She knew that he did get worked up, so she'd try to assign his implications to stress overload.

Sneed continued to puff, then grunted. "Okay then. Keep up the good work."

Eve rolled her eyes. She was a little old to be jerked around between threats and praise.

"Thanks for calling, Mr. Mayor. You have a good rest of your evening."

Eve cut the call and looked at McGruff, who had crawled out of his bed and was focused on the open door. She knew that if she wasn't ready to leave yet, which she wasn't with another set of numbers she wanted to crunch before throwing in the towel, then the dog was probably going to head down to Shaye's office.

"Hang on a second, buddy."

Eve offered him a biscuit while she scribbled on a sticky note and stuck it on his collar, adding a piece of tape to make sure it made the trek down the hall. *Home and whine (oops, wine) in an hour?*

Eve continued working, and twenty minutes later, McGruff tottered back into her office with a reply on his collar. *40 minutes— wine (oops, whine) o'clock.*

❖

Shaye pulled the two slices of apple pie she'd warmed up out of the microwave. There was a glass of wine on the counter in front of her as she reheated the dessert, and Eve was sipping her own drink as she whipped up some cream for a topping. They made a good team, and although she'd never had a dog, Shaye had to admit that scrappy old McGruff made them a comfortable trio.

She was pleased that her talk with her mother, her kindergarten classroom epiphany, and her cop revelation regarding Eve had helped her resolve her thirty-five years of guilt and pain into this feeling of hopefulness, of happiness. This was why she'd moved here. And now, Eve was finding a place in her heart, and darn if that didn't make her smile. She was having a hard time believing it.

Nevertheless, circumstances had flipped the normal order of events on its head—she'd ended up living in Eve's house with Eve before they'd even been on an official date. This was a total inversion of the normal order of things. Shaye wanted to live somewhere else and date Eve. If a relationship didn't work out, she didn't want that to be the reason for her moving out—that would only add to the pain she knew would be unavoidable. But what she really wanted was not to blow this effort at a future with Eve. She wanted the decision to live together permanently to come for one reason only—because they'd grown a love so binding they couldn't live apart.

"I saw you smile. What's putting you in such a good mood?" Eve asked. "Because I want some."

"Just realizing that I'm grateful. Optimistic. And it's been a long time coming."

"I'm glad," Eve said. "Me too. Shall we sit down with the pie and talk about our date night?"

"Okay, but I want to start with you and what's up with the pooch express sticky note...the reference to 'whine' with an *h*. What's up, babe?" The *babe* just slipped out and it felt totally natural to Shaye. Eve's eyes widened and Shaye let her smile transform into a grin. "Yeah. *Babe*. What's going on?"

They sat down and each took a bite before Eve spoke. "Nothing that's not part of the job. Just the mayor calling. Wanting answers about the arsons, like the rest of us."

"I can tell there's more than that. I'd like to support you if you trust me. That's what we're supposed to be doing. Proving we can trust each other. Building that trust."

"You're right." Eve nodded and drew in a breath. "I'm just feeling like Sneed would really like me to name Pauline as a lead suspect—with no evidence. A political move, and I can't play politics."

"As many issues as I have with Pauline, I'd never believe she'd be the one to do it herself. As much as I don't want to think my stepsister was involved, I told you she was telling someone on the phone that it was critical not to leave a trail when I first stopped in to see her. I'm afraid I can imagine her behind the scenes trying to make Sneed look bad with an unidentified arsonist terrorizing the town."

"I agree, but there's no solid evidence," Eve said. "And it may all be in my head, but Sneed's good at the super subtle. I hung up feeling that he was insinuating that my job might be impacted by what I do or don't find. He's feeling the stress of the election. I'm not actually much worried about losing my job if he wins. There would be no point, but Pauline is a different case—it would be personal."

"Yeah, she'd likely find a way to appoint someone else, if not make you miserable and drive you out," Shaye said. "It's a small town and the mayor holds a lot of power. As to stuffing paper and matches through a mail slot—not exactly Pauline's style." Shaye rolled her eyes at the image.

Eve waved her fork back and forth. "Enough of my professional life. I want to talk about my personal life, now that I'm getting one. About *our* personal lives. About our date night."

"I hope we're still on for Saturday night in a week, after the budget proposals are in."

"How could I turn someone down who just called me *babe*?" The warmth in Eve's expression was obvious. "Earl said he'd come and look out for McGruff, so if you agree, maybe we can head down after your library hours on that Saturday afternoon and spend the night in Carmel or Monterey."

"I think I love Earl," Shaye replied.

"Oh, don't give him too much credit. I'm sure there's more to it—God only knows, and I certainly don't want to—like how much motivation the prospect of some sheet sharing with Joye contributed to his dog-sitting, brotherly love."

Shaye chuckled as she took another bite of pie. "Maybe Joye will rub off on him."

"Now there's some wishful thinking." Eve's lips twitched with amusement.

"Spoken like a big sister. You're lucky you have him. I haven't been in contact with my stepbrother, Andy, since I came back. I used to think I had a brother. Losing contact was a casualty of my leaving Paradise Pines behind. I guess I should track him down."

"Andy crosses my professional radar on occasion," Eve said. "He's got issues, but nothing that's led to an arrest. I've got to think that Ginny had some influence on his life after she married Joe." Eve didn't mention that Andy was on her list of arson suspects. She'd seen him placing campaign signs, so he was involved in the election, if only for what Pauline paid him for his labor.

"I do think Mom helped him. I know Sadie helped raise you, but you've never mentioned any other siblings besides Earl, so I'm assuming he's it."

"It's just Earl and me. I had an older brother, Mike, but we lost him in a motorcycle accident when I was twelve. A cop like our dad. When there was no one else to carry on the family tradition—Earl had no interest—I decided to make it my career."

"I'm sorry." Shaye realized that they were both shaped by the losses in their lives—forged into the women they were today. She thought Eve had integrated her past with more insight and grace than she had, but the move back to Paradise Pines was putting so much of her past into perspective. There was her guilt—a guilt that Eve hadn't experienced—but Shaye was seeing that through new eyes. Through the eyes of a forty-year-old. And now, looking at Eve, she thought she might be considering a future that she'd believed she couldn't hope for. She was older and wiser. Shaye was seeing the real Eve beneath the cop label, and she was earning Shaye's trust. *Thank you, Eve.*

"It was a long time ago, and while I loved Mike, I'm not sorry it led me to a job I love," Eve said. "Shall we talk about our date night?"

"Sure. I like your Carmel or Monterey plan. You excel at date night planning."

"Just leave it to an *old-fashioned* cop like me who's smitten with the new librarian."

"Smitten? Now that *is* old-fashioned." Shaye chuckled. "No surprise that she drives a senior-citizen-gray-colored car."

"Okay. Make fun of me. Amend it to captivated, enamored, beguiled, besotted." Eve fell silent and eyed her. "*Twitterpated.*" Then Eve offered a melodious laugh. A sound that Shaye realized she wanted to hear, over and over.

"Well, I'm way too young to be twitterpated." Shaye fought to sound admonishing, but she knew that she was losing that battle. "I might have to rethink this relationship. Where do you come up with that language anyway?"

"Books. You know, those rectangular, bound piles of paper you're so fond of."

"I might have to revoke your library card. And for your information, I'll confess that the librarian is *falling for* the cop too."

"To quote an eleven-year-old, because I'm versatile and definitely young at heart, *dope AF.*" Eve laughed again. Shaye shook her head, her own laughter accompanying Eve's, and she relished the sound.

"Do you know where we can stay on the coast? Not that it matters...as long as my needs are met." Shaye was certain that Eve could hear the husk that had infiltrated her voice. The husk Eve was putting there.

"Needs? And those would be?" Eve's dancing hazel gaze darkened.

"Food...a bed...and you...in the opposite order."

"I strongly suspect that can be arranged." Eve didn't break eye contact as she softly added, "*Babe.*"

## CHAPTER FOURTEEN

Time had passed as a marathon of normal work duties and number crunching for both Eve and Shaye, but finally, a week and a half after discussing this date night, a week and a half during which they'd squeezed in more quick dinners, more sharing, and more flirting, they were finally in Shaye's car on this late Saturday afternoon headed to Carmel.

"You picked the restaurant and I picked the accommodations, so that's the first big test to see if we're compatible on this first date." Eve had rested her arm on the console of Shaye's new car, and Shaye now linked fingers with Eve across the space between them as she navigated the way down the coast toward their destination.

"As if living under the same roof all this time didn't count," Shaye replied with a chuckle. "You already know how I like my coffee, whether my dirty clothes hit the hamper, and maybe even how I squeeze a toothpaste tube."

"I hadn't looked—you don't squeeze it from the middle, do you? Because that's a dealbreaker." Eve clucked her tongue, pretending her indignation at the mere thought of middle-of-the-tube toothpaste squeezers. She'd been looking forward to this time away from their jobs and all the pressures of Paradise Pines, and she was already enjoying herself—the easy bantering.

"And if it's Mickey D's for dinner and Dunkin' for breakfast, we're not compatible?" Shaye glanced sideways at Eve.

"I suppose I could overlook Mickey D's as a personality quirk, in the same category as this flaming crimson car—ground and flattened protein patty pressed between two dry buns smeared with tomato paste is probably marginal, but I would have thought a librarian might have tater tastes expanded beyond french fries." Eve was having trouble keeping her amusement out of her voice and maintaining a tone of false disdain.

"Hey, I love french fries," Shaye said. "That's why I took up running—my french fry addiction." Her twinkling eyes let Eve know that she was having a good time too.

"Now, Dunkin'…doughnuts…" Eve fought to keep her tone serious. "Those are the lifeblood of us cops. I wouldn't dump you over doughnuts. No way."

"That's good, because while we're upscaling to a sea view, white tablecloth restaurant for dinner, I didn't make breakfast reservations—so a doughnut shop can be arranged."

Eve placed her free hand on her chin and pretended to be in deep contemplation. "What if I want to skip breakfast? *Other* plans." She felt a low surge of desire as she contemplated her "other plans."

"And are you going to tell me what could possibly take precedence over a warm glazed doughnut with *a huge hole* in the center?" Shaye's voice had dropped an octave and she'd infused her tone with a suggestive drawl.

Eve choked. "I'll never see a doughnut the same way again." Then she changed the subject and became serious. "I'm probably feeling better than I ever have, but I want you to know that I reserved a place with two bedrooms. It has a small kitchen too, but we can ignore that unless we don't want to. And not far from the beach."

Shaye took her eyes off the highway for a moment and looked at Eve. "You don't want to sleep with me?"

"I want to sleep with you. I want to do so much more than sleep. But I didn't want to be presumptive. I want you to have the choice of sharing a bed tonight, or not."

Eve felt the physical wave of need that had her hoping Shaye wanted to share a bed too. Her body called with a deep low ache, but it was her heart she was listening to because her growing feelings for Shaye and her larger need to try to find a future with Shaye significantly outweighed a night between the sheets if Shaye wasn't ready for that. Eve had booked a place with two bedrooms—she wanted this *Date Night* adventure to help them grow closer at a pace that worked for both of them. She'd decided she was ready to sleep with Shaye, not simply because she'd shut out a personal life and not been with a woman since Pauline but because she needed sex to be more than lust, and while she hadn't defined it, Shaye was certainly so much more than lust. Shaye made her want a personal life again.

Shaye's attention was back on the road. Eve looked out her passenger window, out at the glimmering ocean to the west of Highway 1. They were approaching Monterey, and then it would not be far to Carmel, where they were headed.

Still looking ahead at the highway as she drove, Shaye said, "First, I want you to know that I was tested recently and I'm clear. I want you safe."

"I'm clear too," Eve replied. She appreciated Shaye's willingness to bring up the topic. She'd had other girlfriends and even occasional sexual partners, but climbing the law enforcement ladder had taken most of her focus, and there hadn't been strong enough feelings to override professional considerations and family issues with the girlfriend she'd labeled as serious. And then she'd essentially become a conquest after Pauline's sights were set on her, and probably an acquisition once they'd been together for a while. No consideration regarding her health in the relationship. This was so different. So new. So welcome.

"As to separate beds tonight, or not?...*Or not*," Shaye softly answered. "As to trying to keep to a breakfast schedule in the morning, or not?...*Or not*."

Shaye's response was incentive to the craving deep at Eve's core, and it held the impetus that caused Eve's heart to prance and pirouette. Eve squeezed Shaye's hand as she tamped down her anticipation. They continued down the road in comfortable silence, taking in the scenery.

Finally exiting the highway, Shaye said, "Maybe brunch, if it works out." She turned the Outback into a parking place adjacent to their cottage rental.

"If it works out," Eve echoed. She was feeling like a teenager. Nervous and giddy. For heaven's sake, they were both in their forties. "Okay. Let's go check the place out and then get dinner. That should give us enough energy for whatever comes next. Date night..."

"Yeah, beautiful woman," Shaye replied. "Date night." Shaye grinned at Eve and she grinned back.

❖

Eve opened the cottage door, and they carried their gear in as they looked around. The place was clean and modern, but cozy with a gas fireplace. They found the primary bedroom and deposited their bags. There was a comfortable-looking overstuffed chair with a small side table in one corner, and one wall had large windows with the slatted wooden shades pulled up so the late afternoon sun streamed through and onto the king-sized bed that filled much of the rest of the room.

Eve turned and wandered out to the kitchen so she wouldn't be tempted to push Shaye down onto the bed and ruin their dinner reservation. Shaye came into the kitchen and looked at Eve, hunger in her indigo-hued eyes and anticipation on her face. A tremor of desire traversed Eve's body, and she tried to ignore the pounding pulse that paired with her labored breathing. She waited on Shaye. Shaye stepped closer, and then closer, and then pressed her body up against Eve's as she backed Eve against the edge of the granite countertop. They didn't break eye contact for several seconds.

Finally closing her eyes, Shaye raised a hand and tucked Eve's hair behind her ear before leaning in and breathing warm air into that ear.

"Eve Maguire. *Fucking* chief of police," Shaye whispered. "I want you."

Eve struggled to breathe, struggled to swallow as her need for Shaye escalated. "I thought that you thought the adjective went *after* the 'chief.'" She'd heard Shaye mutter "Chief of fucking police" when she'd first discovered that Eve was a cop.

"Oh, babe, it's not an adjective. It's a verb." Shaye's darkened eyes were dancing with amusement.

Eve knew that if they didn't head out to dinner now, dinner wasn't going to happen. She didn't say a word. She leaned in and gave Shaye a quick kiss on the cheek because she didn't dare kiss those luscious lips. Then she grabbed her purse with one hand and Shaye's hand with her other.

"Hold that thought," Eve said. "I need fuel so I can live up to my chief title *verb*. And you need to eat too, Shaye Hayden, alluring librarian. My impeccable detective skills are telling me that this is going to be a long, rigorous night."

❖

Dinner was delicious, although Eve had offered no indication that she wanted to dally over tiramisu, and Shaye certainly had other things on her mind. They arrived back at the cottage and headed to the bedroom.

It was Eve's turn to use her body to direct Shaye. Front-to-front, Eve's ample breasts pressed against her own, their pelvises fused, and for each forward step that Eve took, Shaye took one backward. She might be losing ground, but Shaye knew that she was gaining exactly what she wanted.

"So, you have plans for the evening?" Shaye asked, knowing exactly what those plans were.

"Dinner was excellent, dessert was lovely, but I'm still hungry." There was no mistaking the intent in the deeper timbre of Eve's voice.

Shaye nodded. "I could manage a snack. Something blond with beautiful as the main ingredient, not just the icing."

When the backs of Shaye's thighs hit the side of the bed, Eve leaned forward and covered Shaye's reclining body with her own. Shaye reached up and placed her hands on each side of Eve's face, pulling her down so their breath mingled, both of them inhaling and exhaling at an accelerated rate. Shaye could feel the rapid rhythm of Eve's heart hammering against her own. Shaye looked into Eve's eyes, dilated and dark. She let her own flutter shut and pursed her lips until they almost met Eve's, then she paused.

"I remember being here before. In a bar parking lot, no bed in sight," Shaye purred. "I wanted you then. I could tell you were more than a one-night stand. You didn't know me, but now you do. Any objections to me having my wicked way with you tonight?"

"I thought seriously about inviting you back to my 4.2 rated hotel room for 10.0 rated sex that night—I was pretty sure it would have received top scores as sex goes. But you're right. I didn't know you. I needed to care for you." Shaye knew that Eve cared for her, but she found that having Eve tell her mattered. Eve slowly unfastened her blouse buttons and grazed Shaye's cleavage above her black bra as Eve undid each closure. "But I think you're mistaken. Now that I know what's hiding beneath the small town, *prim* librarian facade. So much more than someone immersed in overseeing books and the pursuit of information literacy." Eve licked her lips as her eyes twinkled. "I think it's me who's going to be having my wicked way with you."

"Prim librarian?" Shaye laughed. "Now, that's a total stretch—but I can show you prim."

"Hey, sweetheart. If I wanted prim, I'd be facing you in the library, checking out *The Complete Guide to Puritan Living, unabridged*, and I wouldn't be having the thoughts I'm having. You do want that 10.0, don't you?" Eve picked up where they'd left off, moving her mouth closer to Shaye's.

The kiss started off as a bare touch, their air still mixing, their noses gently meeting. When Eve's tongue parted her lips, Shaye opened up, welcoming the taste of Eve into her mouth. Eve's hands held Shaye's hands above her head as she guided her lips in delicate brushstrokes across Shaye's jawline, her chin, and down her throat to her cleavage. She worked her way back up until she met Shaye's aroused gaze.

"Are you doing okay?" Eve asked. "I'm thinking we could move to the shower before this gets to the point of no return. It's been a long day and I want to scrub your back...and other places. We can end up back here, but a rinse off. You're beautiful, not just the exterior that I want to soap and wash and rinse and..."

Shaye locked her mouth on Eve's lips again, a slow sensual kiss with no hint that the point of a shower would be to rinse off. Shaye wasn't sure they'd make it back to the bed before they'd thoroughly *scrubbed* each other, but she had no objection to that.

Eve slid off the side of the bed to a standing position. She'd already slipped off her shoes but was otherwise fully clothed. She'd told Shaye at dinner that she'd packed a dress but then hadn't had the opportunity to change. Shaye didn't care that she was in fitted black slacks—no complaints from her. This wasn't about what they were wearing, and in fact was evolving into what they weren't wearing.

Shaye sat up, slipping one hand into the waistband of Eve's pants as she unbuttoned and unzipped them before lowering them. Eve stepped out of her slacks and pulled Shaye to standing before she unfastened Shaye's skirt. Then Eve took the hem and bunched the fabric up around Shaye's waist with one hand while she cupped Shaye intimately with the other—Shaye couldn't prevent the push of her hips. Eve grasped the entire roll and fed the ring of material down Shaye's thighs and lower legs until it fell to the floor.

"Not fair. I want to be touching you," Shaye managed to say.

"Don't worry, darling. I'm not going to deprive you. Or me. We'll get there. We've got a whole night ahead of us. And no breakfast plans either."

Eve undid Shaye's bra, then helped her pull it off. She hooked a thumb under the elastic on each side of Shaye's silk black briefs, ones that Shaye had carefully selected that morning with no doubt that her intent was to lose them in just this manner—in just the way that Eve now slowly worked them down below the curve of her ass, and then lower, below her knees, below her calves...

Eve took a look at the black silk restraint around Shaye's ankles and stopped, her hungry eyes sparkling with amusement as she drawled, "Well hell, I didn't pack my handcuffs. Maybe we need to postpone this."

Shaye growled. Then she reached out and slipped her fingers into the waistband of Eve's briefs, red ones that screamed for removal. After she tugged them down, Shaye slid her hand between Eve's thighs and let her thumb wander until it found the aroused sensitive tissue she was seeking. Shaye stroked the saturated and primed prelude to the deeper passage into Eve. She wanted more of Eve. So much more.

They ended up back on the bed, both nude. Forget the shower, it was no longer on the immediate agenda—at least not on Shaye's. Not with the ache burning at her center. Shaye worked her way on top of Eve. She trailed her mouth down the beating pulse of Eve's neck until she could place her mouth on Eve's breasts, moistening and then blowing on one, followed by a repeat with the other. With Eve groaning, Shaye sucked each pink peak to full altitude before she gently ringed each nipple. The sensations Shaye delivered with her warm, wet tongue clearly liquefied Eve.

"You're killing me," Eve said. "Who knew the town librarian had talents so far beyond classifying books under the Dewey Decimal system." Her hips rolled up into Shaye before she finally wedged a bent knee between Shaye's thighs, parting them. Eve reached between them and Shaye pulsed to her touch through the next steps of their dance, a fingering waltz, a thumb-led alternating twirl and glide, several slip 'n' slide moves through the drenching slickness of Shaye's folds.

When it began, Shaye knew she was lost. The smoldering that had nested at her core before this ever started had just been an ember. As Shaye rode the hand that fueled the fire, the barely controlled flame exploded into a raging inferno that roared in waves out from the center of her heat, to her pounding heart, her gasping lungs, her quivering limbs.

Shaye tried not to cry out too loudly as the intensity of the firestorm crowned and she came undone. She arched her body and then emitted a groan, low and unrestrained. The blaze finally burned out, leaving her limp and contented. She was a satiated scorched shell, but Shaye pulled herself together and focused on Eve, stretched out beneath her. Shaye slid off and rolled Eve onto her stomach. She moved to settle between Eve's legs before she pulled Eve backward and up onto her knees, a different dance.

"My turn to lead." Shaye placed her hands on Eve's hips and held her steady.

"*Oh, God.*" Eve tried to look back over her shoulder.

Shaye kissed the smooth silk of Eve's ass, reverent kisses. She took her time wandering that pale curve with her nibbling lips. "How's this?"

Eve offered a sensuous moan that spoke to Shaye as surrender. As wanting whatever Shaye had to give.

Shaye worked her way down the backs of Eve's thighs with fingertip strokes that mirrored the movement of Eve's rocking efforts to center her caressing touch. She maintained the mapping of Eve's limbs, never quit engaging high enough to stroke the juncture where legs ended and the core essence of Eve resided.

"*Oh, God.*" Eve's repeated gasp came out as a plea.

"God can't help you now, but I promise to take care of you. I promise to take you where you need to go, to wreak havoc on your beautiful body. I want to show you my…" Shaye had almost added that she wanted to show Eve her *love*, but while the *love* word was certainly niggling at her, this wasn't the time. She didn't want it to come across as between-the-sheets chatter. She wanted Eve to believe her when she finally was ready to label what she was feeling. Shaye needed to believe that she was capable of love. She needed to allow time for her feelings to grow—so she could be sure—that was wise.

Eve whimpered into the mattress. "Oh, babe. You've already shown me that you'll take good care of me. You just might kill me doing it, but I'll leave a note and ask them not to charge you. I'm going willingly."

Shaye lowered her mouth to meet Eve's core, finding the spot that would drive Eve closer to fulfillment before dropping into the passage that led to that point of no return.

Eve's response was throaty and muffled, buried in the bedding.

No more words as Shaye took her apart. She took her time and showed Eve everything she knew, now understanding that maybe all that she'd experienced, even her past shallow female pursuits, had led her to this moment, a time when she could gift this pleasure to Eve.

Afterward, they dozed in each other's arms, both of them emotionally and physically satisfied. That was until they climbed into the shower to finally *scrub* each other thoroughly. When they were back in bed, they began to doze off again as they lay together, warm and content.

"Maybe brunch instead of breakfast tomorrow," Eve said. "I need my beauty sleep."

"That's not what's on the agenda." Shaye rolled so she could look directly into Eve's eyes.

"Don't tell me it's doughnuts," Eve replied and then kissed Shaye into silence.

Shaye finally freed her lips. "Glazed, with that huge center hol—"

Eve snorted and lightly swatted Shaye on the backside before growing serious. "Are you doing okay?"

"I am. And you?" Shaye considered that she probably hadn't been this okay…ever.

"Best *Date Night* of my life. Rates that ten."

"Eleven, twelve, thirteen…"

# CHAPTER FIFTEEN

It was after midnight on Thursday. Eve was dozing but hadn't fallen into a sound sleep yet. She and Shaye had talked about their first date on the drive home from Carmel and how to proceed as they moved forward. Eve knew that Shaye was committed to making them work as a couple, and she was too. That meant Shaye moving out before they made an official relationship decision to live together because that's what Shaye needed—a choice and not a safety necessity. For now, they'd agreed to each sleep in their own beds except maybe following official dates, and they'd done that...except when they hadn't on Tuesday night.

Eve was mature enough to realize there was no need to rush, that this was a healthy way to proceed. There was pleasure to be found in every stage as their relationship evolved. She was having visions of that pleasure when they were two gray-haired old ladies, and then the sound of her phone broke into her relaxed state. She reached for it and answered without trying to focus on the number—not many people had it, and at this time of night, it had to be important.

"Eve Maguire here."

"It's Steve from the volunteer firefighters. Sorry to wake you, but I wanted to call you right away. I'm at the mayor's house. Someone set a fire on his front lawn. Not much of a fire and it's out, but I thought you needed to know. Only a few of us know this, but we found a crumpled receipt with Andy Bromwell's name on it on the ground near the fire."

"Holy smoke" was all Eve could think to say.

"Exactly, Chief." Steve chuckled at her unplanned smoke reference.

"I want you to keep the witnesses to the receipt there on-site."

"I can do that, but I'm not law enforcement…the reason I called you right away."

Eve stopped to consider for a minute. "Steve, I need to step back because of this finding that Pauline's brother might be involved." Steve knew that Pauline was her ex. Practically the entire damn town did. "I'm going to have Grady come and take the lead. Document the fire, secure the site, and interview the witnesses."

Eve contemplated the news of the receipt. Either someone wanted the focus on Pauline, who certainly had her share of detractors, Eve among them, or Andy had actually dropped a receipt. That certainly wasn't impossible from all she knew of Andy and his past issues—and that meant Pauline was undoubtedly behind this. Maybe Andy had had it in his pocket with the matches or whatever incendiary method he'd used. He could have dropped it in the dark when he pulled things out of his pocket.

"I'll turn it over to Hooper and the county sheriff, Jim Greene, in the morning. We'll figure out my level of involvement later, but they need to take the lead. It sounds like it's under control, and I don't want any accusations of a conflict of interest. I'll let the mayor know."

"Sounds smart," Steve replied. "Greg Sneed's out here having a fit. He's aware of the receipt, so I don't see it as a big secret for long. You might want to talk to him soon. Calm him down."

"Let me crawl out of bed, and I'll call him. I'm going to get ahold of Grady first and get him over there. Thanks."

Eve hung up and then sat on the side of the bed. She pulled up Grady's contact information, and when he answered after five rings, she apologized for the time and then explained what had happened, what her plan was, and that she needed him to handle it tonight. She made sure that he'd ask about any video cameras and secure any recorded images. He agreed and she hung up, then repeated her initial statement. "Holy smoke."

McGruff gave her a disgusted look from his bed on the floor, rolled over, and tucked his head back down between his paws.

"You aren't going to get any more sleep than I am if you stay near me. Let's go down to Shaye's room and you can sleep some more in there. She'll want to hear what's going on too." He grunted. As she threw on a robe and dropped her phone into her pocket, McGruff crawled out of his bed and followed her down to the guest room. Eve saw the light under the door and knocked.

"Come on in. I heard your phone ring. Everything okay?"

Eve took in Shaye's tousled hair and couldn't help but smile. She couldn't ignore how her heart thudded at the sight of the sleepy Shaye. Then she refocused.

"Small fire set on the mayor's front lawn. It's all out. You need to know, but it would be good if you didn't talk about this until the news spreads, which it will—a receipt with Andy's name on it was found at the scene. Sneed won't remain quiet about this." Eve knew she could trust Shaye with the information without her breaking the news publicly. Word would be out soon enough.

Shaye's eyes widened as she obviously had just digested that her stepbrother was implicated. Her hand flew to her throat before she swallowed a few times and then spoke. "Pauline? I heard her on the phone telling someone that leaving no trail was critical, that first day I stopped to see her, but that's all she said."

"That could have been her talking about any number of things. We don't know that she was involved, Shaye. Or even that Andy was—it looks very suspicious, but that may have been someone's intent. I'm handing things to Grady tonight and turning it over to Doug Hooper and the county sheriff in the morning. I don't want accusations of a conflict of interest on my part."

Shaye nodded.

"You go back to sleep. McGruff may want to stay in here with you. I'm going out to the living room to call the mayor. He's fit to be tied from what Steve said."

"No, the pooch and I will go out to the kitchen and make you some coffee. I'm not going to go back to sleep right away—we might as well be useful, right, McGruff?" Shaye wiped her eyes as she looked down at him. "Dammit. Andy...I can't believe he'd be such an idiot."

Eve stepped closer and pulled Shaye into her arms, rocking her. She kissed her on the side of the head. "One step at a time, darling. Let's see how it plays out."

❖

Eve sat on her living room sofa, Shaye and McGruff in the kitchen. She closed her eyes and inhaled deeply before dialing the mayor's number.

"Where the hell are you, Eve? Grady just showed up."

That was fast, Eve thought. She owed Grady a huge thanks.

"Pauline Bromwell had her brother set my front yard on fire," Sneed continued. "I want her arrested for the arsons."

"Steve called me. Grady's going to handle it tonight, and—"

"What the fuck!" The mayor was shouting into the phone, and Eve hoped she'd still have a job in the morning.

"Hold on, Greg. If Pauline is involved, you don't want there to be a conflict of interest with me taking the lead—the charges might not hold. That's why Grady's handling it tonight and I'll turn it over in the morning to Hooper and Jim Greene. We need to let the county fire inspector and county sheriff take over. You want this clean—a conflict of interest with Pauline as my ex will only complicate things. You don't need her claiming I framed her out of vengeance for our breakup or for fear that she'd fire me or force me out of my job if she wins."

"I need her arrested and convicted," Sneed barked.

"Then let it play out without my involvement complicating things."

All Eve could hear coming through her phone was Sneed taking a few deep breaths and then sighing.

Finally, he spoke. "Okay, Eve. I guess that makes sense. We don't want to screw this up. I'm trusting that you'll at least keep tabs on things from afar. The election isn't that far off, and voters have a right to know what she's done."

"I can do that, Greg. I'm sure Hooper and Greene won't have an issue keeping me apprised, but I've got to let them do their jobs. Otherwise, we could all lose." As she said it, Eve realized how true that might be. "Is there anything else I can do for you?"

"No. Like I said, I just want her arrested, but I guess you're right that your direct involvement could be a major problem. I'll talk to you later, then."

Eve didn't think that he sounded very satisfied, but she concluded that she was handling it in the best way she could. She would love to be doing her job, but not on this case. Would the *Pauline Bromwell repercussions* never end?

She headed into the kitchen and sat across the table from Shaye, who was sipping on a mug of coffee and had just placed one at Eve's spot before she sat down.

"You know if I drink this, I'm going to be up the rest of the night."

Shaye looked a little sheepish. "That's why I made decaf. I know we're both wound up, but trying to function on no sleep isn't going to improve things."

"I could kiss you," Eve said.

"That isn't going to lead to any more sleep either." A smile played across Shaye's lips as she shook her head.

"I know it's asking a lot, but would you come back to bed with me? No hanky-panky, just you holding me and me holding you," Eve said. "This fire is big—it doesn't get a whole lot more personal for either of us…Andy and Pauline maybe…"

"Here I am, all twitterpated, and you're declaring no hanky-panky. Yeah, I think twitterpated includes a bit of just holding each other," Shaye replied. She sounded tired, and maybe overwhelmed.

Eve wasn't going to define what she was feeling. Pauline had made her cautious, and Eve knew how fearful Shaye had been of becoming involved with a cop. And now Shaye's family was involved with law enforcement. But Eve was feeling better—because of Shaye. She took Shaye's hand and they headed to Eve's room, McGruff escorting them. They crawled into bed.

"How are you doing? Honestly," Eve asked.

Shaye took her time answering. "I'm not sure. I'm feeling rather numb. I don't think that I've really processed it all. I'm just going to have to let it all settle."

"Are you okay settling in next to me? I'd like to hold you."

Shaye moved closer. Eve held her and stroked her back—her moist breathing the giveaway that Shaye was silently crying.

It was midmorning, just a little after ten o'clock, and Eve was tired. She'd headed into her office at the crack of dawn that morning, and Shaye was working in the library trailer. By the time Eve had reached Grady, talked to the mayor, and then spoken with Grady again, she'd had a short night. So had Shaye. Eve had turned the arson case over to the county officials early that morning. She'd explained to both Hooper and Greene why she couldn't be the lead, and they'd both agreed with her. They'd promised to keep her up to speed and even bring her in for consulting if needed, but they'd make the decisions. Between Hooper and Greene, Eve felt comfortable they would do a good job, even if they probably wouldn't be moving fast enough for the mayor.

Eve's cell rang and it brought her out of her thoughts. She looked down at it with the hope that it was Grady or Greene with an update, but it wasn't. She debated about not answering it but decided to get it over with.

"Hi, Joye. I'm in the middle of a few things here. Anything important?"

Joye chuckled. "I bet you're up to your eyeballs right now. What can you tell me for the *Pulse*?"

"You'll have to clarify the topic," Eve told her. She didn't want to assume anything.

"The fire at the mayor's house last night," Joye replied.

"I'm not in charge of the investigation. The county's handling it. You know the county sheriff, Jim Greene."

"I know him. Greg Sneed called me," Joye told her. "He told me about Andy Bromwell's receipt at the scene. He seems to believe that this nails the lid shut on Pauline. He's out there telling people just that from what I'm hearing."

Eve remained silent.

"Plus, you're handing this to the county tells me that you're needing to distance yourself from the case because of a Pauline link too."

"Are you running with the news?" Eve asked. "Quoting the mayor, because you're not getting a quote from me?"

"Don't worry," Joye said. "Sneed was all too happy to be quoted. I've got enough for the story but wanted to see if you had something to add. It sounds like you're keeping your head down though."

"I am. This doesn't need accusations of a conflict of interest... ex-girlfriend, elimination of a mayoral candidate who would probably can me."

"Spoilsport. Those would have made great headlines."

"Sorry." Eve had to chuckle. "Thanks for checking with me. A word of advice, though—ask Greene for any facts he can give you... actual evidence."

She ended the call and headed to the bullpen to see if Grady was there for an update. On her way, she glanced down the hallway into the lobby and was surprised to see Andy Bromwell there.

❖

It was noon and Shaye was on her mind because Eve needed to talk to her. Shaye had planned to work from her office that afternoon, so Eve was listening for her. McGruff would probably detect her approach before she passed Eve's door.

Suddenly, McGruff went on alert and then climbed from his bed, his tail wagging. Eve took a deep breath. It had to be Shaye. Eve headed to her doorway and looked down the hallway. Sure enough, McGruff was right. Eve's heart did a bit of somersaulting—mixed feelings. She was thrilled to see Shaye, but was apprehensive about the conversation she needed to have.

"Hi. I hope you're not as exhausted as I am," Shaye said as she approached Eve.

"I think we're both dragging, but I bet we had more sleep than Grady and a few others. And probably the mayor."

"You're probably right. How did your morning go?" Shaye asked.

"Funny you should ask. Do you have a minute that you can come in and talk to me?"

Shaye's brow furrowed. "Your tone sounds a little ominous. Don't tell me there's more bad news." She came into Eve's office and Eve indicated her visitor's chair and took her own desk chair.

"News—I don't know what to make of it, so come in and let me share."

Shaye inhaled and held her breath, also sitting up straighter, obviously fortifying herself.

"I saw Andy for a few minutes this morning."

Shaye blinked a few times and nodded, then locked her eyes on Eve, a questioning look on her face. Eve could read the concern that shadowed her somber expression.

"So where did you see him? I hope it wasn't in your capacity as a cop—but after what you told me last night, I'm suspecting that it was."

"It was here at the police station, in the lobby, and Andy seemed nervous. Grady's keeping me apprised of the official police department's role. The information about Andy's receipt being found at the scene is no longer under wraps. Sneed's talking about it and he called Joye, so as I said last night, he's doing his best to point the finger at Pauline." Eve shook her head.

Shaye nodded, waiting for Eve to continue. McGruff went over to Shaye, leaning against her leg. She reached down to pet him but kept her gaze on Eve.

"Andy was upset, but there could have been multiple reasons for that."

Shaye arched an eyebrow.

"I've got to consider that I'm the chief of police and he was at the station, so that was probably intimidating. He's had his past run-ins with my officers, but no arrests. He came up to me and told me that he'd heard rumors about a receipt of his being found at Sneed's. He disavowed setting the fire. He also told me that he pockets his receipts and then dumps them into his truck console, and that he doesn't lock his truck here in town—it's twenty years old with nothing really worth stealing. He also told me he was at Romer's Bar yesterday evening where he stopped for a couple of beers about seven o'clock and then finally left around nine to go home, where he claims that he remained the rest of the night. Alone. I'll pass the news to Grady and Greene, and they can handle it from here."

"Did you believe him?" It was obvious that Shaye wanted her to, but Eve knew she'd want the truth more.

"I'm not passing judgment," Eve said. "I don't have to, since Jim Greene is running the law enforcement side of this. It could be true, somebody taking it from his truck. But it could also be a credible but fabricated explanation for discovering you'd dropped a receipt at the scene of a crime. It was dark. It could be that when he pulled whatever he used to start the fire—matches or some other incendiary device—out of his pocket, he didn't notice he'd dropped it. I'm sure he's the top suspect at this point."

Shaye's eyes filled. "Crap. Double crap. I knew this last night when you told me, but it's feeling worse. If he did this, it's got to be with Pauline's influence."

Eve stood and went over to Shaye, pulled her to her feet, and then pulled her in close, wrapping her arms around Shaye. "I'm so sorry. Let's not find him guilty yet—give Greene a chance to do some investigating."

"So how was he?" Shaye sounded so sad.

"He's thin, but seemed to be okay. How long since you've seen him?"

Shaye frowned. "I hate to admit it, but it was probably around the time I left town."

"Over twenty years. He'd have been in his early twenties then?" Eve pursed her lips. That was a long time ago. "Because he's in his early forties now."

"Forty-three."

"He's aged," Eve replied. "I can't say he's had an easy life. It's not a secret that he was using some bad stuff for a while and a lot of alcohol, but I'd thought he'd straightened himself out. Obviously still drinking some if he was at the bar last night. He picks up odd jobs around town, so he's trying. Working."

"Yeah. But probably not the kind of work you want to hear about. From what Pauline told me, he does some labor on her campaign. Posting signs and stuff." Shaye shook her head. "But working for Pauline...could he be stupid enough to set a fire at the mayor's house to remind everyone there's an arsonist on the loose because of the election?"

Shaye stiffened and leaned into Eve. "Oh fuck. It should have dawned on me last night, but I was so shocked and so worn out. It just hit me—do you think he could be the arsonist who set the other fires? Attacked me? He could go to jail for a long, long time."

"I'd thought of that, and so will others," Eve replied. "Do you have any idea if he was the one who attacked you at your house that night?"

"I don't know. I haven't seen him in over two decades. I fell out a window after inhaling a lung full of smoke and then I was kicked. Dazed. The person had on a mask, whispered, and I can't swear if it was a man or a woman, although my impression was a man. So, no clue if it was Andy. I think they called me a bitch—would Andy do that? I guess if he's mad that I disappeared from his life for twenty years." Shaye's tears overflowed. "I hate to think he could do that to me. I knew he'd been through some hard times. I could have been a better support, but I was dealing with my own issues."

"You were trying to take care of yourself, Shaye. And I know that Ginny has always been there for him."

"Gotta love my mom." Shaye wiped at her face with her sleeve, and Eve stepped back and grabbed her a tissue. "Pauline called her Ginny *Mommykins* Bromwell when I stopped by her place that day."

Eve could hear the anger in her voice. "Your mom is a good person. The best."

Shaye nodded. "She is. I don't want this to be Andy or Pauline, for Mom's sake, but Pauline needs some sort of reckoning."

"I need to be honest with you. My experience tells me that they'll pick Andy up very soon if they already haven't done so—I haven't heard that it's happened yet from either Grady or Greene. They'll take him to the county sheriff's office for questioning. I don't know if they'll call you in for a lineup—regarding the fire at your place."

"I don't think I can help, but I'll be honest." Shaye walked over and put her tissue in the trash, then collected another few, stuffing them in the pocket of her blazer. "I'm probably going to need the entire box."

"It's yours, whatever you need," Eve replied before bringing up the next topic that might need Kleenex. "What do you want to do about Ginny? This is going to hit her hard."

Shaye pressed her lips tightly together. She now had McGruff on her lap and she hugged him. "How much can I reveal to her?"

"You can tell Ginny what you know since Sneed's already broken the receipt news to the world—had to implicate Pauline. Do you want me to come with you?"

Shaye nodded. "I'd like that. This is going to hit her hard. Andy. Pauline. I think she might need your support—I might need your support."

"Is she teaching today?" Eve asked.

"Not one of her job-share days. Let me call and see if we can come by. Are you free to go now?"

"I am. And I think the sooner the better. I'll have my phone if there are any updates."

Shaye set McGruff on the ground and stood.

Eve thought Shaye looked overwhelmed and did something she'd never thought she'd do at work, but it felt right. She leaned in and offered Shaye a gentle kiss on the lips. "You're going to get through this, sweetheart." Shaye's pain was breaking her heart, and this shit show would probably only get worse.

There were times when Eve hated being right, and when she answered her phone late that afternoon, she knew this was one of those times. This shitshow was only getting worse. Pauline was always bad news.

"It's bad enough I'm hearing that you're sucking up to my kid, although I'm willing to overlook that because there's no way I'm taking her back from Ginny. I don't have the time. Just don't try to poison Cassie against me."

Eve felt her chest constrict. "Cassie's old enough to form her own opinions. And I wouldn't use her like that. Did you call about Cassie?

Even with Ginny, I'm sure that Cassie would appreciate some attention from you." Eve suspected she was wasting her breath.

"No, I didn't actually call about her." Pauline emitted a loud huff that came through the speaker. "I'm calling to make sure you aren't going to try to pin the mayor's fire on me. If you're going after Andy, leave me out of it. Don't pull some election-influencing stunt to try to save your job."

Eve didn't know whether to believe Pauline's insinuation that she wasn't involved. Pauline's moral compass was compromised, and she could be aggressive at denial. Pauline could just be trying to save herself if Andy had dropped the receipt while executing her orders. Eve had no doubt that Pauline would throw him under the bus.

"I'm stepping back. Jim Greene, the county sheriff, is stepping in. So that there won't be any conflict of interest," Eve said.

Eve heard an unintelligible utterance that she translated as disgust before Pauline finally spoke. "Well, I guess this call is a waste of time, then."

Before Eve could say anything else, she realized the call had ended. It seemed Pauline's plan to intimidate her had just derailed with the information of the handoff to the county. She'd likely lost even more ground with Pauline, but Eve was too tired to care. She just wanted this work day to end. And she didn't want her mind on Pauline. She wanted it on Shaye.

# CHAPTER SIXTEEN

It was the evening after the fire at the mayor's home and Eve was still off dealing with the fallout, even though she wasn't in charge of the investigation. Shaye was back at the house, a glass of wine on the coffee table in front of her, waiting for Eve to arrive.

The lack of sleep last night and the stress of today were taking their toll. McGruff was on the couch next to her. He offered her a kiss and a moment of soulful scrutiny that connected with her. He seemed to understand what she was feeling, and she wondered again about his past. He must have seen his share of torment to be able to read her so well.

"Thanks, McGruff." He was the perfect silent partner, except for his intermittent grunts and groans. She smiled because she wanted to join in his vocal commiseration. After half an hour, Shaye decided she needed to talk to someone. She knew exactly who she'd call. She dialed the number.

"If it isn't Shaye *Hiatus*." Annie answered her phone with her usual teasing tone. "It's been too long since we talked. That last call... it was because Eve was going out on a date. I'm hoping the fact that you're calling me on a Friday night isn't an indication that you're sitting there, home alone. Are you still at her place?"

"I am." Shaye thought about all that had happened since the last time she'd talked with Annie.

"I'm on pins and needles," Annie replied. "Enlighten me—your life is so much more interesting than mine."

"The reason I'm home alone is not because Eve is out on a date. That one she was on when I called before...disaster at the Thai Tanic. Not a disaster for me, and not for Eve either. She realized she kind of likes me."

"Are you telling me that you're Shaye *Hotlips?*"

Shaye rolled her eyes. "You're getting way ahead in the story."

Annie laughed. "That sounds encouraging. Do tell."

"I'm trying, but you keep changing my last name."

"Okay. I'll kick myself and shut up."

"Good," Shaye said. "Eve and I. We're doing okay." Shaye hoped they were. She didn't want to let the stress impact her blooming relationship with Eve. She decided to impart the good things that she and Eve had shared, that had drawn them so much closer. "Short version is that she took me to meet Sadie, her aunt who's in memory care down in the Bay Area, and then to pick up my new Outback. I've got some independence back. I *so* needed some of that."

"Aunt Sadie—that sounds like a serious step on her part. And your new wheels, don't tell me the color because I'm going to guess red."

"Am I that predictable?" Shaye sighed. "Crimson red pearl."

"I wouldn't call you predictable, but every car you've ever owned has been a bit flamboyant. Purple, orange, green…it was a chartreuse green. Now on with the story. I need a little excitement. It's Friday night and Thomas is off bowling, but big plans afterward." Annie's laughter came through the speaker.

"I don't want to hear about you and Thomas and your big plans." Shaye chuckled and took a sip of her wine. "Eve and I had our official first date. *Date night.*"

"Mm-hmm," Annie said. "What was the outcome?"

"We stayed over…Carmel. It was good." Shaye gave herself a moment, remembering how good it had been.

"The dinner. Was it memorable?" Annie asked.

Shaye could hear the tease in Annie's voice. Annie obviously knew it had been more than dinner.

"I don't even remember what I had for dinner," Shaye replied.

Annie laughed again before becoming serious. "That's good, Shaye. And you're finally resolving your issues related to what happened when you were five?"

"Those issues…yeah, I'm making progress. But I called you for another reason."

"I'm all ears," Annie said.

Shaye relayed the news about the mayor's yard fire.

"That doesn't sound like it did much damage."

"They found a receipt belonging to Andy—my stepbrother—at the fire," Shaye said. "Pauline's his sister. I haven't seen him in years."

"That sounds bad for him, Shaye." The sound of Annie sucking in her breath came through the phone speaker.

"Andy claims his truck is usually unlocked and he stores his receipts in the console," Shaye said. "He rushed to the police station this morning after he heard about the receipt implicating him and told Eve his story." Shaye sighed. "But he isn't known for making the best choices in life."

Annie focused directly on the reason for Shaye's greatest anxiety. "How's Ginny? Your mom…that means she's affected. They're her stepkids." Annie's voice was soft, concerned, and it made Shaye want to thank her.

"Exactly. Mom's caught up in this." Shaye suspected Annie could hear her own emotion.

"Is she okay?" Annie asked.

"Eve went with me to see her this afternoon. She was good with Mom. So good." Shaye thought about how kind Eve had been to her mom. And how Eve had held her too, kissed her right there in her office before they headed to her mom's house. "It's been a while since I've seen Mom cry. She's such a strong woman. It hurts." Shaye had gotten her own tears under control before she'd called Annie, but now she was wiping them away again. "I'm worried about her. She realized the worst too—that maybe Andy set all the fires—"

"And burned you out and attacked you. Was that Andy?"

"I honestly don't know," Shaye said. "I guess that's why I called you. Just to talk about it. I don't want it to be him."

"Of course you don't, honey. You're upset." Annie's tone was soothing.

"And Cassie. We still have to talk to her. Pauline's her mom, and Andy's her uncle. She's going to get hit with the blowback. I don't know how to spare her. And she's only eleven."

"I don't think you can. You can only be there for her," Annie said before they fell silent, and Shaye tried to assimilate what had happened and what was coming. Then Annie continued. "I'm going to change the subject. How are you and Eve?"

Shaye decided to be honest and not hold back. The impacts of the latest arson weren't all she needed to discuss if she wanted Annie's feedback. "She's not the cop I'd pegged her for. She's smart and funny and kind. And humble too. Even knows how to blush."

"That sounds like an endorsement, but how are the two of you?"

Shaye tried to sound nonchalant. "We've slept together."

"I kinda got that when you said you couldn't remember what you had for dinner. But that was probably before all this happened with Andy."

"I'm still trying to process what happened...Andy, Mom, Pauline maybe. I don't want it to derail us—Eve and me. It wasn't just sex," Shaye admitted. "I'm falling for her, but I'm worried." Her chest tightened. "I hope I can hold it all together through this fire mess. She's handed it off to the county."

"Do you trust her?" Annie asked. "We talked about you getting to know each other and building trust. Overcoming your aversion to her profession."

"She hasn't given me any reason not to. In fact, she's given me only reasons that I should. But I'm planning on moving out as soon as I can. We've approached this relationship backwards—living together before we dated, but I think we can handle that. It's just all the stress that's coming. That will be the test."

"It's going to boil down to your feelings for her, Shaye. If you can weather the storm. So let them keep growing if you can. And there's no rule book for the order of things. Not that you're wrong about backing up the living situation, but follow your heart."

Shaye laughed. "Same thing that Eve's old aunt said on our visit. Aunt Sadie has her moments."

"Hey, don't knock the wisdom of the elderly. Especially those with memory issues. It's kind of amazing that's something Aunt Sadie didn't forget...'follow your heart.'"

"You know, I keep telling myself to remember what Mom said too—about love, not that I'm ready to say I'm in love."

Shaye felt a pang strike her middle, and then her stomach knotted as she talked to Annie about love. She knew she had more to resolve as her mind and heart fought. Her past was clashing with the present and while she was making major headway, she hadn't fully made peace with her past. At least not yet, but she was hoping with time, she could put it in its proper place. If she was going to have a future with someone, she pictured Eve. One step at a time, she'd been telling herself.

"Your mom is wise. And experienced. What did she say?" Annie asked.

"She said that love is everything," Shaye replied. "I know she sees so much good in her life, but I think she meant that she can't live without love too. Not just romantic love, although she's had three husbands. She treasures her family, friends, and even her students that love her."

"Remember the life wisdom of older women when things get tough, Shaye. There's no rule book—follow your heart." Annie fell silent for a moment. "Love can make you whole. Not just romantic love, because there's different kinds of love, like you just indicated. But the last thing I'd want to lose in my life is love. Love *is* everything."

"Is that you speaking as an *older* woman too?" Shaye asked.

"I am your mentor, you know, so I'll accept it...older, wiser woman. Don't you forget it, either."

❖

Eve came in just as Shaye was ending a call with Annie. She was exhausted but happy to come home to Shaye and McGruff. How her life had changed. She prayed she could count on this as her future, but she was worried about Shaye—after they'd both witnessed her mom's pain, the likely involvement of her stepsiblings, the need to deal with Cassie. Ginny was so strong, but her heart had taken a blow. She'd pulled herself up in the past, and Eve hoped she would do the same now. She'd done so much better than Eve had when life had thrown her curveballs. She'd moved on with her life.

"Hey there, babe. How are you two doing?" Eve plopped down next to Shaye, McGruff on Shaye's other side. He got up and walked across Shaye, stopping to give her a lick on the chin before he continued into Eve's lap and plopped down, offering her a lick too, and then a grunt. "How does he know it's been a tough day?" Eve asked.

"I thought he was a canine cop. Highly honed detecting skills. Sleuth hound. And maybe a little bit of life experience," Shaye replied. "I've got some dinner for you in the kitchen. I even waited for you."

"Dinner—I'd tell you how much I like you, but you probably don't want to hear it, cop and all." Eve worked to keep her tone light.

Shaye looked at her. "I hope we're getting there. But it better not be just about my cooking and your stomach." Shaye maintained a light tone too.

"And what will it be about?" Eve ventured to ask, interested in Shaye's answer. She thought they were exploring that delicate ground before either of them was willing to admit it was really love. But damn if the territory they were treading didn't seem to have a few big potholes that had just appeared in the landscape.

"Well, I could include your hot body and a few unmentionable skills you possess, your flirting and chemistry rating, your knowledge of tempting drink names, even if you do drink old-fashioneds. But that might seem a bit shallow." The humor in Shaye's tone made Eve smile, and then Shaye became more serious. "This is fragile, Eve. I'm not going to lie. And I'm not sure if I know how to navigate history or the present events that might take this to ashes, but I promise you that I'll do my best to do this Aunt Sadie style…follow my heart."

"Me too." Eve nodded. Shaye's was an honest answer, and probably close to the one she would have given. "So back to stomachs from hearts. What's in the kitchen?"

"I got a little carried away after our time with Mom—needed a distraction. So maybe you won't starve. I made chili, cornbread, and salad." Shaye stopped for a moment, taking a deep breath before she went on. "But first, the hors d'oeuvres. Cheese stuffed cherry tomatoes, cranberry-fig goat cheese crostini, asparagus wraps, and stuffed mushrooms…kitchen therapy."

Eve had to chuckle at the embarrassment evident in Shaye's expression as she rattled off all that she'd cooked in the name of therapy. Eve thought about how different this was from her lonely homecomings before Shaye and McGruff. They made Eve happy. "That's an amazing menu. Probably not conducive to maintaining this hot body, but I'm starving and it sounds perfect."

Shaye stood and grabbed Eve's hand, McGruff taking the hint that food might be involved, and they headed to the kitchen to fill their plates for the first round. When they were seated back on the couch because they'd agreed that tonight they were going casual, they started on the finger food.

"So, shall I update you on what I know, or will that ruin your dinner?" Eve asked.

"I'm ready to know. I've been stressing since I got home, so I might as well hear what you can tell me."

"Okay," Eve replied. "Andy hasn't been charged, but he's been picked up by Jim Greene's people for questioning, and he agreed to answer anything and everything, still claiming he's innocent…that his receipts were in his unlocked truck where anybody could have taken one."

"Is that smart without a lawyer?" Shaye asked.

"No lawyer is every cop's best scenario," Eve replied. "But that's not exactly how it played out. Remember Brent Bailey—he said he went to school with you guys?"

Shaye nodded. "Smart kid. Nice. Suffered for being gay, but headed to college like I did after high school. I'm surprised he's back, but good for him."

"He's a lawyer and showed up as Andy's lawyer. Pro bono, he said. Greene did a bit of cursing—don't repeat that—but I'd say Andy is in good hands."

Shaye nodded again.

"You're the only person who has been a witness to an arson, but I relayed to Greene what you told me. That you were dazed, the voice was a whisper, you can't even say if it was a man or woman, and you haven't seen Andy in years. Greene may see if he can jar something loose from you, but I think he knows the odds."

"Did they lock Andy up then?" Shaye asked. "They'd have to keep him at the county jail, right?"

"Actually, Greene didn't. I guess based on just the receipt, the unlocked truck possibility, the good lawyer…not yet. Politics could play a role, so moving it to the county sheriff wasn't a mistake."

"I suspect it was a brilliant move, Eve. Sneed is your boss and would have pressured you to do everything to link this to Pauline."

"Probably not as much brilliant as it was an effort at self-preservation—trying not to end up a political pawn. Speaking of Sneed applying pressure, Pauline called late this afternoon, and I think she had the same thing in mind until I told her it wasn't my case. She hung up on me." Eve shook her head at the thought of the nightmare if either candidate were to gain a foothold in the investigation.

"I can't believe Pauline would do that," Shaye said. Then she rolled her eyes. "Yes, I can. She'd absolutely do that."

"It'll be extremely serious if Greene decides to charge Andy, especially if they decide to go for all the arsons. But he probably wants enough solid evidence to not end up with egg on his face. My experience with Greene is he's cautious, thoughtful, and fair." Eve looked at Shaye and then shoulder bumped her. "You know, those nonexistent cop traits."

"Hey. Don't make me sorry I'm rethinking this cop thing." Shaye bumped her back, and Eve was relieved they could discuss it with a bit of levity.

"If Andy's arrested, he'll probably need bail money if it's set, which Ginny has promised." Eve stopped and thought a moment, then said, "And that's about all I know."

Shaye leaned over and kissed her on the lips. Hard and with passion. Eve kissed her back, realizing it would be easy to escalate this right into bed, but they'd both skipped their meals today.

"Shall we get on with eating this fabulous meal you put together, then take a shower and see where that leads us?" Eve asked. "I have the feeling that this is going to take endurance—a marathon." When Shaye arched an eyebrow and her eyes twinkled, Eve blushed. "I was talking about this whole arson thing."

"And I was thinking of a diversion from this whole arson thing."

Eve nodded and tilted her head, offering Shaye the lead. They quickly finished the hors d'oeuvres and then Eve took over, setting down her plate and taking Shaye's hand. She led Shaye to the shower. Not the one with the dog shampoo, but the one with the handheld massage showerhead.

It didn't take them long to end up totally nude and totally distracted from the events of the day. Eve took her time, grateful that she'd upgraded the size of her hot water tank. With Shaye's pale skin, water-wet and slick, Eve stood facing Shaye, who had her back against the tiled shower wall. After she slipped her leg between Shaye's thighs to widen her stance, Eve took her time and made certain that Shaye experienced the many uses for the pulsing flow of warm water. Shaye's hips rocked as Eve inserted her hand into the rhythm of the cleansing until Shaye arched her back and clasped Eve's shoulders, hanging on through low throaty moans of obvious soaring before the slow slide back to measured breathing. And when Shaye had finally regained control, she took the shower head from Eve and drained the rest of the hot water tank.

Fully satiated with lovemaking and indulged with food by ten o'clock, Eve considered that with the complications that the world was throwing at them, this simple act of leaving that behind and connecting with each other would hopefully help hold them together. She had no doubt that if given the chance, she and Shaye could make this work…if life didn't get in the way. Eve didn't want to race into hasty definitions, maybe because she knew how much could happen to alter things, but her feelings for Shaye were growing. Eve slipped into a night of deep sleep with Shaye in her arms.

# CHAPTER SEVENTEEN

It wasn't until Sunday afternoon that Eve and Shaye went to collect Cassie for an afternoon burger and a debriefing on how she was doing. They'd invited Shaye's mom, but she'd thought that this should be Cassie's time with the two of them. Shaye gave her a hug and headed out to the car to join Eve and Cassie.

After they'd each told Eve what they wanted and collected their drinks, Eve departed to collect the food at the front counter of BurgerTown, and Shaye remained at their table with Cassie.

"How are you doing, Cass?"

Cassie shrugged. "Okay, I guess."

"Is school going okay?"

Cassie just shrugged again.

"And your new writing gig? How about that?" Shaye was working hard to keep the conversation light, but to also engage Cassie. She suspected the conversation would turn to the fires and she wasn't ready for that, but the reason for this lunch was to address any concerns that Cassie might have. Cassie undoubtedly had heard rumors, and she obviously knew that Shaye's mom hadn't remained unaffected because she lived with her.

"Joye is cool. I like working for her—she hasn't published my book story yet, but she said next week probably. Can I ask you something, Aunt Shanelle?"

"Anything," Shaye replied, then added to her response when she saw Cassie's cheeky smirk, the one that had been missing up until now. "That doesn't mean I'm going to answer."

Cassie fidgeted with her hands. "People are saying Uncle Andy has been setting the fires. That Mom had him do it because of the election. Even that you're part of it, getting the librarian job because the old librarian retired, and it was because you had your stepbrother set that fire. Is Eve going to arrest you too?"

Shaye blinked, not having heard those rumors. She'd been holding it all at bay, trying to focus on her Friday night with Eve, on the bright spot in all this chaos on either side of it.

Eve arrived with the burgers and handed them out. "What's up? You talking about me?"

Shaye said "No" at the same time that Cassie said "Yes."

"Well, which is it and what's being said?" Eve focused on Cassie, probably because she'd given the affirmative response, Shaye thought.

"Are you going to arrest Aunt Shanelle?"

"I wasn't planning on it. Why would I? Is she misbehaving again?" Eve asked with raised eyebrows and those dancing eyes that Shaye couldn't resist.

Cassie looked directly at Eve. "You're a cop. You arrest people. I'm not foolish. If Uncle Andy and Mom set those fires, you'll arrest them too."

"I'm not on this case, Cassie, because I know the people involved. The county sheriff is in charge, and I can't tell you what will happen. I know him, and he's always been a good sheriff in my judgment. But I'll be honest with you—if there's enough evidence, he'll make the arrests."

Shaye was still mulling over what Cassie had said about her involvement because of the library fire when Cassie repeated the question about Shaye's arrest to Eve. Eve looked at Shaye and she looked away. Shaye's chest had constricted. Were people really saying that about her? That she was involved.

"No, Cassie," Eve said. "Let me ask you something. Do you think the same person set the fires—because I can tell you that the fire inspector is thinking that's what the evidence shows?"

Cassie nodded.

"Do you know what evidence is and believe it matters?" Eve asked.

Cassie rolled her eyes before saying, "Duh, haven't you ever watched any crime shows?"

Eve smiled at Cassie. "Exactly. So, was Shaye involved in setting her own house and car on fire and the attack on herself, or do you think that people are maybe making things up?"

"Why would she do that to herself?" Cassie asked. "That would be dumb."

"So is it Shaye, or is it the people spreading rumors who aren't using their deductive thinking skills?" Eve reached across the table and took Shaye's hand and winked. Shaye knew that Eve was trying to make her feel better as she walked Cassie through the conversation. Shaye was feeling disconcerted, but that wasn't Eve's fault. In fact, Eve was helping.

"I get it. It's like school. There are knuckleheads," Cassie said. "Some people just like to spread crap."

Shaye started to admonish Cassie for her language when Eve squeezed her hand. "Some people gain their power by being crap spreaders, Cassie. And that's why evidence is important—to establish the truth."

"Is that why you're a cop? To find the evidence and stop the knuckleheads?" Cassie asked.

"Pretty noble of me, huh?" Eve chuckled, and Shaye loved the way she was drawing Cassie out, letting her express how she felt. It was what Cassie needed because she had to be feeling the same type of stress that Shaye was, and she was just a kid. "There's a lot to my story, but discovering the truth is important and part of my reasons."

"Okay," Cassie said. "Now that we've covered that, let's talk about your love life."

Shaye gave Cassie a don't-you-wish look over the top of her drink. "Nice try, kid."

"Who, me? I just want to make sure all this *manure* spreading isn't getting in the way of atrial fibrillation. You know…dope AF, you two." Cassie laughed. "You *are* living together."

Eve turned her attention on Shaye, obviously offering her the chance to address the observation.

"My house burned down. Eve offered me her guest room until they catch the arsonist."

"So, if it's Uncle Andy, you're moving out?" Cassie asked.

Shaye hesitated, then nodded. How to explain it to Cassie, and even to Eve? They were both waiting for her answer. She decided to just lay out her feelings. "I moved in with Eve because I had to for protection. If I live with her in the future, I want that to be for different reasons. Does that make sense?"

"Like true love," Cassie said, then she looked back and forth between them before settling on Shaye. "You could live with us for a while. Ginny is your mom. She could probably use your company— I'm doing my best, but I can tell she's upset. Move in with her and date

Eve. Not that many dates, maybe eight, because you already know each other pretty well and it's so obvious you belong together."

Shaye wondered if Cassie was full of wisdom or just wishful thinking. "Eight? And how is that the magic number?"

"Five, so you've accomplished the *dating*, which I'm smart enough to tell is important to you. Then three more, just so you're an overachiever." Cassie stopped and took a big bite of her burger, then chewed a moment before continuing with her mouth full. "The goal is *together forever*. Right? So don't waste too much time before you know what I know."

"Is that so," Shaye said. "And what is it that you know? And swallow before you choke—it would be a shame to lose such an expert matchmaker." She shook her head as she considered she was taking advice from an eleven-year-old.

"I know the *evidence*—that you two belong together."

Shaye looked at Eve, who was sitting back, an amused expression on her face.

"And just where would you go on these dates?" Eve asked.

"Well, a few could be here to BurgerTown. If you're going to be a good girlfriend, you need to know she likes french fries."

Shaye picked up a fry and waved it around. "I think Cupid's onto something." She took a bite. "Mmm." She didn't break eye contact with Eve.

"I think she approves of that suggestion," Eve said. "Any others?"

"Sure. Invite her over for dinner. Maybe spaghetti—nobody can mess that up. And candles."

Shaye and Eve both nodded, and Cassie added, "And maybe a chaperone like McGruff, because I can tell that you two are going to need a chaperone."

Eve blushed and Shaye wanted to say "Too late to be thinking of that," but she kept her mouth shut in front of Cassie. "Any more ideas?" she asked instead.

"I know you're a good singer, Aunt Shanelle. I still think karaoke night at Romer's Bar is a good idea. They do an early session without alcohol so kids can come one Friday night of the month." Cassie gave Shaye a hopeful look and Shaye knew she'd mentioned kids' night for a reason.

"Might need a chaperone for that one too," Shaye suggested.

"I know just the kid who might accompany us," Eve said with a straight face as Cassie broke into a grin.

"Is that it?" Shaye asked.

"I'm not doing all the work. You two need to figure out the rest… besides, I already got karaoke night in there. But if you're desperate, there's always the beach. And bikinis." Cassie looked hopeful, while Eve looked away.

"I'll keep that in mind, but I suspect the chief of police would only roll around in the sand in public while wearing only a few square inches of cloth under great duress."

"Duress…more like undress," Eve muttered as her color reddened and Shaye enjoyed the entire exchange. "I think it's time to get Cassie back home. She probably has homework to finish before the start of the week."

Cassie shook her head. "It's done. But I think I've given you two enough advice for one day. Except for something Ginny says not to forget."

"Love is everything," she and Shaye said in unison.

❖

After they arrived home, Eve settled on the couch and Shaye sat beside her before McGruff joined them.

"I think that went well," Shaye said, offering her a kiss. "Thanks."

"Thanks for what? The french fries?"

"Definitely the french fries. And for being who you are behind that cop label."

"Cop is part of who I am. Exploring the evidence, seeking the truth." Eve kept her tone light.

Shaye took her hand and Eve intertwined their fingers. Eve wanted a serious conversation after their afternoon at BurgerTown. They needed to talk.

"And the evidence suggests to me that you brought me to the couch to do more than kiss. You want to talk," Shaye said.

"I want this to work, and I've got to give Cassie credit for being pretty smart for an eleven-year-old."

"Let me guess. You've changed your mind…bikinis on the beach." Shaye bumped shoulders with her.

"Don't try to derail me with embarrassing images of myself."

"Never. So, let's talk," Shaye replied.

"I think you should move in with your mom. She needs you right now, and I don't think you're in much danger. With Andy as the prime suspect in Greene's sights, I don't think he'd hurt either of you, plus I don't see any additional motivation to do so. And if it's not him, there's a chance this could never be solved. Also, I think the warning's been delivered and there's no reason for another attack."

"So, you want me out?"

"No. I want you here. But you're so stressed trying to deal with all this. You need to get some normalcy back in your life, and I know that means not being forced to live with me. You want it to be a choice…I get it," Eve said as she squeezed Shaye's hand. "We need those eight dates." I need to know this is going to work for the right reasons too, Eve thought. I need to be sure it's going to turn into a love I can count on.

"And you're going to make me spaghetti? With candles?"

"How hard can mixing noodles with tomato paste and some protein be? And striking a match to a string hanging out of a stick of wax, I can do that," Eve replied.

Shaye laughed. "So romantic."

"I can show you romantic." Eve raised and lowered her eyebrows. "But let's back up like you said and do this the way you need to do it… the way we need to do it. I want that too."

Shaye turned and put a hand on each of Eve's cheeks and looked her in the eye. "I'll call Mom tomorrow." She leaned in and gave Eve a long, slow kiss. "Did you just say that you can show me romantic?"

"I thought we were going to date." Eve closed her eyes and prolonged the kiss.

"Oh, we are. But not until after I move out. In the meantime…"

"You're the boss," Eve said.

"And who said that one of our dates can't be a sleepover? Or two, or three, or…"

Eve stood and took Shaye's hand again, turning toward her bedroom. McGruff looked up from the couch and grunted.

"Great chaperone that you are, McGruff," Shaye told him before she added, "And I'm the boss."

❖

The following week on Saturday evening, Eve was sitting back in BurgerTown with Shaye on that official date number one because they'd officially finished moving Shaye into a small reconfigured office space in Ginny's house late that afternoon. The desk had been moved to the garage, and they'd set up a bed in its place because Shaye had refused to dislodge Cassie.

They all agreed it was temporary. Eve just hoped that Shaye's next move would be back to her house, by choice, and not into a rental because they would have reached the point they both knew it was love—reliable love, deep and true with each of them at the center of the other's world. Eve prayed that it would last. That they weren't moving backwards.

In the meantime, she told herself that this was a great way for Shaye to help support her mom through some trying times with Andy and Pauline under suspicion for the arsons.

"I'm glad you didn't try to cram everything into that little room at your mom's," Eve said.

"I'm glad you have no problem with me leaving some stuff at your house."

"Now you'll be set for date number three," Eve replied, feeling a bit overwhelmed with the fact she was going home to just McGruff. To a dog that she hadn't even had not that long ago. A dog who had been a big reason Shaye had come into her life, and now Shaye had become a big part of her life. Without stopping for McGruff, she would never have ended up in that bar, and Eve wasn't sure how their relationship would have progressed if they'd immediately jumped to conclusions about each other without having the memory, the chemistry, of their unencumbered bar encounter. And then she'd sworn there was no place in her life for Shaye. They'd made it to this point, against so many odds.

"Hey, babe." Shaye handed her a french fry. "I'm feeling a bit overwhelmed too, but this is good for Mom and Cassie, and it's good for us in the long run. As we grow this relationship the correct way. We've come so far. But now I'm ready for you to tell me—what's the plan for date number three?"

"Sleepover," Eve said as she ate the french fry. She hadn't wanted an order of her own. "My hips may be declaring *No* to these deep-fat-fried potato strips, but I have to agree with someone who said 'Mmm' the last time we were here."

Shaye nodded. "And what's on the agenda for date number two? And why is a sleepover the third date?"

"I'm sure the sleepover won't come soon enough for me, but it should be on a weekend, don't you think, so we don't have to get up and race off to work." Eve leaned back as she waited on Shaye's response.

"Agreed. I want one of those brunch mornings the day after,"

Shaye said. "Or after I've spent a cop-friendly night with you, we could always go out and get ourselves a cop-friendly glazed doughnut with a great big center hol—"

"Oh no we don't. It's gonna be brunch." Eve suppressed a laugh in order to insert some admonishment into her tone. "I want brunch in our pj's, and maybe a morning nap. We can have doughnuts delivered for you, though."

"Nap, huh?" Shaye gave her a visual assessment. "Old…or you're planning on a short night."

"You're not going to be able to keep up with me. Now, on to address date number two," Eve said. "Middle of this week if it's okay with you. McGruff's going to be missing you."

"Well, I wouldn't want to upset the pooch."

Eve bit her lower lip. The house wasn't going to be the same without Shaye there. "Me too. I'm going to miss you. So maybe that spaghetti dinner and candlelight…this week?"

"I'll be there," Shaye said. "I'm going to miss you too. I promise to come into the office for part of each day. We're going to take this the way any two girlfriends would, okay?"

Eve smiled. She liked the sound of that word. A word they hadn't actually spoken yet to define their relationship. But yeah. They were definitely girlfriends. *Girlfriends.*

# CHAPTER EIGHTEEN

Tonight was Friday night and officially date number five. They'd shared spaghetti, a weekend sleepover, and been on a dinner date to Thai Tanic in the past two weeks, and the plan was for Cassie to be with them until her mom dropped by and picked her up. They were at Romer's Bar for karaoke night.

"Shaye and I are signing up to sing together," Cassie told Eve as they found a table for the evening. "My very favorite Taylor Swift song, 'It's Nice to Have a Friend.' I wanted to sing 'Lover,' but Ginny said I need to get older first." Cassie rolled her eyes. "As if I haven't been listening to it for years. It came out when I was seven or eight, and I'm so much older now."

"I can hardly wait to hear you two." As Cassie headed to sign up, Eve leaned into Shaye and whispered, "'Lover'? Glad you agreed on something more age appropriate."

Shaye gave Eve her best seductive look. "Do you think that *I'm* old enough?"

Eve was just offering her a laugh when Cassie returned and took Shaye's hand, pulling on her. "Come on, we're up first. There are only a few others signed up too, so far."

The announcer turned on the sound system and announced Cassie and Shaye. They went up front, and Cassie held the mic out to share with Shaye. As the music began, Shaye let Cassie take the lead and accompanied her as Cassie carried the first verse. They'd been practicing, and Shaye thought they'd come up with a decent performance. She hoped that Eve thought so.

She threw back her head at the chorus and joined in with abandon before she locked her focus on Eve and sang directly to her, even though she hoped Eve knew it wasn't simply about friendship. She let the quick beat of the song grip her, a song without a lot of accompanying pomp, stripped down to the rapid delivery of the vocals. This song had been chosen for Cassie but was one she hoped Eve would appreciate too.

Backing off, Shaye let Cassie be the star for each verse. As they finished, the crowd clapped and whistled and stomped. Cassie had a grin a mile wide as they headed back to their seats, and Shaye felt a surge of pleasure that they'd been able to take Cassie's mind off of the cloud hanging over her because of Andy and her mother.

As Cassie headed over to receive congratulations from some friends, Shaye wove her way back to their table. When she was seated again, Eve closed the space between them and kissed her on the lips, her eyes warm and approving. "Definitely another skill besides helping people find a good book and access information. Probably a good thing you weren't singing 'Lover.' We might have had to roll this fifth date into a bonus date number six right now...an emergency sleepover."

Shaye laughed and took Eve's hand, holding it through the other seven singers. When the karaoke was finished, Cassie returned to their table, plopping down in her seat and grabbing Shaye's arm. Her eyes were wide and her posture wasn't relaxed. Shaye would have thought it was from the thrill of the evening, but Cassie's demeanor conveyed more than normal teen excitement related to having a good time.

"What's up?" she asked, worried that someone had said something about the arsons that had upset her.

"Did someone do or say something to you?" Eve asked, looking over at the table with the kids that Cassie had just left.

Cassie shook her head and pointed across the room. "There's Uncle Andy. I haven't seen him in a while. Not since this all began."

"I'd like to talk to him." Shaye turned to Eve. "But you probably don't want to get involved since you've stepped back. Can you stay with Cassie while I try to catch up with him?"

Eve leaned close to Shaye and quietly advised her. "Don't go outside alone, though—stay inside. There are a few empty tables toward the back of the room. I want you safe. And if you feel the least bit threatened, you wave at me or even yell. I'll be watching."

Shaye turned to Cassie. "Mom should be here in about fifteen minutes. If I'm not back, I'll see you at the house, Cassie." She gave Cassie a hug. "You were awesome tonight. I was proud to be your singing partner."

The smile returned to Cassie's face, and Shaye made a point of walking away at a normal pace as she went looking for Andy.

The room buzzed with the conversation of the patrons, and it was difficult to make out details of individuals across the space with the soft glow of subdued lighting. Shaye scanned the crowd, looking for someone who she might recognize as Andy. She hoped she'd know him—it had been about twenty years. She should have asked Cassie if he was alone or with others.

As she moved forward and continued to study faces in the muted light, her attention landed on a man sitting alone at a table in the back of the room. He was nursing a beer and not looking in her direction. Shaye walked closer, determining that he could be someone in his early forties who'd led a challenging life. She wasn't sure it was Andy until he looked up and focused on her, breaking out into a grin and saying, "Shaye?"

Her heart did a few extra beats. His face was tan and thin, with deep wrinkles. His hair was shaggy, but he held her gaze and his eyes were clear. She hadn't seen him in so long, and she realized that while he'd certainly aged, he didn't appear to be the devil he was suspected of being, the person who had started four fires and hurt her. She didn't remember him being skilled at being deceptive, and his grin seemed genuine.

"Hi, Andy. Cassie said she saw you." Shaye continued to study him, trying to get a better read than her first impression, that he was actually the same person she'd known for years. She'd reserve opinion on the arsons, but her inclination doubted that he was the man who'd attacked her. At the same time, she didn't really know him anymore. She had to admit to herself she didn't want it to be him.

"You're as beautiful as ever, Shaye. And you did such a good job up there on the stage with Cassie."

"Thanks, Andy. How have you been?"

Andy pursed his lips before responding. "I've been better. But I've been worse too."

Shaye decided to hold her tongue to see what else he might tell her. She lifted a brow in question, signaling for him to go on.

"I know that your girlfriend is Eve Maguire, chief of police, and Pauline's former girlfriend. I knew her because she dated Pauline—she was always decent to me." Andy ran his hand through his messy hair. "I didn't start those fires, Shaye. Tell that to your girlfriend. Someone must have lifted the receipt from my truck. That's the bad news. I guess the good news is that they haven't arrested me yet."

Shaye nodded again but bit her tongue. She waited for Andy to continue if he wanted to.

"You have to know that your girlfriend passed the case off when they thought Pauline might be involved—and knowing Pauline, she could be. But not me. Cross my heart and hope to die." Andy crossed his chest with his index finger, like they used to do when they were kids.

Shaye closed her eyes a moment and inhaled. That promise used to mean something. She hoped it still did. "You know my house and car were set on fire, and I was attacked for witnessing one of the fires?"

Andy touched her arm. "I'd never do that to you. Never. I always cared for you. And I love your mom—Ginny. She was always there for me. I'd never hurt her either, and hurting you would hurt her. You know that at my age, I'm finally figuring out what's important in life. I think Ginny helped me figure that out—watching her live her life. I know it wasn't always easy for her."

Shaye digested this. "So, what's important in life, Andy?"

He didn't hesitate. "People. Making connections, growing those connections, and loving, being loved."

Shaye looked up from Andy and saw that Eve was working her way toward them. "I think the chief's coming to fetch me. I'd better go. She doesn't want to give anyone an opportunity to say she's involved in a conflict of interest."

"Can I ask you something?" Andy inquired. "Really quickly."

"Not promising to answer, but go for it," she replied.

"Do you love her? If so, don't waste it."

Shaye remained silent as she watched Eve get closer, stop several feet away and nod at Andy. He nodded back. She considered his question as she took measure of the effect Eve's approach had on her, the uptick in her mood. She only offered him a smile as he stood. An answer to that question did not belong to Andy. She had to admit it to herself first, and then it belonged to her and Eve. She had no doubt that she wanted to spend time with Eve, that she was looking at their future because Eve made her happy—that her heart was telling her that she could love Eve. She just had to finish putting her past to rest if she could. She didn't have to address her feelings right now with a label because she wasn't ready to. Not when there were so many other issues to manage right now. Maybe they'd address it when they'd made it through their Cassie-advised, eight-date prelude to a hard look at a future.

"See you, Shaye. Before another twenty years, I hope." He turned to leave. "Be well."

"You too." Then she turned to Eve, who stood waiting for her, and Shaye felt her pulse thrum. She felt fortunate. And hopeful. But she knew how much could go wrong, how life could change things in just an instant.

❖

By midmorning on Wednesday, Eve had talked to both Hooper and Greene, and neither had offered her any new information on the fire at the mayor's house. Hooper reiterated that in his judgment it was the same arsonist, and Greene still wasn't ready to arrest Andy without more evidence. Shaye had come home with her to spend Friday night and had shared what Andy had told her.

The mayor knew it was useless to push on her to name Pauline in the arson attack because Eve had made it clear that Greene was handling the law enforcement aspects. Now Sneed was pushing on Grady instead, so she'd just finished advising her officer to tell the mayor to contact Greene with questions when her phone rang again.

"Hey, Eve. It's Joye. Gotta minute?"

"For you. Sure. What's up?" Eve eased back in her chair and felt a bit of the tension from her earlier morning encounters dissipate as she talked to her.

"First, how are you doing?"

"It depends on the day." Eve chuckled. "It's been a morning focused on the arsons, which I'm not even handling except for being kept informed and advising Grady on his role, not his decisions. Just general advice on how to handle himself. He's never been the lead for Paradise Pines PD before. Experience certainly comes in useful with the politics."

"Politics...you can't be referring to the mayor." Joye's tone conveyed that was exactly what she meant.

"Certainly not me. Although politics is his middle name. And you can't quote me."

"Spoilsport. How are you and Shaye doing with her living at Ginny's?"

Eve could hear something more than just a simple question in Joye's inquiry. She wondered what that was about. "We're doing fine." Eve paused to consider that she meant it. She and Shaye were doing okay, considering all that was impacting them. "Going on dates. I was worried when she moved out how we'd fare, but she was probably right in her desire to back up and make living together a choice, the way a regular relationship would progress. How are you and Earl doing?"

"I haven't seen him since the weekend. He's doing fine. Busy with his business. Busy being Earl."

Eve rolled her eyes and could imagine Joye doing the same on her end of the phone.

"You know, Eve. I started this out as something just for kicks, but underneath all that male machismo, your brother is a good guy. I'm not sure if I should be happy or disgusted with myself for really liking the guy."

"I suspect like any relationship, it all depends on whether your heart's involved and where it ends up. I love Earl, but he's had a hard time settling down. Just be cautious with your feelings," Eve said.

Joye's snort fed into Eve's ear. "Says the *there's no place in my personal life for her* Eve Maguire."

"Well, sue me." Eve shook her head. "You should have seen her singing karaoke with Cassie at the kids' session at Romer's on Friday night. If every lesbian in the world didn't fall in love with her after that performance…"

"Eve." Joye sobered the conversation with the one word. "Are you in love with her?"

Eve didn't just hear the inquiry aspect of the question. She was hearing concern. She swallowed. "I'm close, if not there. I'm trying not to label it yet. I'd say that Post-Pauline repercussions are slowing an acknowledgement that I'm there. Maybe love isn't always as clean when you get older. Wanting it, but scared shitless sometimes."

Eve thought it would be so much easier if Shaye wasn't tied to Pauline, through Andy, through Ginny. If Pauline didn't have the strong potential to be tied up with her future professional life. But she also knew that Shaye had found a place in her heart and she wanted to let those feelings grow. She actually had a personal life, something she hadn't been willing to consider again before Shaye.

"I get it, sweetie. *Post-Pauline Trauma Syndrome.* But you're doing things the right way. Building trust with Shaye. You know she's not Pauline."

"I know," Eve replied. "And while forty-seven years leave me with baggage, as it does everyone, I've got a lot of wisdom under the belt too."

"Wisdom. Focus on that. Because I called for a reason. I need to talk to you. Both you and Earl…together."

"That sounds rather ominous." When Joye didn't counter that statement, Eve's warning bells went off, verifying her impression earlier in their conversation that Joye's questions contained undercurrents of something more than a simple conversation looming.

Joye plowed ahead. "Earl said Saturday morning. Maybe the Coffee Grind?"

Eve thought about that. She had a dinner date, officially number six, with Shaye tonight. Shaye was cooking at Eve's house. Tacos. Eve suspected it would be a full spread—Shaye was a much better cook than she was. Probably enjoyed it more too, although she had to admit that she enjoyed cooking for Shaye.

Eve made a point of groaning. "That shoots an extended Friday night sleepover to smithereens, but I guess there's always Saturday night. The upside is I can count Friday night as the seventh date and Saturday as the eighth. Eight's the magic number."

"And you're counting because…?" Joye asked.

Eve shook her head, knowing she was going to sound ridiculous. "Cassie. Eleven-year-old relationship advisor. Moving Shaye into my house to protect her certainly altered the normal course of how we've both experienced romantic relationships before. Living together wasn't a decision based on a strong romantic relationship."

"Cassie's an astute kid." Joye's entertained chuckle drifted from the phone speaker. "And I can understand what you're saying about the normal course of things."

"When Shaye moved back to Ginny's to allow us a more normal path to a decision about living together, Cassie decided we knew each other well enough already that five official dates was what we needed to have accomplished a regular dating process. And then she added three more dates to make us overachievers."

Joye snorted. "Maybe I need advice from an eleven-year-old on my relationship with a politically challenged, socially challenged, heart-of-gold, big oaf of a guy."

"She's already on your payroll as a budding reporter. You'd just have to expand her job description," Eve said.

"Okay, back to Saturday morning and coffee with that big oaf of a guy. Can I put it on the calendar?"

"I'll make it work." Eve paused for a moment as she thought of the plans she and Shaye had made. She knew Joye wouldn't be pushing for this meeting unless she had something important to discuss. "And I'm going to blame you if Shaye's unhappy."

"Thanks. Say ten o'clock, then?"

After Eve had confirmed and hung up, she wondered again what that was all about. Had Joye found out something about Andy? Pauline? But then Joye had wanted to include Earl, and that didn't compute. Knowing that she'd find out on Saturday, Eve decided there was no point in speculating and stressing about it before then. She whistled at McGruff, and they headed to her Jeep. Before it was time for an afternoon meeting, she'd take time to pick up some lunch and take it to Shaye at the library trailer. Not as an official date, but it was the type of simple everyday thing she wanted to do with Shaye, spend time with her. Her heart was telling her so.

## CHAPTER NINETEEN

As Eve waited for Joye and Earl at the Daily Grind on Saturday morning, she thought about how optimistic she felt regarding Shaye. They'd had a great Friday dinner date that she'd cooked, and while Shaye hadn't spent the night because of Eve's meeting this morning, the plan was for a romantic night tonight.

Shaye was smart and dynamic and caring. She made Eve laugh. And she created a hum in Eve's body with just a simple look. Eve had never wanted anyone the way she wanted Shaye. Eve looked forward to their time together, wanting more. Not just the nights, but the easy meals, the movies, the jogging and biking, the time with Cassie, the pleasure in even the mundane moments of just being with her.

Eve had found Shaye to be the *stable* and *honest* and *loyal* that she'd put on her rational list of necessary partner attributes, and her interactions with Shaye provided an essential flirtation and chemistry that was off the charts…those things that Eve knew her heart needed too. She made Eve want to have a personal life again. With Shaye.

Her thoughts were interrupted when Joye and Earl walked through the door together. Eve didn't ask if they'd just timed it that way or if this was an extension of a long night together. She told herself she didn't want to know. But she would like to know that her brother and her best friend had each found someone to make them happy, as odd as their pairing was. Maybe the heart did know best.

As Joye took her seat across from Eve, she smirked at Eve. "Earl and I happened to arrive at the same time, so stop trying to detect what I did last night, Chief. The bigger question is what you did last night."

Her brother was seated next to Eve and he poked her in the ribs with his elbow. "Yeah, Chief. Did you commit any crimes last night?"

"I cooked eggplant parmesan for Shaye."

"That is a crime," Earl said. "You should have barbecued a thick, juicy steak. I bet Shaye was unhappy."

"I bet she wasn't, and I bet the cow wasn't either." Joye tipped her head toward the counter. "Shall we go order our coffees, and then I'll tell you why I called this meeting."

Eve thought that it was Joye who looked unhappy. She continued to try to tamp down the apprehension she was experiencing. Not wasting any time once they were reseated, Joye cleared her throat, an indication that she was nervous, and Eve's nervousness spiked too.

"Okay. Before I go any further, you need to remember that what happened was all in the past. History. Part of your history, but I'm worried it will impact your present." Joye looked directly at Eve. "Just try to keep in mind that it shouldn't really change anything."

A knot formed in Eve's stomach. This sounded ominous, and Joye was paying significantly more attention to her.

Watching their faces, Joye continued. "I was doing research for the *Pulse*. An election story—I was researching Pauline's background. I dug around and discovered that Pauline's stepmother, Ginny, has been married three times. You probably know this through Shaye. It piqued my interest as part of Pauline's backstory, whether there was anything there for the actual article or not."

Eve knew that finding and pulling threads was part of what made Joye such a good journalist. She wondered where this thread was going.

"Ginny lost her first husband to a work accident and her third husband, Pauline's father, to a heart attack. I was told by one of the old timers in town that she'd lost her second husband in a holdup after a little over two years of marriage." She turned to Earl. "Shaye mentioned this to me when we met for dinner, but you don't know that the shooting happened when Ginny, her husband, and Shaye were on a weekend vacation in San Francisco."

Shaye hadn't disclosed her role in the shooting to Joye that night at the pizza parlor when she'd mentioned the incident, and Joye didn't indicate now what she might know. Eve was grateful because Earl didn't need to know unless Shaye chose to tell him. Eve thought about the morning when they'd been out exercising and Shaye had told her about yelling "Gun!" About how it had impacted her entire life, even bringing Shaye back to Paradise Pines to try to gain some perspective and mend from the trauma—move on. Eve remembered how she had held Shaye on that bench as she shared the story. Shaye had made significant progress in finally forgiving herself.

"Being a nosy journalist, I decided to do a bit more digging." Joye glanced at Earl and then fixed her gaze on Eve, who nodded and waited for more.

After they'd all taken a sip, Joye resumed. "It actually took a lot of digging, but I tracked down the name of a cop who was there, the partner at the time of the involved rookie. It was about thirty-five years ago. Turns out he's deceased, but this partner, now retired, was eager to talk to me. More than eager—lonely retirement...but I digress."

Joye paused for another swallow of her drink, then fixed her eyes on Eve and Earl, who sat across the table from her, waiting to hear her point.

"The partner told me several things about his rookie partner who pulled the trigger. I knew enough from you two to piece some things together. That rookie who was the shooter was named Mike Parsons—your brother." Joye let out a sigh as Eve and Earl let out a collective gasp.

They all sat in silence a moment as the information registered. Eve knew that Mike had been eighteen when she and Earl were adopted by Sadie and Glen, He'd finished high school and was focused on pursuing a law enforcement career. She and Earl were younger and changed their last name to their maternal aunt and uncle's, Maguire. Mike had kept their original family name, Parsons.

The truth of it all hammered in Eve's chest and then rose and settled in her throat. She had trouble swallowing. Uncle Glen and Aunt Sadie had taken them in after the auto accident that took their parents and had helped them redefine their family. She'd known that after Mike had joined the San Francisco police force he'd changed, become despondent and reckless. She'd surmised that whatever had happened had led to his motorcycle accident. But Sadie and Glen had refused to elaborate or discuss it. Losing Mike had hit Eve and Earl hard after losing their parents.

Earl spoke first, looking at Eve. "Well, shit. Joye's saying that our brother was the one who shot Shaye's dad. It might be history, but there's no sticking your head up your backside. This is the past catching up with the present."

Eve didn't respond. She couldn't. The shock of the realization had her throat paralyzed. At least her heart was still beating, even if it was pounding in her ears. Her world had just crashed well beyond the resurrection of the loss of Mike. She just learned that he'd not only made a terrible rookie mistake, but that it was Shaye's dad who had suffered the consequence. Shaye's world was going to crash when Eve told her what had happened, and she was terrified what that meant for their future.

The thought of losing Shaye—it hit Eve. The real possibility of going back to only a professional life…no personal life. The hole was a crippling void. She'd been aware what was growing there in her heart or she wouldn't have gone to bed with Shaye, but this was the moment that she was willing to admit her feelings for Shaye. To define what she knew to be true. She loved Shaye.

Shaye was due any minute. It was Saturday evening and Eve had fretted and stewed since coffee with Joye and Earl that morning. She paced in an effort to keep control of the turmoil that roiled in her gut. Eve searched for the calm that she needed in order to get through what was coming, but it kept slipping out of her grasp as the possible ramifications of what Joye had revealed raced through her mind.

This was supposed to be their eighth date. The third overachiever date according to Cassie, and Eve had hoped that she and Shaye could talk seriously about their future tonight. Instead, she knew that she had to tell Shaye what she knew. Eve didn't know how Shaye would react to the revelations that surrounded an entire sequence of events built into Shaye's adult perceptions of the world. Events with regrets and blame. So much of both. Shaye had recklessly yelled "Gun!" at age five, Eve's brother had accidently shot Shaye's stepfather and changed Shaye's life, and that shooting had triggered the eventual loss of Eve's brother. Eve was filled with regret, but not blame. It was Shaye's reaction that worried her now.

Shaye had made progress in accepting her own childhood role, and she seemed to have made an exception for Eve in the image of the cops she so disliked, but Eve knew even that was fragile. Eve had worked so hard to prove to Shaye that she was a kind, dedicated police officer who performed her job to the best of her abilities and that she could be trusted to do everything in her power to offer Shaye the happiness that she'd craved her entire life. But Shaye had never forgiven the rookie cop who had pulled the trigger, and now Eve had to tell Shaye that it had been her brother. Eve just hoped Shaye would be willing to talk this revelation through with her. That Shaye would be able to put things in perspective.

Pull yourself together, Eve lectured herself. She knew how to handle tough situations, both professionally and in her personal life. Eve snorted as she listened for Shaye's arrival—maybe she owed Pauline a thank you for the maturity she'd gained due to her ex. She knew that working through a situation and her feelings were important, to not simply react, or worse, overreact. Eve was trying to apply those lessons to this situation.

Taking a few deep draws of air, Eve went to answer the door with McGruff at her heels. As she swung the door open, Eve took in Shaye, who looked beautiful and wore a smile that reached her eyes. She was holding a big bouquet of flowers. Shaye was the same gorgeous woman who had taken a seat next to her in that bar, but Eve knew so much more about her now. Eve felt so much more for her, and she wanted her in her life.

They ate some pizza in the kitchen while McGruff begged from the floor. Eve knew that Shaye was wondering what she had to tell her because all she'd been able to tell Shaye last evening was that Joye had made it clear that she'd had something important to say that involved both Eve and Earl.

They finished a vegetarian pizza dinner that Eve had ordered. Eve didn't feel up to engaging in their usual flirting and banter, although she tried to act normal. Then they'd ended up on the living room couch with McGruff settled at one end and Shaye settled a few feet from Eve, a questioning expression on her face.

"Okay, you're not acting your normal self. Tell me what's going on," Shaye said.

"Let me start by saying that what I'm going to tell you changes nothing for me, and I pray that the same holds for you. I know I've had several hours to work through it already, and you're going to need time too, but I hope you can."

Shaye nodded and waited for Eve to begin. It took a moment for Eve to gather herself and start. Shaye sat and listened, and her eyes grew wide while her breathing became louder and more rapid as Eve recounted what Joye had disclosed to her at the Daily Grind that morning. Eve had delivered bad news many times in her professional capacity, and she knew shock when she saw it.

This news seemed to hit Shaye like a Mack truck. Once Eve had disclosed the gist of what she knew, Shaye seemed to withdraw in thought. Eve sat and waited a bit. She wanted to offer Shaye time to digest the information. Information that had upset Eve, but hadn't overshadowed her entire life the way it had overshadowed Shaye's.

❖

*The lights in the convenience store were bright on that rainy day. She'd come in with her dad so he could pay for the gas he'd just put in the car. He'd told her she could pick out a candy, and she had chosen a bag of M&M's. She was just bringing it over to him when a man in a black mask appeared out of nowhere. He was shorter than her dad and all she could see were his eyes before he walked past her and faced the old man at the cash register. She could see the alarm in both her dad's and the old man's faces. Then a policeman came through the door with a gun drawn and she knew that was scary, so she yelled "Gun!" to warn her dad. She heard the loud bang, and then a circle of crimson started leaking onto her dad's shirt before he dropped to his knees and then lay down on the ground. She'd tried to wake him up, but even all the sirens didn't do that. She remembered her mom coming inside from the car and crying. Repeating "David" softly, over and over. She remembered standing there with her bag of M&M's. They never paid for them.*

"Shaye, babe. Are you okay?" Eve reached over to pull her into an embrace.

"I was just having a flashback." Shaye leaned away and held up both hands in a gesture meant to ward Eve off.

"I know you need time to take this in."

Eve had just said *time*. That was how her life worked—*time* doing that in-an-instant body slam that changed everything. Shaye was numb, but maybe that was better than feeling too much. Her sudden new reality was that Eve's brother had been the rookie cop who had killed the only man she remembered ever calling *Dad*. It had completely changed her life. It had changed her mom's life. Shaye didn't know how to handle that.

"I've been thinking about this all afternoon," Eve said. "I decided regrets are normal. Part of the present that might help me move forward. I'm sorry for all the bad things that happened—regrets. But blame serves no purpose because it can't change the past and will only hurt the future."

Shaye didn't know what to say. She didn't have anything to say. She needed to digest what Eve had told her, to sort it out. She needed to figure out what it meant to her and to Eve—to the two of them.

"I need to go." Shaye stood.

"Are you sure you don't want to stay for a little while? We can talk."

"What can you say that can fix this?" Shaye asked.

Eve looked at Shaye. It was a look Shaye hadn't seen before. And Eve's words were ones Shaye hadn't heard from Eve before. "That I love you."

Shaye nodded, then stood and stumbled out the front door without looking back. At least she felt like she was stumbling. That was before she felt like she was falling into a deep hole that contained more conflicting emotion than she could process right now.

# CHAPTER TWENTY

Shaye didn't want to go to her mom's house. She wanted to be alone, not deal with her mother or Cassie tonight. Sometimes she did her best thinking while driving, so she stopped and filled up her car and headed toward the coast.

As she drove, she tried to sort out the chaotic thoughts that raced through her head. Her common sense had warned her not to get involved with Eve because cops had only brought grief to her life. Eve's brother, now that she knew he was the negligent rookie, and Shaye's ex-wife, Cynthia, had turned her life upside down. They'd cut her deeply, carving away pieces of her heart. She'd finally started to heal. She'd finally forgiven her five-year-old self for what had happened, but she hadn't forgiven the carelessness of the cop. And Cynthia had been a lesson in marrying the wrong woman—a cop who had been far less committed to making their marriage work than Shaye had been.

Then there was Eve, who had made her realize that choosing to dislike all police had been a simplistic cop-out. Shaye chuckled as she wiped her eyes, focusing on the term...*cop-out.* She could just refuse to deal with this current revelation, but that would solve nothing, and she'd spent decades not addressing her past. That had left her miserable. She'd come home to Paradise Pines to face her past. Why? Because she'd wanted more in her life. And Eve had offered her that.

So, Shaye didn't want to cop out and just walk away from facing this new revelation about who had been involved thirty-five years ago. Not after the personal progress she'd made. But how was she supposed to process this? She was stunned by this information, this cruel joke that struck her like a physical blow. She needed to let her emotions settle and then carefully think this through in a logical manner. She didn't want to let her emotions run her life—she'd done enough of that.

But then there was the other revelation that had come out of Eve's mouth tonight with undeniable sincerity—maybe even the bigger divulgence, but she hadn't fully processed it yet in light of Joye's news. Shaye could try to walk away as if it was nothing, but even logic told her that Eve's love was not nothing. It was huge. *Eve loved her.* Eve's love…Shaye felt like she was being offered the plug that filled the hole that losing David and Cynthia had left. Was she going to accept it, or just walk away and bleed out? And what about her loving Eve? It would be so easy, and yet so hard if she couldn't sort this out. What if she went all in and then Eve pulled the plug? Shaye needed to remember that love had led to all her past pain in the first place, all of it caused by cops. There was so much in the way of sorting and defining this. She needed to do it logically.

After a bit of further analysis, Shaye decided that she actually had two options. One, don't deal with tonight's revelations. Or two, deal with them. She thought about two immediate actions she could at least take tonight that represented those two options. She could get drunk, or she could call Annie.

As Shaye drove down the road and neared the coast, she saw a neon sign with a flashing red arrow pointing at a bar. Did she want her relationship with Eve to end in the same type of setting where it had begun…in a bar, but all alone tonight? The answer played out from Shaye's unsettled gut and extended right down her leg and into her right foot—she kept that foot on the accelerator.

She found a motel and checked in. She had a clean T-shirt and pair of shorts that she carried in her car, and the hotel clerk gave her a toothbrush. Once she unlocked the hotel room door, she headed to the bed and threw herself down on her back. She stared at the ceiling before she closed her eyes and took a few deep breaths. At least she wasn't sitting alone throwing down drinks. She considered what she would be drinking, and that brought her to the only drink she wanted—an old-fashioned. And of course, that led to images of Eve—the only one who Shaye wanted to be sharing that drink with. Fuck.

Shaye dug her phone out of her purse and dialed.

"If it isn't Shaye *Humdrum*." Annie's voice was warm and teasing.

"Humdrum?"

"Your life must be pretty boring if you're calling me on a Saturday night instead of doing something infinitely more exciting."

"I think I could use a little boring right now." Shaye could hear the stress in her own voice. "There's a reason for the call."

"Okay, honey. What's going on?"

Shaye proceeded to tell Annie all that had transpired during her encounter with Eve this evening. She did her best not to choke up.

"So, your aging mom might have been a factor, but I know the main reason you went home to Paradise Pines was so you could put what happened to your dad in perspective," Annie said. "Part of that was getting a better picture of what happened, then and after. Your mother made it clear that she's had a good life. You only know that because you talked to her, right?"

Shaye thought about how that conversation with her mom had contrasted with her assumptions that she'd ruined her mom's life. "Yeah, right. I'll agree with you."

"Talking...helpful. But you said you didn't stay to talk to Eve."

"I was numb. I didn't know what to say. I need to think," Shaye replied.

"Fair enough. You've been through a lot since you returned to Paradise Pines. The arson at your house and your car. The attack. The suspicion that Andy might be the arsonist. That Pauline might be involved. Those effects on your mom."

"Thanks for reminding me of all my misery." Shaye had been sitting on the edge of the bed and she fell backward onto the mattress, staring at the old grayish popcorn ceiling once again. "I'm guessing you have a reason for bringing all that up."

"Besides tormenting you?" Annie chuckled. "In fact, I do have a purpose."

"And?" Shaye asked.

"Who was there through all that for you? Helping you. Supporting you. Caring about you."

Shaye closed her eyes. The answer wasn't as painful as she would have guessed it would be after learning what Eve's brother had done. "Eve," she whispered.

"Who not only lost her parents at a young age but then lost her brother on top of that horrific event because of the fallout from the incident that took your dad?"

"Eve," Shaye whispered again.

"And who isn't blaming you?"

"You know the answer," Shaye replied.

"And who has concluded that she loves you, in the face of everything that's happened to her too?"

"Eve." Shaye thought again about the fact that Eve had been willing to tell her that she loved her. It mattered that she had, but that revelation was still currently all mixed up with everything else she was facing tonight.

"So, my advice is that you have some figuring out to do. You owe her a conversation. But before you figure out what you're going to say, you need to start figuring out how you feel about her—even if you don't want to label it love, do you want to pursue a future? From what you've told me, you still have one more date before you decide if you want to discuss where you two stand with regard to considering the future—since I don't think you can count tonight as date number eight."

Shaye pursed her lips. She knew she had deep feelings for Eve, but she was so shaken right now, she wasn't ready to label it. Feelings had only left gaping holes in her heart in the past. And after Cynthia, she'd promised herself she'd take this one step at a time. Besides, there was still the election, and if Pauline won, Eve would undoubtedly lose her job and need to move on. She'd be gone and Shaye would be left with the aftermath. "Thanks, Annie. You've given me a lot to think about. I'll make sure I talk to her when I've done some thinking. When I'm ready."

"And, Shaye, regrets are normal, everyone has them. They're part of the present as you reflect back before moving forward. But blame is different—it can't change the past, and it will only get in the way of your future."

"Have you been talking to Eve?" Shaye couldn't help but chuckle as Annie echoed Eve's earlier words.

"Nope. But if two of us are saying it, it must be true."

"I could probably find two people who would say almost anything," Shaye replied.

"But they wouldn't be two people who love you, Shaye."

❖

It was supposed to have been their eighth date that night a week ago when Eve had been left alone with McGruff after Shaye had walked out the door without talking to her about Joye's disclosure. She'd had visions of ending that date on Sunday morning with a plan for proceeding into the future after a long night of lovemaking. Maybe it would have been a plan that incorporated additional dates if that's what Shaye had wanted, but Eve was open to a plan for more than that. Now, she didn't even know if there would be more dates.

Her chest squeezed tight with ache. Shaye was still working through the pain of her past, and Joye's revelation had probably ripped the scab right off her healing. Eve understood that, but if Shaye couldn't have a serious talk about what Joye had uncovered, they didn't stand a chance. Eve knew that Shaye was dealing with her past, her present, and her future. But so was she. She also knew that Shaye needed to come to her...if she was going to.

She hadn't planned on telling Shaye that she loved her until she was certain Shaye was ready to hear it. But everything had gone to hell with last Saturday's revelations, and she'd wanted Shaye to weigh that in when she reacted to Joye's news.

Now it was seven long days later, and Eve's declaration of love hadn't seemed to make any difference. She'd received a text from Shaye on Sunday evening, the day after Shaye had left, simply saying she was okay but needed time alone, to figure some things out. The only thing that had given Eve any hope was that there was a heart emoji at the end of the text. That had to mean something, didn't it? She knew through her contacts that Shaye had called in and missed work on Monday and Tuesday. She'd been back in town the rest of the week but had spent her time at the library trailer, not coming anywhere near her office at the police station.

Eve had fluctuated between ups and downs, hope and despair, resignation and anger, patience and exasperation, love-filled longing and wanting to wring Shaye's neck. She was wallowing in despair and anger, most of it directed at herself. She knew Shaye wasn't Pauline in terms of cheating, but Eve had still let Shaye into her personal life against every admonition she'd given herself. Shaye had slowly crept into her heart. This deep ache was probably what she deserved for letting her guard down. But dammit, how did you tell your heart who to love?

There were so many questions and no answers. Eve finally settled in and tried to watch a movie followed by an unproductive effort to read before giving up and deciding to turn in. A night without much sleep was probably still going to be the outcome. The reality of what had happened thirty-five years ago was devastating, but that Shaye had left without saying anything after Eve had told her that she loved her hurt even more. At the same time, Shaye hadn't rejected her love, at least not yet. She'd said she needed time to sort things out. But the longer Shaye was silent, the more Eve worried about the outcome.

Eve went to bed and finally dozed off at about five o'clock in the morning. The room resonated with old dog snoring when her phone rang. Eve saw that it was seven a.m. She grabbed the cell off the night table next to her bed, and then struggled to wake up as she looked at the caller ID and took the call.

"Hi, Grady. What do you need at this hour on a Sunday morning?" Eve ran her hand through her hair. She was sleep-deprived and cranky. Two hours of sleep wasn't enough. Especially after a long week of very poor sleep.

"Uh, sorry, Chief. It's about Andy Bromwell. Sheriff Greene had him picked up late last night. Greene had his team execute a search warrant—Bromwell's garage at the house he rents. I heard the tip came from the landlord. He had Bromwell's permission to do some work in the garage and saw some suspicious materials, arson related. Greene's team found a can of gasoline, which isn't unusual, but also incendiary devices matching Hooper's findings at the arson sites. Bromwell wasn't there, but they tracked him down and picked him up at a buddy's house. Between his receipt being found at the mayor's arson and now this, there are felony charges being brought."

Eve was fully alert now. Her first thought was of Shaye and how this was going to add to her distress. She assumed Shaye was staying at Ginny's and also assumed that she had no idea about this.

Grady continued. "Greene's running the show, like you want, but thought you might like to drive over to the county sheriff's office and observe the questioning of Bromwell. You can watch from outside the room and you don't have to offer input."

"I'll be there as soon as I get dressed and drive over. Thirty minutes or so."

"I'll tell Greene, and we'll see you in a little while, then."

Calling Shaye crossed Eve's mind, but this wasn't Eve's show and she didn't have that right. Plus, maybe Shaye wouldn't want to hear from her, even about this. She decided to go do the observation and then figure things out after she'd talked with Greene. This was his show and she respected that. Shaye would hear soon enough with or without Eve's heads-up, but maybe she'd be able to answer Shaye's questions—if Shaye wanted to speak to her.

Eve sucked in a deep breath and crawled out of bed. She'd taken a shower last night, so she pulled on some clothes and fed McGruff in less than ten minutes. She paused in the living room as she passed the coffee table where she'd placed the vase with the bouquet that Shaye had brought a week ago. The flowers were still beautiful, like Shaye. Her heart lunged into her throat as she headed out through the front door.

# CHAPTER TWENTY-ONE

Shaye jogged down the street and past the coffee shop where she and Eve had purchased coffees in the past, had sat on the bench across the street, and had savored each other's company in the early morning ambiance. She knew she'd hurt Eve this past week, but she'd needed time to consider what she wanted with Eve. How she felt. She hadn't taken Eve's statement of love lightly. She hadn't called what was growing in her own heart love yet, maybe because she needed to be cautious after all she'd experienced, but she'd gone to Eve's for date number eight with flowers a week ago because she'd believed that she wanted a future with Eve.

Then Joye's revelation had hit her as hard as any physical blow. It had left her stunned. Shaye had walked out because she knew that in the long term, the wrong premature response could only hurt both of them more, and she didn't want to do that.

In the days since, she'd needed to maintain space between herself and Eve because physical space was the only way she could gain the distance to allow a logical perspective on the situation she now found herself in. Eve's brother, a man Eve must have loved, had ended the life of the dad she'd loved and had caused her profound pain for so many years.

She had let her emotions run and ruin so much of her life. She wouldn't let feelings dictate her future again because those had eventually resulted in debilitating pain. She needed to use her head to figure this out—and rational analysis first left her wondering how she'd arrived here. After all the admonishments generated by her history with cops, how the fuck had she allowed herself to become involved with another cop when cops had only caused devastation in her life?

As her feet pounded the pavement, Andy crossed her mind. His buddy had called late last night with the news of the search, the arrest with the cops hauling him off, his denials to the officers. Shaye picked up speed, hoping the early dawn run would dissipate the stresses tethered to her life right now. Her heavy sighs weren't just from the exertion of the exercise. She headed back to her mother's house to try to offer her mom some comfort regarding Andy. Shaye could only address one fire at a time.

Forty minutes later, she was sitting across the kitchen table from her mom and Cassie. She'd shared Joye's investigation findings with her mother when she'd come back to town on Tuesday afternoon, having given herself a few days on the coast earlier in the week to just walk the beach and think. Her mom had been rattled too with the news about David, but Shaye had thought she'd accepted the information with more grace than Shaye had.

Her mom had told her, "That young rookie had to be somebody, and it's no surprise he was somebody's brother. That he was Eve's brother, well, she essentially lost him too that day. I know you need to work through this on your own, though." Then she had let it rest, and they hadn't had time to sit together until this morning.

"Uncle Andy's in deep shit," Cassie declared, leaning back in her chair and crossing her arms over her chest.

Shaye wasn't going to challenge her language because Cassie was just venting, and chewing her out certainly wasn't a way to connect with her right now. They all needed to support each other. She'd watched Eve manage a similar situation when she was trying to reconnect with Cassie—choose your battles had been the lesson Shaye had learned, and there were plenty of battles, and probably lessons to learn too. Besides, Shaye agreed with Cassie's assessment. She decided that she didn't know what to say to comfort them, so they discussed what they could do to help Andy to at least fight the charges if he really wasn't the arsonist.

"Can we get him a lawyer?" Cassie asked.

"Brent Baily represented him after they found Andy's receipt at the mayor's yard fire," Shaye replied. "I'll call him. We can't expect Brent to do this pro bono again. This is big."

"I've got the money," her mom said. "Life insurance from Joe. He took out a policy about a year before his heart attack. He made sure I was well set if something happened to him."

"Brent gave me his cell number and told me to call anytime, so I'll try to catch up with him," Shaye said.

"And Eve," Cassie persisted. "I don't know what's going on,

but you didn't go on any dates this week. You didn't talk about her or McGruff. You look sad. As your karaoke partner and girlfriend advisor, I know things." Cassie formed a heart with her two index fingers and thumbs.

Shaye gazed at Cassie. This kid had no idea how complicated life could get. She was only eleven years old, for crying out loud.

Cassie gazed right back. "You're thinking I'm not old enough to offer you advice. You forget I've lived through all my mom's girlfriends…well, maybe not all. But more than I want to remember. Eve is the winner. Your BAE," Cassie said. Shaye and Ginny gave her a questioning look. "Before anyone else. Don't let her go." Cassie rolled her eyes. "And my girlfriend advice…I'm offering it pro bono."

Shaye watched her mother's lips twitch upward. They were both distracted for a moment from worries of Andy by Cassie's antics, then Cassie continued. "So have you seen her at all this week?"

Shaye glanced from her mother to Cassie and then gave her mom a slight frown. Cassie might be her self-appointed girlfriend advisor, but she was way too young to land in the middle of this. Without answering Cassie, Shaye shook her head to let her mom know that she hadn't.

"I think it's time for you to go focus on Eve." Cassie persisted.

"I agree. It's been a week. Take the afternoon and go talk to her," her mom said. "You don't want to be sorry later that you didn't at least talk, Shaye."

"Yup. And guess what?" Cassie sighed. "If my mom's taught me anything, it's you can't be happy if you don't really care about other people, although she still thinks she can be. She's kinda doing life badly. You've got to decide, Aunt Shanelle. Even I'm smart enough to know that you only have two choices about Eve."

"Yeah, and what are they?" Shaye asked, wondering if there actually could be some positive aspects to come from Pauline's bad behavior, channeled through Cassie. "Let me guess. Eve in my life. Or not." It was one thing to be getting romance advice from her own mother, but from an eleven-year-old too…although a pretty smart one.

"No. You won't admit it yet, but I think you already know that answer, unless you totally blow it." Mirth filled Cassie's eyes. "I was thinking you're going to have to choose if you want the right side of the bed or the left."

"And I think I'm done taking advice from someone barely more than a quarter of my age. I'm out of here."

"Say hi to Eve for me…and the socket dog too." Cassie's laughter followed Shaye out the door.

❖

Shaye was sitting on Eve's front porch when the Jeep pulled into the driveway late Sunday afternoon. Shaye's heart leapt into her throat as she ran her hands over the tops of her thighs and nervously smoothed her pants legs. As she'd been waiting, she'd reminded herself how she'd felt about cops, and for good reason. She'd spent decades loathing the cop who'd ended her dad's life, and she'd lived for three years with the pain of a broken marriage. Who could possibly consider becoming involved with a cop after they'd been through the things that she'd been through?

It would be so much easier if Shaye could just carry all those negative feelings and her anger over to this situation, to let those things rain down on Eve Maguire, chief of police and sister to that reckless rookie who had carved a hole in her heart and riddled all those years of her life with guilt. Eve Maguire was a cop like her former wife. Cynthia's emotional investment had been minimal, and the failed attempt at marriage certainly hadn't bruised Cynthia the way it had hurt Shaye.

If Shaye could just make herself reduce Eve down to this connection that she was to Shaye's pain, there would be no need to even confront the question of whether she could have a future with Eve.

Yet there she was, sitting on Eve's porch, waiting because Shaye had told herself she was an honorable person and she needed to at least talk to Eve. Hell, they'd shared a bed. It had been fabulous sex, but she didn't want to think about that. Plus, she needed to set a good example for Cassie and demonstrate that you didn't just walk away from someone without talking—when you could logically see that things couldn't possibly work. Especially with this new revelation. Because when Shaye had laid out all the facts, when she took emotions out of the mix because feelings had only hurt her, she'd reached that conclusion. She'd even take the blame.

Shaye watched Eve through the Jeep's driver's side window as Eve surveyed her Outback out on the street. Then she noted the moment that Eve saw her waiting, an unrepressed grin flashed for a second across Eve's face before Eve sobered into a neutral expression as she made an unmistakable effort to mask her feelings. Shaye felt the impact of relief surge through her body at Eve's first unguarded positive reaction, although hostility might be a whole lot easier to simply walk away from.

As Eve's eyes locked with hers, Shaye knew that Eve was as vulnerable as she was. But worse, it wasn't all the turmoil that she'd been through over the past week that overtook her, or all the logic and rationale she'd so carefully considered and insulated herself with—the reasons why this wouldn't work. It was the feelings she had for Eve that slammed into her, uprooting her resolve and bowling her over—the feelings that had been sparked in that bar when they'd initially met, flared as Shaye had chastely shared this house with her, and blazed as they grew to know each other, emotionally and physically.

Without the space of their physical distance, a separation that had allowed Shaye to stuff a caricature of Eve into a box where she'd convinced herself that Eve was somehow too closely affiliated with the pain of her past, this in-the-flesh woman in front of Shaye—the one who smelled like Eve, sounded like Eve, exuded the essence of Eve, touched her heart like Eve—hit her like a defibrillator in a cardiac shock sort of way. Hit her with a stunning wake-up slap.

Shaye realized that she owed herself and Eve a talk based on those feelings and not based on all the reasons she'd decided that the two of them wouldn't work. Those reasons they wouldn't work were grounded in events that had occurred prior to Eve—she'd be letting herself be ruled by her past mistakes, the ones that had made her miserable and driven her to Paradise Pines in an effort to move on. Was she to live her life only attuned to negative feelings and not to the positive ones begging for a chance? Had she learned nothing about change?

Shaye gulped and took in the beautiful Eve Maguire standing there waiting. She didn't know if they could make it work after all the history heaped on them, but she knew that Eve's love was something real and amazing, and that she needed to let her feelings play a significant role in her side of this conversation. She needed to listen to her heart.

Shaye stood up from the porch step she'd been sitting on and closed her eyes a moment. She needed to let this conversation run its natural course, wherever that took them.

"Hi. Did you come to see me...or McGruff?" Eve asked, her tone infused with that same vulnerability Shaye had seen in her eyes a moment ago. "Or is this about Andy? That's where I just came from—the county sheriff's office."

"I'm sorry...I wasn't ready." Shaye felt a strong need to clarify her silence. "But you're right—we need to talk."

Eve gave her a solemn, prolonged look, and Shaye couldn't read what she was thinking. Well, Shaye was there to find out. Eve walked past Shaye and opened the door. McGruff greeted them, sitting down and giving Shaye what felt like a welcome-back-to-the-pack wolf howl. He was certainly making a case for feelings over logic.

Eve didn't restrain a flicker of upturned lips. She nodded toward a chair and Shaye sat down, then she took a seat on the couch with McGruff, several feet across the room. Shaye recalled all the times the three of them had shared that couch. The good times. The great times.

"Let's start with Andy." Eve was obviously not going for the topic more fraught with potential pain than Andy's circumstances.

Life truly was a mess if her stepbrother's arrest for multiple incidents of felony arson wasn't the main topic of angst, but Shaye conceded to herself that was the easier opener.

"Is he doing okay?" Shaye asked. "Andy's buddy called Mom. He told us they picked up Andy after searching his garage and finding gasoline and incendiary devices. I don't know what you know about what's going on."

Eve projected her professional chief demeanor now. Shaye didn't like it, but she accepted it. Eve was in a difficult professional position in addition to their personal issues. She'd take what Eve was comfortable imparting.

"I just came from the interrogation and Greene," Eve replied. "I can tell you that Andy didn't confess to knowing how those things had ended up in his garage, much less to the arsons. That was no surprise considering his stance the last time he was questioned about his receipt being found at the scene of the mayor's fire. He claimed again that he isn't the arsonist."

"Does he need a lawyer?" Shaye asked.

"Andy didn't want an attorney, even after he'd been read his rights...claimed he didn't need one. He said he had no clue how those items came to be in his garage—that the lock to the side garage door had been broken since he'd moved in, and the landlord had been there to fix it when he discovered the items. Andy told the interrogator that was all he was going to say."

"Brent Bailey legally represented him earlier. I've already talked with Mom, and I can get back in touch with him."

"I probably won't get any colleague points for addressing your question directly, but hypothetically, if I had a family member in this situation, even if they wanted to go it alone, an attorney would be my recommendation," Eve said. "I think someone in Andy's situation would likely benefit from legal representation moving forward."

Shaye noted the moisture in Eve's eyes as she looked into them and felt the brimming of her own. She knew the liquid was about so much more than just Andy. Shaye had missed looking into those hazel eyes. She was so grateful they weren't hostile. "Thanks. I'll call Brent."

"Just the end to a godawful week, huh?" Eve's smile was crooked. "As you heard, McGruff misses you."

"Now there's an endorsement—the ugliest dog in town misses me." Shaye made an effort to offer Eve a smile as well. "I missed him too." She still wasn't sure where they were headed. After sucking in a lungful of air, she exhaled slowly. She was navigating unfamiliar territory, uncertain where she was going, unclear where Eve was headed. She hoped her smile conveyed the message without actually saying that she'd missed Eve even more than the mutt.

"Did you miss anyone else?" Eve sounded so hesitant. So sad.

"Well, I haven't run into anyone as entertaining as Earl this past week." Shaye just wanted to lighten the mood. They could have this discussion, but she wanted it to carry the connection, the chemistry they shared—if she was going to make a decision based on how she felt and not on all that history that weighed them down.

"Earl? If you want entertaining, then you should spend time with his big sister," Eve replied.

"Yes, I've heard that she's rather entertaining too. In a different way than Earl."

"Care to elaborate?" A touch of teasing came through in Eve's tone.

Shaye didn't want to read too much into it. From that first night in the bar, their conversations had always felt so easy—until Joye's revelation. Until she'd gone silent. Shaye looked around the living room, then stepped back and gave Eve a thorough and exaggerated up-and-down inspection.

"Hmm. Too much elaboration on some of her entertaining skills and they might arrest her." Shaye pictured some of their closest encounters—intertwined and intimate—and she knew that Eve was thinking the same thoughts.

Shaye watched that endearing shade of pink rise in Eve's face. She gave Eve an eyebrow wiggle that she suspected went right to

Eve's center, as intended. She wanted the flirty, sexy Eve back. Shaye laughed at Eve's blushing. She'd love to kiss those pink cheeks…and those pink lips.

"Glad I'm able to cheer you up," Eve grumbled.

"Me too."

Eve grew serious. "The words *flirt* and *chemistry* come to mind. I've learned they're essential measures for ratings on the *entertaining* scale for me, but there needs to be more in a relationship if it's going to work. Stability, honesty, and loyalty. Trust. And communication."

Shaye nodded, but said nothing. Eve hadn't mentioned love. She'd gone silent on Eve for seven days. Did Eve still love her? She owed Eve the chance to say whatever she needed to say. Then she owed her a response.

"And essential…love." Eve didn't say if she still loved Shaye. "I loved and lost my parents. I loved and lost Mike. The magnitude of the sorrow and grief I felt was overwhelming for a while. I know that what happened with your dad caused Mike so much grief because while I didn't know what had happened, I saw him change, and that hurt me too. I believe the sorrow of what he'd done made Mike reckless—he couldn't forgive himself. But you can't blame yourself, Shaye. You were a kid with a natural response to seeing a drawn weapon. I certainly don't blame you. There was so much pain on both sides from the event, but I don't think letting it define the future is the answer."

Shaye nodded again but wanted Eve to finish.

"In forty-seven years, I've learned there will always be things that bring sorrow, but I've also learned that how I handle it matters. After Pauline, I spent a year shutting my personal life down. Maybe I needed it for healing, but not forever. Giving up on love won't fix any of the sorrow I've seen in my life." Eve stopped there and waited for Shaye's response before deciding to say one more thing. "And then I met a woman in a bar who stole my officers' office. And my heart. I wouldn't lie about loving you, Shaye. You've been through so much pain, more than I have, and I know Mike's role in your father's death is shocking. It is for me too. You don't have to say that you love me back, but you need to tell me if you think we have a chance at a future."

That Eve still wanted her—Shaye felt a sweeping swell of relief. Maybe all the meticulous analysis had been to protect herself in case Eve had wanted to abandon any effort at a future. Shaye didn't want to walk away from this in-the-flesh essence of Eve that overtook her whenever she was in Eve's presence—she wanted them to try for a future. But could she forgive Eve's brother for what he'd done? That was a question she'd been considering for a week, but now Shaye realized that wasn't the question she needed to be asking right now. The important question was about Eve. Could she forgive Eve? For what? Loving her brother?

As Shaye analyzed the situation again, she gave Eve the answers. "I don't know if I can forgive your brother. It's taken me thirty-five years to forgive myself. But I can't blame you. Not for his actions. Not for loving him. I'm not going to define what I'm feeling right now—the past week has been emotionally chaotic. But that man who was my dad, he wouldn't have wanted us to give up on seeing if this can work because of what happened. I suspect your brother wouldn't either. So yes. If you're telling me that you have a desire for date number eight, and more, with the bar woman who stole your police station office, then I'm telling you that I do too." Shaye knew this was the right course of action, listening to her heart.

"We can take this at your pace," Eve said. "Exactly eight dates came as a number from an eleven-year-old."

"Maybe only age eleven, but with the title of girlfriend advisor."

As Eve chuckled, McGruff stood. He gave her a long look before sighing and turning around a few times, finally settling back down with a low growl. "The bored dog says listen to your heart."

"I think the bored dog says listen to your stomach."

"You just might be right," Eve replied. "But more important, I think you're the only one who can know what's right for you."

"I know I've lived at your house before, but that was different. I don't want to rush this…and that's not about you. It's about me. I want this to work, but if it doesn't, neither of us needs more pain in our lives. I need to take this at my pace, not based on a calendar—only on my heart." Shaye felt her heart hammering in her chest as she waited for Eve's response.

"I'm okay with that. We have to work through the past, face the future—the election's not that far off—so let's take the present and enjoy it one day at a time for now."

Shaye walked over to Eve and held out her hand. "I want a redo, another official date number eight. Something special, definitely romantic. I want to tell you how beautiful you look wearing your fancy clothes, and then I want you to tell me that I ought to see you without a single stitch on."

Eve took her hand and stood. She leaned in, capturing Shaye's lips with her own, then moved from her lips to Shaye's throat, to her jaw, and then up to her ear. "Not official, then, but I think we need to practice the *without a single stitch on.*"

# CHAPTER TWENTY-TWO

The server collected their empty chicken curry, egg noodle, and mango salad plates before returning with a single bowl of green tea ice cream and two spoons. He was the same young waiter who had served Eve on her prior two dates at Thai Tanic. He'd recognized Eve and offered her an enthusiastic welcome, undoubtedly remembering that she'd rectified the tip that Audrey hadn't left by leaving a lavish one that first time she'd brought Shaye there.

"Perfect finish for a perfect dinner," Eve said.

"Maybe perfect for the dinner, but I've got other things in mind for the perfect finish for our date number eight." Shaye winked at Eve. That sexy wink that registered right where Shaye had aimed it.

They were sitting there on a dinner date after a good week that had followed their talk. They'd spent last Sunday night together in Eve's bed—making tender love, then passionate love, then falling asleep in each other's arms. Nobody had seemed to notice that they'd both been late to work on Monday morning, or at least everyone was smart enough not to comment. Now Eve was looking forward to another night with Shaye, but with the added bonus of a leisurely Sunday morning tomorrow.

During the past days, Shaye had spent time in her office and McGruff had worn a path parading up and down the hallway. They'd had dinner at Shaye's mother's house on Wednesday night, and Eve could only laugh at Cassie's enthusiasm during the entire meal. Cassie had been no good at playing it subtle. Eve had whispered to Shaye in the kitchen while they'd been cleaning up that maybe they ought to change her title from girlfriend advisor to cheerleader.

Eve was relieved and thrilled that they seemed to have worked through what had happened thirty-five years ago, now that the shock had worn off. She was comfortable that Shaye did not blame her and had even made peace with the fact that Eve had loved her brother. The obvious biggest current stress for Shaye, and therefore for Eve as well, was Andy's situation, and yet there was nothing either of them could do about it now that Shaye had made sure that Andy had legal representation.

Shaye interrupted Eve's thoughts. "I think this place is becoming *our* restaurant."

"I like this restaurant. Led to a few revelations on both our parts," Eve said. "And here we are, still afloat."

Eve picked up the two spoons, handed one to Shaye, and scooped up a bite of the ice cream with her own. "Eat up, babe. We've got important things waiting at home."

"You better not be referring to McGruff." Shaye gave her a warning look, not that it wasn't clearly full of humor and anticipation.

Eve took another bite and then placed her hand on her chin in fake contemplation as she watched Shaye. "You have something against my dog?"

"Nope. I totally appreciate his candor. Now, his good looks— extremely questionable. But it's your good looks I have in mind for tonight." Shaye grinned at her and Eve's pulse picked up. She loved their flirting. Their chemistry. She loved Shaye and she needed this to work.

After they finished their last bites of dessert, Eve flagged the server for the bill, paid up, including another generous tip, and they headed to the car. They chatted awhile as Shaye drove, then Eve turned on the radio, wanting to hear Shaye sing along. She possessed several talents that connected with Eve—directly with her heart and right down to her core.

There was nothing like a sexy serenade by your vocally gifted lover to jump-start the next phase of an evening. Even the welcome-home howl from McGruff landed perfectly. This was what Eve was willing to fight for because it was what had been missing from her life. From her entire life because nobody, including Pauline, had made her want to put her personal life before her professional life. Not the way Shaye did.

Eve headed to the kitchen and dumped her purse on the counter before feeding McGruff a treat. She'd just handed him the biscuit and had turned to face the sink to get a drink of water when Shaye came up from behind and placed her hands around Eve's waist, pulling Eve's backside flush with her own front. Eve pushed back against the warm body pressed against her as Shaye destroyed Eve's plan to have a slow romantic encounter in the bedroom, replacing that plan with an explosion of desire that she would be thrilled to have play out here in the kitchen—at least the first round.

"I didn't tell you yet tonight just how absolutely delicious you look in that dress," Eve managed to say as she tried to control her reaction to Shaye. Just keep breathing, she thought.

Shaye lifted Eve's long, loose hair out of the way before she kissed her way along Eve's shoulder and up the back of her neck. After she took her time peppering Eve with those kisses, Shaye slowly lowered Eve's zipper. "I was thinking more along the lines of how absolutely delicious you'll look *without* that dress on tonight."

Shaye managed to remove all Eve's clothing with caressing sweeps of her hands, Eve still sandwiched between Shaye and the counter. She leaned into Eve and pressed Eve's upper body forward until her elbows and forearms rested on the countertop. Eve moaned as Shaye brushed a hand up Eve's inner thigh to find the juncture where sensitive skin met the aching, clenching center of Eve's soaking essence. Pinned in with the pressure of Shaye's body from behind, Eve could only close her eyes and enjoy every sensation Shaye delivered.

Shaye might be a gifted vocalist, but that gift was nothing compared to the way she knew how to play Eve's body as if it was a solo string instrument and Shaye was the bow, rhythmically gliding and sliding at the perfect angle, the perfect pace, in strokes of genius deep into Eve's passage until Eve felt the high point coming on. It started as a low hum, then grew in magnitude as Shaye did not let up, fingers plunging into the depths of the bent-forward Eve. Shaye's thumb performed an exquisite accompaniment through the wet folds to finally reach that swollen spot that only required a minimal massage before the crescendo overtook Eve.

As Eve felt the waves of her peaked pleasure wash through her body, laboring her breathing and weakening her legs, she would have sworn that it was her heartstrings that Shaye had been stroking as well as the physical places that brought such exquisite release. Eve did not want to ever have to give Shaye up, and that thought scared the hell out of her because she knew at forty-seven that there were things in life she could not control.

When she'd recovered enough, Eve straightened and turned, then brought Shaye into her embrace. She'd loved the spontaneity and passion of never making it to the bedroom, of acting like two teenagers who couldn't even make it to a mattress. She felt vibrant and young, but with the maturity to know that she was feeling love with the lust. Eve leaned back to try to determine if Shaye wanted to remain in the kitchen or move to the bedroom because Eve had plans for her too. As Shaye offered an eyebrow dance and a deep kiss, conveying that round two in the kitchen was just fine with her, the phone rang in Eve's purse on the counter.

"Let's ignore it." Eve looked at the kitchen clock and noted it was after eleven. She'd check to see if there was a message before she went to sleep. The world could go on without her for the moment.

"Go ahead and take a peek. You don't have to accept the call, and if it's Earl, we'll whack him silly the next time we see him."

Eve laughed as she extracted the phone from her handbag and glanced at the screen. "It's Cassie." She could feel the internal shift from lighthearted to concern.

"Take it," Shaye said as Eve nodded and accepted the call, putting it on speaker phone.

"Cassie. What's wrong?"

Eve could barely hear Cassie's response as she spoke in a low whisper. "I'm sorry, Eve. I need your help."

"Where are you?" Eve asked as she suppressed the rush of panic that wanted to overtake her before she grabbed a pen and paper in case she needed them.

"Up Coyote Hill hiding behind the big rock."

"Are you alone?"

"I hope so."

Eve wondered what that meant but didn't want to waste time in reaching Cassie. "Are you safe to stay put?"

"I think so."

"Okay. It's going to take Shaye and me about fifteen minutes to get to you. Okay?"

"Okay." Cassie's whisper was barely audible as the call ended.

Shaye was already heading to the guest room to change clothes and Eve followed her down the hallway to throw on clothes of her own and to grab her radio and gun.

They jumped into the Jeep, and as Eve drove, she called Grady to have him meet them in the parking lot below Coyote Hill.

❖

Twelve minutes later, Grady pulled into the lot at the same time that Eve and Shaye arrived. It was adjacent to a large park area, and the hill was the backdrop behind the park. The lot was empty, and the pole lights offered a low glow to the front half of the park, where there were picnic tables as well as several trees and large bushes, but the rest of the landscape was only illuminated by moonlight. The three of them looked around and didn't see anyone else, so while Grady searched the park, Eve and Shaye headed up the hill.

Eve had a flashlight but was reticent to turn it on as long as she could make out where she was going with just the moon's glow. She didn't know what was out there, and she didn't want her flashlight making them an easy target. Shaye followed right behind her, and as they approached the rock, they both softly called out Cassie's name. Cassie stepped out and then ran to them. Eve and Shaye both threw their arms around her as she hugged them and sobbed with relief.

Eve spoke into her radio and brought Grady up to speed before they headed down the hill. At the bottom, they sat at a picnic table and Grady kept watch while Cassie updated them.

"Don't be mad. I know you told me not to go out at night, but with everything that's happening to Andy, and with Ginny so sad, I just came out to think."

"We're just glad you're okay," Eve said as Shaye agreed. "So, what happened that frightened you?"

"I was over there at that table behind that big bush when two men drove into the parking lot in two different cars. They came over and sat at this table and I stayed really quiet so they wouldn't see me. I thought maybe it was a drug deal, but it was one guy selling the other a gun." Cassie stopped and wiped her eyes with her sleeve. Eve and Shaye waited.

"I heard one of them tell the other that he'd gotten the gun money by being paid to set the arson fires. The other guy told him if he was caught, he'd be sent back to prison until he was so old he couldn't..." Cassie stopped and looked at Eve. "It had to do with his manhood and I ignored it, but I knew they were really bad guys. I took a picture of them with my phone. They were here at this table where they were getting a lot of light, so the pictures are okay." Cassie pointed at the parking lot light nearby. "I was afraid if they saw me leaving the park, they might suspect I heard them, so when they got in their cars, I snuck up the hill and called you."

"Great job, Cassie. Not that I'm not really upset with you for being out alone like this at night," Shaye said, giving Cassie another hug.

"Yeah, I know. I'm probably grounded for life. But at least I got the pictures." Cassie tapped on her phone screen and then looked at Eve. "I just sent them to your phone."

Eve took a look. "These are pretty decent shots, Cassie." She thought for a moment and then asked, "Where's Ginny tonight?"

"She had a headache and went to bed, and then I snuck out," Cassie replied. "I'm sorry. Ginny's probably asleep, and now this is going to worry her more...besides Andy."

"You're not off the hook," Shaye said. "But maybe you just helped get Andy off the hook."

"Well, that ought to be worth something." Cassie gave them a hopeful look.

"I'm going to call the county sheriff's office and ask them to have Jim Greene call me as soon as possible so I can update him and send him these pictures. I'll catch a ride with Grady. Shaye can use my Jeep and take you home, Cassie. Ginny has to be told. I'll catch up with you back at my house, Shaye, unless you need me at your mom's."

"Nope. I'll get Cassie in and settled, talk to Mom, and then meet you back at your place," Shaye replied as she took the Jeep keys from Eve.

"The sheriff might need to talk with you tomorrow, Cassie, so get some sleep," Eve said. As Cassie followed Shaye toward the Jeep, Eve added, "Nice job, kid. Even if you're in big trouble. I'm glad you're safe."

"Thanks, Eve. For keeping your word. You said you'd be here if I needed you, and you were."

"I didn't come just because it was part of my job," Eve told her. "I also came because it was you. So anytime you need me...anytime."

❖

It was almost noon on Sunday morning and Shaye was lying in Eve's arms. They hadn't fallen into bed until almost two a.m., both too exhausted to pick up where they'd left off before Cassie's call. Eve smiled. Well, they'd certainly picked things up that morning with Eve making sure Shaye didn't feel the least bit neglected. There might be clothes strewn all over the room, McGruff might be whining at them to get out of bed, and Eve might not have had a cup of coffee yet, but she was hopeful that they both felt satisfied...more than just physically satisfied, although that too.

"Jim Greene should be calling me with an update soon," Eve said. "The fact that he knows exactly who the guy is seemed to have him thinking they shouldn't have too much trouble picking him up."

"I'm anxious for Greene to call you too—to have him tell you that they've got the guy in custody," Shaye replied. "I want to be able to tell Mom that this ex-con named Billy Rachet confessed. To be able to tell her that Andy's been cleared. I can't do that until it's true."

Eve kissed Shaye on the forehead. "Number eight...a date for the scrapbook, wasn't it?"

"You mean the part where we ate egg noodles, or the part where we saved Cassie, or the part where you showed me just what an ace cop you are?" Shaye poked Eve gently in the ribs.

"Ace cop, huh?" Eve chuckled.

"That was this morning...you certainly know how to frisk a girl. Extremely thorough."

"I'm just glad you're finally discovering that there are some redeeming factors to hanging out with a cop." Eve gently poked Shaye back.

"Only hanging with one cop, Eve Maguire. C-o-p—chief of police. Hanging with this uniquely irresistible cop...and that's only because you've grown on me. Now, if you could find your way past that obnoxious deputy dog and bring me coffee in bed..."

Eve rolled out of bed and offered Shaye her most seductive sashay over to the back of her bedroom door where a lightweight robe hung on a hook. "At your service. Part of the job description. Only for you." She fluttered her eyelashes, grabbed her phone, and headed out the door toward the kitchen. She shook her head—she didn't remember ever fluttering her eyelashes. What was Shaye doing to her? The answer didn't escape Eve. Shaye made her feel complete. Like she'd found that piece of her life that had been missing. The piece that made this a home. Eve was happy, and she wanted this to be happy ever after—for both of them.

As Eve waited for the coffee to drip, her phone rang. It was the call she'd been waiting for.

"Hi, Jim. Do you have an update?"

"We picked Billy Rachet up a few hours ago. He knew that he was already in deep trouble, being a felon in possession of a gun. You probably remember, you were the one who originally arrested him for robbery several years ago. I think he figured we were going to get him with or without his cooperation," Greene said. "We promised to pass along the fact that he cooperated if he'd tell us about the arsons. In the end, he confessed to the arsons, writing the library note, and to Shaye's attack."

Greene went on to fill her in on additional details before finishing. "But the bigger news...who paid him."

Greene fell silent and Eve waited. "Was it Pauline Bromwell?" she finally asked.

Greene sighed and his tone held regret. "No Bromwell was involved."

That surprised Eve. "So what aren't you telling me?" She was getting a bad feeling.

"We need to dig deeper, which we're in the process of doing since this is unexpected, but Mayor Sneed is the person he named."

## CHAPTER TWENTY-THREE

Eve spent Sunday afternoon after Shaye's departure trying to make sense of things. She'd held herself together initially when she'd updated Shaye and seen her off, and now she fought to remain calm as she looked at the potential cascade of events Greene's revelation would trigger because she couldn't formulate a response or a plan until she'd done that.

The most obvious had been simmering since Pauline had entered the race, but the blow of undoubtedly losing her chief of police position now moved right into the realm of foreseeable reality if Sneed was guilty. Sneed would be out of the mayoral race, and Pauline was the inevitable shoo-in.

If Eve was not outright fired by Pauline, then her ex would undoubtedly enjoy making her job so onerous she would have little choice except to resign. Eve felt sick as she faced what had turned from conjecture to almost certain truth. A vise-grip headache tempted her to just crawl back into bed, but she fought that powerful urge because simply giving up would accomplish nothing.

The shroud of dread that enveloped her and threatened to physically shut her down was surprising though. It was surprising because while she'd hate to lose the position that she'd worked so hard to achieve and the job she loved, and while she'd hate to leave Paradise Pines to move God only knew how far away to find a similar position, it was the thought of leaving Shaye behind that almost broke her.

Shaye had moved to Paradise Pines for a job, but she'd chosen this town because she needed to make peace with her past. She'd also wanted to help her mother as she aged. There was no way Eve could just expect Shaye to follow her somewhere else, especially considering that Ginny would need Shaye more as time passed. But the inevitable shift in her own future, and the consequences, only solidified for Eve how much she loved Shaye, how much she wanted—no, needed—Shaye in her future. After all they'd been through in their pasts, all the challenges they'd overcome, hadn't they both concluded that they wanted a chance at a future together?

Eve sat on the couch and bawled her eyes out, McGruff at a total loss as to how to comfort her. He looked at her with his sympathetic, soulful eyes and leaned into her, offering her his quiet canine comfort. He wasn't just a couch potato, he was a couch consoler.

When she'd given herself adequate time to blubber, Eve decided it was time to take some action. She'd never been a blubberer in her life, and it rather shocked her. She'd cried as a child when she'd lost her parents, as a teenager when she'd lost her brother, as an adult when she'd lost Uncle Glen, and even a few tears for the loss of what she'd hoped for with Pauline. But this felt different. Like there would be no getting over this loss. Was that what deeply loving someone, body and soul, as part of yourself, did to you? Well, if she was going to hang on to that kind of love, she needed to wipe her face and figure some things out.

Eve took two Advil, loaded McGruff into her Jeep, and headed to her office. She decided to begin by digging deeper into Greg Sneed and the fires, starting with the library fire. She'd done some previous significant digging into the destroyed library, but never in a million years would she have focused on trying to uncover some remote link between Sneed and the arsons.

She already knew from her initial investigation right after that first fire that the burnt library building had a ninety-nine-year lease agreement with the city at a very low rate, and there were still decades left on the lease. The owner was a ninety-three-year-old woman currently in elder care in Ohio. Lydia James was the sole beneficiary of the insurance payout, and nothing had seemed amiss. She'd left Paradise Pines forty-five years ago and had no obvious connections remaining—Eve had explored it and made no headway before. She'd even called the elder care facility, but they'd told her Lydia wasn't very coherent.

Eve called the phone number for Lydia James's care facility in Ohio again and identified herself to the answering service. A nurse returned Eve's call, and Eve explained the situation and what little she'd already learned after the initial fire when she'd reached a dead end. The nurse told her that she could speak with Lydia, but first the nurse needed to verify who Eve was, and then she'd call Eve back.

Eve expressed her surprise and was told that they'd determined that Lydia had needed some major medication adjustments since Eve's prior call, not going into detail. She'd also had surgery and might have been recovering at the time of that first call. Now Lydia had her good days and her not so good days. Today she was having a great day—one of the best she'd had in ages. Eve accepted the offer to talk directly with Lydia. Forty minutes later, Eve's phone rang and she listened for a moment before Lydia was put on the line.

"This is Lydia. Who's there?" The voice warbled a bit, but Eve's hopes rose with Lydia's seeming clarity.

"Hi, Lydia. I'm Eve, and I'm calling from Paradise Pines out in California. I'm a police officer and we've had multiple fires. The library building was the first, and I'm doing some follow-up. I hear it was your building."

"You got that right, girlie. Gosh darn shame. Nice building and I like libraries, so did the city a favor with that lease."

"You certainly did. I'm just wondering if you can tell me if you have any relatives still in Paradise Pines."

"Funny you should ask. A distant cousin removed once or twice I think—I don't remember. Martin, my nephew and heir, passed. Don't ask me all the in-betweens that make this fella that last relative standing because my mind's not sharp anymore, but he's now in my will. Sole inheritor. And still there in Paradise as far as I know."

*Motivation.* An adrenaline rush energized Eve as she posed her pen over a notepad, not that she was likely to forget a name if Lydia had one. "Do you know who it is?" Eve asked.

"I hadn't seen him since he was knee high to a grasshopper. I left there decades ago. Never has come to see me here, but my lawyer said the will was in order now. His name reminded me of my favorite actor…who was it?" Lydia paused for a full fifteen or twenty seconds, then chuckled. "Got it…he was in *To Kill a Mockingbird*—did you see that movie?"

"I did. Gregory Peck," Eve replied, as that feeling of possible success surged. "Does Gregory Sneed sound familiar?"

She heard Lydia chuckle again. "That's who I was trying to name. He's the heir. My lawyer can confirm it—have him call me if you need. I do remember the lawyer's name…chose him because of it. Peter Piper. Made me laugh."

"Thank you, Lydia. You've been a huge help. Have a good rest of your day."

"You know the sayin'—any day I'm here is a good 'un. Call me anytime, girlie." Lydia hung up.

Eve dropped her pen on the blank pad of paper in front of her. She hadn't needed to write down the lawyer's or the mayor's name. The pieces were coming together, not in the way she'd hoped personally, but there was nothing to be done except follow the evidence. Eve remembered her conversation with Cassie about evidence versus crap spreaders. Her moral compass would never allow her to do anything but turn over what she'd just learned to Greene, but Eve couldn't help but feel like she was sealing her fate.

She turned in her office chair and tossed McGruff a biscuit before calling the county sheriff's office and passing along the information. Greene called her back a few minutes later, obviously happy with her update. He assured her that he'd follow up and keep her apprised. There were plans to question Sneed in the morning.

After she'd ended that call, Eve sat a long moment to let her thoughts gel. She was over her blubbering if she could help it. She much preferred taking action and coming up with a plan. Then making the decision that she needed to know what her options were, Eve picked up her phone for the third time.

"What's Paradise Pines' chief of police doing calling me on a Sunday evening?" Joye asked her. "It's either a crisis or you're bored so silly that even that mutt of yours can't entertain you."

Eve sighed. "Probably the crisis category, including a personal one. This is all off the record until I tell you it isn't."

"Off the record, then. How can I help you?"

Eve went on to update Joye on the new revelations about the fires and Sneed's likely involvement.

"I'd tell you I love you because you're helping me make headlines for the *Pulse* faster than I can write up the stories, but oh, sweetie, this is horrible news for you—and for this town."

Eve attempted to swallow down the lump of pain and self-pity that blocked her throat at Joye's affirmation that this was horrible news. "I have a question that needs an honest answer. We both know I'll likely lose my position. I've decided if that's the case, I'm not leaving town. What matters to me the most is right here. Believe it or not, my personal life matters...love matters, especially when it's loving Shaye. I'm looking at other options for work. A career change." Eve gave Joye a strained chuckle. "Maybe piece together a couple of options, but I need to know what those are. Any chance you might need help in some capacity on the paper part-time? I'm toying with other options, but they'll take time to launch and grow. I've got a large nest egg, but I need to start making a plan."

"My turn for off the record because it would be inappropriate as an unbiased journalist for me to say it, but fuck Pauline and fuck Sneed. I'm proud of you, Eve. You've achieved a personal life and a chance at a future that's more important to you than the job you tried to bury yourself in. I know you've been reaching a happy balance, and this sucks, but you're making good choices…Shaye."

Eve thought about all the twists and turns, ups and downs in her life lately, and she knew that if she and Shaye had a chance at a future, she was going to give it her best shot. She still hadn't heard that Shaye loved her, but she thought that without any major additional shocks, they stood a good chance of lasting love on both their parts. She suspected that if and when Shaye declared that she loved her, it would be solid. And that was the only kind of love she wanted.

"I love her. She's had a hard past, but she's strong…smart, funny, kind. Also stable, loyal, honest, three things I need. And I know that I've mentioned the flirting and chemistry—off the charts. She hasn't told me she loves me yet, but she's willing to admit that she wants to try for a future together. As long as we have a chance, I'm not walking away from this."

"I can always use your help at the paper. The *Pulse* is doing well. Dedicated subscribers, growing advertising. Lots of old folks still in town who want a paper subscription, younger folks paying for online. We'll work it out, Eve, but I'll help you however I can."

"Thanks."

"Hey, love is a wonderful thing. I'm glad you know that," Joye said.

"I want this. I need this."

"It's about time, Chief."

Shaye was working in the library trailer late Monday morning and feeling like life was hitting her harder than she could deal with. She considered the multiple insights that could come with an epiphany, how one epiphany could lead to another.

She'd been relaxing in Eve's bed yesterday morning, reflecting on the wonderful time she'd had taking what she needed and giving all she could, and then pondering what their next relationship move should be while Eve was out making coffee. Her head knew that acknowledging that she had fallen in love would be admitting that she had left her heart wide open for a crash landing.

Shaye had been in the middle of these contemplations when Eve had come back into the bedroom and told her that Jim Greene had called, and then Eve had suggested they might want to have coffee out on the patio. Eve's mood had changed from relaxed to reserved.

Shaye wouldn't forget the exact moment that led to her epiphany— she'd been sitting there in a robe, her hair wet from the shower she'd just quickly taken, the patio sun warming her face and the fresh coffee warming her throat when Eve had shared the news that Greg Sneed was being investigated for contracting the arsons.

It had been obvious to Shaye that Eve had already realized the repercussions of the news because she hadn't seemed to be suffering the tectonic shock waves that had rumbled through Shaye's chest as the information had registered. Eve had already settled into despondency.

If the news was true, and there was no reason to believe it wasn't, Sneed would never be elected mayor, leaving Pauline in top contention for the position, and she would fire Eve or drive her from her job. Shaye had been struck with the epiphany that she was going to lose Eve, and then struck with the certainty that losing Eve would leave a gaping hole in her heart…and in her life. There had no longer been any denying the label for what she felt. She loved Eve. Shaye had barely been able to breathe.

So there she was, twenty-four hours later, in her little tin box of a library trying to work and trying harder not to cry any more as she cursed whatever forces had brought her to this point in her life—to the moment when she could finally admit being deeply in love. And to the moment when wanting Eve in her life forever was crashing into the very real likelihood that option was being taken away from her because Eve would be forced to leave. Eve would need to move somewhere else in the country because she'd spent her entire adult life evolving into this current role that had been her life focus. She was well suited to lead—cut out to be a chief of police. Eve loved her job.

Shaye knew she couldn't just walk away from her mom. After all her mother had done for her, and considering that Shaye had been mostly gone for more than twenty years, now wasn't the time to leave again—not at a time in their lives when her mom needed her. And not if she was going to be able to live with herself. Leaving with Eve seemed impossible, but staying without Eve did too. Maybe it was her past, telling her she didn't deserve happiness. Or maybe she could figure out how to live between two worlds, difficult as it would be, because giving up on their love would be so much harder.

The library door opened and Shaye looked up to see who was there. The low dark canine silhouette of McGruff tottered in first, making a beeline for her with a grunt offered at every step. Then a human form blocked the majority of the light leaking in though the open doorway—it was a well-proportioned silhouette with curves that never failed to capture Shaye's attention. The sight of Eve never failed to elevate Shaye's pulse, raise her spirits, and spark her desire.

Shaye wiped her eyes, the ruminating revelations in her chest still weighing on her, but she was glad to see Eve and smiled. "Are you here to arrest someone for a long-overdue book?"

"I just came to browse the bestsellers. To put a hold on my number one pick. I'm glad to see she's available for checking out." Eve gave her an appreciative look.

The laugh rose from somewhere deep inside Shaye. Not coming from just a place of amusement. It centered from that place in her chest that found such deep attachment to Eve. The place that loved Eve's sense of humor. Even when it boomeranged and flustered Eve. Maybe even especially then because a flustered Eve was endearing and relatable and human. It was one of the things that had convinced Shaye from the beginning that there was more to Eve than an arrogant cop designation.

"Bestseller, huh? I'm thinking you might like the digital version more. Two digits. Maybe even three." Shaye offered her a suggestive look.

"I hope you don't say that to all the library card holders."

"Only the ones with gorgeous asses and the word *chief* before their name, and for a price, I'll keep the gorgeous ass info to myself."

"And what kind of blackmail are you proposing for your silence? A kiss?" Eve raised an eyebrow and those kissable lips twitched upward.

"I was thinking of a price closer to a firsthand, lily-white view, and not the shade of blush I'm seeing."

Eve cleared her throat and said, "I'd love to moon you, babe, but I'm here for a reason." Stepping closer, Shaye fell into Eve's arms. Strong embracing arms. They held each other and Shaye breathed in

Eve's scent, mixed with vanilla and spice, before Eve finally stepped back and spoke again.

"Sneed confessed to Greene this morning. We knew the burnt library building was owned by a ninety-three-year-old woman currently in an elder care facility in Ohio. There are still decades left on the ninety-nine-year lease. But guess who's her distant cousin once or twice removed and was the newly named heir in her will?"

"Greg Sneed," Shaye guessed.

"Yup. He figured she doesn't have long left and he didn't want to end up a landlord, inheriting a low-rate lease with little monetary return. He wanted to inherit the insurance cash that she'd collect from the fire."

"Holy shit!" was all that Shaye could think to say.

"Yeah," Eve replied. "He did this when he thought he was the only one who was going to run, similar to his other elections. When he suddenly had competition after the library fire, he had his campaign office mail slot fire set. I guess he figured the library arson was the big one that had already done the damage of rattling the voters. His intention was to assure there would be no attention on himself by being a victim, and also to place it on his opponents."

"It sounds like Sneed was just trying to stay one step ahead of things as it all sort of snowballed," Shaye replied.

"He hired the ex-con, Billy Rachet, who Cassie overheard the other night in the park talking about his role. Sneed worked really hard to blame Pauline."

"What about my house and car, and the attack on me?" Shaye asked.

"It seems that part was all Rachet without Sneed's directive. He left town for a week after the mail slot fire on a job he needed as a condition of his parole, but got to worrying." Eve offered Shaye a sympathetic look. "He was afraid you might eventually identify him. He didn't want to go back to prison, so he acted when he returned. Rather irrational, but desperate people do desperate things."

"And I'd guess that Sneed's lawn blaze was another effort by the mayor to make himself look like a target. The goal was to frame Pauline with Andy's stolen receipt in an effort to assure the mayoral position for himself." Shaye shook her head as she continued to put the pieces together.

"The library trailer and assigning you to my police station office were mitigation efforts once he had rivals—trying to appease the town by minimizing the loss of library services," Eve added.

"After that early library fire, when Sneed's only focus was the insurance money, I bet he was really shocked to suddenly have election competition and an unsolved arson case that made voters unhappy."

"Sneed has withdrawn from the mayoral race, as well as being arrested." Eve pursed her lips as she concluded her news. "That leaves Pauline and Matt Merchant running, and we both know Merchant doesn't stand a chance—young, inexperienced, no connections, minimal support…"

Shaye had pretty much known this was coming, but now that it was clearly spelled out, she could only struggle between her feelings of rage and her sadness. She had no words except the two in her head. *Fuck Pauline.*

She'd come back to Paradise Pines to make peace with her past and to reconnect with her mother. She'd accomplished those, and even more life-changing, she'd found love. As she stood there with Eve, Shaye knew she wasn't willing to give up the chance at a future together. She'd figure out how to juggle between two locations so she could help her mom and Cassie, but she needed to be with Eve. What had her mom said? Love is everything. Look at everything. How did it start? Maybe her mom had meant for her to examine those early feelings and build on them over time.

"I love you, Eve. I don't know how to make this work, but I love you. I'll do everything in my power to be with you, even if it means living between two places so I can help Mom too. And Cassie. But I'm going to find a way to make this work for us. I'll find a job near wherever you need to go. You're the best thing that's ever happened to me."

"I love that you're willing to go where I go and do your best to juggle Ginny and Cassie, and a different job, but you need to be here," Eve said. "You can't move."

Shaye's heart staggered and settled in her throat. She couldn't swallow. It sounded like Eve was willing to give up on them. Then Eve grabbed her and held her in her arms again. She spoke softly into Shaye's ear.

"Let me finish, babe. I'm not leaving. I'm not willing to lose you either. I love you too much. Maybe I'll become a private investigator. I've talked to Joye about part-time work too."

"You're going to cut hair?" Shaye suppressed a chuckle, knowing full well that Eve must mean the newspaper side of Joye's endeavors.

"Hey, not that every customer wouldn't come out better looking than McGruff, but I'll have you know that I'm not a bad writer." Eve's voice was infused with fake huff.

"I bet you'd be great at writing police procedural mysteries. Really great."

"I was thinking that some of my admin skills could come in useful in helping Joye get her paper out." A ghost of amusement crossed Eve's face as she added, "Or maybe Earl will need a plumber's helper."

"God, Earl's errand girl...now you're convincing me how much you really do love me. I just might have to start using the shortened name of this town too—Paradise."

"Yeah, I love you." Eve's pause gave the statement the weight it deserved. "I've never put my personal life first, and you've made me want to. Staying here and figuring out a future is you and me working together to put *us* first." Then Eve laughed. "I hope it doesn't come down to you and me and Earl and a plunger to make this work, but a girl's gotta do what a girl's gotta do for love."

Shaye leaned in and kissed her. Not a quick kiss, or even a gentle kiss, but a prolonged, passionate kiss. She'd been willing to put Eve first, and Eve was willing to put her first. Deep, deep down, she knew that was one true measure of their love.

## CHAPTER TWENTY-FOUR

Eve spent the next week settling into the idea that she was likely going to have to walk away from her job and embark on a new professional life. It didn't cause the devastating internal turmoil she would have thought, even though she had to acknowledge that she loved her job. That was because she loved Shaye more, and while such a huge shift in her professional life would have devastated her when it was her entire focus, she was excited about her prospects of building a personal life with Shaye. Eve knew they both appreciated that they hadn't just meandered into their commitment to their future. Their feelings for each other had been forged through trying times and tested. Eve was confident those feelings were strong and durable.

Shaye hadn't moved back in with her and McGruff yet. They'd decided to continue moving forward one step at a time and not overload on too much change at once. That didn't mean that Shaye wasn't sharing lunches and dinners with Eve, as well as spending frequent nights in Eve's bed. Those nights were wonderful, and they'd often risen early to enjoy exercise and coffee on those early mornings after. What it did mean was that they were going to let the election results play out and face the repercussions day by day with a commitment to each other.

Eve was at her desk this Thursday morning trying to concentrate on creating organized notes for ongoing cases and tying up loose ends on those things she could, so a successor would be able to pick up from wherever she ended up leaving off.

The election was on Tuesday, only five days from now. But after focusing for the past two hours on getting a head start on not leaving chaos behind when the inevitable election results led to the need for her to vacate her job, Eve's mind kept wandering to much more pleasurable thoughts and the prior evening. It wandered to Shaye's warm body next to hers, to the moans of Shaye's desire, to the melodic sound of Shaye's laughter, to the love in Shaye's eyes.

It was in the midst of memories of her hand resting between Shaye's breasts that morning, palpating the pounding of Shaye's heartbeat after a round of wake-up passion, when Eve's phone rang. The screen identified Jim Greene as the caller. He'd understood the political implications for Eve when Sneed had confessed to hiring Billy Rachet and then exited the mayoral race, and he'd kept in touch with her and offered to support her however he could.

"Hi, Jim. How's it going?"

"Moving right along. I've got news and want to bring you up to speed."

Eve assumed it would be an update about Sneed, maybe even news of when sentencing was scheduled because he'd pleaded guilty at his arraignment hearing. She waited for Greene to continue.

"It's about Pauline Bromwell."

"Pauline?" All that Eve could imagine was Pauline already contacting Greene in an effort to establish her alliances as she solidified her planned victory. Or maybe Pauline was seeking advice as to who to replace Eve with, undoubtedly not Grady because he'd had close ties to Eve.

"I just had word from the FBI. They've arrested her here in my jurisdiction. For a white-collar crime."

Eve was shocked. She had major issues with Pauline, but she hadn't seen this coming. Her first thoughts were of Shaye and Ginny and Cassie. Poor Cassie—this was her mother. And then it struck her that she might not lose her job after all.

"You know Bromwell was the senior accountant at the Castlewood Medical Corporation headquarters. It's a big operation with multiple branches. She was arrested along with others, including some medical personnel, for health care fraud."

Eve's shock escalated.

"Eve? Are you there?" Jim asked.

"Yes. Just stunned silent for a moment." *Holy fuck!*

❖

It was election night, and Eve and Shaye were at the Paradise Pizza Parlor with a crowd of others, all waiting on the election results.

It was Tuesday night, and the weekend had been relaxed overall. Ginny and Cassie had been deeply saddened but not stunned by the news regarding Pauline's arrest. Eve knew they were both emotionally exhausted from the roller coaster ride of prior events, and maybe they'd been somewhat prepared after their considerations that Pauline might have been involved with Andy in the arsons.

Shaye's response had been similar to Eve's with that moment of stunned silence followed by an accepting profane acknowledgment. Shaye had even commented that maybe that was what Pauline had been referring to when she'd opened the front door that first day Shaye had seen her. When she had told someone that leaving no trail was critical. It had nothing to do with the arsons. Pauline's new luxury car, the upscale neighborhood, the high-end jewelry—those were probably clues too.

They were all aware that Pauline always operated in her own self-interest, even if this was way beyond her usual selfish actions. As Cassie had labeled it, *A mega bad Mom move with fallout*. Cassie had spent her life being let down by Pauline, and she'd developed her own coping skills. Eve knew that she and Shaye were now integral to those, and she wanted to make sure they offered all the support and prevented any backlash for Cassie that they could.

"They're about to make the final announcement," Joye said as she sat back down at the table between Earl and Shaye. "As if I don't already have the *Pulse*'s headline and article mostly drafted for tomorrow's edition with Matthew Merchant the only candidate left standing. I've got to admit, Mayor Merchant has a certain ring to it."

They all quieted as the current vice mayor stepped up to the microphone at the front of the room and announced Matthew Merchant would be the next mayor before introducing him. Merchant offered a short acceptance speech and turned the mic back to the vice mayor, who ended the official program for the evening. Everyone had expected the news, and the room resonated with toasts and congratulations.

"Well, the kid has a cliff of a learning curve, but I've heard he's okay," Earl said.

"I think he'll get a lot of support," Joye replied.

Shaye poked Eve in the ribs. "He's headed this way."

Merchant walked over to Eve and smiled, holding out his hand. Eve took it and congratulated him. He greeted Joye, who he also knew, and then Eve introduced him to Shaye and Earl. He told them all to call him Matt.

"I just wanted to let you know, Chief Maguire, that I'm grateful for your support and that I'm going to need your help as I step into this position. Kinda overwhelming."

"You're going to do fine, Matt," Eve replied. "And I'm happy to assist you in any way I can."

"So, the next time I'm foolish enough to run out of gas on the highway, you'll be there like you were the last time?" Matt grinned.

Eve grinned too and nodded. "Protect and serve. That's my job." She turned to Shaye, who raised her eyebrows at Eve's reference to her job description. Eve knew that Shaye could tell what she was thinking—she just might have to do a little personal work tonight.

After Matt left their table to talk to others, Earl said, "Well, sis, it looks like you've still got your badge. And darn if I wasn't counting on bringing you on for a little wrench and pipe training."

"I was so looking forward to expanding my résumé under your expert guidance, Earl. But duty calls." Eve offered her brother a look that told him she wasn't the least bit sorry. Everyone laughed and toasted as they finished their drinks.

Eve leaned into Shaye and whispered, "I cleared my calendar in the morning, just in case I oversleep after all the overtime I've been putting in."

"What a coincidence," Shaye replied. "I don't have scheduled library hours in the morning either."

❖

They'd just entered the low-lit living room after the pizza parlor evening, and Shaye laughed as McGruff let them know that he wasn't pleased with their absence by offering a couple of half-hearted howls without giving up his lounging location on the couch. Eve had fed him before she'd left, and he offered no interest in budging for a backyard bush tour, so Eve stepped closer and gave him a gentle coo and pat on the head.

Shaye went weak with the image of what the soft glow of the table lamp illuminated. Eve. McGruff. When contrasted with the myriad of miserable alternatives of where Shaye could have landed in life, with all the ways she could have broken this reality that was right in front of her, the magnitude of her good fortune struck her. These two were her home…and the future she wanted every day for the rest of her life.

Eve walked back across the living room to Shaye. She pulled Shaye close and captured both her hands, their fingers laced together. Shaye fell into those hazel eyes, the usual light sage and honey now saturated to a dark green and sienna, and then Shaye's gaze snagged on the curve of those slightly parted lips. She leaned in to skim them gently. Skin to skin, it was a trifecta of touch—two pairs of hands interwoven and lips touching. Then they pressed together until there was no space between them. They stood like that, Shaye savoring the connection until Eve's thigh slipped between hers, and Shaye wanted so much more of Eve.

"Hey, Chief. Have I told you how much I love you lately?"

Eve collected those words in her mouth as they flowed from Shaye's lips, possessing them as the prelude to a longer silent conversation played out in a slow seductive kiss. Shaye wanted Eve to lock those words away, to hold them as a reminder of who she was to Shaye. Her love. Her lover.

"So, *Chief* is okay with you?" Eve asked when they came up for air, her voice rough and a register lower. Shaye loved when that gravel and whiskey undertone verified how much Eve desired her. God, she would never grow tired of Eve. Not her intelligence or wit or compassion or humbleness or dedication to her job, or the knowledge of what Eve was willing to give up for her.

"If you're keeping your job and I'm moving back in with you, I think I'd better embrace your title, unless you want me to call you *Old-fashioned*."

"I like that too. It reminds me of the first night I laid eyes on you—our first kiss in that bar parking lot. Plus, nobody except you dares to call me that. At least not to my face." Eve's eyes telegraphed her amusement.

"It was an amazing first kiss. No hint of old-fashioned, except maybe the walking away. I didn't want to walk away."

After shifting her demeanor to serious, Eve asked, "Are you ready to come home to McGruff and me now?"

Shaye nodded. "I am."

Still holding Shaye's hand, Eve led Shaye down the hallway to the bedroom. "Another first, then."

Shaye was confused. "I'm not sure what that means. Are you going to teach me something new?" She offered Eve a suggestive smirk-smile. McGruff wandered into the room and Shaye had to add, "Old dogs, new tricks and all."

"I was thinking we've never made love in *our* bedroom. *Our* bed."

And with that, Eve pushed Shaye down on the mattress and captured her surrender with another deep kiss.

Shaye's heart rate accelerated. Eve rolled her over and unzipped her dress; her fingers followed the parting of the cloth in a heated trail.

"You're overdressed for this occasion too." Shaye had trouble getting the words out with Eve's hands caressing her back, undoing her bra. Eve slipped her hands down between Shaye and the mattress to cup her breasts.

Eve halted a moment, then rolled Shaye over and faced her. Eve's eyes slid from the gaping material at Shaye's cleavage up to her eyes. "I can see your point," she purred.

Then in a shared flurry of tugging and pulling and shedding, not slow and provocative because there would be plenty of other occasions for that, they were naked, embraced in each other's arms under the sheets. Love and lust crashed together, fused into the perfect onslaught of emotional and physical desire locked into unwavering trust—this was more than Shaye had ever felt and all that Shaye had ever wanted.

The predawn light barely filtered through the window covering when Eve woke from a short night of sleep to feel Shaye's fingers gliding from her neck down the center of her back as they traversed the ridge-and-dip topography of her spine. Eve tried to regulate her breathing, to control the need to speed up her respiration to match the acceleration of her heart rate, as Shaye's touch approached the landscape of her ass.

That hand and Shaye's mouth had traveled this territory more than once last night, then moved on to map out the drenched heat that was their final destination, to dive into the folds and core passage of Eve. The pace was achingly exquisite, driving Eve higher and higher, to the edge of the precipice before finally tipping her over and into those profound waves of passion. Waves that drowned her in pleasure as she rode them all the way to a whisper, down to that final destination of sated and bemused—bemused because Eve did not know how she kept falling more deeply in love with Shaye. But she did, and best of all, for the first time in her life she felt confident that it was permanent and mutual.

"You're killing me, in the best possible way." Eve rolled over to face Shaye. She pushed Shaye's hair behind her ear and kissed that place where her jaw met her neck.

"Well, I guess I'm safe from murder charges brought by the chief of police, then, because not only would she be the victim but she's an accessory to the crime."

Eve nodded. "And how are you feeling after so little sleep?"

Shaye chuckled. "*Four* hours of sleep. *Four* times you took me past that point of no return. *For*ty years old. With *for*ever on my mind. I'm feeling rather *for*tunate…absolutely euphoric about my life."

Eve trailed her hand across Shaye's breast. She circled her nipple and watched it come to attention.

"We could go for five," Shaye said.

"Five hours of sleep, huh? Well, I guess that some people at forty need…"

Shaye yawned in obvious faux-nonchalance before reaching for Eve and taking her hand—the hand that Eve knew was heading them toward round number five if she kept up the breast massage. Shaye pinned her with an indigo gaze, and one corner of her mouth quirked up before the expansion of the smile captured her entire face.

"At forty, I'm happy to feast on you all night. I'm just so grateful to have found you. I met you with a bruised and damaged heart. There will always be scars, but the journey brought me here to you. Eve—the elixir that helped heal my wounded heart. And a cop elixir at that." Shaye kissed Eve's eyes closed, then caught her mouth in a deep, shared kiss, both of them probing and tasting until Eve needed to come up for air. Shaye kissed her way across Eve's cheek and burrowed her face in the warm curve where Eve's neck met her shoulder.

"I didn't have a personal life, by design," Eve said. "And I certainly didn't want you in any personal life I managed to resurrect. You were so easy to want, you terrified me. How the hell did this happen?" Eve injected humor into her tone.

"You don't sound upset."

Eve wasn't the least bit upset. "I'm grateful, like you. I'm just wondering. Post-Pauline had me locked into an almost solitary focus on my professional life. And then you turned out to be her stepsister."

"And you were her ex. Yet you took me into your home—to protect me." Shaye kissed Eve's temple.

"In the line of duty. Protect and serve. It couldn't have been anything else. Not the chemistry, and certainly not that sexy smile." Eve loved that sexy smile. "And not the fact that McGruff approved of you. I think we owe something to *our* mutt—no escaping the fact that the ugly dog is now an *us* acquisition too. When I stopped to settle the bill and then ended up with McGruff that day after the bar, the receptionist told me, 'We put him back together on the outside. But he needs someone to put him back together on the inside.' It hit me personally. And now I think maybe it applies to all three of us."

"Maybe we owe your bank teller, Audrey, a dinner at our favorite Thai restaurant." Shaye poked Eve. "I knew I didn't want you dating her that night you went out with her. Audrey made me realize I didn't want you dating anyone."

"Dating. Those dates we went on…Cassie's required eight. That's when I couldn't deny that I was falling for you." Eve smiled as she thought of that first night they'd made love—*Date Night*. "I wouldn't have slept with you in Carmel if I hadn't been. And we made it through the crisis of Joye's revelation about Mike. You weren't quite ready to admit you loved me then, but you didn't blame me. Even if it took you *an entire week* to figure that out."

"And then there was Andy, my own stepsibling—godawful stress," Shaye added.

"Yes, we've navigated a lot of that."

"I couldn't admit I loved you until Cassie led you to Sneed as the arsonist. I didn't want to love a cop. Then I couldn't stand the idea of losing the cop I loved."

"Yeah, you were a little slow." Eve chuckled. "I wasn't going to let you lose me, babe."

"You asked how the hell it happened. You and me…two hurting people. An ugly damaged dog. Four fires. A dishonest mayor. An unscrupulous stepsister. Sometimes there's just no stopping love." Shaye grinned at Eve—a grin conveying amusement, and wonder, and joy.

"I listened to Aunt Sadie. I followed my heart," Eve said.

"And my mom told me love is everything. And then she told me to look at everything, at the beginning of everything. I thought she meant for me to consider the sad state of my personal life before I met you, to examine those early feelings and build on them. But I think she meant more. The word—*everything*. The beginning." Shaye's eyes glistened. "Love is e-v-e-rything. E-v-e."

"Well, for me, it's s-h-a-y-e." Eve embraced her, captured her mouth in a slow kiss, tasting her, teasing her, until it was time to take that kiss lower. They made love one more time before they both agreed that a few more hours of sleep would be the perfect finish to a perfect night. Before closing her eyes, Eve muttered into Shaye's ear. "Welcome home."

"Where my heart is," Shaye answered. "Because of you, here in Paradise."

And before either of them could fall fully asleep, McGruff growled his agreement.

# EPILOGUE

"Well, you two *finally* did a few things right, even if it did take almost two years of exhausting pro bono advising." Cassie gave Eve and Shaye a grin.

"And would you care to elaborate?" Shaye asked, her eyes sparkling with amusement at Cassie's comment, or maybe it was just her enjoyment of the entire event, Eve thought. That vitality that Eve had first been attracted to in the bar called Lady Luck was on full display today, and she didn't plan to ever stop loving it.

"At the top of my list is choosing a double fudge chocolate wedding cake." Cassie forked another large mouthful of the cake into her mouth, chewing and swallowing before smacking her lips. "Although I can't believe I had to wait so long—until I became a teenager—for you two to move from girlfriends to legally recognized lovers."

"Maybe at thirteen you should modify that to *wives*." Eve's mouth hitched up before she tamped a smile down. She looked at Shaye, and then at Cassie. Shaye was her legally recognized lover as well as so much more, and that thrilled her, but someone needed to keep the precocious Cassie in check. If only so she didn't embarrass Eve.

Cassie laughed. "Hey, I'm not clueless, so I'll concede—tonight you're finally into *the wife era*."

Earl leaned in and interrupted as he looked at Eve. "Ready for your baby brother to save your blushing backside?"

Eve rolled her eyes and muttered, "My hero," as she wondered what Earl had planned. They'd already done the toasts and he'd done a decent job by surprising her in a public Earl-fashion acknowledgment to the entire reception crowd that maybe some people shouldn't be trying to tell other people who to love...that he'd never seen his sister so happy. Now he turned his attention to Cassie and asked, "Okay, kid. What kind of cake are you recommending for Joye and my wedding?"

Eve's gaze swung from her brother to Joye. It would be just like Earl to not have talked to Joye beforehand and to have expected a conversation with Cassie about a wedding cake flavor to become his proposal.

Luckily, as Eve watched, Joye tilted her head in a nod. "Love works in mysterious ways. But we weren't going to make the announcement until you two had your day."

Earl protested. "Eve needed saving. But I don't want to steal your thunder today, sis."

Eve blew him a kiss across the table. "You owe me a dance after the music starts again, baby bro." Then she turned to Joye. "I love you both. I'm so happy for you."

"Thanks," Joye replied. "But this is your and Shaye's day."

"Hey," Cassie interrupted. "Every day from now on is their day. For the rest of their lives." She looked at Earl and studied him for a moment. Then, while balancing a huge bite of cake on her fork, she pointed it at him and squinted. "Joye's a different case, but with you in the mix, definitely not angel food. And lemon cake might be a little harsh." Earl crossed his arms and waited as Cassie continued. "Now, when I consider your politics, I might say upside down cake, but Joye's the other half and I think she's making you smarter." Cassie leaned back in her chair. "You're way deeper than you want to appear, so I'd say a multilayered cake, but I'm going to leave the rest up to Joye." She paused and pointed the cake laden utensil at Eve and Shaye. "They're the proof that I'm good at this." Then she returned her attention to Earl. "And here's my best advice for you. Defer to Joye." The rest of the table chuckled and nodded.

Earl laughed. "Thanks, kid. Especially that last part." He looked at Joye. "Now, enough of Joye and me. Today is Eve and Shaye's show."

Annie changed the subject. "So, what time does your flight leave tomorrow for that Hawaiian honeymoon, Shaye *Mmmaguire* Hayden?" She drew out the M in Maguire and winked.

"I should have known you'd add the M to your list of new names you'll come up for me," Shaye muttered.

"You better believe it, Shaye *Metamorphosis* Hayden. I'm so happy for you." Annie offered a loving grin, and Eve knew how much she owed Shaye's best friend. "And the next step in this journey of yours—it's the honeymoon. The one where if you're lucky you'll manage to spend a little time on the beach."

"The beach...where else would they be in Hawaii?" Cassie asked, her voice infused with pretend innocence. Eve was searching for an appropriate answer when Earl jumped in.

He managed to keep a straight face. "Volcanoes. They're going from one paradise to another. Hawaii is a paradise born of fire. Can't miss that fire on your honeymoon."

Cassie laughed and rolled her eyes. "Good save, Earl. Kid appropriate—except for maybe the fire part. I know what a honeymoon is. And as I remember, we had some fires around here about the time they met. Fire is what brought Shaye to Paradise Pines. Moved her in with Eve. Got the love affair rolling."

"Well." Ginny spoke up and diverted the conversation. "When is your flight?"

"Not until late tomorrow night," Shaye replied. "We've got a few stops to make first."

They all looked at her and then Eve.

"We're going to leave by midmorning," Eve said. "We want to stop at Breezeland Emergency Veterinary Hospital and show them a few pictures of the current McGruff. I want to thank them for talking me into waffling."

"As if Deputy Dog didn't play a role in convincing you...actually liking you. Not that you're hard to like, but he does have discerning tastes," Shaye replied.

"And he liked Shaye too. No telling where I'd be if he hadn't," Eve told the group. "And he tolerates Earl and Joye, so they've kindly volunteered to take care of him while we're gone."

"I'm gonna spoil that pooch rotten," Joye said. "Maybe even a makeover." She looked at Cassie. "A glow up. You might not recognize him when you get him back."

"If by some miracle you turn him into an unrecognizable Toto, I'll bet we'll still know him by his growl." Eve smiled.

"After Breezeland, we're going to go see Sadie at Golden Days Elder Estate," Shaye said. "I think the chief here might have a teddy bear wrapped in wedding paper, so Sadie can be part of the celebration."

"Rainbow wedding paper," Cassie said. "I helped her find it."

The quartet of musicians had returned from a break and started playing again. Eve and Shaye had danced their first dance as a wedded couple before the cake was served. Everyone at the table paused for a minute and looked in the direction of the music. Eve watched Grady take his wife's hand and lead her out for a dance, and an erotic memory hit her—a flame she'd diligently tried to put out at the time. Obviously without success.

Shaye leaned in and quietly asked, "What's got your attention?"

"Just remembering Grady's wife is a vet tech. And a morning with stitch removal and dog shampoo and a wet T-shirt, a rather revealing wet T-shirt on the woman who is now my wife," Eve whispered back.

Shaye gave her a teasing smile, keeping her volume low. "I thought that wet shirt might get your attention."

"So, it *was* intentional." Eve tsked and offered Shaye her best admonishing expression.

"I was just trying to push your buttons. You were a cop—bad news in my book." Shaye broke into a cheeky grin.

"Well, that was an evil plan, but I think it backfired. Now you're stuck with my attention for the next fifty years."

"Is that all?" Shaye asked.

"Come out on the dance floor with me and we can talk about the fifty years after this first fifty. They're playing our favorite restaurant song."

Shaye listened a moment and then emitted a delighted laugh. "'My Heart Will Go On.' Love song for the Thai Tanic."

Eve held out her hand and Shaye took it. They walked to the dance floor and Eve melted into Shaye's arms. They began to sway as one, their bodies pushed tightly together, and then Shaye crooned softly into Eve's ear until the song ended.

"Tomorrow, and the day after, and the day after that, I'll love you." Shaye's lips feathered the outer rim of Eve's ear, sending a thrum of that love to Eve's heart and downward.

"And in a week, and a month, and in fifty years—because you're stuck with me now." Eve chuckled.

"I know...that life sentence," Shaye said. "And speaking of tomorrow, I've got one more stop I want to make between Sadie's and the airport. We should have plenty of time since it's an eleven p.m. flight."

❖

The illumination was subdued and the digital jukebox music still added the background auditory component that leveled out those eruptions of friendly customer comradery. The mixed aromas of french fry grease and booze and the end-of-the-day crowd still pervaded the Lady Luck. Not much had changed…and yet so much had changed.

It was still over three hours before flight time, and the airport wasn't far. Shaye emerged from the restroom and wandered over to take the empty stool next to the gorgeous blond at the bar. The blond who just happened to be her new wife.

"This seat taken?" she asked. "My name's Shaye. Shaye Maguire Hayden."

"Saving it for you. What are the odds? I happen to be Eve Hayden Maguire."

"Can I get you a drink?" the bartender asked Shaye.

"I'll have what she's having," Shaye said.

Eve chuckled. "Not a Love Potion for Two? Not a Tie Me to the Bedpost?"

"Old-fashioned. That's what I'm partial to." Shaye remembered that first encounter well. "But for future reference, I kind of like the occasional Date Night too."

"Good to know. *For future reference.*" Eve played with those three words from their past.

"Just as long as it's not balsamic vinegar and Kool-Aid. That's not quite the experience I was hoping for." Shaye was thrilled that Eve seemed to recall their first encounter as well as she did.

"And just what kind of experience were you hoping for?" Laughter filled Eve's eyes. "Are we talking about the drink, or something else? I'm kind of rusty at this."

The bartender set Shaye's order in front of her. Eve and Shaye clinked glasses and each took a moment to sip their drink.

"Definitely something else," Shaye replied, letting her voice ooze with suggestion. "And rusty at what? Because rumor has it that you're not rusty at all."

"Are you flirting with me?" Eve asked. "Because rumor has it that you're excellent at that. And creating chemistry."

"I am. It helped me land my wife, and she's not bad at those things either."

"She's a fortunate woman. I met my wife in a bar. Lady Luck."

"Now there's a coincidence." Shaye leaned over and kissed Eve. "So did I. She's the love of my life."

"Mine is too." The corners of Eve's mouth twitched. "And as I remember, there was no kissing in the bar that night. Only in the parking lot."

"I remember. I couldn't forget if I wanted to, which I don't. But I just can't seem to help myself." Shaye leaned in and met Eve's lips again.

They relaxed and sipped their drinks in comfortable silence after their long day. They had plenty of time. They enjoyed a plate of appetizers as they let the alcohol wear off before they drove the last short distance to the airport. This was the perfect place to stop before their honeymoon departure. Shaye thought about how much she'd changed since she was here last. She'd thought it was just another no-name bar that night.

"Okay, are you ready to go?" she asked.

"If you are. I'm so glad we came." Eve led the way toward the door with Shaye right behind her. Eve turned and stood in the subdued light of Lady Luck's parking lot, the muted glow playing off her hair and curves. Shaye couldn't believe how much she loved Eve—the hunger in her eyes…those full, soft lips…who she was as a person. And the way she filled Shaye's heart.

In the dark, Shaye stepped forward and Eve met her, mouth to mouth. In the way they had that first time, they let the warm caress of connection linger before deepening the kiss. As Shaye pressed her breasts and her pelvis into the curves of this beautiful woman, their bodies melded in a perfect pairing. Shaye considered how blessed they were. The primal need, the passion, and their deep abiding love.

They finally broke apart. "You know that if you hadn't already had me in the bar that night, then you had me with that first kiss—right here in this very spot," Eve said. "I wasn't going to forget you. That first kiss lit the spark. I found myself chasing that spark, no matter how hard I tried to fight it. I found myself trying to extinguish the smoldering aftermath."

Shaye reflected that even her past was now full of good memories. "That consummate kiss with consequences. Prelude to the future. I think it ignited those fragile sparks of forever. No getting past *the temptation of Eve*, even when I found out you wore a badge."

"Yeah, babe. You showed up and it was trouble in Paradise." Eve shook her head as she laughed.

"All that irresistible flirting and chemistry," Shaye said.

"Of all the fires…it wasn't just four. It was five."

Shaye took Eve's hand, the one with the wedding ring on it. The look in her eyes as she locked them on Shaye's said it all. It was love. It was everything they needed. Spark to flame to forever.

# About the Author

Julia Underwood (http://www.juliaunderwood.net) grew up loving animals and pursued a degree in veterinary medicine. She's been blessed to have wonderful family members, friends, and a parade of pets to enrich her life. She's an avid writer and reader. The joy of discovering the journey to novel writing cannot be overstated. She hopes her admiration for the love, dedication, and competence women bring to the multitude of roles they fill in this complicated world comes through in her writing.

# Books Available From Bold Strokes Books

**Across the Enchanted Border** by Crin Claxton. Magic, telepathy, swordsmanship, tyranny, and tenderness abound in a tale of two lands separated by the enchanted border. (978-1-63679-804-2)

**Deep Cover** by Kara A. McLeod. Running from your problems by pretending to be someone else only works if the person you're pretending to be doesn't have even bigger problems. (978-1-63679-808-0)

**Good Game** by Suzanne Lenoir. Even though Lauren has sworn off dating gamers, it's becoming hard to resist the multifaceted Sam. An opposites attract lesbian romance. (978-1-63679-764-9)

**Innocence of the Maiden** by Ileandra Young. Three powerful women. Two covens at war. One horrifying murder. When mighty and powerful witches begin to butt heads, who out there is strong enough to mediate? (978-1-63679-765-6)

**Protection in Paradise** by Julia Underwood. When arson forces them together, the flames between chief of police Eve Maguire and librarian Shaye Hayden aren't that easy to extinguish. (978-1-63679-847-9)

**Too Forward** by Krystina Rivers. Just as professional basketball player Jane May's career finally starts heating up, a new relationship with her team's brand consultant could derail the success and happiness she's struggled so long to find. (978-1-63679-717-5)

**Worth Waiting For** by Kristin Keppler. For Peyton and Hanna, reliving the past is painful, but looking back might be the only way to move forward. (978-1-63679-773-1)

**All For Her: Forbidden Romance Novellas** by Gun Brooke, J.J. Hale & Aurora Rey. Explore the angst and excitement of forbidden love few would dare in this heart-stopping novella collection. (978-1-63679-713-7)

**Finding Harmony** by CF Frizzell. Rock star Harper Cushing has to rearrange her grandmother's future and sell the family store out from under her, but she reassesses everything because Gram's helper, Frankie, could be offering the harmony her heart has been missing. (978-1-63679-741-0)

**Gaze** by Kris Bryant. Love at first sight is for dreamers, but the more time Lucky and Brianna spend together, the more they realize the chemistry of a gaze can make anything possible. (978-1-63679-711-3)

**Laying of Hands** by Patricia Evans. The mysterious new writing instructor at camp makes Grace Waters brave enough to wonder what would happen if she dared to write her own story. (978-1-63679-782-3)

**The Naked Truth** by Sandy Lowe. How far are Rowan and Genevieve willing to go and how much will they risk to make their most captivating and forbidden fantasies a reality? (978-1-63679-426-6)

**The Roommate** by Claire Forsythe. Jess Black's boyfriend is handsome and successful. That's why it comes as a shock when she meets a woman on the train who makes her pulse race. (978-1-63679-757-1)

**Seducing the Widow** by Jane Walsh. Former rival debutantes have a second chance at love after fifteen years apart when a spinster persuades her ex-lover to help save her family business. (978-1-63679-747-2)

**Close to Home** by Allisa Bahney. Eli Thomas has to decide if avoiding her hometown forever is worth losing the people who used to mean the most to her, especially Aracely Hernandez, the girl who got away. (978-1-63679-661-1)

**Innis Harbor** by Patricia Evans. When Amir Farzaneh meets and falls in love with Loch, a dark secret lurking in her past reappears, threatening the happiness she'd just started to believe could be hers. (978-1-63679-781-6)

**The Blessed** by Anne Shade. Layla and Suri are brought together by fate to defeat the darkness threatening to tear their world apart. What they don't expect to discover is a love that might set them free. (978-1-63679-715-1)

**The Guardians** by Sheri Lewis Wohl. Dogs, devotion, and determination are all that stand between darkness and light. (978-1-63679-681-9)

**The Mogul Meets Her Match** by Julia Underwood. When CEO Claire Beauchamp goes undercover as a customer of Abby Pita's café to help seal a deal that will solidify her career, she doesn't expect to be so drawn to her. When the truth is revealed, will she break Abby's heart? (978-1-63679-784-7)